The Last Day of the War

The Last Day of the War

Judith Claire Mitchell

PANTHEON BOOKS

New York

Pantheon Books and colophon are registered
trademarks of Random House, Inc.

Library of Congress Cataloging-in Publication Data
Mitchell, Judith Claire, 1952–
The last day of the war / Judith Claire Mitchell.
p.   cm.
ISBN 0-375-42166-1
1. Armenian massacres, 1915–1923—Fiction.   2. World War, 1914–1918—Fiction
3. Americans—France—Fiction.   4. Armenian Americans—Fiction.
5. Paris (France)—Fiction.   6. Jewish women—Fiction.   7. Massacres—Fiction
8. Soldiers—Fiction.   9. Revenge—Fiction.   I. Title.
PS3613.I857L37 2004
813'.6—dc22   2003063960
www.pantheonbooks.com

Book design by Robert C. Olsson

Printed in the United States of America

First Edition

2 4 6 8 9 7 5 3 1

For Don

Let fists be flung like stone
Against the heavens and the heavenly throne!

—Chaim Nachman Bialik,
In the City of Slaughter

CONTENTS

PART ONE

1. The Split Skirt   3
2. Leaving   6
3. Library Crimes   10
4. Clowns   13
5. The Weight of the Package   16
6. Dime-Novel Stuff   21
7. A Woman's Name   27
8. Crazy   30
9. The Denominations   35
10. Along with Those Lies   39

PART TWO

1. The Train to Providence   43
2. Stops Along the Way   48
3. Curses   50
4. The Holy Books Do Not Burn   57
5. Ramela   66
6. Boston   73

Contents

PART THREE

1. The *Espagne* 79
2. *A* as in Amo 84
3. A Tarnished Woman 88
4. Animal, Vegetable, Mineral 94
5. Mind and Matter 96
6. Should This Behavior Continue 99
7. The Last Day of the War 104
8. The White Sisters' Bowling
   League of America 108
9. Counting to One Hundred 113

AN INTERLUDE

Meanwhile, over in France 119

PART FOUR

1. The First Day of the Peace 125
2. A Dive Called Lulu's 127
3. Baptisms 134
4. Trumpets 137
5. Paper Ladles 140
6. Sheep 145
7. *Un Honneur Grand* 149

PART FIVE

1. *Cherchez la Femme* 157
2. Sisterhood 163
3. It Would Be So *Us* 168
4. The Little Vuitton 173
5. An Excellent Haut-Brion 177
6. His *You're Welcome* 184
7. Grips 186
8. Senlis 188
9. Peacock Eggs 196
10. Parlor Games 205

Contents

PART SIX

1. The Hôtel le Marais   215
2. Yah-el   218
3. An Ugly Look   224
4. To Whom It May Concern   228
5. A Girl's Adventures   231
6. While the Getting Is Good   235

PART SEVEN

1. Modern Art   247
2. Springtime in Paris   254
3. The Rest of Their Lives Will Be Like This   259
4. Saints and Virgins   263
5. Precious Cargo   265
6. Springtime in Berlin   268
7. The Gare de l'Est   275
8. Tea   278
9. St. Petersburg   282
10. Loose Ends   285

PART EIGHT

1. Lullabies   291
2. Exclusively Our Red   297
3. Yale, He Says   304
4. April 23, 1919: Nine a.m. at the Château   307
5. Nine a.m. Elsewhere   311
6. A Flashback: The First Day of the War (or, The Hungry Assassin)   314
7. A French Sailor Suit   317
8. The Assassination of Kerim Bey   319

Contents

PART NINE

1. Another Last Day of the War   329
2. Going West   337
3. Magic   340
4. Dinner That Night   343
5. How the Jews Got Their Names   345
6. Requiem   349
Timetable   355
A Note on Sources   359
Acknowledgments   365

Part One

The Split Skirt

ON THE MORNING of her eighteenth birthday, Yael Weiss stole a suit from a St. Louis dry-goods store. She'd never stolen anything before, hadn't planned on stealing anything that morning. Still, she made an elegant job of it. That is, she didn't stuff the suit into a bag or try to conceal it beneath a voluminous skirt. She didn't simply grab it and run. All she did was put the suit on and walk out the door. Left behind in a changing room were the clothes she'd come in with: her white cotton waist, her long floral skirt, her full crinoline. She abandoned even her ribboned straw boater.

Now, back out on Locust Street, she doesn't feel guilty about any of it. That's because it's not an ordinary suit she's taken off in. It's a suffragette suit. And what, after all, do the city fathers, the politicians, the angry preachers, and the enflamed Carrie Nations all have to say about the suffragette suit? They say it's immoral. They say it's corrupting. It's the work of the devil, they say. Well, come to find out—they're right. The suffragette suit *does* lead to a decline in morality. It *is* a corrupting influence. And apparently it works even faster than liquor. Slip one on, and the next thing you know, you're trotting down a staircase, you're whirling out a revolving door, you're hurrying along a hot August sidewalk, happy and unashamed.

Who would have guessed that a woman's suit could generate such bad behavior? At first glance, it appears so respectable. The one Yael's got on is dark green, a typically muted shade in these days of world war and privation and rationing. The jacket is unremarkable too, stopping just beyond the hips, gently nipped at the waist.

But peer at the skirt for a few minutes longer, as Yael did when she first hopped off a streetcar and saw the outfit in the store's display window, and you'll eventually spot the reason for all the controversy and prattle. It's not the short length (the hem a full two inches above the faceless mannequin's salmon pink ankles) that's the problem. It's that the skirt is split down the middle. Divided in two. Not a skirt at all, then. A pair of very wide-legged trousers.

To stand on a street corner and fall frankly in love with this suit is as much a political act as singing the *Internationale* in public. Which, Yael has confided to no one, she actually did last February when Emma Goldman was being transferred from the Manhattan Tombs to the Jefferson City Penitentiary. Learning that Goldman was scheduled to switch trains at Union Station, Yael had skipped geometry class and gone to the terminal, not because she was a Red (she wasn't; she isn't), but because she was dying to know what a woman like Goldman looked like in person. She wanted to see not only the radical who was about to serve two years for protesting the war, but the feminist who had actually painted her name alongside her lover's on their mailbox in Greenwich Village.

At first Yael was disappointed. Away from her podium, Red Emma seemed neither defiant nor dangerous. She was a doughy-faced Russian, middle-aged, with thick legs. As the attorney general's man marched her across the platform and onto the train bound for the pen, Yael found it hard to believe that such a dowdy character even had a lover. But after the train pulled out and the genuine Reds who'd come to support Goldman began belting out their illegal anthem, Yael was glad she'd come. The song was so stirring, so heartfelt, and so catchy she had no choice. She had to hum along.

Yael had been hiding behind a post that day, unseen and unheard. This morning, her politics are far more visible. When she got off the streetcar, a small crowd was gathered in front of the store window. "Disgraceful," a woman was saying, and there were nods and murmured agreement. Joining them, Yael looked at the object of their disapproval and smiled. "No daughter of mine," another woman said, and Yael went inside.

Sauntering up the main aisle, glancing at trinkets in display cases electrically lit, Yael reminded herself she was there just to look, to cast a vote of confidence, as it were, for the maligned suit. No matter how much she liked it, no matter how flattering the suit might turn out to be, she knew she couldn't have it because she couldn't afford it. Her father was David Weiss, owner of Mamzelle, Inc., the largest manufacturer of ladies' corsets in the Midwest, and a year ago price would not have been a concern. But the war had hurt the corset business. Every week, the government commandeered more of the steel Mamzelle needed for her gussets and bones. Every week, more American women donated their corsets to the metal drives, concealing their figures' flaws beneath the new waistless chemises and barrel coats. Meanwhile, Mamzelle's employees were taking jobs at munitions plants, where they got to make parachute silks instead of pink brocade tummy panels. Over dinner, Yael's mother fretted. "They're leaving in droves," she said of the employees, and Yael's father, who coped with this sort of thing by making jokes, said, "Also in streetcars and Fords."

So Yael knew she could not buy the suit. But she trotted upstairs to the Ladies' Ready-made department and tried it on anyway. Back out on the floor, she examined herself in a triptych of mirrors, where she saw that, indeed, she looked well in it. She posed for herself, a little smile, lips slightly apart. She moved her legs slightly apart too. She held up her long dark hair and tried to guess how it would look bobbed. Sleek and sable, she thought. And what if she were to cut thick bangs? Would they distract the eye from the unfortunate curve of her nose?

Sighing, she turned her back on her reflection. She meant to return to the dressing room then, take the suit off, kick it aside, get on with her day. She was already late for her shift at the Red Cross. But each retreating step made it harder for her to do what she intended. It felt too good, giant-stepping in that suit. Her own skirt would now feel like a Victorian hobble.

Avoiding the dressing room, she paced instead from one end of Ready-made to the other. As she did, a plan came to her. She would find a clerk, tell the clerk who her father was, invoke the name of Mamzelle. The clerk, unaware of the family's failing fortunes, would let her take the suit on credit. Then, when she got home, she would wheedle and whine. No need to portray herself as a freethinker who has just found her perfect uniform. She would play the simple girl who craves the latest from Seventh Avenue. Yael kept up with folks like Emma Goldman, it was true, but she also read the women's magazines. She knew how to justify the purchase of new clothes during wartime. "Fashion!" *Good Housekeeping* had exclaimed only recently. "To some the word seems trivial when hearts turn to Flanders Field. Still, what a sorry world it would be if women were not charming."

The only flaw in her plan was this: she did not seem to be stopping to implement it. Rather than turning around and finding a clerk, she was continuing forward, striding out of Ready-made into Custom-made, loping out of Custom-made into Children's. Out of Children's into Toddlers'. Out of Toddlers' into Infants'.

And now down the staircase, hurrying through talking machines and radios. Now dashing through sheet music and player pianos, spinning out the door, rushing back onto Locust, jubilant and giddy, and why wouldn't she be? It was her eighteenth birthday, and in the midst of endless war, dateless nights, meatless Mondays, and wheatless Wednesdays, wasn't she entitled to one self-indulgence, one small pleasure? Wasn't she entitled, just for today, her day, to whatever it was she desired?

CHAPTER TWO

Leaving

WHEN YAEL and the century were both four years old, her parents took her to the St. Louis World's Fair. After hours inside makeshift pavilions and temporary palaces, after improvised meals of ice-cream cones, iced tea, and hot dogs—treats invented just for the Exposition—the sun set and the family walked to the Pike, a wide boulevard illuminated by rows of electric lights, those mechanical moons buzzing like bees. Sitting on her father's shoulders, Yael watched seventy—seventy!—motorcars parade by; in the rumble seat of the very last one, Will Rogers, so chisel-faced, so young, performed his intricate rope tricks. Then, as soon as he was gone, all the lights hissed off and darkness fell. Thousands gasped. And then—more gasps—fireworks exploded, actual words glowing against the black sky: *Good-bye. Farewell.*

On this birthday, she'd woken to a sky that was pale yellow from heat and contained no messages, not even a cloud. Over a breakfast of sugar omelets and twice-boiled coffee, she opened her parents' presents. In an oblong box that might have held a pearl necklace, she found a fountain pen. In a square box that ought to have contained a ring or a cameo, she discovered a bottle of violet ink. "To bring to the Red Cross," her mother said. "For writing to the boys." Then, in honor of the occasion, her mother recalled Yael's birth in an overcrowded lying-in hospital. "A basement delivery room," Esther Weiss said. "That's where they put me. Down in the dungeon with all the other shrieking women. No windows, no fans, not a drop of fresh air."

Nothing but the sodden heat of a midwestern summer. Yael had heard the story countless times, for years had blamed that stifling basement for her troublesome first name, so different, so foreign, so hard to pronounce. *Yael* meant alpine goat; it came from a Hebrew verb meaning to climb, to ascend, and as a child she had assumed that, after nearly two days of blazing hot underground labor, her mother had chosen a name that spoke of snow-capped peaks, icy streams, gamboling kids. But when, at seven or eight, Yael had given voice to that theory, her mother had hooted. "Jews name for the dead," Esther said. "Not for goats."

The Weisses never were practicing Jews. Still, they adhered to certain traditions. David Weiss refused to eat pork. Bacon and ham, yes, but no pork chops, no pork roast. Nothing called pork. Esther Weiss named for the dead. "Once upon a time," she said, "you had an ancestor named Yael, and when she died, the next girl to be born was named Yael in her place, and this continued, generation after generation, until the name was given to my dear departed great-grandmother, and then to my dear departed mother, and then to you." Now, instead of imagining goats when she considered her name, Yael pictured a flitting housefly landing on girl after girl after girl.

She finished breakfast, thanked her parents again for the pen, and caught the streetcar for the Red Cross Center. She already regretted signing up for a shift. It was too hot to knit woolen sweaters or write jaunty letters. As the streetcar jogged through her Benton Park neighborhood, she stared through the open sides at the large brick houses, the gleaming black automobiles, the few remaining milk cows tethered to trees, and thought about how boring the summer had been and would continue to be. Every boy who was worth anything was overseas. For the girls left behind, days were tedious and nights even worse,

7

Yael and her friends sitting through insipid Billie Burke romances or the latest Chaplin (yet another scoop of ice cream dropped down the back décolletage of a rich woman's dress). Already Yael had begun making excuses so she could stay home by herself. She preferred to loll alone in her room, doing absolutely nothing as the light faded and the sky turned that nameless shade of blue she found both lovely and eerie and which, she suspected, was the same color as blood as it traveled the arteries, her blood before it was exposed to oxygen.

While she daydreamed about her ruined summer, the streetcar stopped, and a boy she'd known all her life climbed on. Yael turned her head, trying to become invisible, but he waved and sat by her side. As a boy, Chaim Mandel had been a copper-eyed redhead, and her little girl-friends, already marriage-minded at five or six, assumed the two would someday wed. Weren't they the only Jews in the whole Froebel Method school? Weren't they both bookish and short? A perfect pair, and the little girls chanted rhymes linking the two, mangling their impossible names, changing Chaim to *Hyram,* pronouncing Yael so it rhymed with *jail.* Everyone in St. Louis pronounced her name that way. Even she pronounced it that way unless she was being especially deliberate.

After she exchanged pleasantries with him—at seventeen, Chaim Mandel was a long drink of water with so many freckles he appeared to be rusting and hair so thick it grew upward like a mound of red yarn, and her girlfriends had long ago stopped wishing him on her—Yael resumed staring at the houses and then, as the streetcar grumbled on, at the small shops, the wider streets, the ever-increasing number of cars, but he wouldn't leave her alone. "So, yes, I'm off to work," he said, as if she'd inquired. She had to face him then, adopt an expression of interest. "Yes," he said. "So I'm working in my uncle's offices until I leave St. Louis."

Though he clearly longed for her to press him, she didn't ask why he was leaving or where he was going, and for a moment he appeared hurt. But he had a good nature, could slough off an insult, and so he went on, chatting about his job and then about *Cleopatra,* which was playing in town now. Had she heard about Theda Bara's negligible costumes? he wondered. He made a tiresome joke. "I'm telling you, you'll never see Theda barer," he said, and turned crimson at his own remark.

A redhead's violent blush. Yael couldn't stand it. She fanned herself with her hand as if she'd just noticed the weather. "It's hot," she said. "I'm going to ride the board."

They were downtown by then, where the buildings stood shoulder to shoulder, blocking the sun's rays, though not its heat. Now there was the added discomfort of pickaxes and jackhammers, the racket of new construction. And amid the darkness and racket was Chaim Mandel, who had followed her back to the chain. "So perhaps we could go," he shouted over the din. "To the picture show sometime, I mean. Maybe this week. I'm leaving next week or maybe the week after. You can't know for sure. They won't tell you a thing. But it's definitely soon that I'm leaving."

The way he repeated the word *leaving*—so distinctly, so hope-fully—only the most heartless girl could have refrained from asking. Yael was not quite that girl. "Oh?" she said. "Are you going some-where?"

Again he seemed hurt. "You know where I'm going. You know what it means when a fellow says he's leaving."

She did know, of course she did, and yet she'd missed his meaning until then. "You're lying," she said. "You can't have signed up. You're still a month shy of eighteen."

"Well, I must appear old for my age." He grinned at the ridiculous notion. "I went in and told some stories, and they took me like that."

Not even shaving. Not even close.

He lowered his voice. "And I did a little fiddling with my birth cer-tificate. It's just a matter of some bleach and a few other tricks of the trade. It works on grade reports too."

She thought about that for a moment. News that was too late to put to good use. They'd graduated from high school the month before. She shook her head clear. "I thought you were going to college," she said.

"I know." The grin was gone. "To be honest, it was all fairly spur-of-the-moment. I was with some of the gang and we passed the regis-tration office and they began making these comments: Reds, Jews, malingerers. That sort of thing. And looking at me the whole time."

She felt her eyes burn. The idea of his being goaded into enlisting infuriated her. So did her sudden burst of emotion. She ordered herself to stop being so dramatic. It wasn't as though she was going to miss him. And it wasn't as though he was doomed to harm. Plenty of boys were spending the war on American soil. Training camps in California or Texas. Marching, lifting weights, making new friends. It would be good for him—a nicer class of companions, a pair of visible biceps.

Still, something must have shown on her face. "Oh, Yael," he said, pronouncing it so it rhymed with *jail*. "I had no idea."

She pretended not to have heard him. The jackhammers. The streetcar's bell.

"We'll write," he said earnestly, generously, and she ignored that too. "And I'm still in town for a week, maybe even a fortnight."

The streetcar was slowing. She didn't wait for it to come to a full stop. "Here I am," she cried, though she was nowhere near the Red Cross, and as soon as the one-truck sidled up to the curb, she jumped off.

She was at the corner of Locust and Ninth, in front of a large dry-goods store. A small crowd was scolding a suit in the window. Though a redheaded boy was calling out to her from a departing streetcar, she didn't look back. She half waved without turning. *Good-bye. Farewell.* Then she pushed through the crowd and walked up to that window.

CHAPTER THREE

Library Crimes

Now the suit is hers. And even as she makes what she will someday call her getaway, she knows that some of her excitement is fueled by her assumption that she'll probably be caught or, at the very least, chased. Doesn't she periodically glance over her shoulder? Isn't her heart pounding the same way it would if she were madly in love?

But after a while, when no one has slapped a pair of cuffs on her wrists or so much as called out to her, her heart slows to normal, and she no longer dashes. Now she is merely strolling, and whenever she passes plate glass, she is actually stopping not only to admire herself but also to enjoy the reflections of the others on the street: mature women who stare at her, horrified; young girls who smile at her, envious; men of all ages who leer at her, grateful. But although every man in the vicinity gives her the eye, no store detective approaches. In fact, nobody speaks to her at all until she reaches the Central Branch of the St. Louis Public Library, which she enters so she can cool off.

Standing in the dark vestibule, she gathers her hair off the nape of her neck to let the perspiration evaporate. As she does, some of her excitement evaporates too.

Why should she feel so suddenly blue? Is it guilt, or perhaps disappointment? Was she actually hoping that the God she has never believed in, the God who seems available, plausible, to everyone but herself, would take this opportunity to prove his existence and demonstrate his displeasure by sending a store 'tec to arrest her?

She twists her hair into a topknot held in place with her fingers. She remembers a day long ago, equally warm, when a neighbor child, a little Lutheran girl, urged her to accept the Good News. Sitting on Yael's front porch, the child regaled Yael with all the Bible stories she knew: Adam and Isaac, Jacob and his dreams, Jesus up on the cross. It was an effort to entertain Yael and then rope her in, but Yael wasn't about to fall for it. She listened politely, oohing and aahing at the appropriate places, but the entire time she was asking herself, Does anyone really swallow this eyewash? Even as a child she had no capacity for faith. Even as a child who made wishes on dandelions and avoided cracks in the sidewalk, she knew the difference between making believe and truly believing.

When her friend suggested they pray, Yael agreed only to please her. Following the girl's lead, Yael slid off her cool metal chair, lifted her skirt to her thighs to avoid grass stains, and got down on her knees.

Her father was the one who put a stop to it. He came out of the house, his shirt collar hanging by a stay, his derby slapped on his head in an attempt at decorum. "What are you young ladies doing?" he asked, and, when told, he nodded. "Well, I'm afraid Jews don't kneel, ladies," he said. "Not for kings, not for presidents, not for no one nohow."

Now Yael releases her hair and lets it tumble down her back. She is thinking she might be willing to fall to her knees right here in the library's vestibule were God to tap her on the shoulder and make himself known. She might repent if he did that, return the suit, join a convent, do whatever one did upon accepting the Good News. A conversion would at least give her something to do for the rest of the summer. And if she joined a convent she could cut off her hot, heavy hair. She is thinking about all that, about God and nuns and new hairdos, when the door behind her opens and a man—she can tell by the heavy footfalls—enters the library.

Standing behind her, he lays his hand on the shoulder of her nipped jacket. And now, at last, someone is speaking to her.

"Excuse me, miss," he says in a northern accent and a tone so stern that her heart jolts as if his hand were transmitting an electrical current. She spins around, frightened, excited.

But the man is no emissary of God. Nor is he a detective come to arrest her. He is just an American soldier in a soft overseas cap pulled low on his forehead and marked with two silver bars, an army lieutenant with black eyes and a thick blue-black mustache beneath a strong nose.

The features. The arrogance. Hardly God's emissary. The man is just another Jew, and the worst kind—a Jew from up north.

"Excuse me," he says again, polite words, but the tone is the one he'd use to address a private in his unit. He sounds annoyed, as if he regards her as an impediment to his progress, which, she suddenly realizes, she is, standing there, blocking the entrance. "Can you point me to Periodicals?" he says in the same curt manner. He is peering around her, trying to see into the library.

Still, she responds cordially. "Up and over, Lieutenant." She steps out of his way and points. "Shall I show you?"

He's gone before she can finish personifying midwestern graciousness. He doesn't thank her or raise his hand to his cap. He just continues on his way, no time for courtesy, an important man on an important mission.

She goes inside too. The joy of acquiring new clothes has worn off, along with the delicious fear of imagined apprehension. In the Open Shelf Room, she browses aimlessly. Up one row, down the next, shuffling past books on religion and mythology, migration and colonization, linguistics and cookery. She barely reads the titles on the spines. In one row, she plucks a book from the shelf. In the next row, she forces the book between two others, leaving it where it doesn't belong. This is what the day has come to. She's committing library crimes.

There is only one small thing in which she's interested. At the end of every other row, before she turns down the next, she steps into the main aisle, and there, if she looks through the archway at the end of the Open Shelf Room, she can see into Periodicals, where the rude soldier is seated at a table, reading a newspaper skewered by a long wooden pole. His boots are propped on the chair across from his own. His cap dangles from the toe of his right boot. An odd shadow has fallen over his hair. The shadow is caused, she decides, by the angle of the over-head chandelier. The electric light is making his hair appear half black and half silver.

The odd highlighting intrigues her, as does the fact that were he to glance up at just the right moment, their eyes would meet. But he never glances up. He keeps his head down; he is completely absorbed in the paper. He peruses it intently, from time to time nodding. And once she catches him throwing his head back and laughing, but silently, the way one would in a library.

That's when she knows what he's reading, why he's come here. She is filled with contempt. Some mission! she thinks. This important, important man has come to the great hall of wisdom and knowledge and pushed her aside, he has behaved rudely, disgracefully, unforgivably, all to catch up on the funnies.

CHAPTER FOUR

Clowns

YAEL WILL, of course, come to learn the soldier's name, but never will she learn the name of the old man who, in his way, introduces them. Still, she will not forget what this man looks like. He is gray-haired and slight with sorrowful eyes, and, despite the screening effect of his large droopy mustache, she can tell that at either side of his mouth there are creases so deep they seem more the product of abrupt violence—a scarring knife—than what they actually are, the gradually acquired lines of age and worry.

Even the old man's costume will remain with her: an ill-fitting black jacket that cries out for brushing, a white shirt that needs scrubbing, a tired string tie. He looks like a shabby country clerk come to the big city.

And then there is the package he carries, a bulky bundle wrapped in brown mailing paper and bound with frayed twine. When Yael sees that package, her guess is that it probably contains shirts to be laundered; that's the size and shape of it.

She first encounters him in the row of books pertaining to geography and world events. He is walking toward her and she toward him, but their eyes are on the shelved books, and neither is aware of the other. They collide near Egyptian history.

The man seems unusually stricken by their collision. It's as if he too has been committing library crimes and is afraid she's come to confront him. He apologizes profusely and meekly. She detects an accent she takes to be east European: Greek, Bulgarian, something like that. "No, no," she says. "My fault entirely." He shifts the package, frees enough of his hand to indicate a desire to tip his hat. Then he lowers his head and scurries to the far end of the row.

She walks on too, and so has her back to him when she hears the first cascade of thuds. Turning, she sees he has removed perhaps a half dozen books from one of the shelves, only to have dropped them all. He is crouching now, attempting to retrieve the fallen volumes. He nods at her and mutters another apology, and, as he does, she sees the concern in his eyes. It's as though he thinks the books are made of glass, and he's chipped and cracked them and now he will have to make restitution.

This time she's struck by his face. Not only by the sorrow and fear but also by his resemblance to the soldier. The same jet coloring, the same prominent nose, the very same mustache: thick, long, and black. Another Jew, then. The place, she tells herself, is crawling with them today. Although this man is not the same type as the soldier. This man is the more tolerable type, timid and apologetic and full of the guilt that, after her morning's activities, she ought to be full of.

By the time it occurs to her to stop staring and ruminating and offer to help him, the old man has managed on his own. His arms are filled with the books he's picked up from the floor, as well as his package. It's an awkward pile that reaches his chin, which he uses to hold the top book steady. Then he waddles back to the shelf where, to Yael's amazement and amusement, instead of putting the books down, he removes yet another and adds it to his precarious stack.

The result is predictable; the new book slides to the floor. Then, like Jill after Jack, the other books go tumbling after. So does the package, which the old man snatches by its strings, breaking its fall with his knee.

If he were a clown he'd be the kind with teardrops painted on his stark white face—miserable, hapless, hilariously clumsy—and that's exactly what the librarian will think when she comes to investigate the commotion. May I help you? she'll ask, but *Clown!* is what she'll be thinking—*Clown!* or *Kike!*—and then she'll turn to Yael, intending to exchange a knowing look with one of her own, but she'll take in Yael's own dark hair, dark eyes, the arc of Yael's own nose, and the slight olive tint of Yael's skin—not as olive as the old man's or the soldier's, but olive enough—and she'll rapidly avert her glance.

For this reason—not wanting a librarian to connect her to him— Yael is grateful when the man finally figures out that if he wants to carry so many books at once, he must first relinquish the package. He puts it on the shelf from which the books came. He looks toward Yael again, and she lowers her head, pretends she hasn't been watching his inexpert juggling act. He seems less apologetic now. He nearly scowls at her, and she takes a step back, turns, and leaves the row.

All this hullabaloo. It's kept her from spying on the soldier. She's concerned he may be gone by now, but, no, when she steps into the main aisle he's still there, right where she left him. All that's changed is he's finally put the newspaper aside. He appears to be studying the back of his hand. It takes Yael a moment to realize that he's consulting a wristwatch. Trench coats and men's wristwatches. These are the only good things to have come out of this war.

She is trying to decide what to do. She has an idea about marching right into Periodicals, placing her hand on his shoulder as he placed his on hers. Excuse me, Lieutenant, is that one of those new watches you men have taken to wearing these days? Would you show me how it works? Might I try it on? Will you help me fasten it around my wrist? Will you touch me here, gently, along the veins, where my lifeline begins?

She hears footsteps and pivots. The old man is leaving the Open Shelf Room. As he hurries out, something about him nags at her. He's gone before she realizes what it is: he's quite empty-handed.

Your laundry! she thinks. But she doesn't call out. A library. Good manners. A polite midwestern Jew.

CHAPTER FIVE

The Weight of the Package

At first she can't find the package at all. Then, when she sees where he's left it, she shakes her head. Because what the fellow has done is reshelve all the books he pulled out without noticing he's bricked in his own bundle. Brown paper and string peek out from behind a series of worn leather bindings.

Now she is the one pulling those books from the shelf. *Statements of American Missionaries on the Destruction of the Christian Community* is the title of one. *Fire and Sword in the Caucasus,* the name of another. Another is simply called *Hate.*

As she piles books on the floor, she feels suddenly depleted. It has been a strange and ultimately exhausting morning. She wants a nap, covers pulled over her head. She wants to take off this suit and lie in bed for the rest of her life.

But first she will return the old man's laundry.

The weight of the package surprises her. It clearly contains nothing as insubstantial as clothing. Several sets of brass candlesticks might account for its heft. Perhaps the old man is the observant type who lights candles on Fridays. Or maybe the package holds trench art, spent shells beaten into paperweights by a grandson soldier with time on his hands. Yael gives the bundle a shake. Then, cradling it in both arms, she turns, ready to chase the old fellow down.

Instead, she runs smack into the soldier. He has scrunched his cap in one hand, and the shadows on his hair, the ones she attributed to the library's overhead lights—she sees that they aren't shadows at all. His hair, in the front, is truly half black and half gray. She doesn't mean salt and pepper. She means half and half, fifty-fifty. To the right of his part, hair black as coal. To the left, a shock of pure shining silver. It's as if a miner from Kentucky and one from Nevada have dumped the contents of their carts side by side.

She stares at the two shades, but even then he is oblivious to her presence. He looks around her, beyond her. "Excuse me," she says, but he keeps moving forward, a relentless, insensible shark dressed in khakis. She doesn't know him, and yet she resents being ignored by him. She longs to give him a retaliatory shove, to knock him against the books called *Hate* and *Fire,* see how he likes being pushed around. But she isn't quite the sort of girl who does such things, and even if she were, she can't stop now.

She rushes down the row, out the room, and into the library's foyer, but the old man is gone. Hurrying to the exit, not quite running but taking long strides, knowing they are not only unfeminine but are calling attention to the split legs of her skirt (and she sees people staring, hears whispers, and wants to pause, pirouette, and stick out her tongue, but there's no time), she bolts out the door where the sun is a dagger, the heat a sharp slap, and she looks up Olive, but the old man isn't there. Now to the corner, squinting down Thirteenth—but again nothing, no one. She gives up, decides she will retrace her steps and go back inside, have a librarian place the package in the Lost and Found, toss it into some box filled with single gloves, empty wallets. But when she turns to do this, she runs into the soldier—for, what is it, the third time?— physically runs into him, and she steps back, a bit dazed, and finds herself sneaking another peek at his hair, searching for traces of she doesn't know what. Hair dye? Boot black?

He doesn't say a word. She feels someone ought to. "Well," she says, "we certainly seem to be in each other's way today, don't we, Lieutenant?"

He can't place her; she can tell. He seems ready to push her aside yet again. Then his eyes come to rest on what she's holding.

"What are you doing with that?" he says. "Oh, Christ. Was that you in there? Here, give me that. It's mine."

She can't help it. She smiles. "What?" she says. She too looks down.

"You mean this? This isn't yours. This belongs to—" She scans the street even though she knows she'll see no one to point to. "Someone left this in the library," she says.

"I know," he says. "It was me. I put it down for a second, and when I went back, it was gone."

He is standing so close she can see his upper lip beneath the fringe of his mustache, the gold spokes in his irises. She can smell him, salty but fresh as if someone sprinkled talc over the ocean. He isn't much taller than she is, but he acts as if he towers over her, and when he takes a step forward, she takes a step back.

"It wasn't you," she says, and he takes another step forward. She's more frightened of him now than when she thought he'd come to drag her back to the store or off to a cell or straight down to perdition. It pleases her, then, that her voice doesn't give her away. "Lieutenant," she says, "I happen to know this belongs to somebody else—a third party—and I'm planning on getting it back to him."

"Of course it belongs to somebody else," he says. "I know the somebody else it belongs to. He's an old war chum of mine. We came here together. He had to hurry off, a doctor's appointment, and right after he said so long, I realized he'd forgotten his—" He stops, can't find the words.

"His *this?*" she says.

"Right," he says. "His that. So I went back to get it, and there you were—it *was* you, wasn't it?—scooping it up and running away."

She juts out one hip, rests the package on it. "The gentleman who left this behind was at least in his seventies," she says. "What war did you two fight in together, the Crimean?"

When he tries to take the package, she's able to yank it away and press it tight to her chest. She looks around pointedly. It's the corner of Thirteenth and Olive, a bright summer's day in Missouri. There are people all over the place and not a few of them stopping to acknowledge him. Men tip their hats. Small boys salute.

He helplessly salutes in return. He lowers his voice. "Look, miss," he says. "Be logical. How would I have known exactly where this was if my friend hadn't told me?"

If he drove an automobile the way he argued, he'd kill someone. All the abrupt skids and reverses and veers. "But you just said he *hadn't* told you. You just said he rushed off without a word."

"Before. He told me before. When we first got here."

"But you arrived alone."

"Yes, technically speaking, I did, but he was right inside waiting for me. Think about it. How else would I have known exactly which row to go to?"

"Maybe you were watching him the whole time. Maybe you were casing the joint."

His hand to his chest, to his heart. "The joint? Are you referring to the public library?" He shakes his head, his bicolored hair. "Honestly, miss. I'm an officer in the American army."

"So was Benedict Arnold," she says.

His eyes glitter. She wonders what he sees. A girl clutching a package? A woman giving him a run for his money? Which does he prefer? She is willing to be either.

"Look." A new tactic. "I don't have time for this. Either you give me that or I'll—"

She doesn't know how to describe the blend of anger and excitement she feels. "Or you'll what?" His narrowed eyes, his smoldering indignation. Her modern costume. It's like being an actress; it's like performing in a play. "Or you'll call a copper?" She likes playing against him. "What, you'll get rough with me?"

A bit of an error, that. It's as if she's put the idea into his head, as if she's granted him permission. He takes her wrist as she fantasized him doing only minutes before, except instead of petting her there he's twisting the skin. It doesn't hurt. It's just for effect.

"Ouch," she says anyway.

He is still holding on, but limply now. She wonders if he finds her at all attractive. He is nice-looking enough, but not so handsome that he can be terribly choosy. She might stand a chance.

"Just give me that package, will you?" he says.

She tries not to smile. He's a wretched criminal, all his doubt and reluctance plain on his face. As he pleads with her, the gray hair on the left side of his part falls forward, the shock of old-man silver covering one dark eyebrow. The two tones no longer strike her as odd. In fact, the combination seems touching, the wisdom implied by the gray belied by the youthful black, the gray belied even further by his face, the childish petulance of the out-thrust lower lip. Yael wants to reach up, touch his cheek, brush back the hair. He is the one touching her, though. She looks at her wrist. "Did you not hear me say ouch?" she asks, and he blushes, lets go. On him, she thinks, blushing looks good.

"Look, miss," he says. "I'm sorry, but you need to give me that right now." Then, in another tone: "This instant, young lady." And in still another: "It's a matter of grave national importance."

Hard work not to laugh. "You're crazy," she says. "*I'm* calling a copper."

He has her by the wrist again, tighter this time, hurting now, and the urge to laugh vanishes.

"Stop it!" she says.

He lets go. She's won. The thought doesn't make her entirely happy.

"Give a fellow a break, miss," he says. He takes a step back, leans against the library wall. "I have to be home in Rhode Island tomorrow. I'm supposed to be on the train in . . . God, less than an hour with that"—he points—"and I only just got off it. The train, I mean. I'm beat, miss, I haven't slept a minute, this guy I know chin-wagging in my face the whole way down. Look, what if we do this? You wait here. I'll go find the old fellow who left that behind. I'll find him and bring him back, and you can give it to him. You can put it right in his hands. Then he can put it in *my* hands, which is what he should have done in the first place. You'll have inconvenienced everyone and made me miss my damned train and basically fouled everything up and accomplished nothing at all, but interfered on a really grand scale. That ought to make you feel like a genuine American. What do you say?"

She wants to rub her wrist. "I say fine," she says. "I say let's do that."

"Or," he says, sweetly now, another change in direction, another two-wheeled skid around a corner, "you can save us all the time and trouble and have some pity and compassion and give it to me right now."

"I like the first plan," she says.

His shoulders sag. He blinks and a tear breaks, a genuine tear that coats his eyelashes. She wasn't expecting that. A grown man. A first Loot. She lowers her gaze to his hands: the dark skin, the chewed nails.

"Aw, miss," he says, "the guy wouldn't come back here even if I knew where he went."

"The doctor's," she reminds him.

He glares at her for that. Then he is pouting again. How old is he? she wonders. Five years her senior, at least. She almost feels sorry for him. She tries to concentrate on her throbbing wrist. Otherwise, next thing she knows, she'll be reaching up to dry his tears with her fingertips.

"Damn it to hell, miss," he says, "I am so damned tired."

For a minute they only look at each other. Then—and it's because she feels sorry for him—the idea comes to her. "What's in it?" she says.

CHAPTER SIX

Dime-Novel Stuff

SHE CAN TELL he doesn't understand her. She can tell everything about him just by looking. She jiggles the package. He understands now. "Careful," he says. And then, "I don't know," though it comes out a question.

"Because if you did know and we opened it and you were right, then I suppose I'd be more apt to believe that the old gentleman left it for you. Because how else would you know what was in it if he hadn't told you?"

He thinks it over. "All right," he says. "But we can't open it here. If we're going to open it, it has to be somewhere no one can see us."

"Hah!" she says. "Yes. Let's go someplace secluded. A back alley. How would that be? We can stop along the way, get you a truncheon and some chloroform."

"I'm a white slaver now." He is speaking to the vacant yellow sky. He looks back at her. "I was going to suggest we return to the library." He points with his thumb. "The joint."

This time they enter together. She chooses an isolated table by the far wall of the Reading Room. Though their table is off on its own, there are dozens of occupied tables nearer the entrance. If the soldier *is* a white slaver, if he *does* plan to drug and abduct and destroy her, inside and out, first he will have to drag her limp body past all those library patrons. No one in St. Louis will let him get away with that. And if he has other crimes in mind, such as grabbing the package and bolting, he'll still have to make it past those same dozen tables, those same good Missourians, and with Yael chasing him the whole time, Yael screaming *Stop, thief!* and every other phrase she can think of that will lead to his undoing, khakis or no.

He holds a chair for her. He does that much. She sits and then he sits, the two side by side, their backs to the wall. She puts the package on her lap. No one else can see it there, and everything they say is in a whisper, loud enough so they don't have to put lips to ears but soft enough so no one pays any mind.

"Well?" she says.

"What?"

"Would you like to tell me what's in it?"

"No," he says. "Not really."

"And you need to describe it precisely. You can't just say it's a pair of, say, candlesticks. You have to tell me the design and any distinguishing characteristics."

"It's not a pair of candlesticks."

"Well, then?"

He is miserable, she knows it. What's more, he seems to be of the opinion that she is the one bullying him. But she is only trying to do what is right. She is being generous too. She would be perfectly justified if she walked away this minute, gave the package to the head librarian (gloves, wallets, wayward Shabbos candles).

"Well, come on," she says. "I haven't all day."

"*You* haven't all day? *I'm* the one with a train to catch."

He is looking at her closely now, and she knows from now on, forever and then some, this man who has spent so much of the day pushing her aside will never forget her. She can disappear this very second, vanish from the earth; it doesn't matter. He will remember her face for the rest of his life.

"Well?" she says.

"All right. The damned truth is I don't know what the hell's in it. Now what do we do?"

The cursing, the evasions. She stands in a way that lets him know she will not put up with it. He grabs for her wrist again.

"All right," he says. "Wait. Come on. Sit down." And, when she won't: "Look, the truth is I do know, but only generally. I can't be specific."

She remains standing. She is having such fun.

"All right," he whispers. "All right. It's guns."

Because she can tell everything about him just by looking, she knows he's just told her the truth. She didn't expect it, not the truth, not so quickly, and certainly not his declaring that the package in her arms contains weapons. "They're of German make," he says quietly and unhappily, "and they were used in Turkey in 1915, and I don't know a thing besides that."

"Fine," she says, sitting and sounding far cooler than she is feeling. "Let's put it to the test."

The old man has tied the twine in a big bow, the same way a child does up his shoelaces. No fancy knots, nothing a Boy Scout would point to with pride. Yael pulls at one loop and the bow comes apart; the knot is undone.

"All right, wait," the soldier says. He places his hand over hers, stops her fingers. "Must you really? Look. There's a nine-millimeter Luger, 1908 issue. There's an old broom-handle Mauser. There may be some German egg *handgranaten*."

She looks at her lap. "Are they live?"

"Well, I hope so. Why would the fellow have come all this way to pass us some spent grenades? What the hell would we do with them, put them on the mantel for the amusement of generations to come?"

"You're trying to scare me into giving this over without opening it," she says.

He nods vigorously, the gray shock in motion. "Christ, yes," he says. "Yes, I'm trying to scare you. You ought to be scared. Do I really have to list all the ways you're endangering yourself and everyone else in this place? Look at me, miss. Can't you see how sincere I'm being? Can't you see how important this is?" His eyes dampen again. "Look," he says. "All right. Here's the story. I'm an officer in the AEF. In a few weeks I'll be sent over to France. Once I'm there, I'll be asked to shoot Germans. Are you following so far? These guns were given to the

Turks by the Huns back in 'fifteen. Okay? Are you following? These very guns were used during the massacres. During the deportations. Okay? Do you have any idea what I'm talking about? The deportations? In Turkey?"

She is about to say something scathing—I *do* read the papers, thank you very much—but he doesn't give her the chance.

"All right, then," he says. "So the Germans stood by, taking notes, offering suggestions, lending the Turks their damned weapons. You're using clubs? the Germans said to the Turks. But surely there must be a more efficient way to kill thousands of people at once. Here, try these pistols instead. Do you see what I'm saying, miss? Have I spelled it out enough for you? I don't mind going to France. I'm happy to go and shoot Germans. And if my fate is I die for Europe, then, hell, fine, I'll die for Europe. But I'm not going to die only for Europe. The gun in my hand, at least it'll be a statement, at least it'll be a small sign that we haven't forgotten, that we're aware of who harmed our people and, whenever we can, however we can, we're going to get them back for it."

Again she tries to speak, but now that he's gotten started, he seems unable to stop. And all in a whisper, but a whisper gone hoarse as if he's been screaming at her all afternoon and has injured his voice.

"How has any of this business touched America anyway?" he says. "And don't start in on the *Lusitania*. The *Lusitania*. Are you joking? Fools going off on a pleasure cruise in the middle of hell. And I'm supposed to die for them? Which of them would have died for us? Name one American who tried to avenge our deaths. Name one American who took any kind of action at all. If we had gotten into it, do you know how many of us would have been saved? And even when we did get into it, did we break with Talaat? No, sir. It was Talaat who broke with us."

It's his mentioning Talaat Pasha that does it. She understands at last. *American Missionaries on the Destruction of Christian Communities.* She is stupid, so stupid. "You're Armenian," she says.

He looks at her contemptuously, as if throughout their encounter he's repeatedly mentioned his ethnicity. "Well, yes," he says. "Look at me. Of course I'm Armenian." Then he softens but only a little. "Well, I mean—no, I'm not. I'm American just like you. I'm no crazed foreigner, if that's what you mean. I'm just a regular guy from Providence, Rhode Island."

"And the old man," she says. "He was Armenian too."

"Not was. Is. Much more so than me. I've been here pretty much all my life. He came over only a few years ago. Lost his entire family over there. Saw never-mind-what. I couldn't say it in front of a lady anyway." He looks at her, corrects himself, sneering. "A girl, I mean. But he's American too, now. A farmer from St. Joe."

"But then, I'm rather perplexed." She hears herself, knows she is trying to sound anything but girlish. "Why didn't he simply hand you this?"

"Right, it all seems absurd to you. Dime-novel stuff. Cloak-and-dagger. But he didn't want to meet any of us. He didn't want to be able to identify us or us him. We kept telling him it was okay. The guns are his. He got hold of the lot of them in Anatolia and brought them here. They're yours, we told him. You can give them to anyone you want. Nobody cares. In the infantry lots of fellows carry in their own weapons. In the Caucasus we saw plenty of boys from Fresno with squirrel rifles from home."

"You fought in the Caucasus?"

"But he's been through so much, every last thing makes him suspicious. He has this idea they'll come for him and make him go back. Or torture him, make him divulge our names."

"Dime-novel stuff."

"Yes," he says, "unless you're Armenian. Then it's everyday stuff."

"Well," she says. She doesn't want to fight. She wants to be nice. "He does have a point. Resident aliens have to be careful. They apply different laws to them, you know." She is thinking of Emma Goldman: two years at hard labor just for saying she opposes the war.

"Right," he says. "So maybe that's another thing he's afraid of."

"Yes," she says.

"Yes." And then, in a different tone, "Yes. I fought in the Caucasus." He runs his fingers through the gray forelock. "That's when this happened. Overnight. From the things I saw there. You can't have any idea. I could never tell an American girl."

"I know what went on there," she protests.

"Right," he says, "but it's all romance to you. It's a picture show. But for me—you'd ride into a village and you'd see these things. Rubble and stacks of impaled bodies and the outrages done to the women. One night I went to sleep and the next morning"—he shakes his head, and the silver falls forward—"this had happened."

"You're lying," she says.

"About which part? The part about the Turks slaughtering men and outraging women, two years of it while Americans like you stood by twiddling your thumbs? Or the part about me fighting over there?"

"The part about your hair," she says.

"Oh," he says. "Of course, that's what you'd want to talk about. My hair. What can I say? Everyone has a theory. In St. Petersburg, the Russian foreign minister said it was as if God had touched me while I slept, as if he'd given me a partial coat of armor. He said God knew I was capable of doing heroic things and was giving me a sign that he'd help me part of the way if I'd do the rest on my own. But you know the Russians. They're crazed with religion. Fanatics. It's why they're all revolutionaries."

"You never met the Russian foreign minister," she says.

"Fine," he says. "I never met the Russian foreign minister."

She understands that he has. She's impressed. She tells herself not to be, orders herself not to let tales of czarist Russia distract her. "So, do you agree?" she asks. She touches her own hair, feels the wildness from the day's humidity. She tries not to think about how she must look. "Do you believe you've been touched by God?"

"Christ, no," he says. "I'm just telling you what some people have said."

It seems to her that he keeps bringing things up, and then, when she repeats them, he becomes offended, as if she's accused him of something. She changes the subject. "Who are *we*?" she asks. "Before, you said: divulging *our* names."

"I have some friends who feel the same way I do."

"Other officers in the American army, you mean? Who want to carry old German guns into battle? Is that what you mean? Other officers who are Armenian?"

"Armenian-Americans."

"Hyphenates."

He nods. She sees that he understands her meaning, that she doesn't like the word, this pejorative Teddy Roosevelt coined to describe immigrants with one foot still in the homeland. He understands that her distaste is for TR and the term, not for the hyphenates themselves. It's good to be on the same side at last. She wants to be his ally. The conversation they're having—ravaged women and ruined villages and his hair, which he keeps shaking at her as if inviting her to stroke it—it's the best conversation she's ever had in her life.

CHAPTER SEVEN

A Woman's Name

SHE IS READY to give him the package. She believes him now, understands this all has to do with some political cause that doesn't concern her, a cause she should respect and then forget about, mention to no one. And certainly she no longer wants to peek inside the package. She dislikes guns, can't even begin to think about handling a grenade. She lifts the bundle, ready to pass it to him. But as she does, the strings she previously untied slip to the floor and the brown wrapping paper unfolds and inside she sees another package wrapped and tied the same way—"Like Russian nesting dolls," she says—and then she sees a card tucked under the second bow and on it, in block letters, the name of a woman.

She covers the card with her palm. "There's a name written here," she says. "You tell me the name and I'll give you the package. I won't open it further."

He squints with confusion. "There's a name there?"

"Well, come on. That's a fair solution, don't you think?"

"A name? Written in English?"

"A woman's name. Apparently, your friend addressed the package to her."

"To a woman?"

She nods.

"But that makes no sense. Is it a first name? A last name?"

"First and last."

She doesn't mean to be difficult. She isn't toying with him. She understands how important the package is to him. She wants him to have it; she does. She is in favor of Armenians, is becoming increasingly in favor of them the more time she spends with him. She's never met one before. Until now, she always thought they were dark exotics, like Gypsies, brown men with earrings and shoes that curl up at the toes. Still, she's always sympathized with them. "Clean your plate," mothers all over America say. "Remember the starving Armenians." Yael understands why the soldier is bitter. Read any newspaper. The Turks are killing hundreds of thousands of his people, everyone knows it, and the only way Americans come to their aid is by cleaning their plates, gobbling down every last slice of peach pie, slurping up every last drop of cherry ice cream. America gorges on behalf of dark, swarthy Armenia but storms into battle for blond, blue-eyed Belgium.

She really does read the papers.

And she really is for his people. But having seen the card, she needs this one last thing from him, this last confirmation, this password.

And maybe she also wants to know who this woman is and what his relationship to her is. And maybe she wants him to stay a bit longer. She knows he has a train to catch, but there will be another train tomorrow. In the meantime, he could come home with her. Maybe that's what she wants. That he stay for dinner, that he stay the night. Her eighteenth birthday, her day. And an American soldier. How could her mother refuse her this gift, this guest?

"First name and last?" he says. "And you're sure it's a woman? Because we wouldn't ever involve one of our women in what we're doing."

What we're doing. She doesn't think about it. She is too busy considering what he said just before that and the way he said it: *our women.* So protectively that she glances at his hand, looks for a ring, and there is a gold band but it's on his pinkie, an insignificant finger when it comes to rings, although what does she know about Armenians? They may have all kinds of strange traditions. They may wear their wedding bands on their littlest fingers for reasons she can't begin to guess.

"Give me a hint," he says.

"Her first name begins with an *E*."

"An *E*?" He is leaning toward her. "An *E*?"

She lets the answer roll to the tip of her tongue. She could kiss him the answer, he is that close. She could gently deposit it just inside his ear.

He is thinking so hard he seems in pain. Then, for the first time since they met, he relaxes, he smiles. It's a lopsided smile. It makes him seem bashful. He dips his head to one side like a pigeon.

"Does it say Erinyes?" he asks.

"Oh," she says. The way he says it, it almost rhymes with Pyrenees. "Is that how you pronounce it?"

"Yes," he says. "That's how. It's Greek."

"I thought it was Erin Yes." She shows him the card. "The way he wrote it."

"A girl's name." His smile broadens. "Erin Yes. That's rich. 'Hello, I'm Miss Yes.' Now, there's a girl I'd like to meet."

"Don't make fun of me," she says. But she's smiling too, and she wonders if he admires her ability to laugh at her own foolish mistakes. She wonders if he finds her endearing, even admirable. "How was I supposed to know?" she says. "Do I speak Greek? What does it mean?"

"Nothing," he says. "It's a club I belong to. Will you give me the package now?"

"What sort of club?" she asks. "An Armenian club? A Greek club?"

"Come on," he says. He is still smiling, his head still angled to the side. "Play fair. I told you what was in the package; I guessed the name. I did my part and then some. Come on. Where's my prize?"

She was prepared to give him the package before; now, once again, she is reluctant. The bundle feels so at home on her lap.

The soldier looks into her eyes, makes his pouting face. The full lower lip.

"All right," she says. "You're right. Fair is fair."

She makes sure their fingers touch when she passes it to him. She feels pounds lighter when it's gone. Her lap is cold. "So," she says, crossing her legs lavishly, something else one can do in a split skirt. "Tell me about this Erinyes of yours. What does it mean?"

She imagines him leaning back in his chair as he tells her the story, impassioned words rushing at her the way they did when he told her about Armenians in Turkey, American apathy, the frightened farmer from St. Joe.

He smiles again, his head to one side, and she finds it impossible not to cock her own head in the opposite direction. He leans forward. He presses his face close to hers. Once more, the gray shock tumbles forward.

"You really want to know what it means?" he says.

She nods. She does.

"Then go look it up," he says. "And then go to hell."

He shambles to his feet. The outer layer of brown wrapping paper rustles to the floor. He places his cap on his head, hiding the gray. He tucks the package beneath his arm. Kicking the wrapping out of his way, he leaves the library, stomping, angry, echoing: a hungry man late for his train.

CHAPTER EIGHT

Crazy

CRAZY. The streetcar carries Yael home and that's what she thinks, that the soldier was crazy. Worse than that; he was dangerous. He was—what is the word?—mercurial. One minute arrogant, the next nearly sniveling. And what about the way he twisted her wrist? And what about the language he used? Damn this and Christ that and telling her to go to hell. She was doing the right thing based on her assessment of the circumstances, the right thing based on what she had witnessed, and he should have understood, should have seen that her heart was in the right place. Instead, he'd sworn at her.

What had he expected her to do? Did he think she could read minds? Did he think she could see through two layers of brown wrap-

ping paper? How was she to know what was transpiring in the library?
Cloak-and-dagger, cops and robbers, eastern intrigue. The need to
exchange arms in the Turkish history section of the Open Shelf Room,
for heaven's sake. The need to kill your enemies in battle with their
very own guns, as if life were an epic poem full of symbolism and double meanings. The soldier was crazy.

Or maybe a poet.

But probably crazy.

And the old man too. Both of them were crazy. Because after the
soldier had stalked off, she went to the Reference Room and looked up
Erinyes as he'd ordered her to, and the definition made her mouth fall
open. Because not only was the soldier crazy and not only was the old
man crazy, but apparently they were affiliated with an entire group of
crazy people, because the Erinyes, as it turned out, were creatures from
Greek mythology, a trio of beautiful but vicious goddesses whose job it
was to track down and punish the guilty. The Erinyes dressed in black.
Their eyes dripped blood. Their hair was a tangle of snakes, and their
favorite weapon was the scourge. (And, she noticed with great satisfaction, the book said *goddesses*: that is, women, which meant she'd been
right, damn him, when she'd said that Erinyes was a woman's name. He
could have at least given her that much. He made her feel ignorant, but
she'd been right, at least in a way.)

The streetcar lurches to a halt. College boys, it seems, have pulled
down the pole. Now every time it rounds a corner, the motorman has to
pull the brake, climb to the roof, and put the pole back. The other passengers groan at each unscheduled stop, but Yael barely notices. She is
thinking only of the soldier.

She knows she upset him, but, really, what genuine harm did she do?
A bit of frustration. At the worst, a missed train. And what kind of hero
was this man, this Armenian? What kind of warrior? One small set-
back, and right away the brave man is crying. A girl confronts him, and
suddenly there's a tear in his eye. God save the American Expeditionary
Forces if this is a typical officer.

That tear, though. She thinks about it, that lone silver drop caught in
his thick black eyelashes like a sliver of ice clinging to a twig in winter,
and she knows this image, as well as the way it is making her feel, is so
damned yokel, so damned clichéd (and now her thoughts are punctu-

ated as they've never been before with the word *damned*, and this is the soldier's fault too). But what is a cliché except something so true that everyone who has ever lived has at one time spoken it or felt it or at the very least recognized it? The soldier's tear touched her. Why isn't she allowed to feel clichéd feelings in response? Just because others have beaten her to it? Why would anyone want to deprive her of these first steps into the overdone half-baked world of love?

Because she *is* in love, she is certain of it. Maybe she won't be in love tomorrow, but she is in love now, on this halting, lurching streetcar, at this very moment, and she repeats the word inside her head until she can no longer remember if it's really a word, and she has to stop and think about it, has to reassure herself that, yes, it's definitely a word. *Love.* From the French *oeuf*. *Oeuf* meaning egg. As in egg *handgranate*.

And what if that *oeuf-handgranate* should go off in the club car of a train bound for Providence, Rhode Island? She is thinking about that as the streetcar lumbers up the hill to the stop nearest her house. What kind of person risks such a disaster? Only someone who's crazy. Crazy and soft. And too easily angered. And downright sentimental.

The little Lutheran girl who taught Yael how to pray years ago—one of the Bible stories that girl had recited was about a general's wife who invited a murderous tyrant into her tent, lulled him to sleep with warm milk, and then hammered a tent peg clean through his skull. An obscure story, the little girl had admitted, but perhaps of interest because the general's wife was named Jael. Maybe Yael's parents had named her for this woman. Yael said she didn't think so. She mentioned her own theory—goats—and her mother's—houseflies. Still, she never forgot that general's wife, Jael with her milk and her hammer and her tent peg. Now *there* was a goddess of vengeance!

This soldier by contrast was so soft that he had entered into negotiations with a little girl from St. Louis to get back what was his. He had pleaded with that girl. Could there be a clearer sign he wasn't up to the challenge he'd set for himself? She can imagine his fate. A battle in France, and he sneaks up on a Hun, puts the 1908 Luger to the cowering German's forehead, pulls back the trigger. And then the German says ouch and the lieutenant blanches; he apologizes, he backs away, his head cocked to one side, and he weeps, not blood, but his commonplace tears. And what is the result? The lieutenant, her lieutenant, winds up shot by the dissembling Hun. Because her lieutenant doesn't have it in him to aim that Luger at the space between some wretched Boche's eyes and fire.

Because—a pistol. Don't you have to be awfully close to do a fellow in with a pistol? Not a repeater, not a Big Bertha, but a small gun, a Luger. Don't you have to stand so close that you see your enemy's eyes and the tears he is shedding, which are nothing special, just salt and water, the same as your own?

She has somehow reached her front door. She opens it, passes through the parlor, climbs the stairs. Her mother is in the second-floor hallway, washing the woodwork, perspiring through her dark dress. "What in the world are you wearing?" she shouts as Yael continues up the next flight of stairs to her room.

Beneath the dormered ceiling, she stares out her window, stares down the hill, past rooftops decorated with ornate brass lightning rods, spiked iron pigeon deflectors. She doesn't see any of them. She is too busy imagining the soldier's arrival in Providence. She is too busy thinking, Just who are his comrades? Why was he so afraid to return home to Rhode Island without the weapons? A man on a mission, and the mission had come this close to failing. Well, what if it had failed? What did he fear his friends would have done to him then, all those other snake-headed Erinyes men?

And, she thinks the next day at the Red Cross Center (knitting needles clicking, gossip bouncing off walls), even though he had told her to go to hell, the truth was that *he* was the one going there. Literally going. Wasn't the Western Front hell on earth? The trenches where men lived for days in their waste, where men set up house in their graves. Men in muck, men in cold, men using their dead comrades as decoys and shields and umbrellas and blankets. And the waiting, which people said was the worst part of all.

The British reported that the average lieutenant's life span at the front was two weeks. They were speaking, of course, of their own men, their *leftenants*. Surely Americans fared better. Still, she could no longer concentrate on her scarf.

She puts down her needles. "I'm dizzy," she tells the girl next to her. "I have a blinding headache. I'm going home early."

Before she leaves, she glances at the bulletin board by the door. Thumbtacked on top of newspaper articles about battles won and local boys lost, on top of posters about paper drives, metal drives, and food conservation, is a clipping from the latest issue of *Current Opinion*. It says:

1,000 WOMEN ARE WANTED
FOR OVERSEAS CANTEEN WORK

PARIS—The Y.M.C.A. War Work Council has issued an appeal for more women workers. Dr. John R. Mott, general secretary of the Red Triangle Organization, states that the finest type of woman is needed for work in the Y.M.'s overseas canteens.

High-minded, unselfish devotion and absolute willingness to do the humblest task, combined with the ability to rise to any emergency, are necessary for success. A knowledge of French is helpful but not required.

The U.S. government will not issue passports to women under the age of twenty-five.

The soldier is crazy and the old man is crazy and the men who belong to Erinyes are all crazy too, but she is the craziest of all. Days pass, then a week, and she keeps thinking about him, worrying about him, arguing with him in her mind. She conjures him and kisses her pillow as if it has his face, as if it has arms to hold her.

The only French she knows is *hinky dinky parlay voo*. She has never been fond of the humblest of tasks. She's not twenty-five, she's eighteen.

But she can teach herself French, she can learn it. She can learn to tolerate serving meals in canteens as well. And she knows how to become twenty-five.

She accompanies Chaim Mandel to *Cleopatra* (where the costumes, if negligible, are also achingly beautiful, spiderwebs held in place with emeralds and diamonds), and in the dark theater she lets him kiss her and she promises to be there, waving, when his train takes him away.

Before they part, she gives him her birth certificate, handwritten, blue ink ("Be glad it's not black," he says. "Black is impossible"), and a short week later he has used bleach and a feather to erase the year of her birth. The document now maintains she was born in early August of the year 1893. A seven-year difference. There is something significant, something biblical, about that number. Seven years of fat, seven years of lean. Seven years and eligible for a United States passport.

The day she goes to City Hall and slips the altered birth certificate beneath the iron bars of a clerk's cage, she learns that this clerk is crazy too. Or maybe just gullible. "Be glad you look so young," he says. "Someday you'll be happy for it, believe you me."

When she tells him she also wishes to petition for a name change, he laughs.

"Weiss to White," he repeats. "Very clever. Typical of you people. The other day I had one of you here, says he wants to go from Shonberg to Belmont. Had to get him to explain that one. Very clever, you people, I'll give you that much."

She takes no offense. She knows he means to be nice. He *is* being nice.

"And lookit here," he says when he returns with various forms and applications and seals and petitions. "You see this? I fixed up the first name for you too. The way it's writ down here"—he means the birth certificate, the ornate loops of the professional scrivener—"it looks like *Y-A-E-L*. See what I mean? The *L* looks like the *E*, the *E* looks like the *L*. Anyways, I fixed it up. I did, didn't I? Unless it's some Jew name I never did hear of?"

She stands on her toes. She sees what he's done.

"Yes," she says, a polite midwestern Jew on her last day of being one. "Thank you so much. You fixed it up perfectly."

CHAPTER NINE

The Denominations

THE DAY her passport arrives, she hands it to her father and tells him he will have to address his letters to this girl, this Yale White. The

YMCA will recognize her by no other name. She fears he'll be hurt. It's his name, after all. But he doesn't say a word. "It will be easier," she says, and he shrugs. The only thing that concerns him is the one thing she thought he wouldn't notice: the line asking for her religion. Methodist, it says.

"You didn't have to do this." They are sitting at the dining-room table. He's having a glass of hot tea. He opens the sugar bowl, takes a tiny cube with a small pair of silver tongs. She reaches into the bowl with her fingers. "The YMCA has to take you regardless," he tells her. His sugar cube plunks into the tea. Her sugar cube melts on her tongue. "They have to take everyone. Jews, coloreds, even Chinamen. It's the law."

"I know," she says. "It just seemed like less trouble this way. You can't amount to anything in the organization unless you're a true Trinitarian. It says so in their charter. You can't even serve on their board."

"You aspire to a position of importance with the YMCA?"

"No," she says.

"Methodist," he says. "How did you come up with Methodist?"

She doesn't know. She supposes it was the local Methodist church, its white facade, its lean spire—a church as simple and plain as a working woman's dress, a suffragette's suit. "I had to pick something," she says.

"Episcopalian," he tells her. "That's higher up their ladder."

"Really? I didn't know there was an order."

"Of course there's an order. You don't know there's always an order?" A beat. "So, what you're telling me is there was no Methodist in your madness?"

She laughs, and then they are silent. He returns her passport. He gets up. He is leaving.

"Why do you suppose there are so many?" she says. "Denominations, I mean."

"I don't know." He has stopped in the doorway and turned back to face her. "But there are." He begins to count them off. "Methodists, Episcopalians . . ."

"Lutherans," she says, thinking of the little girl who tried to share the Good News, thinking of almost all her friends, really. Lutherans, all of them. All descended from Prussians. And she thinks about how the once-mighty have fallen. No one speaks of St. Louis's great German language experiment any longer. People boycott sauerkraut. Berlin Street has been renamed Pershing.

"Presbyterians," her father says.

She is willing—no, happy—to play. "Baptists," she tells him.

"Anabaptists."

"Like the Quakers."

"And the Shakers."

"And the Pennsylvania Dutch."

"And the Amish," he says. "And the Mennonites."

"And the Congregationalists. I mean, they're not Anabaptists. Just another one."

"Right. And the Campbellites."

"And the Calvinists."

"I don't think there are any more Calvinists."

"They're extinct?"

"Yes, like the dinosaurs and the Pilgrims and the Puritans."

"And the Huguenots?"

"I think there may still be Huguenots. Up in Canada."

"And I know there are still snake people."

"Snake people?"

"The ones who dance with snakes. What do you call them?"

"*Meshugge.*"

"Yes," she says, happy for an opportunity to say the word out loud. "Crazy."

"And the Mormons. Also crazy. A hundred wives."

"And the Seventh-Day Adventists."

"Again, crazy."

"And the Transcendentalists."

"Less crazy," he says. "In a good way, crazy."

"Like all the poets."

"Like H. David Thoreau. My namesake."

"Really?"

"No, not really. I was named for a dead uncle."

"Oh."

"And Walt Whitman."

She brightens. "You know him? I like him. I have some of him by heart. 'Do I contradict myself? / Very well then I contradict myself. / (I am large, I contain multitudes.)'"

"So you do," says her father.

She names other Transcendentalists. "All the Bostonians. The Beechers."

"The Lowells."

"Damn it," she says. "That's what I should have said I was. Instead of Methodist."

He overlooks the cussing. "A Transcendentalist?" he says.

"A Unitarian. Isn't that what the Beechers and Lowells are?"

"You may be right."

"Or are they Universalists?"

"That could be too."

They grow quiet again.

"Well?" he says. "Are we done? Are the denominations now closed?"

She doesn't want to be done. She says, "I'll bet there are more." Armenians, for instance. And Russians and Greeks, the Orthodox Church. They haven't even got round to them. And the Roman Church. You could go on forever. Every time you thought you had them all, you came up with another. "There are always more," she says.

"And what about what they believe in? What do you think about that?"

She's caught unaware, doesn't know how to answer. She knows only the most basic Christian tenets: Turn the other cheek. Love thy neighbor. Perfectly nice tenets. Better than anything her own people believe in. Although what do her own people believe in? She has no idea. She only knows what they don't believe in. Pork chops. Kneeling. Naming for the living.

"I don't know what any of it means," she says.

"Who does?" he says. "You want to know what it means? It means nobody likes the idea of dying. It means people die, soldiers, babies, and nobody understands why." He looks over her head, at something against the far wall or in the air. "Well," he says. "And how do you plan to tell all this to your mother?"

He's smiling as he says this. She can tell from his expression that he knows the answer to his own question, and she waits for him to share it with her, to provide a primer on how she and her mother should talk to each other, a guide to how this family fits together. She is eager to hear what he has to tell her; they've never spoken to each other like this before.

But it's only a punch line he leaves her with.

"You just go up to her," he says, "and you say to her, Mama? You've heard of somebody being christened? Well, I've just been christianed."

CHAPTER TEN

Along with Those Lies

THE NAME Esther Weiss means white star, but Esther has always been more like a planet, stolid and steadfast, a woman who doesn't like to stray from her prescribed orbit. "If you're going, you're going," she says, as she washes dishes and gazes out the window over the sink, taking in the remains of her summer garden, the absurdly large squashes, the still brilliant delphiniums. "My parting advice is never love your children. The minute your back is turned, they find ways to leave you."

"Oh, for heaven's sake," Yael says. "It's not forever."

Esther plunges a handful of spoons into dishwater. "Says you. Bring a pillow. I hear the pillows on the boats are hard as rocks."

"I don't think we even get pillows," Yael says. "I think we're supposed to sleep in our helmets in case of torpedoes."

"Oh, now I feel better," Esther says. She turns on the spigots. The hot water reddens her hands.

Later, from her bedroom window, Yael watches remnants of sunlight dissipate until the sky has turned the eerie blue of which she's so fond. Then she lights a lamp and sits at her desk and unfolds the Y's application. With the pen and violet ink her parents gave her for her birthday, now a full month gone by, she writes of her patriotism and her belief in self-determination. She writes of her compassion for poor little Belgium and her longing to do God's work on the Western Front.

Along with those lies, she writes these:

NAME: *Yale White*
DATE OF BIRTH: *August 5, 1893*
LANGUAGES SPOKEN: *Un peu de français, et l'anglais, of course*
RELIGIOUS AFFILIATION: *Southern Methodist*

She is crazy and she is a thief and she is a liar. But most of all crazy. Because the reason she is going overseas, the reason she is becoming seven years older and bilingual and Christian is this: if the soldier is going to France, and if France is hell, and if he told her to go to hell—well then, hasn't he asked her please to come with him?

Part Two

CHAPTER ONE

The Train to Providence

WHEN LIEUTENANT DOUBLEDAY HAGOPIAN arrives at St. Louis's Union Station he is woefully late, thoroughly out of breath, and cradling a bundle of weapons in his arms. Sweat rivers down his back, a painful stitch nags at his side, and he is aching with hunger.

He hasn't once thought about the girl in the library. He is much too preoccupied with how he is feeling, which is, in a word, lousy. *Vad* if you want it in Armenian, the language that often comes to him when he's feeling this way—angry, miserable, put-upon. *Vad*, in his father's voice, perpetually gruff, comically green.

And yet, to his astonishment, good news awaits him at the station. The train to Providence, a ticket agent tells him, has been delayed to accommodate troop movement. There's the Commercial Express now, shimmying on its track, the last few recruits marching aboard.

A miracle, thinks Doubleday Hagopian (the accent's on the *gop* and the *-ian* means *son of*, and as for the first name, he goes by Dub and don't even ask how he's come by it). He doesn't generally believe in miracles, of course, but it does seem that this time some compassionate and all-seeing Someone has caught wind of his problem and come to his rescue. It's as if a big divine finger is holding the train in place until Dub gets his ass on board. Thank God for small favors, Dub thinks.

Not that he lets himself get carried away. He isn't *that* happy, isn't *that* grateful. He is a man who believes that small favors are the only kind God bestows nowadays. And, he believes, God is damned parsimonious even with those. He doesn't have to wait long for proof of the latter. "Sorry, Lieutenant," a conductor says, when Dub steps onto the train and asks for a compartment, "but every sleeper's been nabbed." Dub swears. Running from the library, he spurred himself onward with fantasies of clean linens, a lock on his door, and, above all else, silence. Instead, he's going to have to sit up all night on a train stuffed to bursting with soldiers.

He swears again as he walks through the cars, the air cottony from humidity and coal dust and warm breath. He can't help but hear all the crude jokes and chest-thumping. How loudly the recruits claim they're looking forward to fighting, this hodgepodge of bodies and odors and drawls jamming the aisles, none of them making an effort to get out of his way. There are no empty seats, and a depressing thought comes to him. The only thing worse than sitting up all night among these soldiers will be standing up all night among them.

It's not until he reaches the next-to-last car that he spots Raffi Soghokian in a window seat, his back to the aisle, his forehead pressed to the pane, his eyes fixed on the now empty platform. Raffi's hat, though, is saving the aisle seat beside him, and Dub feels a mixture of relief and disappointment. So much for standing the whole way. So much too for a silent journey.

Despite this last unhappy thought, he makes himself smile. He whistles once as if calling a dog. "Say, Ivan," he says (Ivan because Raffi's hat is a peaked Russian infantry cap with a khaki leather bill and the Russian tricolored cockade), "that seat for me?"

When Raffi turns, Dub sees that the skin under his eyes is thin and sallow. The eyes themselves are bleary. *Kheghj eh,* thinks Dub. How exhausted the poor bastard is. How miserable. Dub's smile broadens a little.

Dub knows the cause of Raffi's misery. While Dub was dispatched to the library, Raffi spent the day with the women's auxiliary of the local Armenian Revolutionary Federation. The ladies had raised cartloads of money for Erinyes by reading tea leaves at local fairs and selling candy and cakes, but then they refused to send their check to Boston by post. They didn't trust the mail system, they wrote (in a letter they'd mailed), but it was clear that what they really wanted was to personally present their donation to a bona fide freedom fighter. They wanted a handsome warrior to stand in their chairwoman's parlor and deliver a speech in the old mother tongue in which he praised their generosity and fervor and baked goods. What they got instead—a subtle rebuke from Aram Kazarian, although they didn't recognize it as such and neither did Raffi—was the most unpleasant and graceless *fedayee* in the American branch of Operation Erinyes.

Two hours of dishing out flattery, consuming sweets, and minding his manners; Dub relishes the toll it must have taken. No wonder Raffi is irritable. Not that Raffi is ever anything but. Irritable is the vehicle in which Raffi Soghokian navigates life.

And he's not only perpetually irritable, he's perpetually irritating, as well. "Christ," he says now in his pedantic English. "You cannot genuinely be intending to tell me that you are only just now boarding this train."

Dub is still smiling, but he is also still standing, being made to cool his heels, and he gestures impatiently at the hat. "Come on," he says, "or I'll sit on it."

"*Khent es,*" Raffi mutters. He folds his arms across his chest. "And here I am concluding long ago that you have already boarded and found yourself another seat without telling me. Or that maybe you are so severely screwing up your assignment today you are deciding never to show your face to me again."

Dub takes the hat off the seat and tosses it onto the overhead rack. He sits heavily, gracelessly, but he's still smiling. "What do you mean, screwing up?" he says. "I'm here, aren't I?" He juts his chin toward the package now in his lap. "I've got this, haven't I? Where's the screw-up?"

"It must be someplace, *tratsi.* Are you not hours late?"

"One hour late. Hour. Singular."

"Very well." A grim smile, a gold front tooth gleaming. "You are singularly late."

But unlike Dub, Raffi is incapable of feigning equanimity when he is exasperated, and his smile dissolves quickly. Raffi is wildly exasperated, partially because Dub is so late, but mainly because Dub has been off doing something important and romantic (a clandestine rendezvous, a cache of weapons, a task involving synchronized watches) while Raffi has been enduring a ladies' coffee. After which he returned directly to this station and sat on a bench, where he had nothing to do but worry about his pulse, which he could feel racing from resentment and too much caffeine and halvah, and look for Dub. When the train pulled in, he'd gone on board, taken his seat, and continued to look for Dub. He has been in this station for hours now, like a piece of luggage dropped off early, a worn-out valise bloated with folderol, womanly gewgaws.

He's no good with people; that's his problem. He told Aram Kazarian as much, Aram who should have known it by now. He begged

Aram to let him be the one to pick up the guns in the library. Synchronized watches! He would have done anything for such an adventure. And unlike Dub Hagopian, Raffi had earned an adventure. "I really don't care one way or the other," Dub had piped up—he'd been eating a sardine and tomato sandwich in the back room at Lulu's and had crumbs and grease in his mustache—and Raffi had pounced. "You see, Aslan? He admits he doesn't care. What is a *fedayee* who doesn't care? An oxymoron, that's what. A bourgeois American who is playing games." But Aram, the *aslan*—the lion—was mulish. No, he said in every language he knew. *Non, nein, nyet, voch.* "Dub to the library. You to the old ladies."

"So," Dub says now, as he settles in, every prissy adjustment of his creased trousers, his pressed tunic, and the package on his lap making Raffi want to strike him, "did you get the check?"

Rubbing it in, and Raffi nods curtly, says nothing.

"Oh, come on. At least you got to eat."

Nothing. Just the bragging of the recruits in the aisle, only a whistle, two blasts, then the engine full throttle.

"*Eench eh?*" Dub says. "You're not talking to me now?"

When Raffi doesn't respond, Dub laughs. It's another goddamn miracle, he tells himself, another small favor. The day began shitty and then it got shittier, but look how it's ending up. It will take thirty-some hours for the two of them to get back to Providence, and if all that time Raffi is sulking and silent . . .

"*Park Asdudzo,*" Dub says, and he sighs like a man who has just unbuttoned his trousers after a feast. "God is good."

AND YET, a quick moment after acknowledging God's most recent small favor, Dub Hagopian is melancholy again. First of all, he's hungry. Second, his seat cushion is so thin that whenever the train jitters over a nick in the tracks, he feels booted in the ass. And then there's the package on his lap. It's awkward and bulky and quite a bit closer to certain cherished parts of his body than he'd like. Also, it extends into the aisle, its corners grazing the thighs of passengers squeezing by, who invariably glare at him, requiring him to glare back if they are civilians or corporals, to apologize if they are captains or colonels.

He would prefer to stow the package on the overhead rack or under his seat (under Raffi's seat would be even better), but he can't. He has to hold it tightly on his lap as if it were a toddler prone to squirming and mischief. He can't leave it to go find something to eat. He can't trust a conductor to safeguard it so he might run to the toilet for a quick minute. He certainly can't ask Raffi for help. *Hey, keep an eye on this for me, will you, tratsi?* If Raffi got hold of the package, he'd find a way to present it to Aram Kazarian as his own. He'd sneak off the train while Dub dozed and somehow manage to beat the Commercial Express to Providence. Once there, he would hand the package to Aram along with the check from the ladies. "No thanks needed, Aslan. Unlike some, I would never let our noble cause down."

Dub would rather sit here and piss himself sopping.

He lets his head fall back against the white tidy. Closing his eyes, he tries to sleep.

Find a package on a shelf. Bring the package home. It was such a simple assignment, really. Yet Raffi was right, he had screwed up, although how could he be blamed for the screw-up? It had not been his fault, but still, he'd come perilously close to returning home empty-handed.

His fingers tighten their grip on the string. And now he does think about that girl in the library. That pain in the ass, he thinks. That goddamn shit in the mouth. It's all too humiliating, not only the way she nearly thwarted him but also the range of degrading methods he had to employ to wrest the package from her. Crocodile tears, little-boy pouts, and the lie he'd told about how his hair had turned gray. And then, giving in to his anger and passion and doubts, finally confessing far too much of the truth. He dislikes admitting how near he came to failing, tells himself that he needs to stop thinking this way, ought to concentrate instead on what matters: his ultimate victory, how at the last minute he prevailed, and now the package is his, and he will not let it go, not for a minute, not for a second, not until he is the one standing in the Providence train station putting it into the damaged but welcoming hands of Aram Kazarian.

The train rocks and rattles through the last snippets of northern Missouri. Dub places his cap over his nose and mouth as if it's a mask. His trapped breath is hot and damp on his skin, but the cap mitigates the stench and sting of coal dust. He tries not to think about guns and blasting gelatin. Or about his growling belly. Or about his needling bladder. His father's lugubrious voice comes to him, his father appealing to God's mercy. *Der voghormya. Der voghormya.* On the train goes, past farms and fields, past cattails and cornstalks. On it goes, past slaughterhouse after slaughterhouse full of doomed, lowing cattle.

CHAPTER TWO

Stops Along the Way

FIRST IS East St. Louis, where, the year before, neighbor turned against neighbor and white men beat colored men, looting their stores, burning their homes, wielding clubs, tying nooses. Next come small towns like Troy and St. Jacob and Greenup. Then a slightly larger town, Terre Haute; later still, Indianapolis; and, by ten at night, Piqua, where highway workers recently unearthed the remains of a pioneer family killed in an Indian raid. "May we always remember our ancestors, who endured great hardships and, in some cases, as with the Dilbones, made the supreme sacrifice," a town father will intone at a memorial service.

Pioneers, Raffi is thinking. Only eight years ago, in 1910, he was fifteen years old and a pioneer himself. He thinks of it often, his family's voyage from Turkey to America. After spending two weeks in a lower bunk in steerage, lice raining down on their heads, the four Soghokians stumbled off the boat in New York, and though they were as queasy and rubber-legged as a quartet of drunkards sprung from the tank on a Sunday morning, they got right back on another boat, the one that took them to the port of Providence.

After weeks of vermin and vomiting, after a lifetime of humiliation, his parents believed they were saved. "Providence is meaning heaven," his father crowed in his broken English. "From Turkish hell to American heaven we come."

The local branch of the Kharput Society had already found them an apartment, a generous thing to have done, everyone told him, given that the Soghokians hailed not from Kharput but from the little town of Peri in the Dersim region. The apartment was on the top floor of a shabby triple-decker on Smith Hill. It consisted of two small rooms, one for Raffi's parents and sister, the other a kitchen where, for the first few nights, Raffi slept on a bed fashioned from everyone's coats. Later, a cot was moved in and out. He didn't mind either of his beds, such as they were. It was Smith Hill he minded.

The city of Providence had been built on seven hills, people repeatedly told him with inexplicable pride. Like Rome, they said, when Raffi looked at them contemptuously. Like Constantinople, they'd add, nodding energetically and meaningfully, as if this comparison was supposed to make him feel that he was, in a way, back home.

Rome, he thought. Constantinople. What were they but a pair of corrupt empires?

It wasn't only the constant reminders of Constantinople that irked him. It was the way these immigrants tried so hard to elevate pathetic Smith Hill to the same level as that far more illustrious city. As if puny Smith Hill was the same, just as good, when in fact Smith Hill was ridiculous. Why had the Armenian community settled on the seediest of Providence's seven hills? he wondered. Why not Fruit Hill, with its flowering orchards and arbors? Why not College Hill, with its ivy league university, or Mount Pleasant, with its farms and fat grazing sheep? Why Smith Hill, this bump in the road, this pimple with a name like an alias, with its soft tarry streets, its sooty factories, its ramshackle and grime?

On the ship he'd imagined something so very different. Eating meals from the same bucket he'd thrown up in that morning, he would comfort himself with fantasies of becoming a companion to people both wealthy and interesting. In several years, he would enroll at Harvard. Several years after that he would buy a Ford, have an office, and be a professional: a doctor, a lawyer. In the meantime he would spend his days talking philosophy with other formerly oppressed souls who were now breathing free. He would confab with exotics, befriend red Indians. But none of this had come to pass, because all of what he'd heard about America turned out to be lies. Despite the names of the streets and waterways (Narragansett Bay, Wampanoag Trail, Cowesett Square), there were no redmen to be found anywhere in Providence, certainly not on Smith Hill, unless you counted the red-faced Irishmen raging against England or the Russians, those Reds, raging against the czar. Worst of all, the Soghokians' apartment was near a colony of Levites, and these Levites were not even the well-to-do intellectuals one expected to encounter in America—artistic children of bankers from London—but were instead filthy sheenies from Salonika, goat-eyed Asiatics from back home. So this was America, this was heaven—Smith Hill, where the unwanted of the world bobbed in America's melting pot like so many calcified turds. And Raffi, who wanted only to turn around and go back to Peri, swimming all the way if he had to—Raffi, who now realized he'd done the absolutely wrong thing by flee-ing the *yergir,* the earth of the old country—Raffi, it appeared, was going to spend the rest of his life as just another bobbing turd.

Dub Hagopian was something else altogether. Not exactly a turd—he'd have grown prudish and squeamish at the very description—but neither had he melted upon being dropped in the cauldron. Perhaps, Raffi thought, Dub would someday have children who would become a part of the American slop, but Dub himself never would, even though—and here was the pitiful part, here was Dub in a nutshell, as the Americans said—he didn't seem to know it.

CHAPTER THREE

Curses

THEY'D MET a few days after the Soghokians first arrived on Smith Hill. Dub, also fifteen, was walking home from school when he turned off Chalkstone Avenue and saw Raffi by a pile of used furniture that the Kharputs had trucked over and dumped on the curb. Raffi was circling a dilapidated brown armchair and a doubled-over mattress. He looked like someone trying to recall an incantation that would persuade furni-ture to climb three flights of stairs on its own.

Dub knew Raffi at once for a greenhorn. Only someone fresh off the boat would be wearing that long threadbare coat, such old worn-out shoes. Only an immigrant would let himself be seen in public with that dirty sheepskin astrakhan on his head. Dub had little use for the crop of *Spiurka Hai* washing up on Smith Hill in 1910. They were such a morose and seething lot. Still, something about this particular kid made Dub feel sorry for him. It was the grotesque hat, he thought. Someone ought to say something about it.

He introduced himself, offered to help with the furniture. "*Shenorha-gal em,*" Raffi said, though he hardly sounded thankful, "but I am not requiring an assistant."

"Could have fooled me," Dub said.

From the start, Raffi unnerved him. It wasn't the stiff turns of phrase or the accent, that strange blend of diasporan Armenian and Oxford don. It was more Raffi's skill at figuring out Dub's weak spots and going right for them. From the beginning, it was as if someone were whispering in Raffi's ear, *Here's where it hurts. Poke him right here.*

"What kind of name is Dub?" Raffi said, homing right in on that sore spot, shining a mean-spirited light on that abrupt, ugly syllable, only one letter shy of *dumb,* too close for comfort to *dud,* and, in the early days of the century, a slang expression meaning *hayseed.* "It is hardly Armenian."

"It's for Abner Doubleday." Dub tried to sound proud. "You know, the great American general."

The name had been foisted on him in 1896 by an Ellis Island immigration officer. "Hampartzum?" the officer had chided Dub's parents, who cowered and nodded and smiled, their heads cocked to one side, a gesture of surrender they'd each perfected in Turkey and so inevitably passed on to their son. The officer grimaced. "You can't saddle the little beggar with a moniker like Hampartzum."

The prior ship had come in from Italy, and this man had just sent a McClellan Bonfiglio, a Fremont Caponegro, and a Sheridan Montebello out into the New World. Now he patted Hampartzum Hagopian's raven hair and, as the two-year-old recoiled, consulted his list.

"He invented baseball," Dub said. "You know the Red Sox, don't you?"

"I know the Red Sultan," said Raffi. Dub rolled his eyes. He knew the Red Sultan too—Abdul Hamit II, called red because of the Christian blood the tyrant liked wading in. Did Raffi want him to recite these details, prove himself? "We are leaving Turkey thanks to his massacres," Raffi said.

Dub was willing to give Raffi this much: "Yeah, we left because of his massacres too."

"Yes, but when?"

"In 'ninety-six," Dub said, but cautiously. He was suddenly doubting his own history. "From Erzurum. I don't remember much of it. I was only a baby."

He was still a baby. Or no, he was a lousy pitcher who had just lobbed a ball over the plate. And Raffi was swinging away, Raffi had knocked it over the wall and was now trotting lazily, leisurely, from base to base. "Yes," Raffi said, "we are living also through those same times. My parents, however, are not letting anyone chase us away so soon. For those massacres we are staying in our home and remaining defiant. No, I am speaking of last year's catastrophe. Much worse than 'ninety-six. When the church is burning in Adana with all the people locked inside, we are losing dear family. My sister. Her husband."

He suddenly stopped speaking. Dub thought it was emotion silencing him and again he felt sorry for the kid. It wasn't emotion, though. It never was that. It was just that for a moment Raffi thought he'd detected the same meaty fragrance he'd smelled the year before on the day he and his father rode into luckless Adana hoping to find Maro alive. Approaching the city, Raffi had inhaled a pleasing aroma. Roast lamb, he thought, and wondered if the Turks were having a feast, hundreds of lambs roasted out in the square to celebrate their destroying the church. Such a conflagration! Such a triumph! All those Christians inside to witness the children's first communions. The Turks barred the doors and lit torches.

As he and his father rode closer to the church, the smell became stench—revolting, sick-making. Then he understood it was the burnt bodies he was smelling. That kind of meat. But at a distance he hadn't known, and one of the secrets he would take to his grave was this: when he'd first breathed in the fragrance, his mouth had begun to water.

"Jeez, your sister," Dub was saying, and he felt genuinely bad, even though he also was envious—he wished he too could claim a murdered sibling. His parents could cite cousins, other relations killed in the *yer-gir*, but Dub himself had no memory of the old country, and he felt he was failing a test he hadn't wanted to take, losing a game he never agreed to play: *How Armenian are you?*

The aroma, real or imagined, was gone now, and Raffi waited for his stomach to right itself. "You see now why I am not interested in your precious Red Sox," he said. "Unlike you, I have no capacity for child-ish games."

"Yeah, but that's what's so swell about your being here now," Dub said. "You don't have to worry about all that anymore." He gestured like an umpire. "Safe!" he said.

Raffi's eyes grew dark; like a growling animal he bared his front teeth, which were crooked and coffee-stained. "And you are truly believing this? You are truly feeling no shame for running away?"

He hadn't run away, Dub thought. How could he have run? He'd been two; he'd been carried onto the boat in his mother's arms. "Yeah, I believe it," he said. "I mean, the fearful head survives, right?" He was repeating a lesson he'd learned at the dinner table. "Those of us who got out—you, me—we're the ones who were smart enough to see what was going on and be afraid enough to save our skins. We could read the writing on the wall."

"You are like the jackass who went to Jerusalem forty times," Raffi said. Another old saw, passed around dinner tables. "He still came home a jackass."

There had recently been a court case in New England. *Halladjian et al. v. United States of America*—this guy Halladjian challenging the Immigration Bureau's contention that Armenians were yellow Asiatics, not white men, and therefore ineligible for citizenship. The judge had ruled for the Armenians. Just because a people hailed from Turkey, Judge Francis Cabot Lowell had pointed out, it didn't make them Asi-atics. Hadn't Europe's arts and letters come from that same part of Asia? Hadn't Christianity come from there too? Hadn't Armenians in America proven themselves adaptable, educable, quite well-behaved? And weren't those traits the traits of white men?

Had it not been for the Halladjian decision, would Raffi Soghokian have even been permitted to put a single one of his shabbily clad toes on American soil? The greenhorn should have been grateful to guys like Dub, guys who came before him and whose exemplary conduct and good grades had informed Judge Lowell's ruling. Instead, Raffi Soghokian—as much an *esh* as the guy running the Immigration Bureau—stood here belittling the Red Sox and calling Dub names. And now he was turning his back to Dub, bending over, showing Dub his ass as he tried to lift the mattress that lay along the curb.

"You can't do that alone," Dub said.

"I am doing it," Raffi said. "I am needing no help."

"Who's offering any?"

Dub stuffed his hands in his coat pockets. It was a woolen coat, like Raffi's, but far less bedraggled. Still, it was only wool, not raccoon like the coats worn by the fellows who went to Brown up on College Hill. Raccoon coats and knit scarves so long they swept the ground. Model Ts, Bearcats, and Moons. Blondes in the passenger seats, goggled and gloved and giggling.

There were white men, Dub knew, and then there were white men.

The corner of the mattress slipped out of Raffi's hands. He spat on his palms and rubbed them together as if traction, not insufficient strength, were his problem. He went at the mattress again, grunting, swearing, and suddenly it was resting on one of his shoulders.

He seemed as surprised by his success as Dub. The bulk of the mattress hung over his shoulder, down his back. He stumbled, then steadied himself. His face turned crimson. He began to sway from side to side to avoid tumbling over. He could not take a single step forward.

Hands still in his pockets, Dub waited for the inevitable collapse, the literal downfall of Raffi Soghokian. He wished for it, could barely wait for it, was pretty sure the wish would be granted in the next few seconds. His confidence made him feel chatty and benevolent. "You speak good English," he said, as Raffi staggered this way and that. "Most of the *Spiurka Hai* never use articles. They can spit out their names that are always five city blocks long, but none of them can ever manage a *the* or an *a*."

"Yes, yes, my English is excellent," Raffi said. He was red-faced and out of breath. He knew speaking was depleting his energy and distracting him from his task, yet he couldn't resist. He was tired of hearing how splendid his English was, as if he didn't already know it. He was tired of the incredulity of Americans. Why wouldn't his English be splendid? Hadn't he traveled from home every year to study at a Christian school? Hadn't his teacher at that school studied in England? The mattress slipped again, just a little. He caught it and took a deep breath. He had it now. He straightened up, and it remained on his shoulder. "Perhaps your own Armenian is poor," he suggested. "Maybe this is why you are anticipating the same from me regarding my English. But please do not be making such a mistake. I shall never be permitting myself such mediocrity."

As he said this, his knees began to buckle and his arms to tremble. The mattress began to slide again, to slip slowly from his grasp. Dub didn't say a word. He just waited to see what it looked like: a wish coming true.

AND YET, in the end, he didn't let either of them fall, not the mattress and not Raffi. Why not? he wonders to this day. Was it something admirable like loyalty, some innate understanding of their connection, their brotherhood? Or was he just a big sap? Whatever the reason, while originally he'd been hanging around so he could see Raffi topple flat on his ass, he ended up doing all he could to prevent that from happening. Raffi began to go down, and Dub found himself rushing behind him. He bent at the knees as Raffi had done. He grunted as Raffi had grunted. He held his breath and lifted the back of the mattress up off the sidewalk.

Standing again, he let out his breath. The spent springs and matted stuffing were suspended between the two of them now, heavy but manageable, and Dub felt victorious and strong. He was about to say something—*See, not so bad letting someone else lessen your burden*—when Raffi, still purple-faced, abruptly let go of his end, walked away, and Dub, suddenly holding every bit of the dead, flaccid weight, fell backward, his tailbone hitting the sidewalk hard, a sharp eyetooth puncturing his tongue.

He sat in the gutter, dazed, and spat blood. "So graceful," Raffi said, and he laughed.

Dub swore at him, not in his superior English and not in his perfectly good Armenian, but in the Turkish he'd picked up outside the coffee-houses, Turkish being the best language there was when the worst language was needed. He swore again, impugning Raffi's mother, and grabbed hold of Raffi's ankles, tackled him, pulled him down. Then Raffi was on him, flailing, kicking, biting, and Dub, who was neither a dirty fighter nor an avid fighter but, still, a guy who could throw a punch when he had to, wrested an arm free and jabbed straight up and hard. He was aiming for the scimitar of a nose, but he hit the mouth instead and, along with a trickle of blood, one of the stained and serrated front teeth fell from Raffi's mouth and landed on Dub's cheek. Dub flinched and flicked it off as if a crawling insect had lighted on him.

He wasn't sure when the little sister had come running out onto the sidewalk. He saw her only when she was standing beside them, her deep-set eyes frightened and underscored by black shadows, all her hair hidden beneath a dark kerchief tied under her chin. She was ten, he'd later find out, but she appeared years younger, and yet when he looked at her thin face he also knew exactly what she'd look like when she was much older, six or seven decades hence: pale, bony, wizened. Bitter and alone and afraid on her deathbed.

He saw her fear. He saw her grim future. What he didn't see was his own future, his own fate. A curse was about to come crashing down on his head, but he didn't know it, and so he failed to get out of its way.

Something about the tooth damp on his cheek and the big-eyed little girl watching him flick it into the gutter had made him stop fighting. Now the boys were sitting side by side on the curb. "Don't think you are so powerful that you are unilaterally disengaging that tooth," Raffi said. He tongued the empty space in his mouth, felt the nubby root. "It is being killed long ago when I am pummeling to an inch of his life a Mohammedan lout who defamed my mother as you did. It is on the verge of falling out for many years. By now a breeze could have knocked it to the ground with no trouble."

He spat again, long strings of silvery pink. He smiled a mean half smile. It made him appear both frightening and foolish, the angry grin with the new idiot gap.

Dub spat too. *Abush!* he thought. From now on he would take a different route home from school.

It was Raffi who changed Dub's mind, Raffi who sealed Dub's fate, planting the curse upon him as if with a kiss. Raffi did this by uttering magic words, seductive, irresistible.

"Do not attempt to do this again ever," Raffi said.

"Don't do what again?" Dub said. "Try to help you or beat the shit out of you?"

Raffi spat more blood and then he said (and here came the magic, thus was the spell cast, the curse brought down on Dub Hagopian's young head, which was then covered with nothing but pitch-black hair, not a gray strand to be found), "Still, *tratsi*, if maybe you are sticking with me, we will be turning you into a true Armenian after all."

CHAPTER FOUR

The Holy Books Do Not Burn

AFTER THIS comes a period of détente, of something more closely resembling friendship. On Sundays, Dub and Raffi meet up at church. They sit in gray plumes of incense and crane their necks to look at girls. They whisper about breasts and in some cases burgeoning mustaches.

When they can stand it no longer, they leave.

When the boys duck outside, they feel smug and clever. That they are missing the interminable Divine Liturgy fills them with joy. That week after week they have escaped without having to recite the Nicene Creed makes them feel more rebellious than George Washington, Gavrilo Princip, and all the freedom fighters of Bash Abaran rolled into one.

Best of all is knowing they've walked out on the Der Hayr and his lily-livered sermons. They pledged weeks before that they would never again listen to his treasonous claptrap.

"Jesus told Peter to put away the sword," the Der Hayr had cried. "And yet there are those of you who insist that taking up the sword is the only honorable response to the violence against us. To those of you,

I say, take up the sword, yes. But make certain that it is the Christian sword."

The Christian sword. The boys had leaned forward. This is what they wanted to hear. Retaliation, revenge. Instruction on how to strike back. But as the priest went on, they'd slunk down.

"The Christian sword is prayer," the priest said. "The Christian sword is fasting. The Christian sword is repentance. The Christian sword is Lent."

Now they leave church before they have to hear any more of this cowardly tripe. In the pocket park across the street they sit on a bench until *badarak* is over. Sometimes they stop first at Derounian's and buy a bag of *lokhum*, the two boys counting out pennies, checking their change, carefully splitting the cost down the middle. In the park, they make a mess eating the candy. Powdered sugar falls on their good shirts. Syrup clings to the stubble of their new beards.

Getting to know Raffi Soghokian does little to alter Dub's initial impression, but it helps Dub get used to him. "What is transpiring to our people upon coming to America?" Raffi asks. He licks his fingers, shakes his head. "In the East we have a grand reputation for bellicosity, but here we are timid, so grateful for crumbs. In the East our priests say, Take arms, take arms! Here the priest tells us to fast. Not only are we having to get screwed up the ass by the infidel, we are having to get screwed up the ass on an empty stomach."

"It's because we're in America," Dub says for the millionth time. "We have laws here. Courts."

"Yes," Raffi says. "Here we are allowed to beg a judge to acknowledge that a people from the Caucasus are actually Caucasians."

Dub shrugs. Really, on these Sundays he doesn't want to debate. What he wants is to eat candy and listen to Raffi's stories. Without exception, Raffi's stories are harrowing and unnerving, and yet they are also extraordinarily entertaining. In Raffi's stories, Kurds swoop down on his sleepy village of Peri to steal silver and torture prelates. Christian virgins are slung over the backs of mountain ponies and carried off into the hills. Turkish *mudirs* with curved swords leave the severed heads of village elders on doorsteps the way milkmen in Providence drop off bottles of cream. All the stories begin the same way. *One dreadful day in Peri*, Raffi will say, and then Dub knows it's time to sit back and listen. Although lately, a separate part of Dub's brain has taken to pondering the word *dreadful*. "This dreary autumn weather is just dreadful," murmurs Dub's French teacher, an unmarried woman of Irish extraction who wears a tiny crucifix on a gold chain so short the cross rests in the soft concave of her throat. She stands in profile to the class— upturned nose, sharp chin, and her breasts, her hips—and stares out the window, distracted and blue and violating her own dictum that English never be spoken in this classroom. "This dreadful autumn weather," she says.

But here is Raffi's version of *dreadful*. *One dreadful day in Peri several of my friends were beaten by grown men for sport. Or, one dreadful day in Peri a little Christian girl was stripped naked and made to endure unspeakable things before an audience of jeering men. Or, one dreadful day in Peri they pulled out the priest's beard hair by hair.*

Dreadful, Dub thinks. The word stays with him after he and Raffi part. Doesn't that word actually refer to the manner in which one is supposed to approach God? Full of dread. Dread-fully. Awe-fully. Dub tries to make a connection. Perhaps by letting dreadful things happen to his people, God hopes his people will repent their sins, whatever they are, and thereby learn to approach him more dread-fully.

Dub doesn't know what to do with these thoughts. With whom can he discuss God—or, for that matter, etymology? Not his French teacher, whose only passion is the simpler poems of Baudelaire. Not even the Der Hayr, who has no thoughts of his own, can only recite prescribed Bible verses or echo the words of church leaders long gone. It's just as well. Dub wouldn't know how to say what he's thinking anyway. He prefers to stop thinking. He just listens. *One dreadful day in Peri*, Raffi begins, and Dub leans against the green slats of the bench. Raffi's words have the same effect on him as *once upon a time* or the words with which his mother, like all Armenian mothers, used to begin her bedtime tales: *Gar oo chagar*. Once there was and was not. Or the way God began his own series of horrific but entertaining stories: *In the beginning*.

NOT THAT DUB would ever suggest to Raffi that his stories have anything in common with the Bible. This is because Raffi is a mistheist. That's what he says.

"You mean atheist," Dub says, but Raffi shakes his head.

"An atheist is not believing in God," he says. "I am, I am believing in him. It's only that I am also hating him."

"Even so," Dub says, "there's no such word as mistheist."

Raffi is exasperated. "The prefix *mis-* as in *misanthrope.* The suffix *-theist* as in *monotheist.* Mistheist."

On this October Sunday, the sun is bright and the park is full of yesterday's puddles. Mistheist, Dub is thinking. Maybe he's wrong. Maybe there is such a word. As he is thinking this, he notices a leaf fall from an elm tree shading the bench. He watches it descend. It lands in Raffi's hair.

Raffi doesn't notice. He's too busy talking. "I'll tell you about the day I am turning from a deiphile into a mistheist." He reaches into his pocket and pulls out a pack of Fatimas and a book of matches. He offers the pack to Dub, gallantly, graciously, but with a big leaf on top of his head, a leaf the size of a mother's outstretched hand, a bright orange leaf that Dub should call to Raffi's attention but doesn't.

Raffi lights both their cigarettes. "So, the day I am becoming a mistheist," he says. "Well. It was another dreadful day in Peri. Early springtime of this very year, and girls are beginning to disappear again. My parents are not permitting Ramela to leave the house or even to look out a window. I too am exhorted not to go to the window, nor may I return to school. That kind of life, it can make you die from so much boredom. So on this one day I am deciding I am no longer caring, and I dare to look outside. And what am I seeing but a group of peasants, and they have sliced off the Vartapet's ear."

Raffi does not try to imbue his narratives with great feeling. He prefers the monotone of a bored professor relaying facts he's relayed countless times to yet another roomful of unworthy freshmen.

"The Vartapet's sister just had a new baby, you see. And the Turks, for a change—such good Mohammedans—they are all drunk. I am opening the window only a small segment so I can hear what they are saying. I am on my knees, crouching down so they cannot see me. And I am listening to them, and I am hearing them order the Vartapet to name the baby Fatima." He gestures with the cigarette. "Fatima is not only a product name," he says. "It is also the name of Mohammed's daughter. But you are aware of that, I am assuming."

On Raffi's head, there is now the tiniest bright green bug walking along the leaf's spine. It looks like a passenger on a huge raft.

"Yeah," Dub says, "I know that."

"Such fools," Raffi says. "They are waving their bloody swords at the Vartapet and they are ranting, 'If she doesn't name that baby Fatima, you tell her we are dismembering next the other ear.' The Vartapet, he is saying, Oh, no, no, no, meaning that, No, he will not say a word to his sister. So they make him run around the square. He is dressed in his long robe and he is obeying them, he is running around like a dog in the circus show, and he is bleeding the whole time from the side of his head and chanting '*Hrashapar Asdvadz, hrashapar Asdvadz.*' You know what that is meaning, I presume?"

Dub rolls his eyes. The green bug is still inching along the middle of the leaf. "Of course I know."

"It is meaning ever-protecting God. And I am watching all this, and I am thinking, What? Is the Vartapet being facetious? Is he making a big joke? Did he truly say *ever-protecting* in the middle of being tortured? And of course the Turks are calling out as they always do, 'Your savior, it seems, is not listening, priest. Only Allah can help you now. Swear to Allah you will name the baby Fatima, or off with the other ear.' And the Vartapet? As he runs past them, he is saying, 'We will name the baby Varjouhi.'"

"Vengeance," Dub says, before he can be quizzed.

"And I am hearing all this, and I am thinking, Hmmm, in my understanding of Christian theology, Varjouhi would not please this God of ours any more than Fatima would displease him. Blessed are the peacemakers, isn't that what our God tells us? Vengeance is mine, is that not correct? So why would it please this God of ours to have a Christian child named in honor of that which he is holding for only himself? But then, who am I to say these things? What do I know? This man is the priest, after all, not I. It is his profession to know what is pleasing to our wonderful God. I am only a boy; I am fourteen years old. All I know is what I am seeing with my eyes, and what I am seeing is that God, wherever he is, may be pleased by the Vartapet's defiance, but the Turks, they are not pleased, and they are right here, and they are coming at the Vartapet again with their swords. The Vartapet, he is cowering and squealing, and he is covering his remaining ear with both his hands. Except this time when they are coming to him, they don't use their swords. No. Instead of cutting off the remaining ear as they are promising, now they are setting on fire the bottom of his robe, and then they are chasing him and making him run faster and faster until he is ablaze, he is a flame with feet, and the whole time he is still crying, '*Hrashapar Asdvadz*.'"

"Ah," Dub says. He can carry off a bored monotone too. "So God didn't protect him, and now you're an atheist."

"Mistheist. No. Wait. I am not yet finished. There is still more to follow. Later that same dreadful day—it is now early evening, and I am looking again out the window, and there is a group of our neighbors. Not only peasants this time, shopkeepers too. Businessmen, you know. They have accumulated together in the middle of the square. The Vartapet's body has been removed, and his ear they are long ago kicking aside. It is already black by then, that ear. Soon a dog is coming by to carry it away. But at this time it is still there, and these men have convened in the square, and I am seeing that they have taken the precious books from the church—the ancient Bibles and illuminated manuscripts—and they have built them into a tower. And one of these men has with him a candle from the church. I know this man. He used to give to me rides atop his shoulders."

"Piggybacks."

"However you want to say it. And now, here he is, this nice man in the square with the other nice men in the square, and he is holding a long candle, and he touches the candle to the topmost book, and I am waiting for the flames to—" Raffi gestures with his hands, his fingers dancing, rising. "But nothing. The books do not ignite."

"What do you mean?" Dub says.

"Just what I am saying. They are putting flame to the page, but the books do not burn."

Despite the indifferent tone in which Raffi tells the story, Dub leans forward. It's like watching one of the new picture shows at the nickel theater. Dub knows what will happen next. The flames will finally catch. They will engulf and consume the books. Raffi will ride off into the sunset detesting God. Then the screen will go black, and there will be nothing but the *click-click-click* of the spent reel. Dub knows all this, and yet he's caught up. He is rooting for those doomed books.

"The Turks are enraged," Raffi says. "They are shouting at the man with the candle. He is bending again, applying the flame lower, elsewhere. But again, nothing. The books are still refusing to burn."

There is a tightening through Dub. Even his bones are clenched. He flexes his fingers. He holds his breath. When he realizes that he is doing all this, he makes himself stop. He slouches, he exhales. He doesn't want Raffi to know that he's spellbound, that he has such hope for those pages, for those poems and bright ink.

"And the Turks are commanding the man once more, and he is trying once again; he holds the candle to a book at the bottom, but nothing. Not a book, not a page, not a word."

Has Dub's jaw dropped? Is he gripping the edge of the bench? He can no longer monitor himself, not when the holy books have continued to defy fire. Raffi is also caught up; there's the slightest rise to his voice. Even the green bug has stepped off the edge of the leaf, is skiddling among the black strands of Raffi's hair as if seeking a better position for the story's climax.

"So that is that," Raffi says. "The books are surviving."

Dub maintains his composure. He refuses to reveal his joy on behalf of the victorious books. He doesn't cheer, certainly doesn't whisper the word that is lodged in his head and won't go away. He will not say *miracle*.

"So what do you think the Turks are doing next?" Raffi asks.

"How should I know?" He sounds detached and is proud to have managed it.

"Come on, *tratsi*. Have a wild guess."

"They all converted to Christianity right there on the spot." Sardonic now and even prouder.

"Ha," Raffi says. "Very amusing. No, they are not converting to Christianity. They are doing something even more outlandish to believe. I am sorry to have to be telling you this, but each one is thereupon lowering his trousers and pulling out—what is the word? His *jugik*."

"Prick."

"Yes, that is correct. Each one is pulling out his prick, and then, all together, as if one of them is giving the signal, they all in harmony are urinating upon the Bibles."

"You ought to say pissing," Dub says. "Urinating is something a doctor would say."

"However you want to say these things, it is remaining the most pitiful sight. But what else can they do? The holy books of the Christians are defeating them. Can you imagine the height of their anger? Thus, they are driven to perform this most disgusting and pitiful display. Although they at least are out in the street. I am inside, hiding like a whipped dog. So who is truly pitiful?"

Dub shrugs, conceding the point.

"So *that* is when I am beginning to hate God," Raffi says. "Then, at that exact moment. God is letting the priest burn, but the books praising his name, these he is saving? Is this not despicable? Who would not become a mistheist then? Who could remain loyal to this God of ours?"

In the ensuing silence Dub can hear muffled chanting, heart-tearing music: the blessing of the souls. He stubs out his cigarette. "We ought to get back."

He won't tell Raffi about the leaf. Let him go inside like that, let him look foolish, let him greet the Der Hayr that way. The leaf, Dub could not help noticing, had fallen onto Raffi's head while he'd been declaring his hatred for God. It was as if God had heard him, and, more tickled than offended by this belligerent pipsqueak, he'd winked at Dub, whispered, "Watch this," and down came the leaf.

But at the heavy wooden doors, Dub reconsiders. If Raffi is made to look like a fool, Dub is a fool by association. He reaches up, takes the leaf, and hands it to Raffi. "Here," he says. "Somebody left you a present." The whereabouts of the green bug—that he doesn't know.

AT THE KITCHEN table that night, Dub repeats Raffi's story to his father. "Do you believe it?" he asks in Armenian, and Vartan Hagopian says that, sadly, he does.

"Raffi may not have actually been at the window, watching and listening," Vartan says. "That's hard to imagine. Did his family live right on the village square? I don't think so. But the basic facts, murder and mayhem? Oh, yes. Things like that happened far too often. It's why we left. You know that."

Dub knows all about murder and mayhem. That's not what he's wondering about. "But the books," he says. "How could that have happened? Books touched with a candle but nothing ignites? Is it supposed to be some kind of miracle?"

He is embarrassed to say such a word to his father, laughs as he says it, is afraid his father will laugh at him. But he does say it, he does—he takes the chance. Because that's what Dub wants to hear. He wants to hear about God's special love for the Christians of Turkey and, thus, for his parents and himself. He wants to hear about the power of the spirit and about the mysterious ways in which the Christian God, the only God, expresses his love. Armenia, as every Armenian knows, was the first nation—the first!—to embrace Christianity. And her reward has been suffering, so much suffering, century upon century. He wants the suffering to be alleviated every now and then by God's intervention, by a miracle, a wink, a leaf, just the way a rare nugget of gold is occasionally found in stakes consisting mostly of pyrite and sand.

"Oh, the candle," Vartan says. "Well, there is a scientific explanation for that. The ancient books were made of parchment. Animal skin. Did you know that?"

Dub supposes he did.

"And parchment, especially old parchment, is much more difficult to burn than paper. Had the Turks been more patient and taken the time to build a proper bonfire, those books would have caught."

Vartan's eyes grow distant. He is somewhere else. He is back home, the *yergir*.

"An Armenian would have applied himself more diligently to the task at hand," he says. He is applying himself diligently to the task as he speaks. He is setting a fire; he is taking his time; he is steadfast and determined and strong. "We are much harder workers than the Mohammedans," he says. "An Armenian would not have given up on a pile of Korans quite so easily, let me assure you." He balls his hand into a fist. "An Armenian would have known that parchment is so flammable it is sometimes used in bombs."

He brings his fist down on the kitchen table. The vibrations running through the table legs run through Dub's legs as well.

"An Armenian," his father says, and he hits the table again until Dub's mother comes in, takes his fist, holds it still against her breasts, kisses the knuckles—"*Eench eh?*" she says. "What did my poor table ever do to you?"—but Vartan pulls his hand away, and he points a finger at Dub. "An Armenian," Dub's father says, "would have blown that damned village to pieces."

CHAPTER FIVE

Ramela

URBANA. Coschocton. Altoona.

Little Ramela Soghokian, eighteen by now, sits on her front step watching fireflies pop and die against the sky, while under her breath she recites the names of the depots Raffi and Dub's train has passed through. She has all the stations memorized as if they were lyrics to one of the nonsense songs that are so popular these days. Ramela Soghokian loves nonsense songs. Gibberish, she believes, is like so many balls of cotton stuck inside your head. It fills the empty spaces between your wild thoughts. It is padding to lessen the impact when your jagged memories career into one another. Gibberish cures your headaches. It muffles the commands of whispering voices.

"*Jada!*" she sings, whenever the voices try to make her remember Turkey. "*Jada! Jada!*" Once a man lifted her, swung her around, by her braid. "*Jada jada jing-jing-jing!*" Ever since then she's kept her hair chopped short as a schoolboy's. It's her mother's despair, but Ramela keeps hacking away at it, and—astounding but true—in America it's now the style.

Or maybe an idea comes to her in the middle of the afternoon, a disembodied voice explaining that if she slashes each of her fingers with a razor and mingles the blood from the right hand with the blood of the left, then back in the *yergir* God will reunite five children with five mothers. When a voice says such a thing to her, what she does—before she can succumb, before she can obey—is sings the words to some other silly song, maybe "Yacki Hacki Wicki Wacki Woo," until the thought itself is revealed to be as foolish, truly, as the lyrics.

This evening, however, she prefers to sing train stations. She likes the names of the depots. Some of them rhyme. Urbana. Altoona. So many others involve the color green. Greenville, Greenup, Greencast, Greenfield, Greenburg. Also Limedale. And there's one station named for Dub: St. Jacob, and doesn't Hagopian mean son of Jacob? Also, she spends a good deal of time muttering *Coshocton* over and over: Coshocton, which is not only a city where the train stops but is also the sound the train makes to get there. Neighbors pass by, try to greet her, but she's lost in the syllables. *Co-shoc-ton, co-shoc-ton, co-shoc-ton.*

Faraway stations, faraway states. Missouri, Illinois, Ohio. These are places she'll never see because she will never board a train. And not only a train. She will never get on a bus or let someone drive her from here to there by automobile. She won't even ride the local tram. Engines, motors: these are for men. She herself is going nowhere. Once she heard an American say disapprovingly of a girl: she sure gets around. It meant the same as what the Turkish peasants used to shout at her mother, that shy timid woman: Armenian whore! Ramela is not going to get around ever. She is staying put, here on Smith Hill.

This evening she came outside at six. The sun was still in the sky. If the Commercial Express was on time, Dub and Raffi were now in Pennsylvania Station. Ramela has read all about New York City's new terminal; she knows how beautiful it is. But she can't imagine her brother and Dub taking the time to stop and marvel as they walk through the concourse. Raffi, she is certain, will never notice the arteries of tracks beneath the glass floors. Dub won't look up and admire the billowing quilt of glass patches and iron thread that constitutes the grand ceiling. In the waiting room, they will not think to run their hands along the limestone walls that shine as if coated with crushed diamonds. Instead, they will be doing the same as always—bickering, squabbling like an old married couple, these lifelong adversaries, these competitors and best friends, her brother and her fiancé.

It's too bad, Ramela muses, safe on her front step, that Raffi and Dub will get to walk through Pennsylvania Station, but she never will.

She is the one who appreciates beauty. Even now, she is transfixed by a sky the color of nickels and dimes, and though the sun is still out, the moon is too, a delicate spray of white in one low corner. It's as if that moon, like any romantic, wants to watch the sun set. The moon is like Ramela, a timorous spectator with no light of its own.

Only the timorous appreciate beauty. This is Ramela's conviction. The brave don't appreciate it; how could they, when they don't even notice it? They are, by nature, oblivious. If a brave man ever noticed, really noticed, what went on in this world, he could never remain brave. If he noticed, if he let the world sink in, not just the beauty but the rest of it too, he would turn into Ramela, a girl sitting on a stoop, trembling at the prospect of what she's got to do next.

RAMELA SOGHOKIAN is in love with Dub Hagopian. To date she has extracted from him a promise to marry her, but with a caveat attached. *I will marry you if.* That was her marriage proposal. *I will marry you if.*

Dub's list of *if*s has been extensive and impossible to fulfill. I will marry you if you stop talking to God. I will marry you if you stop hurting yourself. I will marry you if you stop cutting off your hair, if you stop cutting into your flesh, if you forget your sister, your childhood, your homeland. I will marry you if you turn into someone else.

She is trying. She is trying to do every last thing he has asked. But so many *if*s. The sun sets and she sits on the steps and pulls down the cuffs of her blouse so the blood stitches along the blue veins of her wrist won't show. Too many *if*s. He leaves her nothing.

How can we have children if you're doing that? he says. He holds her arms up to her face and makes her look at her own flesh—as if she doesn't know what she's done. He doesn't mean to be cruel. He is tortured on her behalf. Isn't that love, to want her not to bleed? To want her not to burn? How can she not forgive him for wanting such things for her? How can she not love him for loving her? She's never wanted anything else but his love. She roots for him to defeat her, even as she disobeys him.

"How can I be a happy American girl when back in the *yergir* Armenian women suffer so?" she asks him. She is only repeating the question God asks her nearly every night. Softening it, actually. How *dare* you be happy? is how God always puts it. "My sister burned up in a church," she reminds Dub, just as God reminds her daily, constantly, minute by minute.

Dub says, "That's your sister's tragedy, not yours."

SHE FIRST CAME to him when she was thirteen. She sat right next to him on the steps of his building. He was surprised to see her. As far as he was concerned, she was still a petrified kid watching him knock out her big brother's tooth.

They talked a bit. She liked his hair, she said. By then it had begun, the lopsided graying. He pointed to the left side, the gray side. "Thanks to your brother," he said. She smiled but shook her head and touched the left side of his chest, pressing gently, presumptuously. "It's not Raffi," she said. "It's the part above your heart that's turning. God dwells inside your heart. He talks to you this way. Didn't Moses return from Sinai hoary?"

Another crazy Soghokian, Dub thought. But he smiled as if she'd paid him a compliment that had pleased him.

"I want to show you something," she said. "I want to show you something I've done."

"All right," he said. He expected an embroidered handkerchief or a miniature painting. "Let's see."

The sky was purple and mottled that night like the skin of an eggplant cooked on a stove's burner. Ramela began to unbutton her blouse. Dub was too stunned to move. Her fingers flew rapidly. She opened her blouse. She was bare underneath. He should have turned his head, abandoned her there, gone into the house, not come out until she was gone, but he stayed and he looked.

At first he thought the thick white triangle on her left breast was a birthmark. But he forced himself to look closer, and then he understood what he was seeing. She'd burned herself with a clothes iron.

She took his hand, pressed it against the burn. She kept her hand on his. He felt the warm oozing from the blistering flesh. He felt, too, the hardening nipple. And so he had touched his first, his only, Armenian girl.

A car rumbled by and struck the two of them with its headlamps. He tried to pull his hand away, but she wouldn't permit it. She didn't flinch. She held him fast. Then, when he stopped resisting, she abruptly released him. Her hands retreated into the lap of her dress, the fingers daintily entwined. "Do you think you would ever want to marry me?" she asked politely and sweetly. He looked at her chest. The blister glistened. "Raffi, my whole family, they all think so highly of you. You're so smart. And smiled upon by Christ too, I believe. It would be wonderful to have babies with you."

"You're a baby yourself," he said. He stood up at last. She stood too, as if he'd invited her to accompany him. He took her upstairs, led her directly into his small bedroom. He had her sit on his bed. Her blouse remained opened. He found the jar of petroleum jelly he used for his own nightly purposes and applied the ointment to the burn, just the burn, with care and in silence. They both watched his fingertips making circles on the wet, white triangle. The friction made his fingertips warm. He stopped when he thought he'd done what he could. He buttoned her shirt. The buttons were tiny and round like rosary beads, and they were hard for him to master with the ointment still slicking his fingers. He finally managed, though; he buttoned her up. Then he watched, chagrined, as the jelly stained through the thin cotton blouse.

It was as if she regarded it as their first date. She began coming by after that. She'd never left Smith Hill, she told him. Not once, not once since arriving. He couldn't believe that, didn't see how it was possible. He took pity on her then. He thought, Maybe if she sees the world. He showed her what he could of it, this small industrial city. The East Side. The harbor. She refused to go by streetcar. No motors, she said. No engines. So they went on his bicycle, an old wooden Chillion, Ramela up on the handlebars. She was terrified, trying the whole time not to scream. She didn't tell him about that, though. They would reach their chosen destination—*his* chosen destination—and he would park the bike somewhere safe, by a school, by a bank, and she would beam at him as if she were having the most fun, and then they'd stroll past the great homes. He showed her the Athenaeum and the Nightingale House. When it grew dark they would sit in Prospect Park and listen to trains pull into the station below. Sometimes she showed him new burns, new cuts. Once she had carved slogans on her thin arms with sewing needles, and he railed, he yelled, he wept. In the park, she asked him to make love to her.

He said no, always no.

But it was also in that park that she asked him, again, to marry her, and there that, one evening, he said that if she stopped hurting herself, he might. Not now, he said. And I'm not saying for sure. "All right," she said. "Then I won't listen to God anymore."

When the massacres began again, he decided to fight in the Caucasus. "Marry me before you go," she said.

"Maybe when I come back," he said. "If you haven't hurt yourself. If there isn't a mark on you." She looked at him hesitantly. "You tell God I'll be the one shedding blood for us now," he said. "My blood, not yours. You tell him you're busy doing other things."

"Like what?" she said, as if God might inquire.

"I don't know," he said. "Learn to cook. Learn to play the piano. I don't know. What do girls do?"

"PLEASE, *MEDZ-HAYRIG*," Ramela had said to Aram Kazarian that morning. "Please, don't ask me to do this. Dub will be so angry."

She had called him grandpa from the first day she'd met him, a guest at the Soghokians' dinner table in 1910. He had come to ask permission to take Raffi under his wing, into Erinyes. Her parents assented eagerly. Ramela had looked at Aram's silver mane and remarkable blue eyes. She hadn't fully understood the cause's aims then, but she looked at the man her father called Lion and she knew what her life was lacking. "*Medz-hayrig*," she said. "I want to fight too."

They'd all laughed at her, and soon after she lost her interest in joining the men. And not long after that, she started receiving her orders from another.

But Aram thinks she is still a member of his own regiment. He did not understand her reluctance. "*Mais, chérie,*" he said, "why in the world will Dub be angry at you for meeting his train?"

She tried to explain, but she couldn't. She knew far fewer languages than the men in her life; still, she knew one too many and that was her downfall. When she tried to speak Armenian, English came out. When she attempted to make a point in English, out came Armenian. It used to happen all the time in school. It was one of the reasons she'd quit before reaching sixth grade.

Now Aram was speaking in French. The tiniest bit of French made her mind screech to a halt. All of Aram's *bien sûr*s and *d'accord*s and *sans blague*s paralyzed her. Just think of it as Aram's version of *eench eh*,

Raffi advised, but she couldn't. Raffi had all the brains in the family, all the intellect, all the schooling, and, on top of that, all the common sense. Ramela's brain (like her father's, like her mother's) was a rabbit. When prey animals like rabbits get frightened, they don't move a muscle. They freeze.

"But *Medz-hayrig*," she said, "please, I don't want to. Please, ask someone else."

"Ramela," Aram said. "I have unexpected business to attend to in Boston, and someone has to meet the boys' train. Who better than you? Who else will they trust without hesitation?" When still she demurred, he laughed outright. "Aren't you the one who always calls me a leader of men?" he said. "Well, here I am, Hokees. I am leading. Why aren't you following?"

"I said leader of *men*," Ramela said, and he laughed again, her beloved *Medz-hayrig*, belittling her, hurting her feelings.

"Yes, you're certainly not a man," he said. "Now you see why we don't let women join us. With men, when I issue commands, they salute. With women, no matter what I say, they argue." He sighed, though he was still smiling. "You are far too tough for me, Ramela," he said. His blue eyes glinted and charmed her. "Surely, you are sufficiently tough to meet your own brother and his friend at a train station?"

She had been unable to resist any longer. And now, so soon, it's time for her to go. She wraps her arms around her knees. What will happen if she disobeys Aram? What will happen if she is not at the station when Raffi and Dub arrive? Surely nothing so terrible. Won't Raffi and Dub simply assume Aram has been delayed and make their way home on their own?

On the other hand, what will happen if she goes? She thinks of how angry Dub will be when he sees her at the station. This is what's scaring her so. Not only the idea of leaving the front steps so late at night, all on her own, but the prospect of Dub's anger. Dub is the one who truly asks very little of her. He has asked just one thing, and she fails him repeatedly.

"But God tells me to disobey you," she said. He had just come home from the Caucasus. He'd been immediately furious with her. She had to go down on her knees, kiss his fingertips, beg him to forgive her. He did, at last, or at least said he did. But, oh, he was furious. "Look at you, look at you," he kept saying, turning her wrists, pushing up her sleeves. He tried to return her grandfather's ring, but she said she would throw it in the river if he took it off his little finger.

"I'll never marry you if you aren't going to obey me," he said. He spoke very slowly and in Armenian. He had acquired a Russian accent, which nearly made her smile in the midst of their terrible quarrel. "A wife has to put her husband above everyone else, isn't that so?" he said.

"Above God?" she asked. It was heretical, evil, and thrilling.

"You're a woman," he said. "You answer to me. I handle God."

She had promised. She had tried. When God sent his messages, she tried to ignore them. She sang songs: *jada jada jing-jing-jing*. But she was so weak, such a rabbit.

"Do you want me to marry you or don't you?" Dub would say. And God whispering in her other ear the whole time, pulling at her, trying to drag her in the opposite direction.

Now she folds her hands in her lap. She doesn't move a muscle. She tries to be good, to be perfect, but daily, constantly, minute by minute, she fails. And so she recites stations. *Co-shoc-ton, Co-shoc-ton.* And then, at a loss, in despair, she does exactly what Dub doesn't want her to do. With all her heart, she begins to pray.

CHAPTER SIX

Boston

DUB ARRIVES in Providence hours late, sweaty and sour yet excited. Home at last and he is so eager to see Aram. He holds the package of guns and grenades in both arms, proudly. But as he steps out of the car, onto the platform, he can't find the old lion anywhere. He's disappointed, to say the least. He has been looking forward to this moment for thirty-some hours.

And then, compounding his disappointment, he spots Ramela. She is standing at the far end of the platform, wearing a dark drab dress, suspiciously long-sleeved on this hot August night. She lifts a hand tentatively, then drops it. She hides both arms behind her back. Slowly, head down, she begins to come toward him.

"Is that my sister?" Raffi asks. He is directly behind Dub, nearly leaning against his shoulder. "Here? By herself?"

Behind them, the whistle blows as the train readies to leave. The shrill blast startles Dub, but he doesn't let himself jump or turn his head. He won't take his eyes from Ramela. How many times has she told him that God has suggested she throw herself beneath the wheels of the streetcar as it rumbles down Smith Hill? If she does, God says, he will clothe bones in the desert with warm, healed flesh. Just a wish, Dub tells her, her own wishes given voice. Now Dub can hear the train begin to move, slowly, ploddingly, and at the same time, he sees her come at him, faster and faster. Then suddenly she is running, and Dub waits, his heart slamming in his chest, and then, when she's close enough, he hands off the package to Raffi, catches Ramela at the wrist, takes her in his arms, and holds her as tightly as he can until the train is gone.

She takes it as a display of affection and forgiveness. She embraces him in return. She kisses him, small frantic kisses, and between those kisses she apologizes. Aram, she says. A fund-raising event in Boston, at Koko's, everyone there, Aram had to go too. She didn't want to come, she says, she swears she didn't. Aram made her. She knows Dub doesn't want her involved with the men's work, the politics. It was Aram, though, Aram who wouldn't listen.

"I don't want you hurting yourself," Dub says. He's relieved it's Aram, not God, she's obeyed tonight. He wants to laugh, to cry. "I never said you couldn't deliver a message for Aram."

"I didn't know what to do," she says. "I love you. I'm scared to lose you."

Love, he thinks. When it comes to love, she's an all-American girl; she has arranged her own marriage. She takes the Armenian word for arranged marriage literally. *Khosgob* means word-tie—to give your word that you are tied to another. But instead of her parents hiring a *meechnort* and binding their daughter to a man with promises of a dowry, it's Ramela doing all the binding and tying. She has tied Dub up with her own words—*God tells me to, God wants me to*—and with her deeds. A clothes iron, a razor blade, a few sewing needles.

74

"It's all right," he says. "It's fine. We're both fine."

"Only because you're finally home again," she says.

What harm in agreeing with her? And it's the truth. Had he not come home then, had he not been on this train, who knows what she'd have done to herself? "Because I'm home again," he says.

By the time he's quieted her down, Raffi is long gone. He is back on the train, being carried to its next and final stop, Boston, with a small arsenal of guns and grenades on his lap. Dub can nearly admire him for it.

He kisses her hair. The sacrifice he's just made. The chill deep within his belly whenever he sees her. Aren't these signs of love? "Come on," he says. He is tired, he'd prefer to take the streetcar, but instead he puts his arm around her shoulders. "Let's walk up the hill."

Part Three

The *Espagne*

By November 9, 1918, Turkey has surrendered, the Kaiser has abdicated, and the *New York Times* is reporting the war all but over. In France, American soldiers are so elated they ignore the maddening pings of frozen raindrops on the domes of their tin derbies and rush with joyful fury into the final pointless skirmishes of the war, some so exuberant they forgo their customary ration of pre-battle whiskey. They take the field feeling invincible, and in so doing they become modern Americans, men who believe no harm will dare befall them.

On that same day, in Brooklyn, New York, Yale White, née Yael Weiss, now a volunteer with the YMCA, is feeling less invincible than she usually does. She stands at the rail of the *Espagne* (the most luxurious ship sailing the Atlantic, now that the *Vaterland* and *Lusitania* are gone) and looks down at the throng of rowdy young men on the pier below. These are good-natured men who have managed to miss the fighting and are slightly ashamed of themselves, but not so ashamed as to hide away and go about their business. Instead, they are out here, screaming their heads off. *Bon voyage!* they shout at the departing female volunteers. *Bonne chance!* but without attempting the sissy French accent. They also blow kisses and grasp at their chests as if to keep their hearts from tumbling out, falling and shattering on the slats of the pier.

It's all a big joke, those kisses, those friable hearts. The girls like it fine, and this includes Yale's new cabinmate, who is standing by her side and screeching back down at the men.

Yale's cabinmate is, if not beautiful, striking. And certainly she's energetic. Her hair is banged and bobbed and dyed the color of ginger beer. Her figure is thin as broth, but she herself is hardly as dull. As she shouts whatever comes into her head, she spins, twirls, gestures. After she's said her piece, whatever that piece may have been, she lifts her arms over her head and raises them up in the air, as if she has completed not a sentence but an aria.

Her name, she told Yale only minutes before, when the two met in their little stateroom, is Mary Brennan White. Yale was not happy to hear it. "Did you say White?" she asked, as if dipping a toe into potentially treacherous waters. She sat down on the cot by her open valise. She sat very still. "My name's White too," she said.

"Whose isn't?" said Mary Brennan White. The young woman was sprawled on her own cot. She had already finished unpacking. She hadn't brought much. A bathing costume. A string of fake pearls. Now she was in her uniform trying on her helmet. "I've met thousands of Whites," she said. She posed as if modeling a bonnet. "And not one of them has ever turned out to be a relation." Then, on her stomach, hanging off the edge of her mattress, she removed the helmet and spun it on the floor as if practicing to someday torment a turtle. "But we may as well go through the exercise. My father's George White, presently of Palmyra, New York, originally of some English shrop or shire."

"We're not from there," Yale said. She felt unable to move. "Still," she said. "*Quelle coincidence, non?*"

"*Non, ce n'est pas une coincidence.* Come to find out, the Y assigns its rooms in alphabetical order. Adams and Adderly, I met those two up top earlier. Carothers and Carmichael. It goes on and on. Robinson, Rosenberg. Poor Miss Robinson. But anyway, that's how they go about it. As if we girls were so many files in a cabinet." She smiled, her upper lip growing fuller, a pink unfurling. "You and I, Miss White," she said, batting her eyelashes like Theda Bara, "were administratively meant for each other."

The *Espagne*'s bullying horn had put an end to the conversation. The two White girls, along with all the other Y-girls aboard (Adams, Adderly, Robinson, Rosenberg, dozens of Y-girls in long green skirts and constricting peplum jackets, the sleeves decorated with the YMCA's red triangle), plus all the other volunteers, Hello Girls and Red Cross nurses, women from church groups, sorority coeds—all these girls swarmed the rail where their supervisors waited for them, handing out red, white, or blue crepe-paper streamers.

Yale's streamer is red, and she can't make it wave. It's harder than you'd think to persuade a wan strip of paper to undulate rhythmically. It taxes parts of the wrist and arm not usually taxed.

Yale feels both foolish and apprehensive. She thinks Mary Brennan

White may be a spy. Would the YMCA do that, send an agent into the cabins of girls suspected of lying on their applications? Yale thinks it just might.

She releases the stupid ribbon. She tries to send it off with a flourish, giving it her best effort, propelling it upward, putting some vigor into the toss, the way a person might release a sparrow she's just nursed back to health. Fly, little streamer, fly. But there is no wind and the boneless thing just falls, slow motion, down to the stagnant sea.

Meanwhile, Mary Brennan White—spy or floozy, Yale can't make up her mind—flings her own streamer about her neck like a scarf. Then she leans as far over the rail as she can without falling into the sea herself. Megaphoning her mouth with her hands, she shouts down to the men. "Darling, come with me!" she yells. And, "Dearest—yes, you!— how can I live without you?"

Other Y-girls get into the act. They cry, "Sweetheart, is this really the end?" Or, "Beloved, all is forgiven!" Even the Hello Girls, those dreary women willing to spend twelve hours a day manning switchboards inside dark tents, have begun to chant. "Stow away! Stow away!" they call, not as an accusation but as a suggestion to the men.

Yale wants to call down too. She wants to be one of the gang. But she can think of nothing to say. Like a hussy's slip, her age is showing. Never mind the Y's claim that a Y-girl's main duties are distributing chocolate and selling cigarettes and helping illiterates write letters back home. Yale has already come to realize what a Y-girl's main duty is.

It's to flirt, and she's awful at it, a fact that became evident during her training in New York City. She didn't mind working the Times Square Canteen. New York hardly intimidated her. St. Louis, after all, was no Podunk. Nor did she mind her lowly assignments. She poured coffee for doughboys, wiped down tables, took her turn mopping the floor. She'd expected these things to be part of her job.

Oh, but the flirting. She disliked it for the same reason she'd always disliked math: she knew she would have no use for it later in life. She was, she'd discovered, the kind of girl who fell in love like a rock hurled from a cliff into a river. She had eyes for no men; she wanted only her lieutenant, her soldier—or someone just like him, though so far she'd met no one who even came close. His passion for certain politics. His hair. The bad manners. She wanted it all. Why bother learning the formulas and all the little tricks and shortcuts? she asked herself as she mopped up, just as she'd asked herself when she'd been forced to study geometry.

Serious conversation was different. She didn't mind talking to the boys if they were genuinely talking. But even then she wasn't like the other girls. She didn't avoid the grim subjects. Trenches and duckboards and sandbags, those were the things she wanted to know about. What did it feel like to shoot someone? The doughboys wouldn't discuss any of it. They only grinned and clowned and showed her pictures of their wives back on their farms, snapshots of their mothers standing stiff and unsmiling on the family porch. They went on and on about how much they missed their setters and spaniels.

She sighed in their faces. They didn't seem to understand this meant she was bored. They just kept on talking. They were soldiers; they thought it was their right. Sometimes she would get so frustrated she'd interrupt them. "Tell me about Paris," she'd say. She wanted to hear about red wine and edible snails and bawdy theatricals where actresses performed without hosiery. The men would only tell her about the Eiffel Tower. Or they would talk about churches. Did she know the French had placed fake panels over the masterpieces that were Notre Dame's doors so the Huns couldn't harm them? Don't even bother going by with your Brownie if those doors are what you're after, the boys said.

For a while she sought out men with pinned sleeves or empty trouser legs. She thought they'd be more contemplative than the others, would talk about the lessons of war or at least the mysterious aching of phantom limbs. She was fascinated by that. But they were just like the others. Even with one arm gone, nothing but grinning and clowning. She would eventually give up. "Would you like to dance?" she'd ask, trying to be the good Y-girl, flirty and fun. The crippled boys held her tightly. They hummed "Till We Meet Again" into her hair. She followed their simple box steps and thought about how much she wanted to be dancing with her lieutenant, his crazy striped hair, his lousy disposition, his devotion to something important. She wondered where he was right then. She wondered if he knew how to dance.

Now her limp, flimsy ribbon is floating like bright red seaweed in the dark strip of ocean between liner and dock, and Mary Brennan White is pulling at her sleeve.

"Come on, Yale," she says. "Get in on the fun. Are you always so quiet? Come on! We're going to Paris!"

Yale smiles as best she can and scans the crowd for the one thing that might cheer her. Of course he's not there. She's been looking for him the entire time she's been in New York. He's never there.

"That one," Mary Brennan White says. "See over there, the little gob with the bouquet of violets? Look how he's looking up at you. Yell something to him. Give the poor boy something to dream about later when he's alone in bed."

"Miss White," Yale says. She is teasing; she hopes it comes out that way. "Did you skip over the part in the Y's literature where it says we're supposed to be the finest of women?"

Her cabinmate puts her hands to her face. "Is that what it said? Shoot, and I thought it said the funnest."

Hard not to laugh, hard not to be charmed. Yale gives in. She leans over the rail and sees other discarded streamers stuck to the side of the ship, which is still dazzle-painted for camouflage purposes. She looks farther down and studies the audience of rowdies. Save for the gob with the violets, who is shielding his eyes with a hand as he hunts the top deck for someone—his sister? his sweetheart?—the men seem to be long-shoremen, scruffy and whiskered, recent arrivals from the less desirable cities of Europe. *Show us some shin!* one of them shouts. It's all so problematic. Does one embrace such men (workers, the salt of the earth) or snub them? What would Red Emma call out under these circumstances?

Yale wants to please Emma Goldman, who is still in the Jeff City prison. At the same time, she wants to impress Mary Brennan White, who has snagged the bouquet of violets just now catapulted upward by the young sailor. Yale admires both the throw and that catch, although she knows the flowers were meant for some other girl.

At last Yale steps forward. She has finally come up with something to shout. Cupping her hands by her mouth, she adopts the same posture as the other Miss White: up on her toes, hands on the rail. "Free love!" she cries. She is thinking of Emma's mailbox in Greenwich Village, which is not very far away from this pier. She is picturing the names of the lovers stenciled there. She shouts it again: "Free love!"

The unimaginative Hello Girls pick it up. Then all the rest—the nurses, the coeds, then the men on the dock, until everyone is yelling,

"Free love! Free love!"—although none of them, Yale suspects, knows what it really means: the end of female enslavement, the advent of equality, suffrage, split skirts. But they are all shouting it anyway. They are all drunk on sea air, and Mary Brennan White slips an arm around Yale's shoulders and squeezes her as she shouts along too, for free love, free love, free love.

CHAPTER TWO

A as in Amo

AMO WINSTON cannot believe her ears. On her previous tours of France, Miss Winston, a forty-year-old Y-matron, has never encountered such unruly young women. Free love? Is that what they are shrieking now? Bohemians, she thinks, and shakes her head while she squinches her lips to one side.

When she realizes what she's done, she immediately unsquinches them. In civilian life, she is an aesthetician in Des Moines, where she sells beauty creams at the Utica Dry Goods Store. She is an expert when it comes to the care of skin; she knows certain expressions produce wrinkles no lotion can ever erase. She is constantly aware of this, always monitoring herself, ordering her heart not to allow itself deep emotions lest they show up several years thereafter on her face. But suppressing feelings is a struggle for a woman who so readily experiences them all, from devotion to chagrin to fierce moral outrage.

Amo Winston tells herself to calm down. Relax, she commands herself. Breathe. She slackens her jaw and unclenches her teeth. She lets her lips drift apart. There, that's better, she thinks, mouth agape, head lolling.

And then she snaps to. She thinks, But you know, Amo, this only goes to prove that the end of a war is not entirely a good thing.

Nobody, least of all a patriot like Amo Winston, would ever say that out loud. Still, Amo can't be the only one who is thinking it. A war

84

ends, and the next thing you know you've got chaos. You'd guess it would be just the opposite—that peace would eliminate chaos and restore civility and decorum, and everyone would be grateful and eager to return to life as they once knew it—but you'd be wrong. Instead, what really happens is the generation that's gone out and done the fighting starts to feel it ought to have a say now in the way things are run, and that's when everything falls apart. Take these girls at the rail with their exposed calves and shrill voices. These girls think all they're doing is being carefree and modern, but what they really are doing is holding society's values up to the light and, employing naught but their naked and inexperienced eyes, arrogantly determining which of these values are precious and which are paste. And then they are blithely casting the latter, along with their streamers, into the sea.

Amo Winston fears for the future, she truly does, although not for the immediate future. She is, after all, a Y-matron, which means she has a degree of authority over these girls. Her plan is to exercise that authority as long as she can: benevolently, of course, but definitely, consistently, unrelentingly. There will be no bohemianism on her watch. No naked calves either. She will announce all this later at morning chapel.

Some things, however, cannot be postponed. Miss Winston knows she must deal right this minute with the two girls she's identified as the ringleaders, the ones who have initiated a chant as contagious as the Spanish flu. She marches right up to them, her smile as thin and false as the panels concealing the doors of Notre Dame. "Amo Winston," she says, extending her hand. "*A* as in amen, *mo* as in motivation."

That's all it takes. Once they know they've been picked out by someone less malleable, less easily charmed than the others, the taller yellow-haired one becomes meek, while the littler dark-haired one's neck blossoms red.

"Well," Amo Winston says upon hearing their names in return, "two Miss Whites. Well, well. Our cup runneth over."

She grills them a bit to keep them off balance. How old are they? They claim they're both twenty-five. How long have they been with the YMCA? Not long at all, they admit. And what were their reasons for signing up? The poor lonely boys, they both say. Neither mentions the Red Triangle's evangelical mission, which doesn't surprise Amo Winston one bit. No doubt they're freethinkers as well as free lovers. "Keep your voices down to a civilized roar," she instructs them. Miss White and Miss White, she repeats to herself as she walks away. Miss Black and Miss Black is more like it. Miss Scarlet and Miss Scarlet. Again her lips squinch to one side, so far over that the squared tip of her nose also crinkles. She maintains the expression for a moment, unaware she's doing so. But it's a frightful expression, and no one who passes by fails to notice it, including the lay minister of approximately fifty years and 250 pounds who is approaching her now. "Miss Winston!" he cries. He takes her hand as if to check her pulse. "You look so distressed!" he says.

Her tense face is transformed. "Nothing the sight of an old friend can't cure," she says. She is lit from within now, her eyes lighthouse beams. "Oh, Reverend Bliss, you old thing! I had no idea we'd be traveling together again." She allows herself this little white lie just as she allows him a comradely embrace. He is an imposing man, large in the manner of President Taft, his pink face composed mostly of cheeks and chins, his chest and belly straining the buttons on his uniform, his roly-poly thighs testing the inner seams of his jodhpurs. To be held by him is to be wrapped head to toe in a thick stole. "Oh, Reverend Bliss," she says again, loving the sound of his title. "I would confide what I just heard from those girls, those two over there, but I can't bring myself to repeat such language."

He is not only warm and not only a man who shares her deepest convictions. Reverend Alban Bliss is also a celebrity. He writes for *Good Housekeeping*, his opinions sandwiched between articles about electric suction sweepers and the benefits of hairnets made of pure human hair. "Woman must not come to man with a vote in her hand," he wrote in his column not long ago, "but with that same humble devotion which Mary the Mother showed Christ on the Cross." How many times has she quoted those words? And although he is only a lay minister, he has performed more trench conversions than any ordained man of the cloth. Bullets may whisk past his head, his prayers may be muffled by his gas mask, but never has he turned from a man who has made the decision. Nor has he ever been wounded during his ministrations. His voice is so loud, the boys say, it deflects shrapnel.

He is married, but his wife does not travel with him. She stays home in Indiana, attending to their five children, all boys.

When Alban Bliss releases Amo Winston from his hug—the old bear—she looks shyly down at the toes of her boots while patting her hair, which is arranged in an old-fashioned pompadour, tall and rigid and pinned a thousand times over a rat. Her hair is as lustrous and thick as it was during their last crossing, and she is grateful for this. She believes Alban Bliss admires its sheen and overlooks the fact that it is stark white—in fact, has grown even whiter since their last voyage, twelve months earlier. She has been assured that in sunlight the color flatters her type of complexion, that in sunlight the hue is opalescent, ivory with hints of lilac and pale blue. Perhaps, Miss Winston thinks hopefully, it will be a sunny voyage. Is he admiring her hair even now? She fixes those light beams on him again.

"You know," he says, "if you wish to unburden yourself, as it were, regarding those two volunteers, this old vagabond is always ready and willing to listen." She wonders what he means by this, what he is *really* trying to tell her. "I've spent much time in No Man's Land," he adds. He's lonely, that's what he's getting at. But, no, that's not what he's saying. It's this: "There are no words or deeds that can shock me."

He is trying to send her a message—signaling—and she must signal back. "Perhaps I would feel better if I shared what I heard," she allows. "Perhaps you could advise me how best to supervise these flibbertigibbets of mine. Maybe directly following evening chapel tonight I shall summon the courage and get down on my knees and confess to you like a Catholic."

"Although if you did, you would be confessing their sins, not a sin of your own," he reminds her.

"Now, Alban," she says. "Don't you start thinking I'm without sin. I'm not perfect, you know—only human like everyone else."

"Now, Miss Winston," he says, and she fears she has made a mistake—two mistakes. He is going to scold her for using his Christian name without invitation, and he is going to tell her that he didn't for a moment think her perfect, that only the Lord Jesus Christ is perfect and she ought to remember that.

But, in fact, what he says is, "You mustn't ask the impossible of me. Who could know you and find you anything but flawless?" He slides his fingers along one half of his waxy mustache, and his wedding ring glimmers. She is chastened again. He bows slightly before he goes. Miss

Winston waves adieu, a lace hankie peeking out from her cuff like a magician's overeager scarf. When he is gone, she removes the hankie and dabs at her eyes. Then she opens her mouth, relaxes her jaw, and lets her head roll on her neck like a flower on a delicate stem.

CHAPTER THREE

A Tarnished Woman

BACK IN THE girls' cabin, Mary Brennan White has an announcement to make. From here on she wishes to be called Brennan. Yale doesn't ask why. She of all people requires no explanation. Still, she's concerned. Is it a trap, a ruse to trick her into discussing her own nom de guerre? "A rose by any other name" is all she says. "Call me anything but late for supper," Brennan replies. Yale smiles, then opens her valise and gets on with her unpacking.

But Mary Brennan White wants to talk about her declared preference, Brennan over Mary. First of all, she tells Yale, there are too many Marys in the world. Second of all, there's that unfortunate association with virginity.

Brennan reclines on her cot, Yale's pillow from home propped behind her blonde head. "Okay?" she asks, meaning the pillow. "Of course," Yale says. She has a feeling she might as well get used to Brennan White all over her things. The cabin is tiny, although it does have a porthole and a private if minuscule loo, and she knows that they're lucky to have them. Except for those two amenities, the place is a cell. There are the two cots, each with a pilly olive-drab blanket. There is a single bureau, nicked and marred, soldiers on previous crossings having carved their sweethearts' names into the wood. Mary. Mary. Mary.

She is not just another Mary, Brennan says, suddenly back on her feet. Even in a cell, she manages to whirl as she talks. She is not, she says, just another girl. She stops to sniff the royal blue petals of her violets, which she tossed on the top of the bureau when they returned to the cabin. Then she goes to the porthole, leans against the wall there. She puts a hand on her hip, tilts back her head. She says, "I'm the kind of girl people call names."

"Oh, surely not," Yale says, but Brennan holds up her hand.

No, she says, it's true. And what's more, she likes it: not being called names but the things she does to get herself called those names. "Who wants to be a prig?" she says.

She has her nose in the air as she says this, priggishly delighting in her tawdry ways. It's a long and narrow nose, in some ways like Yale's, but straighter through the bridge, and where Yale's turns down at the end, Brennan's turns up. Also, there is the faintest smattering of freckles.

"I may be common," Brennan says with relish and so fluidly that Yale knows she's said these exact words before, "but Lord knows I'm not *common*."

Yale continues to unpack as Brennan natters on, a girl with a lot to say and the need to find many places from which to say it. Now she is sitting on Yale's cot, next on her own cot, then she is standing at Yale's side, trying on one of Yale's hats. Her terrible comportment, she explains as she adjusts the brim, is well known throughout Palmyra. There was a certain dalliance with a man rather prominent—quite the talk of the town, doncha know. Brennan sighs. Palmyra! she says. She takes off Yale's hat and places it, cockeyed, on Yale's head. How she loathes that stifling city where she was raised by her pharmacist father.

"George White," Yale says, to show she's been listening.

Half an orphan since birth, doncha know, Brennan goes on, and she smiles as if her mother's death on the delivery table is the jolliest of facts. Palmyra! she sighs once more. It's such a provincial burg, everyone acting like the Erie Canal is the world's eighth wonder. And the way people gossip there! She herself despises gossip. Not that she cares what people say about her. Why would she? She's not like other people, she marches to a different drummer, she's not ashamed of anything she's done. She's voluntarily telling Yale all about it, isn't she? The prominent citizen with whom she'd dallied—a descendant of both the Durfees and the Wilcoxes, as he didn't hesitate to tell you every other minute—he was married, of course. Not that she'd known about *that* till the end. Well, she'd known, yes, she'd known, but she'd thought they were no longer officially together, the man and his wife. And by the time she found out that the wife was gone for reasons other than the dissolution of the marriage—drying out, Brennan mouths, which, she hastens to add, full voice, isn't gossip but a simple fact and what does it matter anyway; Yale doesn't know the woman, does she, so what harm is Brennan doing?—at any rate, when she found out the marriage was still intact, Brennan says, she broke it off fast. She'd been gulled, that was what had happened.

Should she be ashamed of that? For trusting Billy Wilcox? Well, maybe she should be, and God knows she felt rotten about it, still does to this day, and she will never trust a man ever again, that she swears on her dear mother's grave, but still, is trusting someone really a crime? Well, it isn't, of course, so she will continue to tell her story to anyone, maybe even to that humorless Amo Winston, maybe even to that gargantuan lay minister, the Reverend Alban Bliss—Alban Blimp is more like it; has Yale seen him yet?—just to see if they keel right over at the thought of a girl like Brennan White prancing about in one of their precious uniforms. And if the YMCA should decide to reject her the same way the citizens of Palmyra had, the way her own father had—if Alban Bliss and his kind should decide to make her an example of all that is wrong with the new generation—well, that would be fine with her. Did she mention she was the kind of girl who didn't give a good goddamn what people thought?

"Only, please, God, please"—her arms are in the air; she is dancing her prayer—"first let me get to see Paree!"

While Brennan twirls about, flops down, bounces back up—a dancer, a dervish, a cyclone—Yale remains fixed and dull. She flinches when Brennan funnels too close with those flying elbows, those careless sweeping gestures. She worries there might not be enough oxygen in the little cabin to keep both of them going. She isn't sure what she thinks about Brennan and her torrid affair. "Well, we all make mistakes," she says.

For a moment Brennan seems interested. "What mistakes have you made?" she asks. But Yale can't think of any, and soon Brennan is talking about herself again. "I've never gone to college," Brennan says. "I'm a different kind of smart."

"Me too," Yale says.

"And I don't ever want to get married. And I'm not going to Paris to meet a man, like everyone else is. I'm going to meet men. Hundreds of men. It's Paris, right? And I'm free, white, and twenty-one plus four."

"Me too."

There's a sudden pause in the flurry. "You too, what?"

Yale is startled to have the spotlight back on her. "Well, not hundreds of men," she says. "I'm already in love with just one. But me too, twenty-one plus four."

Brennan raises an eyebrow, a gesture conveying such frank disbelief that Yale feels like a counterfeiter who's just handed a treasury agent a wad of damp bills. But the gesture also fills Yale with admiration, not only for cynicism so eloquently expressed—a lone brow arched upward—but for the brow itself, so high and inquisitive, so meticulously shaped and penciled.

"Right," Brennan says. "You said that before, at the rail, to that meddlesome matron. Twenty-five years old, you said. She didn't believe a word of it either, did you happen to notice?"

Yale tries lifting a brow of her own—I see your skepticism and I raise it one brow—but she has no control over those particular muscles, and when she tries to raise the right brow the left shoots up along with it, and she knows that, rather than coming off jaded, she is making herself appear even more wide-eyed and innocent than she is. She raises a single shoulder instead. "Oh," she says, "people are always saying that: me looking young for my age. It's the way I wear my hair."

Brennan raises the lone brow again as if to demonstrate how. Then she is hanging off her cot, snaking an arm beneath the mattress and fishing out a pack of Pall Malls. Snaking her arm beneath the mattress again, this time pulling out a round lighter of darkened brass with a three-dimensional figure of a naked woman hammered into it. The naked woman is neither a goddess nor a classical figure. She is simply a woman with breasts that sag despite their being fashioned from metal and a belly that is rounded but not large enough to conceal anything directly below it.

Brennan seems unaware that her fingers are running over the most intimate part of the woman's tarnished form. She flicks the wheel above the woman's head, and a blue flame streaks out. "A gift from that prominent citizen I was mentioning," she says.

She inhales and blows a smoke ring toward the ceiling. She clearly means to be both blasé and instructional. She tosses both pack and lighter onto Yale's cot. "Help yourself, darling," she says. "Nothing makes a girl look more mature."

Yale feels a grid of red prickle her neck. She turns down the offer and turns her back. It's vexing, the way her body has taken to betraying her. How glad she is that she chose not to bob her hair.

She continues unpacking, removing nightgowns, a robe, several pairs of gloves (wool mittens for visits to the front, cotton whites for visits to the theater). As she arranges her belongings in a drawer, she wonders why people are so bloody obsessed with her age. It seems such a trivial thing to worry about given these tragic times. The war is not officially over, for one thing. And even if it should end tomorrow or the day after, as everyone keeps saying it will, the world will remain a tragic place. Millions of boys will still be dead. Emma Goldman will still be in jail. Armenian children will still be starving in Turkey.

They will be starving in Armenia too. Because Armenia is actually a small country now. Situated to the south of Russia, the brand-new Republic of Armenia is squeezed between the brand-new Republic of Georgia and the brand-new Republic of Azerbaijan.

Since meeting the soldier in the library, Yale has become quite the expert on his suddenly existent homeland, as well as on his people's travails during the centuries past. Like most Americans, she has long known about the deportations of 1915, how women and children were marched across blazing sands, ostensibly to a new home in the desert, and how most of them perished before reaching their destination. Now she knows the terrible details of that enforced trek. She knows that starving marchers foraged for bits of food in their own excrement. She knows that children ate their dead mothers' flesh, that girls threw themselves into the Euphrates to end their nightly violations, that old women drowned themselves in wells for the same reason. She knows that sun-scorched skin turns not black, as one might guess, but a deep green before it peels from the bones.

It touches her, reaches her; she could talk about it forever. Not that she has ever done so. No one she knows would want to discuss such a morbid topic. But she *could* talk about it if she chose to, that's her point. She could quote Lord Bryce for hours. She could paraphrase the reports of all the heartsick German tourists and gasping American missionaries. She could recite lines from poems: *then someone brought a jug of kerosene/human justice I spit in your face*. The fellow who wrote that one—a report in verse of Christian women forced to dance naked before being burned alive—he was killed on April 24, 1915, along with so many other Armenian men. See that? She can even rattle off dates the way she never could in history class. The day Missouri entered the union? Early eighteen-something-or-other. The day the Young Turks staged their coup, tossed out Abdul Hamit, the evil Red Sultan, and installed Talaat and Enver and Djemal in his place, those dissemblers, those tyrants, that triumvir promising equal rights while secretly arranging for horrors no one could imagine?

That would be January 26, 1913.

She looks into her near-empty valise. She is down to the last few items: hair ribbons, hairpins, the half-dozen bars of Ivory she packed in case there was no soap in Europe. Brennan, meanwhile, is back to her flitting, even more dangerous now because she has a lit cigarette in her hand. And because now she is asking Yale personal questions.

It's only small talk, the sort of harmless inquisition new acquaintances are routinely subjected to. Yet every question feels like a challenge, an obstacle course requiring Yale to be so swift, so nimble, she can hardly think. So, Brennan says, Yale is twenty-five? Then how has Yale spent the last seven years since high school? Oh, Yale says, unfolding, then refolding handkerchiefs, she's been working for her father. How interesting, says Brennan. And what did that job entail? Oh, Yale says, mainly she ran the office, wrote copy for his advertisements, that sort of thing. Advertising, says Brennan. How fascinating. And what were those advertisements for, what product does her father make? Oh, he makes airplane parts, Yale says.

Brennan crosses the room to stand at Yale's side. Smoke curls into Yale's face. Yale waits. Her neck reddens. She promises herself she will never cut her hair, never pin it up, never.

But Brennan is not suspicious. She is only impressed and a little bit envious. "I've always wanted to go up in a plane," she says.

CHAPTER FOUR

Animal, Vegetable, Mineral

Flying's fun," Yale allows. She gathers her courage and looks Brennan in the eye. What she sees surprises her. Hook, line, and sinker, she thinks. Brennan may be a dervish, a summer storm, an acrobat, but Yale is a tightrope walker, and she's just crossed from one end of the wire to the other without missing a step.

She closes the bureau drawer and begins to push her near-empty suitcase beneath her cot. Maybe she is becoming invincible. Maybe she's a modern American after all.

Then Brennan says, "So what are you, anyway?" and, up on her wire, Yale stumbles. "What do you mean, what am I?" she asks, flummoxed, flustered. "Do you mean as in animal, vegetable, or mineral?"

Brennan snorts. "Right." She is back on Yale's cot now, head on Yale's pillow, arm crooked beneath her neck. She kicks off her boots, lets them fly, one at a time, across the small cabin. She blows a smoke ring; it undulates above her like a harem girl's hips. "Yes," she says. "We're playing Twenty Questions, and—wait, I've got it—you're the village idiot." She laughs as if Yale has been telling a joke. "No, of course that's not what I mean. I mean, what are you? You know what I mean. I mean, what church do you go to?"

Oh! Yale wants to say. Oh, so that's how you people gather this information. A question posed in code. An outsider exposed by her perplexed squint, her dumbbell response.

To keep busy, to avoid looking at Brennan, she taps a cigarette from the pack on her cot and holds it as Brennan does, between two fingers. "Oh, we're Methodists," she says.

She has trained for this moment. Her final few weeks in St. Louis, she attended Methodist funerals. She would have gone to regular Sunday services, but she thought it might be too risky. Wouldn't the congregation know they'd never seen her before? Mightn't they question her, ask for a membership card, check to see if her dues were paid up?

94

Funerals were safer. A hearty turnout spoke well of the dead, especially given the influenza pandemic, which kept so many from attending any public gathering. What family member would discourage her participation? Besides, might not the deceased have befriended a Jew? If one of her school friends died, God forbid, wouldn't Yale show up at the church?

She might not have been good at flirting, but she did have a certain knack for mourning. She did not shy away from receiving lines. She joined right in, offering what always felt like the sincerest of condolences. She was moved by the widowers particularly, old men who had been alone for only a few days but whose eyes were already bewildered and helpless and whose suits already smelled slightly of mildew.

Yet here she is now, feeling a bit bewildered and helpless herself. It isn't only Brennan's question throwing her off balance. It's her own blushing and the way her voice spiked up when she finally came out with the answer—"Oh, we're Methodists." Her voice had become a childlike soprano, and there had even been the hint of a question mark at the end.

But as was the case with all those grieving Methodists back in St. Louis, Brennan White doesn't suspect a thing. In fact, Brennan seems not to care, really, what Yale is. Animal, vegetable, Methodist—Brennan appears not the least interested. And it dawns on Yale that Brennan has asked the question only so she can say what *she* is. There is a lesson to be learned here, Yale thinks. Maybe nobody really gives a damn about anyone else when it comes right down to it. Although what if she had inadvertently blurted out the truth? She is pretty sure Mary Brennan White would have cared about *that*.

"Well, I'm Episcopalian on George White's side, you'll be happy to know," Brennan is saying, "but on my dead mother's side I'm Catholic, famine Irish to boot, and if that means you think I ought to be your maid instead of your roommate, you'll just have to get by it somehow. You're officially stuck with me." She raises the lone brow again, indicates the cigarette Yale is still holding. "Are you going to light that or just use it to conduct a symphony?"

Yale comes to Brennan, allows Brennan to flick the obscene lighter scant inches away from her nose. She inhales shallowly, exhales lavishly, chokes moderately. She glances at Brennan, anticipating disdain, but sees another look altogether. It's a look that Yale recognizes because she's seen it before, and suddenly she knows where: her mother, when the family moved into their neighborhood. All those Lutherans descended from Prussians—not one had greeted the Weisses. For the first several months not one had spoken to them on the street. They stayed on anyway. Her mother planted her garden and her feet. She nurtured her delphiniums and her four-foot-high black-eyed Susans as if to say to the neighbors, Well, then try to ignore these. Soon people were coming to her for advice. Fertilizer, weed removal, the proper way to prune roses. If you want to see a breathtaking example of Chinese wisteria, people said, you simply have to walk past the Jews'.

Bravado, then. It was bravado enabling Esther Weiss to stay on like that. It's the same with Brennan. Her expression isn't contempt or suspicion or pride. It's pure bravado, and Yale has just figured out what bravado is. It's abject terror brushed with a thin coat of who-gives-a-damn and topped with a dollop of if-you-don't-like-it-lump-it.

Yale wants to reassure Brennan that there's nothing to fear, at least not from her. But how to do it without giving herself away? "Oh, religion," she ventures, waving the cigarette for emphasis. "I don't judge people based on that bushwa."

"Liar," Brennan says, but she smiles, that generous pink unfurling. She is relieved, she is pleased, she is grateful. "You're full of bunk," Brennan White says. "Even I wouldn't want to room with a damned Papist."

CHAPTER FIVE

Mind and Matter

I T TAKES the average landlubber three days to grow a pair of sea legs, three wrenching days when death seems preferable, when one fantasizes pitching oneself overboard and letting oneself go under (drowning is said to be such a pleasant way to die). Everyone knows this about mal de mer—three wretched days—but Brennan and Yale aren't concerned. They are American girls, they are invincible, and they have made a decision. They have decided to be immune to seasickness.

"Mind over matter," says Yale.

If Brennan nods, it is only because she doesn't wish to get into a philosophical debate. The truth is she has no faith in her mind's ability to triumph over anything. It's matter she trusts. It's the forces outside herself. She has faith in the primitive. She believes in animated nature: in lunar gods, solar gods, gods of the sky and the wind and the sea.

Not that she erects any shrines to these gods. She indulges in no rituals, whispers no prayers to Odin or Ares. She just believes she's constantly being watched and judged by sprites, fairies, old Norse deities, the stars, small animals, every molecule comprising everything there is. When she does wrong, these forces punish her. Thus, her recent ordeal. She did wrong—her married man—and so of course she'd been punished: heartbreak, heartache, and then, the distressing aftermath. But when she stops doing wrong, when she ignores the tugging of her own mind, her own heart, her own needs, and does what she's supposed to do, when she lives her life right, then the forces are kind to her, because basically the forces understand love, they understand desire, and while they want Brennan to be a moral person—as they define moral, which is quite similar to the way Brennan defines moral—they also want her to have a good time.

Chief among these forces, Brennan thinks, is her mother. Her mother's ghost. She knows that in life her mother was a Catholic, and that a true Catholic would be horrified at the nature of Brennan's cobbled theology. But she also knows that, upon marrying her father, her mother stopped going to church, stopped practicing, became a lapsed Catholic, and this is both a condition and a phrase that Brennan likes. The ocean laps; you sit in laps; Catholics lapse and turn into good-natured ghosts, guardian angels.

Of course, she doesn't really believe any of this. But at the same time she believes it all, and this is why Brennan is certain she won't get seasick. It's because the forces have already punished her. She has lost (in order of importance, least to most) her reputation, her home, her father,

Billy Wilcox. Now it is time for the gods, the goddesses, the clouds, the sky, the small animals, the angels to say, *Whoa, Nelly! That's more than enough!* Brennan has paid for her transgressions, and now, she is convinced, the gods of the sea will spare her their undignified initiation.

If Yale were privy to any of this, she'd nod and say, "That's what I said. Mind over matter."

Meaning that Yale feels she and Brennan are too strong and determined to succumb. Also, Yale is under the impression that the unpleasantness strikes as soon as the ship enters the high seas. Certainly this is the case for many of the others on board, all those poor volunteers turning as green as their uniforms, gasping in mid-conversation and sprinting to their cabins or the rail, whichever is closer, all ladylike delicacy forgotten.

Poor slobs, Brennan and Yale say to each other. They bring the sick girls hot tea and sour pickles, the latter at the ship's doctor's behest. (He's a long-bearded Frenchman who wears a uniform from some prior war, including a saber, and believes in the old cures.) Then they go off, just the two of them, and explore.

The ship is a mess. In the dining room, the carpeting has been pulled up, leaving scuffed flooring and rows of bashed-in carpet nails. The grand ballroom has been stripped of all furnishings save for several massive crystal chandeliers, under which soldiers have been falling out for the past year, mornings for drills, afternoons for cootie inspection.

They are among a handful of girls hearty enough to make it to morning chapel. The chapel, so-called, is a former officers' bar, and although the billiard table and spittoons have been carted away, stale cigar smoke still clings to the crimson flocked wallpaper, where, above a portable pulpit, the French crew has hung a portrait of Jesus. The savior has long wavy blond hair, large sad brown eyes. "He looks like a golden retriever," Brennan says, not necessarily disapprovingly, as the two girls sit in white folding chairs, eating stale crullers and waiting for services to begin.

CHAPTER SIX

Should This Behavior Continue

THERE'S SOMETHING about seeing Amo Winston come in and storm up to the lectern that makes them want to giggle the way schoolchildren invariably do at events where sobriety's required. Amo Winston drones on about manners and hemlines and rules. Uniforms must be worn at all times, even in bed, she says, and something about the way she says it makes it impossible for the two girls to look at each other without laughing. After sundown, Miss Winston says, there is to be no singing because the war isn't over; U-boats might find them yet, and although this isn't remotely funny, Brennan bites her lip and Yale covers her mouth with her hand. Then Alban Bliss steps up, and the podium that concealed nearly all of thin Miss Winston is a mere stripe down the front of his uniform. For a quick second Yale and Brennan dare exchange glances, and Brennan mouths *blimp*, and Yale has to turn away quickly, keeping her eyes away from the podium, knowing she will never again see Alban Bliss as anything but a giant balloon propelled by hot air, by gas.

When he preaches, Alban Bliss shouts as if he is in a huge hall addressing thousands. "I have been over there, ladies," he bellows. "I have seen our boys emerge from out a withering fire. I who am no ordained minister of the Gospel, but merely a worker through the YMCA in the cause of God, have learned from these boys what religion is. God is no longer the policeman we have made him for so many years. To our boys, God is a chum who won't let a pal down."

By now, Yale has recovered herself enough to look at the lay minister. Spittle flies from his lips. He pumps both fists in the style of the old speakers: William Jennings Bryan, Robert La Follette. Yale averts her face and narrows her eyes, the way one does when caught in a squall. At the same time she sees Amo Winston leaning forward in her wooden chair in the first row, nodding, taking a handkerchief from her sleeve, dabbing at her eyes, wiping the end of her nose.

"And now here are you women, sailing off to care for these boys," the Reverend Bliss thunders. "I beg you to bring with you your female touch of tenderness. As women wearing the Red Triangle, I beseech you to epitomize grace, love, and purity."

"Oh, brother," Brennan says, and Amo Winston turns around in her seat.

"I will always remember," Alban Bliss roars, "the poor lad who, seconds before perishing in my arms, declared that to him YMCA meant You Must Cry Amen. Ladies, you are our boys' Amen-girls, and while your job may be that of canteen worker, your calling is nothing less than this: your calling is to bring Christ to men."

Certainly Brennan means to whisper. It's just that to whisper yet still be heard while Alban Bliss is going on, one has to whisper fairly loudly. And how was Brennan to know that Alban Bliss was going to pause that very moment for effect?

"My calling," Brennan says, in that rare and surprising silence, "is to bring *me* to men. Christ's on his own."

"TROUBLE!" Amo Winston announces. That's what the two White girls are. She knew it right from the start, and she will report them should this behavior continue. The girls are outside the chapel now, where Amo Winston has dragged them as if they actually were ill-behaved children. "Trouble!" Amo Winston says again. Yale makes a squeak of protest, but a finger comes jabbing at her nose. "Don't deny it, and don't give me that innocent face. She's the mouthpiece, I know, but you're in on it too. Lying to me like the dickens before. Twenty-five years old! Butter wouldn't melt."

"It's my hair," Yale begins, but Miss Winston is talking over her.

"What you don't know," Amo Winston says, "is that in civilian life I happen to be the head aesthetician at the Utica Dry Goods Store in Des Moines, Iowa. I happen to be able to tell a person's age just by looking."

"I once knew a man who worked for the carnival," Brennan says. "He could do that too."

Yale focuses only upon Miss Winston. Her skin *is* very nice, white as the bark of a birch tree perhaps, but completely unlined and without any brown spots or other marks of aging. And yet, despite this, Miss Winston looks every bit the middle-aged spinster. It's her thin lips, the white pompadour, and the several long hairs emerging from her chin. It's the eyes too, the hooded skin above them. But most of all, it's the prudery. Carnival workers? Miss Winston is saying. Yes. Of course Miss White would be acquainted with persons of that ilk.

Brennan returns Miss Winston's strained, angry smile. "All I said was, Christ could take care of himself," Brennan says. "Don't you agree? Don't you think he can?"

It's then that the conversation takes the turn that catches Yale completely off guard. "Excuse me, Miss White," Amo Winston says. "Excuse me, but would you like to henceforth be excused from chapel? Perhaps I can introduce you to the Jewesses on board. You can spend your time with them. You needn't bother yourself with matters of salvation."

Yale feels her ears prick up. She thinks of cats, stalking and being stalked, the way their own ears prick up, how those ears rotate toward the danger, the rest of their bodies immobile except, perhaps, for a barely perceptible quivering at the very end of the tail.

"Oh, come now, Miss Winston," Brennan says. "I didn't say I wanted to crucify him. I only said I don't want to compete with him for dates."

Miss Winston nods. "Keep it up, Miss White. Please do. Soon you'll be having me believing you're actually one of them. For the record, you never said. You're not a Hebrew, are you? Or are you?"

The way Amo Winston says *Hebrew*—it's as if that's the worst thing you can call another person. And maybe from Amo Winston's perspective it is. Maybe from Brennan's it is too. Yale knows she should keep still, say nothing. But she can no longer help herself. She takes one step forward and says, through gritted teeth—this is all she can think to say—"You are not a kind person, Miss Winston."

For the briefest moment Amo Winston's entire mouth scoots to one side of her face and her eyes become as protuberant as a fish's. Then her mouth scoots back where it belongs, and she says, sweet as pie, "I'm simply asking a question, Miss White."

"Well, it's an unkind question," Yale says.

Miss Winston's tone has changed completely. She speaks to Yale confidentially, almost maternally. "It's not as if it hasn't happened before, dear. People going to Europe, thinking no one will know them, and they can all of a sudden be what they're not. Women trying to catch a man of quality, move up in the world. Who will ever know? That's what they tell themselves. Even colored girls; I've seen it. But mostly the Jews. I can't count the number who've tried to pass on my watch."

Miss Winston is taking pity on poor little Yale, trying to teach her the facts of life. Yale has had the wool pulled over her eyes, Miss Winston believes. Now she needs to see Brennan for what she is, which is, of course, what she isn't and what Yale is, or at least used to be. There's an expression Yale heard soldiers use in the Times Square Canteen when they thought none of the girls were listening and they wanted to describe how the army always got everything as wrong as could be. Miss Winston's got it all bass-ackward.

"Brennan isn't passing," Yale says. *Bravado.* "We have the same last name. What she is, I am. What I am, she is."

Miss Winston will have none of it. "Oh, please, Miss White. It's a ridiculously common name. People from a myriad of backgrounds share that name. It doesn't mean a thing."

This is when the first wave of nausea overtakes Yale. She tells herself the queasiness is only her imagination, but she knows it's not true. She tells herself the queasiness is caused by Amo Winston and her accusations and insinuations, and maybe that's part of it, but it's more than that, and Yale knows it. She tries to fight it, gulping the cold sea air. At the same time, she tries to come up with a response that cannot be challenged. "Well, it does in our case," she says. "We have the same name because we're sisters, and we're neither of us anything but what we say we are, and if you start spreading this kind of rumor about us, I'll have your job."

She is so angry—and feels so lousy—she believes she can do it. One word from her, and Amo Winston will be drummed out of the YMCA. Slander! Yale will cry, and then, a shipboard ceremony, the red triangle ripped from Amo Winston's sleeve. Yale pictures pirates, poking épées, a plank.

And so she is surprised to see Amo smiling. "Sisters!" Amo Winston says, as if the word is delicious, as if it's been dipped in chocolate. Yale feels dizzy, feverish. Her vision is blurring. The floor is in motion.

"Yes," Amo Winston says. "Yes, of course you are sisters. Although isn't it odd you didn't think to mention it earlier?"

"Didn't we?" Yale puts a hand against the wall.

"No, I don't believe you did. Although I do believe you mentioned that you're both twenty-five." Miss Winston nods. "Which would mean you are twins."

Yale feels her forehead grow wet with cold perspiration as she tries to think how to get out of this, what, if anything, she knows about twinship, when Brennan, who up till now has been merely observing the skirmish like a picnicker on the hilltop overlooking Gettysburg, turns into the cavalry and charges to the rescue. "Miss Winston," Brennan says, "Yale said we are sisters. And we've already told you our ages. The rest we leave to your keen powers of deduction." She takes Yale by the arm. "Come, darling," she says. "You look more peaked than Mount Vesuvius and equally ready to blow."

Amo Winston opens her mouth. She never really thought Brennan White was Hebrew when all this began. She was just trying to make a point. But—how ironic, or perhaps she's more astute about these things than she's realized—it's so obvious now. And that's just the trouble with those people trying to pass. Sooner or later they're all found out. As for the other one—the little liar, the freethinker—Yale White must have known the truth all along. Because look how vehemently she's denied Brennan's true race, look at the extremes she's gone to, the preposterous lie she's told just so Amo wouldn't figure it out. Such misguided loyalty. To claim sisterhood! Twinship!

The girls are already in retreat, Yale clattering down the iron stairs, Brennan White a step behind, laughing. It's that laughter, rude and disrespectful and reverberating, that drowns out Amo Winston's final words.

She stands at the top of the metal staircase. A hymn seeps out from under the chapel's door, Alban Bliss's basso profundo sweetened by the sopranos of the volunteers, like sugar in rich black coffee. Is she disturbing them, yelling like this? Even if she is, she can't help it. She aims her voice right at Yale. She pities Brennan, but it's the defender she abominates and names. "Liar!" she calls. She squinches her mouth all the way to the side, aims, and hits Yale square in the back. *"Teenager!"*

CHAPTER SEVEN

The Last Day of the War

TWO MORNINGS LATER, the Great War ends. In France, at eleven on the dot, every gun is laid down. Somewhere, the last boy who is going to die on the field closes his eyes. A few seconds later, farmers tiptoe outside and try to figure out what in God's name they will plant on their ravaged acreage come spring.

On such a day an American girl ought to be happy. Even a girl who has been suffering with mal de mer for forty-eight hours ought to be able to see the larger picture and offer up a few words of thanks. But neither Brennan nor Yale is happy or thankful. Yale lies in bed, a damp cloth over her eyes. Brennan, who fell victim to the ailment shortly after Yale did, is curled on the bathroom floor. Everything hurts: their bones, their teeth, their raw red throats. The cloth touching their skin is killing. Even odors cause pain. They have thrown their sour pickles out the porthole, but let them recall the stink of the pickle juice and once again they are retching.

"It's day three," Yale bleats. "They said we'd be cured by day three."

From the music seeping into their room through the ceiling, Yale guesses that most everyone else on the *Espagne* has recovered. A band consisting mostly of percussionists—drums, pianos, the accompaniment of pounding feet and voices lifted in song—is playing "Over There," and has played that song so frequently for the past several hours that, even when the musicians take a break, the lyrics knock around inside Yale, the drums rum-tumming against her temples and the backs of her eyes.

It's even worse when the band launches into a thumping version of "Home Sweet Home." The song has been banned all these months, the army fearing the troops would fall to pieces should they hear the tune. Now Yale hears the melody and she's the one falling apart because she finds the sentiment as sickening as the Atlantic. Be it ever so humble, she thinks of her stomach. But she also thinks of Esther, to whom, despite her illness, she's been writing daily postcards full of unmitigated cheer.

Day two of the voyage. Having wonderful time. Am working hard on my French. Well, adieu—must wash hair.

The band plays a second chorus of "Home Sweet Home." Yale removes the compress so she can hang off the bed and get sick into the wastepaper basket she's pulled to her bedside. There is nothing in her stomach. She contains only the sea, pale foam.

SOMETIME AFTERWARD, the band still playing, she falls asleep, and when she opens her eyes it's midnight and she's fine.

She sits up in bed. She listens and hears nothing. There is no music, not even the screech of gulls. It seems as though, while she slept, the ship, the sea, and the seabirds all grew as peaceful as the world itself. The war is twelve hours over.

She ought to change out of her uniform, she thinks. Sick as she was, she obeyed orders and slept in it, and now it is wrinkled and matted with perspiration. She ought to strip it off, have it laundered. She ought to draw a bath and clean herself too. Instead, she sits in bed and wishes she'd kept her pickle; she's that hungry. She glances around the darkened cabin. She is cold, she realizes, and then sees why. The porthole has been thrown open.

"I've been waiting for you," Brennan says. She is sitting in her cot, wearing only her cheap lacy bloomers and a cheaper and lacier camisole. She's resting on Yale's pillow. "Let's go up top," she says. "I'm starved batty."

Even now she doesn't put on her uniform. She slips her YMCA-issued oilskin greatcoat over her underthings and steps into her boots, although she doesn't bother with the laces. Yale puts on her coat too, and wears her boots open, the same as Brennan. The leather tongues hang to the side, loose and flapping. The girls slosh up the metal stairs.

On the top deck, the *Espagne* is wet and deserted, but the girls don't mind. It feels good, having the damp cold to themselves. They open their mouths to catch raindrops like turkeys. They stand by the rail, luxuriating in their sogginess. "Look out there," Brennan says. "It's so beautiful."

"Oh, it is," Yale says, although she sees nothing she considers beautiful. Sea and sky are the same leaden gray, such a precise match it's as if the whole world has been patched together by a skinflint tailor willing to spare only his gloomiest serge. Even the foam produced when the angry and muscular ocean slaps the side of the ship is gray.

Yet then suddenly—a brilliant white flash under the water's surface.

"It's as if whichever god of the sea is on duty tonight is flicking a switch down there and turning on a string of electric lights," Brennan says, a touch of reverence in her voice.

"What do you mean, whichever God?"

"Neptune," Brennan says. "Poseidon. The Celts have Aegir. There must be others. The Norse must have one. There's ours, of course. The God of Job and Jonah."

Yale envisions picture-book illustrations: gods with wreathed white hair, tridents, bare feet. She imagines them all lined up, each waiting for his turn to sit on the underwater throne like women lined up at the baker's, the butcher's. "You know a lot of gods," she says.

"I worship them all," Brennan tells her.

"You worship multiple sea gods?"

"I do. I'm a Pagan. I'm a Deist. I'm also a Druid. I worship the trees."

"Funny," Yale says, "you don't look Druish." She waits. "It's a joke," she says.

"But I do." Brennan looks thoughtful. "I do look Druish. Nobody looks more Gaelic than I do. That's what was so odd the other morning with that Amo Winston." She shakes her head. "Christ, Yale, you look more Jewish than I do. Not that you look Jewish either. You're perfectly pretty. You have an exotic quality to you. You could almost be Spanish. I'm only just saying, compared to me."

"It's the way I wear my hair," Yale says. It's another joke, not a very good one, but a joke, and Brennan gets it and laughs.

Sometimes Yale thinks her secrets are like red shoes on her feet or a long feather boa wrapped around her neck, things no one could miss if they would only really look at her. Other times she feels she has no secrets at all. At those times her lies feel like truths, like an integral part of her, the way a man's wedding band is said to become as much a part of his hand as his fingers. She is thinking of Alban Bliss's ring now. She saw it in chapel, surrounded by flesh, something that would never come off. She is thinking of her soldier's pinkie ring too.

"Did I tell you before that I'm in love?" she says, but at the same time Brennan shouts, "Look!"

It's a whale, and he's massive and majestic and yet also extraordinarily ugly. He's the same gray as everything else, although not as purely gray; rather, he is mottled and barnacled, and there is also an eye, a huge and solitary eye. As soon as that eye takes in the girls, the whale vanishes.

Yale wants to stay by the rail. She is hoping for another exciting disturbance. What comes after phosphorescence and whales? Flying fish? Mermaids? A U-boat, perhaps? But Brennan is hungry. Brennan is thirsty. "Let's find some pie and some whiskey," she says. Her face is dripping, although whether from raindrops or sea spray, Yale isn't certain. She licks her own lips, tastes salt. She looks up, feels immediately spat in the eye.

"All right," she says.

"We'll have a toast," says Brennan. "We'll drink to the last day of the war and the first real day of our voyage. Or—no, I know what. We'll raise a glass to sisters. To twins." She mimes lifting that glass. "To Castor and Pollux," she says.

"But, Brennan," Yale says. The spell of the sea has been broken. Yale's stomach is growling. "Castor and Pollux were brothers, not sisters."

"All right, all right," Brennan says. "To Dorothy and Lillian Gish."

They are laughing, falling against each other as they go. The slick deck and those flapping, sloshing boots make it hard to walk. "But, Brennan," Yale says. "The Gish girls aren't twins."

"But, Yale," Brennan tells her. "Neither are we."

CHAPTER EIGHT

The White Sisters'
Bowling League of America

THE DOORS to the dining room are locked. Brennan futilely wriggles one of Yale's hairpins in the latch. "Damn it," she says. "Where the hell is everyone?"

Everyone is in bed. They hadn't thought of that. They thought it was the last day of the war and so there would be parties, dancing, carrying on. That noisy band thumping fox-trots till dawn.

The problem is that it's not really, not exactly, the last day of the war. No peace treaty was signed on Armistice Day, and until there's a peace treaty, the war will go on and wartime regulations will remain in effect. Sleeping in uniforms. No singing after sundown. And the same early lights-out as before. While Brennan and Yale try to jimmy the dining-room locks, all the other girls on the *Espagne* are asleep fully dressed, helmets by every pillow, boots at the foot of every bed.

The only doors that open when they try the knobs are the doors to the grand ballroom. Why these? Yale wonders. Maybe a drowsy steward forgot to secure them, Brennan suggests. Maybe a minor goddess of good times is feeling sympathetic tonight. The White twins, Brennan says, are never to question their good luck. In this vale of tears, she tells Yale, when good luck comes along, they are to fill their fists.

The ballroom is as empty as it was the first morning out, save for an upright piano pushed into one corner. "Look!" Brennan says, as excited as she was minutes ago, spotting that whale. On top of the piano are a dozen or so glass plates containing leftover pieces of chocolate layer cake. There are also a number of goblets containing various amounts of abandoned champagne. The same drowsy steward who forgot to lock the doors must have overlooked this spinet when he cleaned up after the day's celebration.

"Pie and whiskey," Brennan says, and she and Yale each take off their drenched heavy coats and nab themselves a plate and a glass. The champagne is warm and flat, but Yale doesn't know any better and drinks two glasses in quick succession.

"You'll want to look out for cigarette butts," Brennan says. She is sitting on the piano bench in her underclothes. She presses a white key so slowly, so gently, it makes no sound. "Also, a woman of your purported age would know fine beverages are sipped slowly."

Yale tries to raise one eyebrow. She takes a third glass, checks for doused butts. She wonders who sipped from these glasses before her. A good way to catch the flu, she thinks. It doesn't stop her, though. She's feeling invincible again. She has survived mal de mer, and the war is over. Nothing can go wrong tonight. She sits next to Brennan, who is pressing a black key this time. A note comes forth, muffled and minor, unsure of itself. Yale looks into the ballroom's shadows. "I can see the people who danced here before the war," she says, "in their ball gowns and jewels. Before President Wilson drafted this poor ship into the navy."

"I can see the people who will dance here in the future," Brennan says. She licks frosting off her finger, then plays another black note, more vibration than music. They've eaten almost every slice of cake they've found. "Come on," she says. She wipes crumbs from her lips, puts on her coat. "Let's go play billiards."

Yale is dizzy, but not from champagne. It's from Brennan, all this energy. She slings on her coat and follows her out to the top deck, into the rain, knowing all the while that they can't play billiards. The sporting facilities on the lowest deck are closed for the voyage. Amo Winston said so in chapel. A big sign on the top deck says so as well. There was a time when Yale would have pointed to that sign and refused to descend the stairs. That time might have been only three days ago. But now Yale is following Brennan down the tinny steps, treading softly so the stamped metal won't clang beneath her floppy boots. Also, so the two glasses of champagne she carries, one in each hand, won't spill.

The bottom deck, like the rest of the ship, is empty. The girls walk along a dark hallway until Brennan finds a light switch. When she flips it on, the electric lights sputter and spark, and the two girls see a row of doors with round windows, the glass of each window gridded with wire. Yale peeks through one, expecting a room full of explosives, bombs, crates marked DANGER! All she sees are wooden weights, mats, medicine balls. A sign on another room says it's a Turkish bath. Stand on your toes, peer inside, and you can see towels and, in the distance, red wooden benches.

Brennan shakes the knob. "I want in," she says.

Sitting around and sweating. Yale says she doesn't see the fun in that. But Brennan keeps rattling the door. "It would be like going to confession naked," she says. "You wouldn't have to say a word. Your sins would just seep out your pores."

Yale has never seen a confessional. Now she imagines herself kneeling before a wooden booth in a vast cathedral, her hair wet and hanging down her back, she herself wearing only a white towel. She pictures steam filling the booth as she shivers on the cold stone floor. She realizes this is not a new image, not entirely. This is the image that has always come to her when she hears words like *spirit* or *soul*. She has always thought of these things as shapeless, white, steamy. Water right after it's boiled.

"Look," Brennan says. "There's the billiard table out in the open, just waiting for us." She circles the table as if it were a shrine. She runs her fingers along the green felt, touches the rosewood corners, strokes the ivory sights. "Let's play," she says.

But the balls and cues have been stowed for the trip. "Too bad," Yale says. Her wet coat is heavy; it's begun to hurt her shoulders. She is thinking they ought to go to bed, get some sleep. And that they might stop, before they do, for a little more cake and champagne. She's already consumed most of her fourth glass. "We'll have to call it a night."

"We'll have to make do with the bowling lane," Brennan counters.

Like the billiard table, the alley is out in the open, but in this case, so are the requisite accessories. Bowling balls, solid and ripe, are lined up on a wooden rack.

"Are you crazy?" Yale says. "The whole world will come running."

But Brennan has made up her mind. No dinner, no celebration, no steam bath, no billiards. She is going to do something fun tonight. She is going to bowl.

Oh, don't worry, she tells Yale. No one will hear them. They're nowhere near the sleeping quarters. They're surrounded by rooms filled with nothing but steamer trunks and rations and scrip.

"And horses," Yale says. "I swear as we were walking along I heard a horse."

And horses, Brennan agrees. Horses who won't say a word, not if Brennan and Yale bowl quietly, delicately. "Come on," she says. "I promise to bowl like the finest of women."

"You're going to get us sent home," Yale tells her. "I thought you were desperate to make it to Paris."

But Brennan is begging. "Yale," she says, "I have never once in my life been bowling."

"Then you have no idea the ruckus it makes." Yale feels as if she is the older one, the big sister, the first twin. "I'm telling you. We'll get thrown off the ship."

Brennan and her eyebrow. "Oh, come on. You honestly think they'll put us in a little lifeboat off the side and leave us to our own devices because we've bowled illicitly?" She puts a hand on her hip. "Please," she says. "I've been lying on the floor for three days. I've missed the end of the war. I'm going to die from starvation. I think I'm entitled to bowl. The gods of the sea want me to bowl."

Yale has to admit that she understands. Her own arms have begun to feel like those crepe-paper streamers, perfectly limp, as if their more critical bones have been removed and discarded. She is beginning to yearn for some substance. She is beginning to crave the weight of a bowling ball in her hand.

"I will perish if I don't bowl this very second," says Brennan.

THE BALL in Brennan's arms looks like a dark severed head. "Oof," she says, and drops it heavily onto the rack, a terrible, echoing thud. Yale freezes, but nobody comes, and Brennan picks up the next ball in the rack and then the next, groaning and grunting and cursing until she finally finds a ball so light she nearly stumbles from the ease of it. She turns to Yale. She cradles the ball in her arms. "There," she says. "Now, shall we?"

Now, shall we? It's their call to arms, this demure question, heard not round the world but in an isolated and, as it turns out, impressively soundproofed corner of a former luxury liner turned battleship. *Now, shall we?*, and two YMCA girls remove their soaking topcoats, slip off their galumphing boots, and take turns heaving the lightest of the *Espagne*'s bowling balls at a platoon of wooden pins. In her bloomers and camisole, Brennan has the advantage. Yale's long skirt interferes when she tries to thrust her lead leg forward. The sleeves of her jacket are tight. She thinks of her suffragette suit, its superior skirt, hanging in a wardrobe back home.

"Take off your clothes," Brennan says.

Yale looks around.

"No one is coming. They'd be here by now if they were. And if somebody comes, we'll hear them before they see us, and we'll throw on our coats." She smiles her generous smile. "Come on, darling. Come on, sis—you can do it."

Yale sighs, but she also steps out of her skirt. She takes off her jacket, unbuttons her shirtwaist.

"That corset," Brennan says. She reaches out, flicking her fingers down along the bones. "Why in heaven's name do you still wear one?"

Yale steps back, a finger length out of reach. She repeats what she's always been told, that a corset is good for the organs, that it keeps them aligned.

Brennan says, "That's a lie."

She hasn't known it for a lie until now. But Yale is a skilled liar and as such she knows truth when she hears it. The stomachaches, the bruising, the need for fainting couches at the top of every long flight of stairs. The daily press of her father's bones upon hers. Of course it's a lie.

"And even if it *were* good for the organs, which any dolt knows it isn't," Brennan says, "it's no good for the White Sisters' Bowling League of America."

Yale's fourth glass of champagne is long gone. She takes a sip from the fifth, the last she brought with her, then raises her arms over her head. Brennan unhooks the back stays, one by one.

"There," she says. "Now we're properly sportif in our matching team uniforms."

Camisoles and bloomers. They resume their play. They hurl the ball with all their strength. They throw it so hard it bounces down the lane. They chase after it, one retrieving it, the other resetting pins. Then they dash back to the throw line, breathless, elated.

They have no idea how to keep score. But keeping score, that's a man's way of playing, isn't it? No winner or loser for them. They are women, they are twin sisters, they are playing for fun, they are playing for peace and the vote and the noise and the mess. They are playing for Wilson's Fourteen Points and for each other and for the sheer joy of shattering the precious geometry of the pins.

Nobody comes. They get in no trouble. "Kill the Boche!" Brennan cries, even though the Allies have already killed them or at least killed enough of them.

"And the Turks," Yale shouts. "And get those two lousy so-and-so's on the ends." She means the perpetual wobblers on either side of the wooden flank, the pins that keep taunting her, swaying as if to fall but always regaining their balance.

Afterward, winded and sweaty (and Yale dressed again except for her corset, which she's thrown overboard as if it died at sea, although the tossing was less ceremonial than all that—no wreaths, no prayers, just a casual tossing, the way you'd get rid of any item you didn't need while you were in the middle of the ocean, a sour pickle or a bouquet of violets that never were meant for you), the girls climb the stairs and return to the ballroom for stale warm nightcaps. The ship is as quiet as it has been since they left their cabin, and they feel compelled to speak softly. "We can do this every night," Brennan whispers, though as it turns out they will not do it even once more. Still, they clink glasses and drink to cake and champagne and twins and bowling. Then, arms around each other's waists, they make their way back to their room.

CHAPTER NINE

Counting to One Hundred

THE LIGHT in the ballroom was so dim they did not see Alban Bliss in the corner farthest from the piano, his breath held, his uniform trousers down round his ankles, his hand gently placed over Amo Winston's mouth. "Those are the ones I was telling you about," Miss Winston hisses as soon as the two girls leave and he once again allows her to speak. "The tall one is the Jew who's passing, with that dyed-blonde hair—so typical—and the littler one's the Jew lover who is covering for her. I'm telling you, Alban, there's not a good Christian bone in their bodies."

"Now, now, Miss Winston," Mr. Bliss says. He is disturbed for a number of reasons, not least because he is longing to come out with a joke about a good Christian bone being in *her* body. It is a terrible, shocking thing to have come into his head. "You must be a mother to them," he says. "Everyone can be saved. Perhaps you can accomplish that; perhaps they've been sent to you for that very reason. You must try to love them despite their sins."

A sermon in the midst of lovemaking: another woman might find it off-putting. But he makes Amo Winston weak with passion when he speaks this way. "As you love me despite mine?" she moans. He doesn't reply. He's hard at work again, picking up where he left off, lifting her in his bearish paws, pressing her spine against the wall so that, with each of his hearty thrusts, she can feel her vertebrae bruise. This would be so much easier in her stateroom, she thinks, the two of them supine and a nice soft mattress beneath her. If only the Reverend were less fearful of their cabins. The other Y-matrons were too nearby, he said when he asked her to meet him up here at one in the morning. Why, Alban! she'd said, I could never! But he'd told her he had faith in her; he believed she could. How had he known the door would be unlocked? she wonders now. But the real question is how could they have possibly forgotten to turn that lock once they were inside? Too avid for each other, she supposes, rueful and pleased, even as her poor spine feels close to splintering. They must take more care in the future. Because here it is, one in the morning, and who shows up but those two haunts. And the worst of it is, she can't even call them on the carpet for it, give them what-for about their traipsing round the ship at such an hour, so long after lights-out. How can she?

Jew and Jew lover, Miss Winston thinks, to take her mind off her backbone and the fact that, by now, she's grown just a touch bored by Alban's stamina. Devils, she thinks. Spies. And then, at last, the Reverend has achieved satisfaction, and they come apart, turn their backs to each other, rearrange their uniforms. He kisses her hand before he leaves, and tells her to count to one hundred, then back down to one before she follows. Then he shuts the ballroom doors inch by inch. The doors make no sound when they catch, not a squeak, not a click.

Alone now in the wet dark, Alban Bliss finally recognizes how close a call he had in there. In the moment, he and Amo standing stock-still in the dark, he was certain those girls hadn't seen them. Now, in the disapproving rain, he's less sure, and by the time he reaches his cabin he is nearly panting with worry. He drops to his knees, clasps his hands. Never again, he promises, he swears. Just the agreed-upon rendezvous the following night and then—never again.

Up in the ballroom, Amo Winston is dutifully counting to herself. Fifty-eight. Fifty-seven. She hears a wail and jumps, hand to heart. She waits, mouth open, heart beating. At last she decides it was just a sea mammal of some sort, a lonely seal, a walrus floating along. She resumes her counting. Fifty-seven, isn't that where she was? She stops again. Was she counting up or counting down? She's lost track. Where is she? She thinks it's sad, quite sad indeed, that there's no one nearby who can answer her question.

An Interlude

Meanwhile, over in France

NOVEMBER 11, 1918. The eleventh hour of the eleventh day of the eleventh month. Students will memorize that date, recite it, celebrate it. On that day there will be parades and bank holidays and speeches amid streamers and bunting. Eventually there will also be White Sales.

The only trouble is that no war actually ends on that day. It's not the last day of the war; at best, it's the first day of the last stage of the war. A cease-fire, and that's momentous, of course it is, especially for those experiencing the chill and the mud and the bombs and the gas. But there's still the peace process to go through, still a treaty to be drawn up.

Several treaties, in fact. Versailles, Saint-Germain, Neuilly, Trianon, Sèvres. One treaty for each defeated belligerent.

The first of the treaties, the Treaty of Versailles between the Allies and Germany—that treaty won't be signed until June 1919. The last of the treaties, the Treaty of Sèvres between the Allies and Turkey, not until 1920; and even then Turkey will so blatantly ignore its terms that the worthless thing will have to be revoked and replaced by the Treaty of Lausanne in July 1923.

So: July 1923. Maybe that's the last day of the war.

But surely the last day is not November 11. The Paris Peace Conference won't even commence until three full months after the so-called last day of the war. Sullen boys in AEF uniforms will have to endure one more Thanksgiving, one more Christmas, one more New Year's in the desolation of the Western Front, nothing to do but shiver and drink and go joyriding in stolen motor trucks.

It's not until the afternoon of January 18, 1919, that Allied delegates from around the world finally converge on the Quai d'Orsay and take their seats in the French Foreign Ministry's newly named Salon de la Paix. Only then do they hear Poincaré so succinctly sum up the reasons for this war, so firmly and aptly state the only way to end it, once and for all.

"Justice," the French president proclaims, "banishes the dreams of imperialism."

Yes, the delegates agree to a man. This is why towns have been obliterated, economies ruined, women widowed, children orphaned. This is why a generation of young men have died by so many new and horrifying means. To rid the world, once and for all, of the nineteenth-century disease of imperialism. To usher in, at long last, a century of self-determination for all the world's oppressed peoples.

This is the only hope the world has, and the delegates in Paris will accept nothing less. It's all they talk of, all they long for: the end of imperialism and self-determination for all oppressed peoples.

With, however, the following exceptions:

Great Britain intends to retain Australia, New Zealand, Canada, Ireland, India, Burma, Ceylon, Aden, Yemen, Gibraltar, Malta, Malaysia, Honduras, her West Indies islands, Papua, New Guinea, Tonga and Fiji, Hong Kong, and pretty much all of Africa. She'd also like mandates over most of what will soon be called the Middle East.

France can't give up Tunis, Cameroon, Somaliland, Madagascar, Morocco, New Caldonia, Tahiti, her Caribbean islands, or Indochina. She also demands Alsace-Lorraine, expects the Saar basin, and insists on Cilicia and Syria.

Italy plans to keep Eritrea, Tripoli, and Mogadishu. Also, she's got her eyes on the southern Tyrol, Trieste, Istria, Zara, Sevenico, Albania, the larger part of the Dalmatian Islands, the Trentino as far as the Brenner Pass, and a port called Fiume.

The Kingdom of the Serbs-Croats and Slovenes wants Fiume too, as well as Bosnia, Herzegovina, Montenegro, and the Banat of Temesvar. Romania also wants the Banat of Temesvar. In addition, she wants Bessarabia, southern Dobrudja, Bukowina, and Transylvania. Transylvania wants Hungary. As does the new Czecho-Slovak Republic, which also wants Bohemia, Moravia, Teschen, and parts of Saxony and Silesia. The Romanians, Ruthenians, and Magyars likewise want parts of Saxony and Silesia.

So do the Poles. Nor can the Poles live without Posen, West Prussia, Vilna, or Danzig. And while the great Paderewski has given up piano, he cannot be expected to give up Lemberg in the Ukraine and Cholm in Little Russia. He is also squabbling with the Bohemians over Teschen.

Albania wants certain territories which, at the moment, belong to Serbia, Montenegro, and Greece.

Greece must have northern Epirus, Thrace, and Smyrna. And should the world make her a gift of Constantinople as it hints it might—well, to such a gift, who could say no?

Japan feels entitled to the Caroline and Marshall islands, Kiao Chau, and the Shantung peninsula. Upon receiving the latter, however, she promises she will forthwith hand it over to China. Really, she will.

China would prefer the Shantung outright.

Belgium yearns for the left bank of the Scheldt and the peninsula of Maastricht. She also wants to hold on to the Congo. Switzerland insists the Rhine be declared a Neutral Stream so she can have a path to the sea. Denmark wants to keep Greenland and Iceland and longs to take Schleswig. Norway has aspirations to Spitzbergen. Sweden pines for the Aaland Islands. As does the new Republic of Finland.

And the United States?

The United States watches the squabbling with dismay. President Wilson grows weak and infirm. His physicians say he will die if he presses on, but press on he does, press on he must. He begs his European allies to give up these claims. He pleads that his Fourteen Points be adopted. He goes on his knees on behalf of the League of Nations. He placates his friends, soothes his enemies, fights with Congress, speaks to all who will listen about reason and compassion.

Because the United States truly wants nothing for herself, nothing at all, only justice and peace and, above all else (unless you count the Philippines, Guam, Samoa, Guantánamo, Puerto Rico, and Panama, so long as you overlook the Mexicans, the North American Indians, and let's not even bring up the former slaves), the end of imperialism and self-determination for all the world's oppressed peoples.

Part Four

The First Day of the Peace

ALTHOUGH the first three weeks of 1919 have been snowy, windy, rainy, and unrelentingly gray, the sun comes out on the first day of the peace conference. In his apartment at the hôtel Crillon, Dub Hagopian gets out of bed and peers through the curtains, disbelieving his own eyes. The sky is actually blue, the swollen river green, and the captured tanks in the place de la Concorde gleam like polished silver. And although the American flag is still at half-mast (Teddy Roosevelt, just the other day), it seems brighter, crisper, pluckier than it has in weeks.

It's one of those small favors God likes to dole out, and for a moment Dub feels buoyed, eager to get outside and enjoy the day, which he has off from his army duties. Then he looks at his watch and sees it's nearly noon. He can't remember when he has last slept so late, and his elation disappears; instead he feels slothful, selfish, sinful. So— shame and self-recrimination. Those are his abiding feelings on this stunningly bright morning.

He takes a quick bath, returns to his room, puts on his uniform. At the white and gold desk in his suite, he reviews the notes he jotted the night before, Aram Kazarian's voice scratchy and staticky over the hotel telephone. He needs to be at the Gare du Nord at four. Less than three hours, then, he has to himself. Not a lot of time, but he will make the most of it. That's what he tells himself, sternly, grimly, a man who means business. You *will* go out. You *will* have a nice day.

His first stop is a bistro that recently hung out its *réouverture* banner. The proprietor had been shaky up there on his ladder, an old guy, gray-haired and pot-bellied, who from a distance looked like Aram. Based on that alone, Dub decided he would lunch there, help the old man start anew. A good deed and a good meal, the former to do right by the world, the latter to do right by Dub's stomach.

But of course—just his luck—the lunch disappoints. Score one for the world, zero for Dub. The owner, who looks nothing like Aram up close, is a depressed Frenchman with multiple black mourning ribbons pinned to his sleeve and a long list of unavailables chalked on his board. Butter, milk, sugar, eggs. Dub orders the *poulet,* and the old man brings him a tough, bony hen along with several dry slices of the sour brown bread everyone's serving these days. Dub eats what's put in front of him, but as he downs his last sip of chicory coffee, he feels so glum he considers forgoing the sunshine and heading instead to the office, where the mood is always dark and sour but at least justifiably so.

The U.S. Translation Bureau is housed in American Headquarters on the rue Royale, right above Maxim's. Dub's desk of dark pitted wood is shoved into a corner of a room that used to be the restaurant's *cabinet particulaire.* Tête-à-têtes once took place here, marriage proposals, seductions. Now it's all politics.

Dub has been working for Translation since coming to Paris in August. He has not spent a day in the trenches. The truth is he's never seen a minute of combat in his life. Now he suspects he never will. He's not sure how he's supposed to feel about that, and, as usual, he has no one he can talk to about it.

If he did, he'd defend himself. It's not like he's ducked or shirked. Certainly he didn't go after this cushy position in Translation. Like everyone else, he expected Saint-Mihiel or the Marne and would not have said a word had he ended up in one of those hellholes. But the army claimed it preferred Dub behind a mound of communiqués, memos, and letters. It didn't want him battling Germans but attending parties, standing behind men like Mr. Lansing or Colonel House, sipping cocktails while whispering the meaning of assorted French idioms into their illustrious ears.

Of course, truth be known (and Dub does know the truth), this assignment (this plum) was secured by Aram. "*Il n'était rien, mon cher,*" Aram said modestly when Dub asked how the job had come about. Just a few strings tugged by an aging if still moderately influential resident of France, coupled with Dub's bona fide language skills. "It's a great boon to the Americans to have you," Aram said, patting Dub's hand with his own deformed mitt, "while at the same time, of course, we are being entirely selfish. Erinyes needs you in Paris."

No fighting. No heroism. A desk and some dictionaries his only equipment. "Thank you," he said to Aram then, just as he says to the owner of the bistro now. "Thank you, yes, it is all to my liking."

CHAPTER TWO

A Dive Called Lulu's

DUB MET ARAM KAZARIAN in 1911 at the most dilapidated coffeehouse on all of Smith Hill, a dive called Lulu's after its owner, Hamal Aloojian. Dub's presence there, late at night, while his parents assumed he was asleep in his bed, was of course due to Raffi Soghokian.

Raffi was dying to see the itinerant belly dancers. THIS NITE! ONE TIME! NOT TO MISS! the sign outside Lulu's read. "I can't," Dub had protested. Like Raffi, he was sixteen by then, but he was still squeamish about certain things, and he repeated something his father had told him hundreds of times: "The coffeehouses are for roughnecks and bachelors." Then Raffi pointed out that the two of them *were* bachelors, so they'd gone inside, although the minute they passed through the split and silvered wooden doors and smelled the smoke and liquor, heard the loud Armenian voices, male and argumentative, they felt sheepish and scared and were ready to turn around and go home, and they probably would have, had they not been accosted by the father of one of Dub's schoolmates.

Henry Garabedian was a serious kid with glasses and a stammer, the kind of boy who would never sneak out at night, much less to a place like Lulu's. In fact, Henry was so self-righteous, so pious, that he had preached to his father before his father had gone out that very night, reminding him that the hootchy-kootchy had originally been a sacred birthing ritual, a muscle dance women were meant to perform only for other women. "It's a sin against our women to watch those dancers," Henry Garabedian had said.

Henry Garabedian's father blamed this kind of talk on the revolutionaries running around Providence, delivering lectures about the violence in the *yergir*, filling the heads of the new generation with far too much Armenian history. Giving those revolutionaries money was one thing; you had to throw them a few dimes or they'd never leave you alone. But genuinely embracing the cause when one was thousands of miles from Turkey, that was another.

He wished his Henry could relax, have some fun, like these two boys who obviously understood that this was a modern age, a new century, and that women—some women, anyway—were happy to gyrate their hips and ripple their bellies for men, and why not, given that those men were equally happy to dance up to those women and press spit-moistened coins to their faces? Boys of sixteen should want to have fun of this kind, thought Garabedian's father, who approached Dub and Raffi as soon as he saw them. "I know you," he said to Dub in Armenian. "You're Henry's school friend, the French scholar. I am happy to see you have taken time away from your books. Here, come with me. Parlay voo beer?"

A hand pressed to the scruff of each of their necks, Garabedian's father shepherded the boys past rickety tables where men played tavloo and drank coffee or brandy or beer. He took them to his own table, where two men were busy at an inlaid game board. *"Eench eh?"* one of the men said.

"This is the big French scholar from Henry's school." Garabedian's father shook Dub's neck, making Dub's head bobble as if he were a marionette. He pulled up two chairs. "Sit," he said. He poured two glasses of beer. "Drink."

He talked to the boys as if they were all old cronies. He told them how business was going—very well, very well. No matter what went on in the world, people would always need pencils, would always need pens. And he was working on a new invention; it would change the world, he told them. Pens where the ink flow was governed by clicking down on a tiny lever. He showed Dub his hands, stained blue and black. "My father was an ironmonger in Marash," he said. "The Garabedians are not afraid of dirt on their hands." He snatched Dub's hand and showed it to the other men, who reluctantly looked up from the board. "Here is the pretty hand of a big French scholar," Garabedian's father said. Then he held up his own hand, the blackened fingers. "And here is the hand of a peasant from Marash." Releasing Dub, he pulled a pen from his pocket.

"You didn't invent that," Dub said. "I've read about those kinds of pens."

"Yes, but mine works," said Garabedian's father. He rolled up his sleeve and, wrist to elbow, wrote his name on his forearm. The pen left pools of ink that ran down his skin, but the name was, for the most part, legible. The men looked up from their game again and made sounds of admiration. "Here," Garabedian's father said to Dub. "You roll up your sleeve."

Raffi and Dub exchanged glances. Dub rolled up his sleeve. Garabedian's father took Dub's arm and drew, from wrist to elbow, a naked woman. Her features smeared, the sharp nib scratched, but there she was. Garabedian's father blew on her so she would dry. The other men were laughing. "So?" Garabedian's father said. "You like her?"

Dub regarded himself. "Too hairy," he said.

"*Medz dzidzik,*" Raffi said affably, a phrase Dub didn't know. Then Raffi smiled, exposing the new gold tooth that, thanks to last year's fist-fight with Dub, now took center stage in his mouth.

"Well, of course," Garabedian's father said. "Why wouldn't I give her big tits? God created women in infinite variety, but when I get to play God"—he waved his pen as if it were a scepter—"I make them only one way." He winked at Dub, and Dub grimaced. He couldn't abide a man who winked. Then Garabedian's father curled his hand into a fist and joggled it down by his crotch. "Later you will like her," he said. "When you go home. Am I right?"

Dub blushed. He was unaware of how fiercely he was frowning. Garabedian's father resented the frown. He was disappointed in Dub. The kid was just like Henry after all. Up on his high horse, a know-it-all, and holier than everyone else.

Dub wanted to roll down his sleeve, but he was afraid the ink would stain his shirt. How would he explain that to his mother? He turned his attention to his beer, drinking it down as if it were lemonade, even though it was repulsive, not only the taste but also the woman coming straight at him as he tipped the glass to his lips. And when one of the tavloo players ordered another round, Dub drained his second glass too.

It was then Aram Kazarian came out from the back room. There wasn't a door there, just opaque red curtains, and when Aram passed through them it was as if a famed actor had entered the room. Not that he preened or strutted. Not that he spoke a word. But the room grew hushed and every head turned, and there was whispering, nudges.

Lion, the men called him as he crossed the floor. Aslan. And some men stood when he was near them, while others offered their hands. It gave Dub time to look the man over. If he was a lion, he was an old lion. His hair was a long thick mane, yes, but it was also silver, and his shoulders were bent, and his face deeply lined, the creases going every which way, recording all the expressions from a long life, the early years of which had been spent in the sun and winds of the Caucasus. And as the man came even closer to Dub's table, Dub saw that both hands were missing fingers.

An old and maimed lion, and not only that: a small lion, short and compact, no more than five foot five. A fop lion too, in his tailor-made suit, the likes of which had never been seen on Smith Hill, not even on a landlord. Dub's first thought regarding Aram was that the Armenian people could do better in the hero department.

As if he'd heard Dub's disparaging thoughts and was going to dispel them right there and then, Aram Kazarian walked straight to Dub's table. Dub felt his pulse quicken, was certain he was about to be scolded, humiliated inside this run-down dive. But Aram Kazarian had not come for him, did not even notice him. Aram leaned over the table, his palms flat on its surface, his few fingers splayed. Dub counted six altogether. Two on the right hand, four on the left.

An explosion, Dub thought. A gun misfiring. Dub had figured out by now that the man was an old freedom fighter: the respect in the room, the confidence in his bearing, the weathered face, the injuries. But even so, Dub told himself, the missing fingers might have come from something less glamorous. Maybe just an old farm accident. Dub was resisting; he did not like the idea of being awed by a *fedayee*. Dub believed in justice, in lawsuits, in court cases. His hero was Halladjian. His savior was Judge Francis Cabot Lowell. Still, he could not take his eyes off the knots of scar tissue from which no flesh or bone protruded.

Aram Kazarian remained unaware that Dub was gaping at him, thinking about him, sizing him up. He was otherwise occupied, his face in the face of Garabedian's father. "Monsieur," he said pleasantly, though the two were nose to nose, mustache to mustache. "Tonight before I depart for Paris I am personally collecting overdue pledges. May I ask if you have something for me?"

Garabedian's father hit his forehead with the heel of his palm. *"Abush!"* he said. "What's wrong with this head? Again I forgot my checkbook." He pressed his inky hands together, smiled expansively. "Tomorrow, Aslan, you come to my office. The girl at the desk, she'll have it for you."

"He won't be here tomorrow," one of the tavloo players said.

"He's leaving for Paris," said the other. "He just told you."

"Abush!" Garabedian's father hit himself again. "This head! Next time you come, Aslan, I'll give you double." Then he excused himself. Another beer, he said. A piss in the alley, he said. He'd heard thunder, he said; he would go out, see if it was raining, report back with the news.

"He is having hard times, Aslan," the first tavloo player explained after Garabedian's father had fled. "All his money into his new invention."

"A pledge is a pledge," Aram said. He was still leaning over the table, was still smiling pleasantly. Nothing but a fund-raiser, Dub thought. That's all the old lion was: a fund-raiser, and not very successful at it.

Raffi, meanwhile, was all aflutter, as swoony as a girl who has bumped into a Broadway star at a most improbable place: at the green-grocer's, on the streetcar. He had recognized Aram Kazarian the moment those red curtains parted. Now he was struggling to control his breathing, regain his voice; also trying to think of something brilliant to say. Something so smart and so witty or, better yet, something so brave and profound that the *aslan* would never forget him. *And so that's when I met the young man who so reminded me of myself at the same age and recognized him to be the son of my spirit, my heart, my soul.*

"Aslan," Raffi finally managed, an adolescent cracking, his voice traveling scales as it hadn't for months. "I am honored to make your acquaintance."

Aram extended the two-fingered hand. Though he longed to kiss it, Raffi only pumped the thumb and the one lonely finger. The tavloo players were laughing at him, this weak-kneed, tongue-tied boy, and amid his admiration and love for the one man, Raffi found himself able to loathe these two others and think how he'd like to give each one a smack in the mouth. But Aram Kazarian was beginning to turn away, to look for other deadbeats and Raffi grew desperate. "Aslan," he said. "Ever since I came to this country, I've regretted leaving home. I've never been to Lulu's before, and now I see that coming tonight was dictated by fate. Aslan, I want to return home and fight alongside you. I want to become *madagh*."

Though Dub hadn't known the Armenian words for big tits, he did know this word. Literally, it was the ram, the sheep, the goat boiled in a cauldron, an animal grateful to be sacrificed because it knew the community would partake of its flesh and thus thrive. Dub knew too what it meant when a man said he wanted to become *madagh*, and he looked at Raffi with surprise. Raffi had lived in Rhode Island for a year now; he had told Dub all those dreadful stories of home. How could he still yearn to go back to the old days, the old ways? He pictured Raffi dressed as a *fedayee*, the flat red tarboosh draped with a tinseled bandanna, the baggy trousers embroidered with red and yellow, the long winding sash. And, of course, the array of weapons: the bandoliers filled with cartridges crisscrossing the chest, the curved sword of Damascus hanging from the dagger belt, a Mosin rifle or two slung over the shoulder. Raffi would collapse under the weight of all those weapons as he had once nearly collapsed under the weight of a mattress.

Dub was relieved to see that Aram Kazarian had reached the same conclusion. "You have a good life in this country," Aram said. "Only a fool would want to go back now." He ruffled Raffi's hair with a clawlike hand. "It's late," he said. "You should be home in bed."

THAT NIGHT at Lulu's, Dub was as different from Raffi as he knew how to be. He didn't want to become *madagh*. He wanted to become a lawyer. He might have too, if only he hadn't decided to take another swig of the disgusting warm beer.

The glass to his mouth. That's when the old lion looked at him. It was the first time Dub noticed Aram's eyes. How could he have missed them? Maybe they had to be aimed at you before you could appreciate how blue they were. Maybe they were only that blue when they were focused on you. Dub had known Armenians with light hair and eyes, descendants of women raped centuries ago by Crusaders passing through the Armenian steppes on their way to Jerusalem. But Dub had never seen an Armenian with eyes quite this blue, blue like a child's crayon, blue like wildflowers, such unforgettable blue eyes, and those eyes were wide and amused and fixed on Dub's arm.

Dub felt overwhelmed by the need both to save face and to distinguish himself from Raffi. Also, he was a little bit drunk. He never would have spoken up otherwise; he was not the type to be rude to his elders. But now he put his glass down. His hand was shaking a little because he knew what he was about to say and he was not used to being a smart-ass. "I want to become *madagh* too," he said, smarmy, sarcastic. "In fact, I'd cut off my right arm for the cause, but given its current condition"—and he raised it, showed it around—"I suspect the cause wouldn't want it."

He got what he hoped for: the tavloo players laughed, Raffi glared. He hadn't thought about what reaction he wanted from Aram. Maybe it was for Aram to go away. Maybe it was for Aram to blush like a schoolgirl. But Aram stayed put. He continued to smile pleasantly. He'd been smiling pleasantly the entire time he'd been standing over the table. "Ah," he said. "Another victim of our dear Monsieur Garabedian, I see." Then he crooked one of his few fingers and summoned Dub to follow him.

Dub didn't move.

"You," Aram said.

Dub stood then. He felt like a child. He longed to race out the door and join Garabedian's father in his investigation of the weather.

"He's taking him to the back room," one of the tavloo players said.

"He should give the girls some money while he's there," the other player said. "He'll come back with his mustache grown in."

Raffi began to stand as well. "No," Aram said, "not you." He was still smiling. "Don't worry," he added. "The women will be out momentarily." And when Raffi began to object, to assert his lack of interest in the belly dance, to insist he'd come to Lulu's not for the girls but for the cause, then Aram said, suddenly not so pleasant, "In that case go collect Garabedian's debt," and the tavloo players laughed harder at that than they'd laughed at any other joke all night.

CHAPTER THREE

Baptisms

BEHIND THE RED curtains, three dancers in full-length kimonos sat on overturned whiskey crates, playing cards with their *duduk* player. The musician muttered a greeting as Aram and Dub passed by single file, but the women didn't glance up. Dub glanced down, though. Never, he thought, would he have offered these women his money. They were each the age of his mother. They should have been home with their children. They should not have been wearing their hair loose down their backs. He tried to imagine licking a coin, affixing it to one of their cheeks.

"They are actually Syrian," Aram said over his shoulder.

Dub followed Aram into another room, a back room behind the back room. Here there were more crates and, on an overturned barrel, a partially eaten meal: torn pita and a small pile of olive pits. Also on the barrel were several piles of cash. Two young men Dub recognized from the neighborhood were sorting through the money, separating ones from fives, stacking coins. A tower of nickels curved perilously to one side. One of the young men ran two fingers along the tower, straightening it, saving it. "So, Aslan?" he said in accented English. "Do you do miracle? Do you make blood come out from stone?"

Aram smiled. He spoke a nearly perfect and unaccented English. Still, this one time he needed help. He turned to Dub. "Is there a word denoting a rich man who refuses to pay what he has promised?" he asked.

"Piker," Dub said.

"Mr. Garabedian is a piker," Aram said to the neighborhood guys.

"Is bad," the young man said. "Is give to Providence very bad name."

"Every city has its dogs," Aram said. Then he put the two-fingered hand on Dub's back and pushed him to the far corner of the room where a large steel washbasin, one side dented, rusty pipes exposed, was bolted to the wall. He turned on the faucets; brown water streamed forth from each. Nothing was said, but Dub knew to offer up his arm, and Aram took it, holding it with his right hand, that pincer, that wrench, beneath the water. The spray was so icy cold it felt hot. Dub watched the good fingers of Aram's left hand go at him, rub his skin clean and raw.

It wasn't easy. The ink woman did not wash away all that fast. Aram needed a weapon to get rid of her entirely, had to employ a dish brush with stiff wiry bristles. Dub stood through it all like a stoic, eyes open, not moving. It was as if Aram were performing a medical procedure and Dub's only role, only hope, was to remain immobile and endure and, after it was over, to recover, get better, grow stronger. Meanwhile, he felt passive and childish, but more than those things he felt cared for. And most of all he felt chosen.

"Not that there's anything wrong with beautiful girls," Aram said, after the ink woman had finally faded. He dried Dub's arm with a rough white towel. He shrugged again, his palms upward. "I may have been born in the *yergir*, but I am now a Frenchman, am I not?"

DUB WAS SITTING on a crate, eating *basterma* with the others, when Raffi burst in, both fists full. The two guys from the neighborhood jumped to their feet, and Dub saw their hands move toward their breast pockets. Reaching for guns, Dub realized, and his heart went berserk. Raffi must have realized it too, because he raised both his arms, and then everyone could see that in one fist, blue with leaking ink, he held a newfangled pen and in the other a fan of five-dollar bills. The men from the neighborhood sat down again, and Raffi grinned and his gold tooth glistened. He tossed the bills onto the table. "Blood from stone," one of the neighborhood guys said.

"And how did you accomplish this miracle?" Aram asked.

Raffi's grin broadened. "I told him if he didn't do right by us, then tomorrow, after school, Dub would make Henry's nose and mouth into one."

"You said *I* would?" Dub said.

Raffi shrugged apologetically, but to Aram, not Dub. "I would have said I'd do it, but this Henry Garabedian and Dub are schoolboys together. I myself am a working man; I'm never around the schoolyard." It was true. He worked at Acme, the Jorjorian brothers' plating plant. He spent his days stirring the baths, inhaling the poisonous fumes rising off the vats of gold soup. Good honest work, backbreaking but respectable, the immigrants' path to success, and he resented every minute of it. It was *this* he was made for—threats and bill collecting and working for the *aslan*—and he could not stop smiling. This evening, his life: how bizarre it was, how remarkable, how ironic. He had to come to America before he could meet and join up with Aram Kazarian.

"Aslan," said Raffi, and here, although he did not fall to his knees, did not snatch and kiss the great man's hand, he did bow slightly, and the neighborhood boys snickered. In a matter of months those boys would be looking to Raffi for guidance and approval, looking for Raffi to convey the wishes, the thoughts, the commands of Aram Kazarian. "Aslan," said Raffi, "my friend and I, we await our next assignment."

"Your next assignment?" Aram Kazarian said. "Your next assignment is to go home and get some sleep, the both of you."

THEY IGNORED that one—they stayed and counted money instead— but otherwise they've been doing Aram's bidding, running Aram's errands, ever since. These days Raffi runs his in humbled Berlin, where (the men of Erinyes happen to know) at least seven of the most prominent Turkish fugitives are hiding from the Allies in luxurious apartments, living on money stolen from Armenian bank accounts. Dub, meanwhile, is here in France. In a way, you could say he is the lawyer he long ago planned to be. The errands he performs for Erinyes are lawyerlike. He collects evidence pertaining to war crimes. He writes letters meant to persuade and convince. Whenever the opportunity presents itself, Dub tries to argue Erinyes' case.

Today, Erinyes is sending him out on a fact-finding mission, like a junior associate in a big-city law firm. This is why he will soon be rendezvousing with a train at the Gare du Nord.

But first he pays his bill and makes ready to leave the bistro. He hears his mother's voice, feels her hands pushing him out the door. *Outside it shines, inside it whines.* He checks his watch. Two hours left to himself. Get out there, he thinks. Take a walk. Have some fun for once in your miserable life.

CHAPTER FOUR

Trumpets

THE ENTIRE CITY is headed to the Quai d'Orsay to rubberneck the opening session of the Peace Conference. All Dub has to do is swim with the tide. He crosses the Pont Alexandre III. It's cold and he can see his breath when he exhales, but the sun is still beaming overhead. He has to look away from the gold eagles along the bridge, that's how brightly their gilt plumage shines.

At the Quai he regards the crowd with dismay and once again considers turning around, going to the office, doing something useful until it's time to make his excuses and head to the station. Instead, he squares his shoulders and plunges through hundreds of delirious Frenchies, wrangling a premium spot for himself. He is directly behind the row of gendarmes who have formed a human barricade at the curbstones. Their hands on the hilts of their swords, their blue capes rippling in the wind, they are, even he will admit, a glorious sight.

Nonetheless, they're impeding his view. The only way he can see the entrance to the Ministry is by standing high on his toes and peeking between the heads of the two cops right in front of him. It's difficult, this stretching and balancing. The people behind him push forward. They are going to knock him down, crush him; he ought to get out. But just then the limousines begin creeping down the street, and the crowd surges forward, and Dub decides to stay put. It's a matter of principle. He will not turn over his spot to these Europeans whom his people— and by "his people" he means the American Expeditionary Force—had to rescue from their own folly and history and moronic generals. He holds his ground, although he still must shift from side to side if he wants to see each sedan as it pulls up to the Ministry's entrance.

When the plenipotentiaries emerge from the back seats of their cars, there's an accompanying fanfare of trumpets. Very dramatic, there's no doubt about it, and the drama is heightened by the fact that the early arrivals are from the small countries, and it's like a costume pageant,

Indians in turbans and kurtas, Asiatics in borrowed cutaways, Arabs in black robes and white headdresses secured by gold bands. Dub recognizes some of the delegates from newspaper photographs, others from parties he has attended. He wants to nudge the Frenchman next to him, point everyone out. *Regardez, monsieur. C'est Nguyen le Patriote. Et regardez maintenant—c'est une vue rare: le roi Faisal sans son ami T. E. Lawrence.*

But he's not a man who strikes up conversations with strangers, so he continues to crane his neck and try to guess which delegation is coming next. He can tell whether he's right by the small flags mounted with tiny suction cups on the hoods of the cars.

He doesn't waste his time looking for the flags of Germany, Austria, or Turkey. None of the defeated powers has been invited to tell its side of things. Nor will he be seeing the flag of his people—and this time he means the Armenians—because the Allies have refused to invite the foundling Republic of Armenia. The result of this exclusion has led to what Dub considers a ridiculous if predictable reaction from the men who meet at Aram's château to talk about vengeance. In the past these men scoffed at diplomacy. But now that the Allies have denied them a seat in the Salon of Peace, they've changed their tune. They are children, these old men; whatever the world won't give them, that's what they want. For the time being, they've stopped crying "Guns!" They've stopped advocating street murder. Now all they want is to sit with, be one of, the peacemakers. They write letters to everyone they can think of, explaining why Armenia deserves a seat, a voice, an invitation to the party.

"Our volunteers," they write to the French government, "fought in the French *Légion étrangère,* in the *Légion d'Orient,* and in the Caucasus, where, without mentioning the 150,000 Armenians in the Russian armies, about 50,000 Armenian volunteers under Andranik, Nazarbekov, and others fought for the cause of the Entente."

"Sir," they tell the *Times* of London, "the name of Armenia is not on the list of the nations admitted to the Peace Conference, and our sorrow and disappointment are deep beyond expression."

This change in tactics is fine with Dub. Letters to the editor are his strong suit. He prefers revision and proofreading to vitriol and target practice. While the men of Erinyes meet in Aram's parlor, Dub hides out in Aram's study, adding the *a*'s and *the*'s his compatriots can't seem to get the hang of. And it does not go unnoticed by Aram and the others that a letter fine-tuned by Dub Hagopian is a letter that invariably receives a considered reply. Unfortunately, the replies are almost always apologias, pages of sympathy and handwringing and impotence.

So the Republic of Armenia has not been and will not be seated. It's the Russian flag, actually, that Dub's looking for. He knows the Russian question has been fiercely debated these past few weeks. Should the Russians be invited at all? And if they are to be invited, then who is to receive the invitation? The Bolsheviks in St. Petersburg? The White Russians clinging on in the south? The exiled nobility already in Paris? He doesn't know how the powers resolved the debate, so he's playing a game. Will this next car be full of Russians? Well, then, how about the one after that?

He hasn't thought about Russia like this in a long time. But now, although he is standing on a street in Paris, he is drifting off to St. Petersburg. Behind him the Seine is green, but he is seeing the frozen Neva, rose-cheeked children scoring its whitened surface with the blades of their skates. He skated that river himself one winter, along with Konstantin Kobakov's children, those fat little boys, noisy and ill-mannered, delighted and delightful. That had been a good day.

And now Dub realizes why he's come here today. He wants to see Kostya Kobakov. He wants Kostya to hop out of a big fancy limousine, healthy and fit. "Surely you know he's gone," Aram has said kindly, gently, and more than once. "You can't possibly believe he survived the revolution." And Dub has always said that, yes, yes, of course he knew, and it's true, he does know, and yet it's equally true that he is standing on the Quai d'Orsay hoping to see Kostya in the ruddy flesh. It's Kostya who has taught him to understand the purpose of funerals and wakes, to appreciate the disquieting comfort of an open coffin. Unless and until he sees Kostya laid out, he will go on doggedly remembering him as vibrant and boyish and very much alive. And so damned pleased to be working in the czar's foreign ministry. And, of course, he will also remember Kostya's concern for the Armenian cause.

Now more than anything Dub wants Kostya to show up in Paris, alive and well and waving his black lamb's wool hat to the crowd. Now *that* would justify an alarum of trumpets. But in the next limousine it's only the Poles, Dmowski grinning at Paderewski as the former musician winces at the assault of the horns.

CHAPTER FIVE

Paper Ladles

Dᴜʙ ᴘᴀʏꜱ the Poles no attention. He is wincing too, but only because
he is remembering the day he left home for Russia, the late spring of
1915, and he's embarrassed at how naive he'd been then, twenty-one
years old but just as innocent as lads in fairy tales who think they can
bump off dragons with slingshots and plucky dispositions. Dub figured
he'd go to the Caucasus, do in some Turks, and come home unscathed,
ready at last to marry Ramela Soghokian, the damsel he'd have rescued
via this display of courage. Surely he would feel something akin to love
for her by then. Surely all that adventure on her behalf would spark
something in his heart more gratifying than pity.

He said good-bye to his parents on a dock in Providence. He had
their blessings, at least with respect to the war. Everyone knew about
the deportations and slaughters by then; no one could object if a son
wanted to do something about them. In fact, who could remain proud
of a son who did nothing while all that butchery took place?

As for marrying Ramela—well, that he'd neglected to mention to
his parents. If he had told them, they would have regretted, perhaps
rescinded, their decision to forgo the *meechnort,* to let him find a wife
on his own. He knew they'd never have chosen Ramela. Whenever
they saw Dub with her, they laughed nervously. "Is nice girl, your
friend's sister," his father might say, but then he'd touch his finger to
his temple. "Is nice girl, poor mouse, but also *khent,* no?"

Now, while the warship *Kursk* waited for Russia's new recruits,
Armenian boys knelt and Armenian mothers draped crucifixes blessed
by the Der Hayr around their necks and kissed their hands three times.
In the name of the Father, the Son, and the Holy Ghost. American lob-
stermen watched and either sniggered or crossed themselves.

Dub's parents were too western for such rituals. No kneeling, no
chanting. His mother kissed him hard on the cheek. His father waved a

small American flag. "What's America got to do with it?" Dub said. His father shrugged. "You want I should wave Russia's?"

Also on that day, Ramela slipped her grandfather's ring onto Dub's littlest finger, the only finger it fit. "I still promise," she said, "if you will still promise too." "Yeah," he said, "only make sure you remember what that promise was." He knew she wanted him to take her into his arms in front of both families, make at least that much of a declaration. He wouldn't do it. If he touched her at all it would be to shake her hand. It's a deal, he would say, pumping it like a businessman. My blood spilled so you can stop spilling yours. My life risked so you will no longer risk your own. He put his hand in his pocket, where he rubbed his fingers together, feeling the ring. It was like a cinder in the eye; you couldn't leave it alone because you so badly wanted it gone. Then Aram said it was time, and the youngest members of the Providence branch of Erinyes followed him onto the ponderous ship.

North from the port of Providence, north past Canada, north past the Arctic Circle, the magnetic pole, north past Point Barrow. The ship was heavy with *chemadahns* and other explosives, and the journey was slow. During the day, the Armenian-Americans drilled on the top deck; at night they sang folk songs. *Better to die without bread than surrender to the pitiless infidels.* Dub found the songs tawdry and grating. The melodies, such as they were—no choruses, no repeated refrains—were said to be haunting, but he thought they were monotonous and self-pitying. He liked it when the bored Russians countered with some of the new jazz they'd picked up in New York. "Listen to dat big bass drum," the Russians sang while comets streaked, exploded, died directly over their heads. "An' ain't dat ol' trombone goin' some?"

Aram Kazarian never sang. His talent was talking. After drills, he gathered the men around him. They sat cross-legged on the deck. They were like children at story time. *Gar oo chagar*, Aram might as well have intoned. Once there was and was not a peace conference in Berlin. Did the volunteers remember it? The Congress of Berlin, back in 1858, when the British and Germans and French summoned the weak nations of the world to the peace table. Not only the Armenians but all of them: the Serbs, the Bulgarians, even the Armenians' perpetual enemies, the despised Azeris. The Europeans smiled and made promises. At last you'll get what you're owed, they said. Your own states, your own names. The end of imperialism. Self-determination for all the world's oppressed peoples.

Just put down your weapons, they said. Put down your weapons, and then you may come to Berlin and we will let you take your fair share.

Dub shivered in his inadequate coat. Raffi stood by Aram's side, his arms crossed over his chest like a *fedayee*'s bandoliers.

"And we believed them," Aram said, "and we trusted them. So we left our guns and swords behind, and we brought nothing but our appeals and petitions. They were masterpieces, these documents of ours. They were as persuasive as a mathematician's proof. They were as heart-wrenching as your own child's first words. And some of us also brought a single page torn from our Bibles, the page containing that sublime admonition, Thou shalt not kill."

The men on the *Kursk* murmured. Above their heads a phosphorescent cloud had begun to pulse, but the men didn't know this, they didn't look up, they looked only at Aram, his silver-white mane also aglow in the night.

"When we arrived in Berlin with these beautiful papers," Aram said, "we saw we were the only ones who had respected the edict to leave our weapons home. We felt pleased with ourselves; we waited to be rewarded for our obedience and spirit of cooperation. How optimistic we were as we approached the peace table. And then we looked and there on the table"—Aram paused and his voice dropped—"that's when we saw it."

"*Eench eh*, Aslan?"

"A big bowl of *heriseh* in the center of the table."

"*Heriseh?* At the Congress of Berlin? You're telling us that at the Congress of Berlin there was a bowl of stew on the peace table?"

"Beloved Armenians," Aram said, "hear my words and understand their meaning."

Dub and Raffi had heard this speech before. Fund-raisers at Lulu's or Koko's. Coffees at Exchange Place. It was not a story original to Aram. It was one of Khrimian Hayrig's old sermons. But the prelate was dead now and the story still needed telling, and Aram told it well. Every time Aram told it, Raffi listened carefully, not so much to the words, which he knew by heart, as to the inflections and every shift in volume and intensity. Aram's delivery was what interested him. Aram was aging, and Raffi imagined it might not be long before he'd be the one telling the story.

Dub, on the other hand, was transfixed by the sky. Stars throbbed and flamed and perished, and then their remains descended toward the horizon, all those remnants of stars now melded together, a thick purple curtain. Then the curtain was gone just like that, as if it had never existed, as if he'd been seeing things.

"One by one," Aram said, "the representatives of the other small nations drew their forbidden swords and dipped them into the *heriseh*. And right before our astonished eyes, their swords turned into iron ladles, and they boldly took their portions and departed. But when our turn came, we had nothing to dip into the *heriseh* except our appeals and petitions, our flimsy paper ladles, and naturally, once we immersed them in the stew, they fell to pieces."

Crimson streaks drizzled down the sky as if the stars were shedding blood. The sky was a battlefield, but only Dub was aware of it. He went to the rail and looked up. Aram, from his crate, leaned forward. "Beloved Armenians," he said, "we must use our brains and our words, but we must also use our fists and our guns. Remember the new commandment our priests have taught us."

Take weapons, take weapons, again take weapons! A chant, a roar. And the sky a starless black scrim.

ON THE FOURTEENTH day out, a Russian ice cutter preceding her, the *Kursk* docked at the frozen port of Archangel. The recruits from America purchased equipment, practiced shooting their rifles, bought and clumsily altered their Russian uniforms. Then they marched to Archangel's train station, a cavern lit by white votives, a darkened hall where travelers rushed for trains while old women slipped into alcoves and knelt before gold-leafed icons. The recruits pushed past the travelers, tiptoed past the supplicants, and boarded a luxurious coach (silver samovars at each end, lap robes on every seat).

Now at last they were heading south, from the frozen White Sea toward the roiling Black Sea. At Vladikavkaz, where snow swaddled the ground, Cossacks in skirted jackets waited for them with barebacked mountain ponies and one touring car, and while most of the Cossacks and recruits rode off on the tiny steeds, a single Cossack chauffeured Raffi, Dub, and Aram to the town of Diliman. That touring car was so large that there was a marble-topped desk and a bed in the back seat, yet so cold that Dub had to sit on his hands the whole journey. He had to raise his collar, buttoning it so it covered his chin. Every exhalation seemed to freeze in his mustache. Still, he was grateful for those white puffs of carbon monoxide coming from his mouth. He focused on them. It was because he was afraid to look at anything else. The gorgeous scenery terrified him. Steppes and plateaus, ridges and necks, saddles and defiles. The country seemed fashioned by a mad sculptor, and the sculptor's most lunatic forms were those mountains, the absurd scale of them.

Those mountains didn't scare Raffi. Certainly they didn't scare Aram. Aram pointed out the window continuously. Look up there, he said. He had a story for every precipice, every peak. The village above them, where, if they squinted, they could see a bride on a palanquin strapped to a cow? Did they know what he once witnessed in that very village? It was the aftermath of a Turkish massacre, a row of iron stakes in the square, and on each stake an impaled Armenian girl, her belly slit, her long hair loose and thick with blood, and many of those women still alive and begging for water. "The first killing I ever did," Aram said. "Virgins who blessed me as I took aim."

Or there, he said, referring to a series of mud huts suspended along a ledge like a row of eagles' nests. The Khevsurs lived there, little men who celebrated all three sabbaths, the Friday night of the Mohammedans, the Saturday morning of the Jews, the Sunday of the Christians—these funny, strange men who had somehow missed the entire point of practicing a given faith and yet, at the same time, had gotten it exactly right.

Dub couldn't bring himself to look up at that bride, at those huts. But neither could he look down, because then he'd have to see the Terek thousands of feet below them, a river in name only because, really, the Terek behaved like an ocean trapped in a gorge. It crashed and it frothed, trying to escape, tearing at the boulders confining it. The sound of that crashing made Dub tremble, especially each time the Cossack let go of the wheel to light a new cigarette.

Afraid to look up, afraid to look down. Still, he was certain that he would not be too frightened to march into war. It was one thing to die because a Cossack in a get-up straight out of a vaudeville skit needed a smoke. It was another matter entirely to perish on a battlefield to end the suffering of innocents who resembled his parents and little Ramela Soghokian. A death like that, he'd put up with.

Also, he was pretty darned sure a death like that was never going to befall him. When he finally found himself in battle, Dub planned only to kill. He had no serious plans to be killed.

As an Armenian boy aware of his history and aware of the ongoing slaughter in the desert, he believed killing Turks was his job, maybe even his birthright. But he was an American boy too, so a job to him was something you came home from at the end of the day. Hard work followed by the six o'clock whistle, followed by leisure time: feet up, a crisp newspaper, a cigar. The pursuit of happiness: that was his birthright as well.

CHAPTER SIX

Sheep

WHEN DUB, Raffi, and Aram stumble out of the Cossack's cartoonish automobile, they are greeted by a distraught Russian officer. "What's he saying?" Raffi asks Dub, and Dub says, "I don't know. Something like, Thank God you're here. Something about General Yudenich wanting Aram to talk some sense into General Nazarbekov."

What would one think upon hearing this? Dub and Raffi assume that Nazarbekov is planning an operation that is far too daring, much too dangerous, that the famous general's enthusiasm for the enemy's blood has grown so extreme that even Yudenich knows it must be curbed. General Nazarbekov is, after all, renowned for his bravery. Only days before, with merely six Armenian *druzhini* and two Cossack battalions under his command, he single-handedly took Urmia and Baskale from Halil Bey, leaving one thousand Turks dead on the field. A great fighter, a greater leader of men, this General Nazarbekov whose birth name was Nazarbekian. Of course one would assume that each time he pursued the Turk, he would escalate the violence, attempt a campaign so much fiercer, so much crueler than the last that it might eventually border on the inhuman.

Aram is being asked to calm the general's bloodlust—that's what Dub and Raffi believe, Dub with relief, Raffi with regret. It's not the case, though; quite the opposite. Nazarbekov, a former *fedayee*, a great and victorious general, is not planning a greater and bloodier adventure. What he is planning is no further adventure at all. Nazarbekov, it seems, has decided he is through with all that, so he is doing nothing but sit inside his tent. He won't talk to his aides. He refuses to rally his troops. He won't look at a map or even eat his dinner, although he still has several glasses of Armenian brandy each evening.

His men are confounded. After Urmia and Baskale, even the lowliest foot soldier knows the next step is to press the advantage, march on at once, and take Van. And they also know time is of the essence; they've got to go now. But the general sits in his tent, and the men spend their days cleaning their rifles, walking their horses, going into the village for supplies, souvenirs, and to bait the Jews living there just to keep their blood at the proper boiling point. Then they return to camp, where they eat goat kebabs and potatoes, but mostly potatoes. Their bellies are going to get huge if this goes on much longer. A humiliating prospect: returning home from war fat as a pasha.

"What's he saying now?" Raffi asks Dub, as the distraught officer accompanies Aram to the general's tent.

"I don't know. Something like, Oh, Monsieur Kazarian, you fought with the old man; only you can talk the general out of his stupor."

"It's some type of strategy," Raffi says of Nazarbekov's behavior. But when Aram emerges from the general's tent, he's got a brandy snifter in his hand and a heartbroken look on his face.

A telegram from Yudenich arrives the next morning: NAZARBEKOV. TAKE VAN AT ONCE. For several hours the telegram has its effect. "All right, all right," the general says. A rallying cry of sorts, and the men mount their horses. Dub and Raffi ride with Aram and the general in the touring car. The crisis seems averted.

But while the general begins the day barking commands, the barking grows softer as the day goes on until it becomes a yipping, a mewling, and then the men realize their pace is slowing and their leader has turned from a dog to a pup, from an advancing general to a dawdling schoolboy, the kind who neglects chores to pick flowers or consider the patterns of clouds. And then, only several miles outside of Van, where the battle they should have initiated rages without them (they can actually hear the gunfire now, even the horses strain at their reins, want to charge forward), the general abruptly changes directions, runs from the fighting, and leads his platoon to Bitlis. What can Aram do then? He telegrams St. Petersburg, and soon an emissary of Yudenich arrives in person, asking to see not Nazarbekov but Kazarian (whom he insists on calling Kazarov), and when the meeting ends, the emissary has relieved Nazarbekov of all his Cossacks and nearly all his Armenians.

Aram leaves Bitlis the next day along with the emissary who refuses to get his name right. They are off on a new mission they won't talk about. Raffi and the other Americans leave Bitlis that day too, joining one of the Armenian *druzhini* now under the command of Andranik. With this new unit, Raffi will help chase the exhausted Turk out of Van, then participate in the victorious battle for Sevan and Sorp. He will kill men and horses and then, after a few months of what will someday become known as the Lull in the Caucasus, he will return to Providence, the hero he always knew he could be.

As for Dub, he is punished for his language skills. Flawless in French, competent in Russian, he's asked to stay on with Nazarbekov. Aram tries to comfort him. "Yudenich needs someone with whom he can communicate," Aram says, before leaving Dub on his own, and suddenly Dub is no longer a soldier but a diplomat, a canvas tent his lonely embassy. But just as he's been a soldier with no war to fight, he's a diplomat with no duties to perform. He never hears from Yudenich. Nazarbekov has no use for him. Nor does he get on with his new comrades. He is not from Russia as they are. In their considered and collective opinion, he isn't even really Armenian.

The Armenians who remain in his outfit are peasants. They are skilled at manual labor, digging ditches, laying railroad tracks. They work during the mornings, visit whores in the late afternoon. To wash the women from their flesh, they strip off their uniforms and jump into an icy lake. They tumble, holler, do handstands.

I died in a battle I can't remember and was relegated to hell, Dub thinks. These men, their squat buttocks, their bouncing genitals. He hides in his tent whenever he can, reading novels in Russian, composing letters to Ramela. *It is very exciting here. My work is extremely important.* When his eyes burn from working in the dark, he goes outside, stretches in the grass, stares up at the white sky.

He no longer finds the peaks of the granite mountains too frightening to contemplate. In fact, he has contemplated them in every way possible: (1) symbols of man reaching up to God; (2) symbols of God reaching down to man; (3) symbols of God's glory; (4) symbols of man's insignificance. Lately, the only things that intrigues him are the sheep walking single file along the narrow roads cut into those impossible mountains. How fearless they are, these rotund animals trudging along what might as well be the edge of a knife.

The Neva, the Terek, the mountains in Russia. Sheep that seem to be on the brink of falling to their doom but never do. That's what Dub is thinking about when Captain Edmund Harden, Dub's colleague in the American Translation Bureau, comes up from behind him and slaps him hard on the back. So it is in this way, abruptly, rudely, unceremoniously, that Dub is forced to return to the Quai d'Orsay. He is unable to say whether he is glad or disappointed. He is unable to say where on the planet he'd be happy to find himself.

CHAPTER SEVEN

Un Honneur Grand

N OT CONTENT just to slap Dub on the back, Captain Harden also punches him on the arm. It's sheer joy motivating Harden's attacks. The man is grinning daffily. "Hagopian!" he shouts. He has to bellow to be heard over the crowd. "Am I glad to see you, old man!"

Ned Harden is a whisker-free fellow in his early thirties, a six-footer with a strong jaw and pale eyes whose only unappealing physical feature is hair that's so fine and white-blond it can barely be perceived on bright days like this one. Today, then, he appears bald and eyelash-less and somewhat scalded. Other than that, though, he's a good-looking man, and wealthy too. He grew up not all that far from Providence, in a part of Connecticut that is lush and groomed and rolling, a part of the world where the houses have houses: small cottages for the gardeners and the drivers, large barns for the automobiles and the horses. He speaks with a slight British accent.

"My Godfrey!" he shouts. He waves his hand at the throng. "Will you take a gander at all this?"

"It's something, isn't it?" Dub shouts back.

"I'll say. All these great men coming together in one place. It's downright humbling."

Like Dub, Ned Harden got his job at Translation due to some string-pulling; unlike Dub, Ned's language skills are virtually nonexistent. But he's a perfectly nice guy, and most of the others in the linguistic pool think he's just fine, and even if some of them don't, even if occasionally one or two of them feel a touch of resentment over Ned's being far more familiar with certain Roosevelts than the declensions of most irregular French verbs, they all know he's the kind of guy who can do his old army buddies some good once they get back to the States. Also, his ersatz British accent slays them. "All right, men," says Colonel McIntosh, Translation's director, before the lot of them head out to a meeting. "I'll be wrestling with Venizelos's Cretan French, Kendricks will battle Diamandy's Romanian French, Hagopian here will decipher Dmowski's Polish French and, you, Harden, you just tell us what the hell Lloyd George is blithering on about."

Dub likes Ned Harden too. What he finds especially appealing right now is what a hick Ned is, deep inside. This fellow who sups with Roosevelts is genuinely moved by the parade of plenipotentiaries. "Every important fellow on the planet is here," Ned gushes. "And for such a grand cause. And then you've got all these plain folks, hoi polloi who've come to cheer them on. And, honestly, Hagopian, the way the Frogs regard us Americans, I can hardly take a step without someone trying to shake my hand. They really love us, don't they?"

"This week," Dub says. He looks down the street. "Say, what was the upshot with the Russians?" he asks. "I haven't seen them yet."

"No invite," Ned says. "France won that battle. And a lot of the Orientals are showing up missing as well. The Japanese are still on their way. McIntosh told me the Koreans are walking here. Literally walking." He laughs. "Rotsa ruck, huh?" Up on his toes, a hand on Dub's shoulder for balance, he peers into the street. "Godfrey Crow, what a sight." A beat. A sigh. "I'm going in, did you know?"

"Where? The Ministry, you mean?"

"Mmm. Colonel House asked me the other day. I know, I know. *C'est un honneur grand.* Mantoux will be doing the official translating, of course, but the colonel wanted one of us in there. A safety net, so to speak."

Dub feels slighted. Rank, he supposes. Rank and Roosevelts. Even Colonel House needs a job after the war. "A safety net? You mean in case any colloquialisms fall through the cracks?"

"Right-o," Ned says. He is suddenly sober and somber. "Of course, I'm looking forward to it. It's going to be grand in there. A man inside—well, he's going to have some stories for the grandkiddies, that's for sure."

Another car is coming. Dub rises up, looks at the flags. It's as if his eyes haven't absorbed the message his ears have. His eyes still want Russia. Instead they get three bold stripes, white, green, red. Idiot! he thinks. *Dmbo!* You've just been told the Russians aren't coming, and still you're looking for them, still wishing for Kostya.

Flat-footed again, he senses Ned waiting for something, wanting something. "Well," he says, "that's just dandy, Ned. Congratulations."

"Yes," Ned says. "Thank you. It really is a splendid honor, isn't it?"

There is a trumpet fanfare. It makes Ned jump.

"Hey," Dub says. "Easy."

"It doesn't feel right, the thing of it is," Ned says. "You're so much better at this sort of thing than I am. I feel as though I ought to turn the honor over to you."

"Well," Dub says, "that's nice of you. But even if you could, I can't."

"Really? You can't?"

"I've got this damned errand to run. I have to go meet a train." He points as two men wriggle out of the limousine. "Orlando and Sonnino," he says.

Ned shakes his head. "An Italian Jew. What will they come up with next?" But a disquieting thought is occurring to him. If the Italians have arrived, it means the Powers are showing up now. The English will be here any minute. Then Wilson. "Listen, Dub," Ned says. "You've got to do this for me."

"Do what?" Dub says, and he smiles at Ned, and only then does he see that Ned is frantic.

"I can't do it," Ned says. "You know I can't. I won't be able to keep up. It's hard enough at the office, but at least one's got dictionaries there, plus plenty of time, and of course, you boys are always so helpful. And then at parties—Lord, those parties! But at parties, of course, one can joke, one can say, *Monsieur le President, plus lentement, plus lentement,* don't you know I'm blotto? But, Hagopian, one can't quite pull out that excuse in there, can one? And one can't start flipping through a dictionary in there either. They're going to be talking about all sorts of heady things. There'll be terminology, Hagopian. I mean, how the hell does one say imperialism in French anyway?"

"*L'impérialisme.*"

"You see? I knew that," Ned says. "It just leaves one's head when one feels pressure."

Dub would be backing away were there a place to back away to. "I wish I could help you, Neddie," he says, "but I just can't. I've got this train. I'm sorry, really. I'd love to be in there."

"Shit," Ned says.

"Can't you run back to Translation? Get Kendricks or someone?"

"It's about to begin any minute. It's supposed to start at three." He frowns, then almost at once, he brightens. "Listen," he says. "This train of yours. Why don't I go meet it instead?"

Dub smiles. "Good try, but no. It's got to be me."

"But why? I can meet someone getting off a train. That's one of the rare things I happen to be quite good at. Just tell me who to look for."

"It won't work," Dub says.

Ned's eyes narrow; another new thought is coming to him. "I'll wager it's not even a Translation matter, is it?"

"It's still important," Dub says. "And I've got the day's leave."

"It's a girl, isn't it? Come on, admit it. Selfish bastard."

"Hardly. Jesus, Ned."

The crowd has begun to scream now. By tomorrow, Ned Harden thinks, not a soul in Paris will be able to croak out a word. Paris will have become a city of mutes. A wonderful prospect. Of course, by tomorrow, Ned may be mute too. He is screaming over the crowd. "Come on, Hagopian! Just this one time, help me out. Your fellow on the train will be all right. He'll wait awhile, and then he'll take a taxi to wherever he's going. He'll find his way. You'll explain what happened when you see him. Tell him you're a soldier in Woody's army, and there was a last-minute change in your orders. You had to translate at the bloody Peace Conference. Who won't understand that?"

Dub is shaking his head, his mouth forming the words *no* and *can't* and *sorry*. But if Ned can't hear Dub's words, he has suddenly heard his own, and one word in particular has stopped him short.

What the hell is he doing? he asks himself. Why is he begging and pleading? He's a captain and he's talking to a goddamn lieutenant. All he has to do is issue an order.

This happens to Ned Harden repeatedly. It's because he's a civilian at heart, a true democrat despite his background, his birth, and his rank. "You can't let them walk all over you," more than one higher-up has told him. "Deep down, the boys want you to be in charge."

He waits for the first lull in the shrieking. "Lieutenant," he says. "I'm sorry, but I think this is going to have to be an order."

At first Dub smiles. But then Ned repeats himself—"I *am* giving you an order," he says, nodding vigorously to show he honestly and sincerely means what he's saying—and Dub is suddenly furious. *How do you say imperialism in French!* It's wrong, a guy like Ned in the Bureau, taking up space, doubling the work of everyone else. And now this. Insult to injury.

Dub whips his hat off his head, punches the crown with his fist. "I don't care what you're giving me," he shouts. "I've got to meet this goddamn train, and I'm going to meet it. The guy I'm meeting has important papers for me."

"Bullshit!" Ned shouts back.

The crowd roars so loudly that Dub spins around, turning his back on Harden, and sees the Union Jacks on the car in front of the Ministry, and then out of that car comes Lloyd George with his lopsided gait and his top hat pulled down to the bridge of his nose, and after him comes Balfour, who, if Dub were a real *fedayee,* he'd shoot right now with the Luger he is wearing under his tunic—Balfour, that liar, that hypocrite, that betrayer. Then another roar from the crowd, a roar with substance, a roar with a body, a roar that nearly knocks Dub off his feet, and he looks at the next car, the final car as it inches along so it won't arrive at the curb before the Brit chauffeur pulls away, so its entrance will be as grand as it should be.

The gendarmes along the curb have taken their hands from their swords and linked arms, a blue human chain fighting the surging throng. Dub feels himself shoved from behind like a kid in the ocean at the mercy of waves. For a moment he thinks about letting the crowd knock him down. He has a comic image of himself on all fours, crawling like crazy through the legs of the French until he reaches the crowd's perimeter and can stand and tear hellbent for the Solferino metro station, while Ned scratches his white-blond head and tries to figure out where his underling's run off to.

He thinks too about not going to the station at all. He thinks about staying here, helping Ned out of a jam. He looks at the Stars and Stripes suctioned to the American limousine, those miniature flags as plucky as the ones hanging half-mast for TR, and he thinks he ought to stay. Do a favor for a fellow American. Just for a change.

He can't do it, though. Not today, anyway. He turns to tell Ned to buck up, be a man, get his goddamn rear end into the goddamn Salon of goddamn Peace. But before he can speak, he sees that the daffy grin has returned to Ned's face.

Dub can't figure out where it's come from, Ned's sudden glee. It's not their proximity to Wilson, Dub knows, because Ned isn't even looking at the president's car. In fact, he has his back to the car; he is no longer facing the street but has turned around to face the crowd and is looking over Dub's shoulder, at something behind Dub, with such a wide, dopey grin it's clear the guy thinks his troubles are over.

Dub turns around expecting to see someone from the language pool, Kendricks or McIntosh unwittingly shown up, but he sees no one he recognizes, only the gaping mouths of French men and women, every one of them howling or weeping with joy. If this were a silent movie—no sound, only these faces—the audience would think that everyone at the Quai was in great pain. Everyone, that is, except for Ned Harden.

"Well, Lieutenant," Ned bellows, chuffing Dub on the shoulder, "apparently your friend from the train has come here to meet you. I had it right the first time, didn't I? *Cherchez la femme,* eh?"

The horns are off-key now, the trumpeters as undone as everyone else at the sight of their savior, the venerated Thomas Woodrow Wilson, who is standing on the running board of his limousine, sunlight reflecting off his glasses as he waves his top hat to them all. The crowd pulses like a heart. The chanting buffets Dub. *Vive! Vive! Vive!*

Then Ned points, and this time Dub sees the petite figure behind him, the young girl standing in his shadow, smiling up at him. "*Bonjour,* Lieutenant," she says in a strong midwestern accent. "Fancy meeting you here."

Part Five

Cherchez la Femme

SHE IS A Y-girl now, but otherwise she is as he remembers. That is, she's just as silly and presumptuous and in the wrong place at the wrong time as she was back in the States. She smiles at him as if he waved her over, as if they are old friends with a long-standing engagement. *I've a brilliant idea: let's meet at the Quai d'Orsay at the most chaotic time in the history of the world.*

Her hair is pulled back, but it's as messy as he remembers it, dark strands corkscrewing around her cheeks. She brushes a lock from the corner of her mouth, which is moistened with red lipstick. "Now, don't you dare pretend you don't know me, Lieutenant," the red lips shout up at him.

"Oh, he knows you all right," Ned Harden shouts back. "He was just about to go running off to meet you. Well, Hagopian? Aren't you going to introduce me?"

He can't, of course, given that he doesn't know her name, doesn't know her. She laughs, and her eyes crinkle away; she is all teeth and gums. Even Dub can't deny there is something endearing about the way she is letting her happiness show, this one person in the mob whose joy comes not from seeing the American president but from seeing him. She is nearly bouncing at the sight of him; Dub wants to put his hands on her shoulders, hold her in place. "Yale White!" she shouts. She looks from one man to the other. "Yale White!" she repeats at the top of her lungs, now looking only at Dub.

Yale White, thinks Ned Harden. He suppresses the urge to tell her that she and his alma mater share the same name. Some Elis, you can't get them to shut up about the place, but Ned doesn't like to come off too privileged. He goes in another direction. "Any relation to our own Harry White?" he yells.

For a moment she seems not to know how to answer this perfectly straightforward inquiry. Then there is a glittering through her olive-drab eyes, and the red mouth purses, and Dub thinks, Good God, she is going to confirm the connection. Why, yes, she seems about to say, the American plenipotentiary, the ex-French ambassador, the illustrious Mr. Henry White—why, yes, indeed, the man is her father, her uncle, her cousin's third cousin. Dub is sure she is about to say something like that, and he is about to be impressed, perhaps even intimidated. Perhaps he is even about to regret treating her so discourteously in St. Louis. Harry White's daughter—Jesus Christ!—wouldn't that be a helpful person to know! But then a different look crosses her face, and she shakes her head vigorously. More strands of hair fall loose from her queue.

"Oh, gosh," she says. "If I were related to *that* Mr. White I don't think I'd be standing out here in the cold. No, I imagine I'd be sitting inside the Ministry, nice and warm, making small talk with Monsieur Clemenceau and company."

She infuses her answer with laughter. It's as if she doesn't mind letting the world know she considers the three of them dopes, not only the captain for imagining she might be related to such a great man, and not only herself for failing to be, but Dub too, just because he's a part of their group. The combination of her impudence and self-ridicule tickles Dub, and he smiles back at her.

He is thoroughly surprised, and not because this girl of all girls has turned up in Paris. The entire world, after all, is in Paris. Every day on the short walk from the Crillon to the rue Royale, he sees nothing less than the whole of mankind: Poilus on crutches; Tommies with swagger sticks; Scots in plaid kilts and bare knees; Portuguese in green-gray; Poles in azure; Belgians with tassels bobbing from their caps; Aussies whose slouch hats are pinned up, even though this means their right ears are burnt purple by the icy wind, those pigheaded idiots. And then there are the colonials and exotics: the Koreans in blue *chogoris;* the Ethiopians in white robes; the Senegalese in red fezzes, their cheeks slashed and scarred. Everywhere, a hodgepodge of tunics, leggings, and silly headgear.

He has stared at them all. He has studied every face that's gone by. He has been looking for someone in particular, someone whose whereabouts has baffled Erinyes ever since a German liner spirited away eight Young Turks several days before Turkey's surrender.

Erinyes has known all along that seven of those fugitives, including the criminal triumvir of Talaat, Enver, and Djemal, are hiding in Berlin. But the eighth fugitive, Kerim Bey, the former police chief of Adana—they've long suspected that he may be somewhere in Paris. On the one hand, Paris is an audacious and perhaps suicidal place for a Turk to be hiding. On the other hand, it makes perfect sense. Kerim Bey is married to a Parisian. It has been rumored that the marriage had estranged him from his comrades. "Mark my words," the men who meet weekly at Aram's château say, "that French wife of his will be his downfall." And then someone adds, especially if Aram's French wife, Seta, whom they adore, is serving them cheese or strawberries, "It's the first time I feel any empathy for the cur," or, "Of course I wish untold suffering upon the monster, but still—a French wife! That is too extreme."

Last night, Aram called Dub to inform him that the German branch of Erinyes had finally located Kerim Bey. "In Berlin," Aram shouted across the wires. "Just like the others, after all. But you'll never guess where he was spotted. At the train station buying tickets to Paris! So one might say we were right all along. Only our timing was off." And the whole while, Dub is scribbling the vital information on a pad: *Orient Express/4 p.m./Gare du Nord*. And thinking, There goes my day off.

An American expression you hear every day in the army: if it starts out bad, it ends up shit. Look at this day: the wasted morning, the bony chicken, running into Ned, and now this girl. It's uncanny the way she has once again materialized just in time to foul him up royally.

And yet, Dub is smiling. That's what surprises him. Not encountering this girl but how damned pleased he is to have encountered her, this virtual stranger, this consummate pest. He can't explain the feeling of pleasure to himself any more than he was able to explain his pressing mission to Ned. All he knows is that his pleasure confuses him. Happiness, he almost wants to call it. And he thinks about the unhappiness that accompanies all his memories, even his fantasies, involving Ramela. Sometimes, after leaving the bed of a woman (the various Red Cross workers he's been with, several French farm girls now working the big city), he finds himself fantasizing that Ramela will be waiting for him back at the Crillon. "*Parev*, Dub," she will say, when he wheels through the revolving doors. "So sorry to barge in on you like this, but you know how it is. God orders you to go visit someone, he buys you a ticket and personally packs your bags, then he drives you down to the pier in his holy taxi and waves while you sail off—well, what are you going to do, say no to God?" Depressing, the words he so mean-spiritedly puts into her mouth, and also the fact that even though it's his fantasy, he still finds himself without any choice. Even in fantasies, he has to act glad to see her. He has to murmur reassurances into her midnight hair. He has to surrender to her, give her his heart, arms, bed. In his dreams, ever chivalrous, he sleeps on the floor.

But this girl, this Miss Yes, this Miss White. Seeing her makes him feel light, and he runs over his plans for the evening: the dinner he's scheduled with Trevor Hamilton and Stephen Lindsey at the Majestic. It had seemed like a good idea when he arranged it. Now he'd much rather take this little Miss White out on the town. The difficulty she gave him back in Missouri. Her showing up now. Her perfectly imperfect timing. If he doesn't leave soon, he's going to miss that train and will not be able to follow Kerim Bey to his new Paris residence. The prey lost, only a day after being found.

What does she have against him making a train?

She owes him a debt, that much is clear, and even as he worries about his train, about Kerim Bey, he is working out how he'll accept repayment. He'll show her Maxim's and let her peek upstairs into the room where he works, a room cluttered with heavy wooden desks and papers and officers. Women always love seeing American HQ. And then, many drinks later, he will remind her what the boys in France insist YMCA really stands for: You Must Come Across. That's what he'll whisper in this one's ear.

IT'S NED HARDEN who, once again, brings him back to the Quai. "Well," Ned says. "Hadn't you better be going inside now, Lieutenant? You're not here on holiday, after all." He winks extravagantly. "You've a job to do. And don't worry about Miss White. I'll entertain her while you're indisposed."

Yale's mouth opens. "Lieutenant," she says. "You're attending the session?"

The way both Ned and the girl are looking at him, he hates to disappoint either of them. Yet he makes one last effort. "You've got it all wrong, Captain," he says. "Miss White is not the party I'm to meet. I've got to get going immediately. I told you I need to pick up some documents."

"Well, look here," Ned says. He is feeling pleased with himself, feeling every bit the officer he somehow has come to be. "If that's really the case—and I'm not saying I believe it for one minute, mind you—but if it is the case, why are we arguing when the solution to both our dilemmas stands right before us? There's this train, you insist? Well, let's have your old friend Miss White here hook up with your party and explain your delay. I know you don't trust me to do the job, but surely you trust Miss White."

Yale places her hand on Dub's arm. "Oh, gladly," she says. "Please. Is there something I can do for you, Lieutenant? You've really got to let me if there is."

She is touching his sleeve. She is looking into his eyes. He is thinking that sending her is a terrible solution, but at least a solution, and he is thinking that he must have known he was going to do this the minute he recognized her. That's why he was so happy to see her. He's already told her about Erinyes, after all. The gun beneath his tunic right now— she held that gun, along with several others, on her lap. No ill fortune has befallen him or the cause since that first small confession of his.

She has not let go of his sleeve. She is ardent and earnest. "I'd be truly grateful if you'd let me be of service, Lieutenant. I do feel I owe you a favor for—well, I just do. And anyway, it's my job, isn't it? To help our fighting men. I'm not here on holiday either. Helping our boys is what I do."

She's risen up on her heels as if what he needs from her lies on a shelf high over her head. I will reach it; I won't drop it; I will give it to you. He presses down on her shoulders as he wanted to earlier. He gets her back on solid footing, then takes her by the elbow and leads her a few paces away, nearly knocking several old women to the ground to accomplish it.

"It's complicated," he says. "You don't know who Kerim Bey is, but he's—"

"But I do know," she says. "I know them all, all the ones who escaped when Turkey fell. Kerim Bey was the police chief in the Adana region. He was there when that church burned, that awful fire. He was behind the whole thing, isn't that what they say? And then, when the Young Turks came to power—"

She goes on, telling him his own history. He's both annoyed and impressed. Most Americans can name only the unholy triumvirate. Beyond that, they are hopeless.

"If it involves bringing Kerim Bey to justice," she says, "then I definitely want to help." She remembers Brennan rattling the door to the officers' steam room on the *Espagne,* remembers what Brennan said then. "I want in," she says.

"I am going to trust you." He leans closer. "You're a little hound dog, anyway, I know that much about you." He is talking fast. She is nodding faster. "Listen," he says. "Kerim Bey is arriving at the Gare du Nord on this afternoon's train from Berlin. We need to know where in the city he's staying. You say you know what he looks like?" She is nodding, but he tells her anyway. "Fiftyish," he says, "and immense, and carrying most of the weight in his chest. He's cut off his facial hair. His wife will be with him. Very striking. Dark, in the French manner, and wearing a long red fur. And much taller than he is. An improbable couple. And then the child. Also dark, but in the eastern manner. Three years old, whatever a three-year-old looks like. They walk on their own by then, don't they? And what else? Western attire, a receding hairline—"

"A fat man with a pretty wife and a three-year-old with a receding hairline."

He doesn't laugh. "We need his Paris address."

"You want me to tail him?"

"However you do it. We need to know where he's putting up."

"All right," she says.

"It won't be dangerous," he says. "And look, here are some francs for a taxi. But perhaps you can just glance at the hotel label on his luggage. Just stand by the baggage gate; he'll have to pass by." The same advice Aram gave him the night before. "But if you do need to taxi behind him, be sure to keep up. You don't even have to hide, really. He'll never suspect you."

"And let's say I get this address."

"You will, won't you?"

"I will. Then where shall I meet you? To report in?"

"Can you come by the Majestic later? The dining room there? Come at seven, and if they won't let you in, make the guard at the door fetch me."

"What's your name?" she says. "Lieutenant what?"

He tells her, and she nods very seriously, as if his were a handsome name and not the clerical joke he knows it to be. Her newfound solemnity makes him think once again of Ramela. He'd have lost his man, though, before ever asking Ramela to go to the station. The idea of Ramela having to see the face of her sister's murderer . . .

"Will you do this for me, Miss White?" he asks.

She is shining with excitement and conviction and the cold. "I will, Lieutenant Hagopian."

"And you won't tell a soul?"

"Not a soul. And don't worry." She takes his cold hand into her cold hand and somehow warms him. "You can't imagine what I can do when I put my mind to it." She is bouncing again. "I think," she says, "spying is going to be something I'm good at."

CHAPTER TWO

Sisterhood

BRENNAN WHITE adores Paris. She loves its boulevards and bars. She enjoys the casino and the cathedrals and the few museums that have reopened. And unlike most of the other American women she's met here, she is not put off by the crippled buskers in tattered horizon blue, the beggars with no arms who play harmonicas held round their necks with wires. She talks to them, learns their names, drops large chunks of her pay into their inverted caps. She's even fascinated by the street-walkers, not only the girls from the city but the white widows from the country, young women who have come to work in Paris so they can pay the mortgages on their parents' farms or feed their fatherless children. Sometimes there are so many of these nice young women wishing to sashay among the tables of a particular café, they have to take turns. "*Après vous,*" they say to one another. "*Merci, madame,*" they say. "*Vous êtes très gentile.*"

"Sisterhood," Brennan says to Yale. "Ain't it swell?"

She means it. Turns out, she loves having a twin sister. That's how people refer to her now. She and Yale, they're the twins. It's a helpful thing to be. A person gets more dates when she's a twin because, it appears, a twin stays in a man's mind far longer than a single girl does. And then, at the end of an evening, a twin has someone with whom she can rehash the night's events. And sometimes having a twin prevents a girl from doing something out of loneliness or spite that later she'll only regret.

Brennan is having such a good time in Paris she doesn't even mind the room she and Yale have been assigned at YMCA headquarters on the rue d'Aguesseau. It is the worst room in the place, dingy and small and shaped like a trapezoid, the east and west walls angling away from each other. If she dwells on those walls, she gets dizzy and remembers those wretched first three days at sea.

"Don't dwell on it, then," Yale says, and Brennan stops dwelling and feels fine.

This is why she likes having a twin. Someone who talks to her straight, calms her down, doesn't let her get away with anything.

As for the rest of their room, it's drearily ordinary. Two beds, each with a hard, lumpy horsehair mattress ("and the hair apparently still attached to the horse," Yale says to everyone, until Brennan threatens to kill her if she repeats the joke one more time), plus an unsteady wardrobe where their few outfits hang squashed together. They share all their clothes now. And there's a bureau where they mingle their underthings, their stockings. The top of the bureau is covered with gloves, empty cigarette packs, a play card from a bawdy theatrical revue. They also have a container of cold cream that was foisted upon them by Amo Winston. "It's never too early to start worrying about wrinkles," she said, smiling pointedly at Yale.

Amo Winston is the only thing Brennan dislikes about their room. The matron has a larger room directly across the hall. "So she can watch us," Yale says, and Brennan agrees, although she also thinks it might have something to do with the Y's penchant for alphabetized personnel. But whatever the reason for Miss Winston's proximity, whenever the twins come home late, whenever they stay up even later, giggling, passing a flask, blowing cigarette smoke out the window, Amo Winston eventually knocks on their door to ask if they know what time it is.

They don't care what time it is. They are having nothing but fun. When she joined the Y, her heart broken and her reputation a mess, Brennan feared she would never have fun again. But here she is, having it. She is having fun with this kid from Missouri.

It is, she thinks, astonishing. No matter what they do, they turn it into a good time. Spreading mustard on ham sandwiches for hours on end? Squeezing lemons for lemonade until your fingers crack and ache? Not so bad if the two of you are, at the same time, joking and flirting with some of the boys. Yale, who insists she doesn't know how to flirt, goes on and on about how the Y's dances aren't dances at all, but football games, and guess who's the football?—and everyone laughs as she staggers about, acting out what she's saying, playing the girl flung from boy to boy each time the bandleader's whistle blows. And then, the next thing you know, someone lets loose with a two-fingered whistle, and suddenly you are being led in an impromptu fox-trot right there in the canteen, and then everyone joins in, and you have all abandoned the ham, the mustard, the lemons, and everyone in the room is dancing and singing "That Little Good-for-Nothing's Good for Something After All," which you have come to think of as your song.

It's just the most *regular* time you've ever had.

Or maybe one day, after the army begins assigning soldiers to work the canteens (because what else do the soldiers have to do now?), you and your twin sister are sent out to visit the boys stationed in the small outlying towns. Your duties are few and ill-defined. You're supposed to smile a lot and go to dances in the evenings. They pay you to do this; they actually do. Well, if you weren't with your twin, you would have to charm a man into escorting you everywhere. With your twin, though, it's perfectly proper for the two of you to go everywhere on your own. You aren't fearful. You don't get lonely. You can even go out after dark. You can dine in one of the many private homes that have been turned into restaurants. You can walk into somebody's bedroom and have your chop and French-fried potatoes and peas (the peas served as a separate course after the chop). That's where the French serve meals these days, in the bedrooms, your table alongside the bed. It's an adventure. It's absurd. (Those peas rattling around all by their lonesome on the plate.) Sometimes, it's sad. (They always take you through the kitchen, where old men sit on low stools, drinking wine by the stove, and there is never a young man to be seen.) Then you order brandy, and you go out and tease the old men, you and your twin, and you make them feel like young men, and once again it's all such a laugh.

One week you are taken by motor truck to visit the front. You are driven along rutted dirt paths periodically lined with heaps of rubble. The first time you see such a path, the truck has covered half a mile of it before it dawns on you that this was once a paved street and each mound of debris was once someone's house. Each family who lived on the street must have come by after the final air raid and gathered up the stone and metal and wood from their homes, somehow distinguishing their ruins from the ruins of their neighbors, and piled the junk on their now useless parcels of land.

"My Lord," you say. And if you begin to tremble, your twin holds your hand until, after a while, you can take it back and smoke a cigarette.

And maybe one day, outside one of these towns, you begin to see trenches raking the land, as if one of the angry gods you sometimes believe in has clawed the earth with his fingernails. Later that same afternoon, everyone gets out of the truck to search for souvenirs. There are six of you altogether, four men and you and your sister, and everyone is looking for Kaiser cocks, which is what the men call the *Pickelhaubes,* those funny Prussian helmets with the little spike. "That's my specialty," you cry out, "finding cocks." Let them think you don't know what it means, that you think you are referring only to a little spike on a hat. Or let them think that you *do* know what it means. You're only happy that they think you're a grand girl, a fun girl, and they are now letting you and your sister lead the way. The two of you dance about, leaping like ballerinas over coils of barbed wire. You pass your flask around and cry out whenever you spot a glimmering object. Mostly they're only old fuses you're finding, and soon the fellows are collecting the fuses.

Later, you run into another group of souvenir hunters. "Be careful, will ya?" the captain of that group says. "Stay on this side of the wire. Look where you're going. It's dangerous here." He shakes his head, as if you're to blame for everything. "Women," he says. "Jesus." After that, you do stay on the right side of the wire, but still you run about recklessly like a child during recess. It's so easy to dance here. There are no trees. No vegetation at all. Halfway across the field you notice a little French boy, perhaps six or seven, watching you. You slip your flask into your pocket. The little boy wants to make friends. Now he joins your party, wedging himself between you and your sister. He has made himself the middle link in a chain. But he's the dominant link. He pulls you both along. He points out the shell craters so you don't turn your ankle. The little boy chatters incessantly and so rapidly you can't catch a word except for the times he cries, "*Et puis—boom-boom!*" and closes his eyes and drops his head to one side, doing his impression of yet another neighbor buying the farm, or at least that's what you're thinking until your twin whispers over his head, "Who is he saying went west? Do you think it's his parents?"

He seems too cheerful for that, you decide. He is running you past stumps and heaps of jagged bricks until, all of a sudden, you find your-self looking at a shattered bronze church bell. Your party encircles it. "*Boom-boom!*" the boy says.

"He's trying to tell us the priest bought it, I'll bet," says your sister.

Before you leave, each member of your little party takes a piece of the bell. One man takes the clapper. It weighs plenty, but, still, what a fine souvenir. The little boy takes a piece of the bell too. Perhaps he's been waiting for uniformed Americans to come give him permission.

You put your slice of bronze in your pocket. You are thinking that you'd like to put the little boy in your pocket as well, that you'd like to take him home with you. You are feeling sudden tenderness for the child, and then you think of Billy Wilcox, the children you once imag-ined you'd have with him, and you grab hold of the bronze, and it is as if you were touching something genuinely holy—a thread of Jesus' shroud, a frond from the Garden of Eden—and you feel suddenly, deeply, palpably Christian. And you think of Billy again, and you feel such forgiveness, and then such a need to be forgiven.

You walk back to the truck. No one utters a word, not even the little boy, unless it's a quick shout to keep one of you from tripping over a wire, stepping into a hole. You have all formed a chain now. All your arms are linked.

That night, as you recline on a bed you've been told Black Jack Pershing once slept in, you say to your twin, "I am going to say something ghastly now. I had a wonderful day in No Man's Land." And your twin blows a smoke ring to the ceiling and says, "I know exactly what you mean." Then you start to sing, and your twin sings with you, because, after all, your songs are her songs.

> But now she's Over There; she's joined the Y.M.,
> She's given up her life for duty's call.
> And the ones who used to sneer,
> Are the people who now cheer,
> That little good-for-nothing's good for something after all!

So, of course, given that you're happy and content and calm in your own crazy way, and at peace in a way that may not appear peaceful to others but is peaceful for you, peaceful in a way you've never been at peace before, what do you go and do? You being you?

You ruin it all. You muck it up. On the day of the first plenary session of the Peace Conference, you suggest that the two of you go and watch the dignitaries show up on the Quai. "You never know," you say to your twin, "who we might run into."

CHAPTER THREE

It Would Be So *Us*

THE TRAIN from Berlin is late. Yale and Brennan fidget on a bench on a platform between two empty tracks. For a while they busy themselves by admiring the architecture, especially the arched ceiling, its suspended gas lamps. Then bored and, for the first time since they met, cross with each other, they smoke the cigarettes they now routinely swipe from the canteen. They play with Brennan's brass cigarette lighter, making the naked girl perform her fire trick for them. They pass Brennan's flask.

"Something awful's going to come from all this," Brennan says. She crosses her legs, looks away. She is very angry, mostly with herself. It's her fault that Yale saw the Armenian lieutenant that afternoon. Her fault that she and Yale are now waiting for the train of some international criminal she's never heard of and whose acquaintance she doesn't wish to make. For not only was it she, Mary Brennan White, who suggested they spend their afternoon watching the famous arrive at the Peace Conference. She was also the one who actually spotted the lieutenant, spotted him and, damn her eyes, pointed him out. "Look," she said, not thinking it through. "That soldier over there, the one waving his cap all around. That has to be the fellow you're always going on about, doesn't it? Look at his hair. He's striped like a skunk."

She could shoot herself. But she's been hearing about this soldier for months now, so she'd been momentarily excited to see him. For a minute it was as if she'd been the one searching for him. But still, why couldn't she ever think anything through?

Yale looks up to the station's smoky dome. She wonders how the French keep it clean. "Don't be that way, Brennan," she says. "Nothing awful will happen. It's just a small favor for a doughboy. Then we'll be going."

"We've already been here forever. Where is this alleged train? We're going to sit here forever and freeze to death and catch the flu and die and miss supper."

"I'll tell you a story," Yale says.

"Please, darling, not the one about how you met him."

"I'll tell you about the decline and fall of the Ottoman Empire and the rise of the Republic of Armenia."

"But I'm so thoroughly not interested, darling."

"But it's an adventure tale, and you're the great adventuress. Really, it's even more exciting than breaking into a bowling lane, if you can only imagine."

"I'm not an adventuress," Brennan grouses. "I was only bowling. It was harmless fun. This is evil." She drinks. "I don't even know where the Republic of Armenia is," she says.

"It's at the bottom of Russia. Between Georgia and Azerbaijan."

"Oh," Brennan says. "That solves that."

Yale has never seen Brennan so crotchety or cautious. Her time of the month, Yale would assume, except that their cycles coincide now, twin sisters and moon sisters both, and they were struck down the week before.

"Think about it a minute, will you?" Brennan says. "What's he going to do with this man's address, send him a Christmas card? He can't be up to any good."

"Did you know the Armenians celebrate Christmas in January?" Yale says.

She has no idea what Lieutenant Hagopian intends to do with Kerim Bey's address. Hand it over to some Allied authority, she imagines. Alert the police to the fugitive's presence so they can arrest him and ship him back to Turkey. Mustafa Kemal, Turkey's new leader, has acknowledged the former government's sins and promised the West trials and hangings.

Or perhaps the men from Erinyes plan to picket the man's dwelling.

That last—it's a joke. Shooting the Turk, she knows, is also a possibility. The Erinyes were seekers of vengeance. The scourge was their favorite weapon, and now their namesakes collect guns and grenades. So, political assassination—she can't deny to herself that it's a possibility too.

At the same time, Dub is an American boy, a U.S. lieutenant. Surely he has his limits.

The sun is beginning to set over the domed roof. Yale sips from the flask. "He's trying to keep an eye on a war criminal," she says. "He wants to make sure a murderer of thousands—hundreds of thousands—doesn't escape justice. How is that evil?"

Brennan nods like a person who is listening, but all she is doing is reading the posters mounted on the station's walls, the advertisements for wines, aperitifs, artificial legs. She is also thinking that while she has no objection to trials or hangings or what-have-you, and that she is definitely in favor of Turkey doing its best to right its wrongs, there are certain wrongs that, once committed, are irrevocable. She and Turkey are in the same boat when it comes to righting their wrongs, she thinks. There is really nothing for either of them but to try to do better in the future.

"Fine," Brennan says. "You're right. He's a goddamn hero." Meanwhile, she's squinting up at the big board. A workman in railroad blue is changing the numbers with a long, hooked pole. Next to the name of the train from Berlin, though, nothing's changed at all. It's as if the workman doesn't even wish to acknowledge the reference to Berlin. The train, the board says, is still due in at 4:05 p.m.

"There's a dance tonight," Brennan says, as if the dance were posted along with the names of the trains.

"Oh, so what?" Yale says. "There's a dance every night. I get so bored watching the desiccated and despicable Amo Winston throwing herself at the unctuous and extremely married Alban Bliss."

"He's the one who's married, not her," Brennan says. "He's the one who stood up before God and everyone else on earth and took a vow. He's the one with the responsibility to his wife, not Amo." A sip from the flask. "Desiccated and despicable though she may be," she says.

"Well, you go dancing if you want," Yale says. "You don't have to wait here with me."

"Maybe I will," Brennan says. "Anyway," she adds, "if I were going to spend my time fretting about a suffering people, the suffering people I'd be fretting about would be the Irish. Loyalty to my own mother, doncha know. As my twin sister, you might share those sentiments."

"You never so much as mention your mother," Yale says.

Brennan is irritated by this. It's as if Yale is saying that Brennan's earlier discretion has cost her the right to bring up her mother now. "Well, what's there to say, really?" Brennan says. "I never knew her. For years they let me think she was fine and strong and giving birth to me was what did her in. But come to learn she was terribly weak." Brennan raises the flask. "The Irish Curse got her like it'll get me."

She hears herself then, blubbering about her ma, and she hates that sort of sentimentality, so she makes herself quit. It's deliberate, her never talking about her mother, and she knows the only reason she did so now was because she needed an excuse to bring up the Irish question. She wanted to remind Yale that Armenians are hardly the only people to feel unwelcome in their own land or to be punished for their religion or to be made to suffer and starve and leave their homes. It disgusts her, though, that she exploited her heart's secret pain, mentioning her mother just to win an argument. And it hurts her too that Yale isn't asking more questions, isn't probing and prodding and begging Brennan to unburden herself. But Yale is oblivious to Brennan's heart's pain, Brennan can see that. Yale is lost to this soldier, that man, his cause.

Yale is trying to figure out what the Irish Curse is. Is it the potato famine? Is it the British? Yale doesn't want to confess her ignorance. She doesn't want to hear, once again, how if she were really twenty-five, she would know all about everything: cigarettes, booze, Irish Curses. So she says nothing, even though she would like very much to know more about Brennan's family. Not only Brennan's mother. The father too. The pharmacist. She is curious about both of them. What combination of genes and rearing produced Brennan White? But Brennan's unhappy expression discourages Yale from pursuing the matter. If Brennan wants to talk about her family, Yale figures, Brennan will. It's not as if Brennan were the reticent type.

"In any event," Brennan says, "I have no intention of ruining my time in Paris by going around fretting about any suffering people, be they Armenian or Irish or Ubangis with dinner plates stuffed in their lips. There are too many suffering people in this world and not a thing that can be done for any of them."

Brennan flicks her lighter, and the naked woman obediently gives forth her small flame, her one and only skill. "She reminds me of you," Billy Wilcox said when he gave it to her. "How so?" Brennan asked, but he never really explained. She flicks the lighter again. "Your lieutenant is married too," she tells Yale.

"What are you talking about? How do you know that?"

"I told you on the *Espagne* that I can see the future. He's married or he's something else just as bad. He's got a girl back home or maybe he will never marry someone who isn't Armenian. His momma will have a fit if he dares to, and he won't ever do anything to upset his precious mother. Just wait. There will be something."

The sun has dropped to the horizon, turning the glass dome orange, making Yale feel as though she is sitting inside an elegant pumpkin. She stamps out her cigarette. "They aren't all Billy," she says.

"What experience could you possibly have had that allows you to say that?"

Yale pats Brennan's shoulder. It looks like an act of tenderness and sisterly warmth, but really it's an act of restraint. Yale is longing to shove Brennan off the bench. "Why don't you go back to the rue d'Aguesseau, darling," she says. "You don't have to keep me company. I'll be fine on my own."

Brennan flicks the lighter again, then again. "Right," she says. "As if I'd leave you here waiting on a depraved murderer of thousands." Another flick. "And father of one," she says.

The sun is gone. They smoke two more cigarettes. They drink to stay warm, although they both know that, according to science and the YMCA's temperance bulletins, whiskey only makes a person colder in the long run. Twice they hear the approach of a train, but each time it comes in on the track behind them, and they turn and watch the passengers disembark, crippled soldiers on leave, a new flock of widows to work the cafés. Suitcases of fine leather and suitcases of cardboard are passed to porters from compartment windows.

Each time, when the whistle blows and the train is about to depart, Brennan says the same thing. "Let's get on. Let's see where it takes us. Let's see where we wind up."

"Stop it," Yale says when the second train readies for Brussels.

"No, really. Getting on and just turning up somewhere. It would be so *us*."

"I have something important to do here," says Yale.

Brennan lifts the flask to her lips and takes the last swig. She shudders as the whiskey goes down. Lately she has begun to notice something. The only thing that makes her body hurt more than whiskey is the absence of whiskey. She shivers and wipes her mouth with her coat sleeve.

CHAPTER FOUR

The Little Vuitton

It's nearly six when the Berlin train arrives. Even Brennan, who has never seen his likeness, recognizes Kerim Bey at once. He is, as promised, huge and barrel-chested. He walks with a stick, favoring his left leg. He keeps his head down, makes eye contact with no one. It's the

tall wife, her sleeping child in her arms, who summons the commis-
sionaire, points out the family's luggage.

The porter loads the bags onto his cart. It is elegant luggage, brown
patterned leather, and the pieces are mostly large and bulging, although
there is a dainty traveling case as well.

"Now I've seen it all," Brennan says. "Mohammedans with Vuitton."

"Well, the wife is French," Yale says. She is still seated on the bench.
She is waiting to make her move. She only wishes she knew what that
move ought to be. Should she follow the family? Stay with the luggage
cart? She is nervous. She feels big and conspicuous.

The small family seems pressed for time. They are hurrying to the
end of the quai, expressionless, silent. They look at no one, not even
each other. The husband and wife could be strangers who happen to be
walking side by side.

"Come on," Yale says. She may be speaking more to herself than to
Brennan. She rises and follows the couple. It's as easy as that. She turns
once to look over her shoulder and make sure Brennan is coming along,
and it's a relief to see that she is. It occurred to her that Brennan might
stay on the bench, sulking and forcing Yale to choose between friendship and what she is already thinking of as duty. Brennan, however, is
trotting behind her, scowling but keeping up, and the two of them have
no trouble staying only a few feet behind the fugitive and his French
wife and their small child, whose face is smothered in red fur.

There's a shortage of taxis in Paris just as there is a shortage of
everything else, but there are two cabs at the taxi stand, and two cabs
are sufficient for Yale's purpose. As Kerim Bey holds the door of the
first cab for his wife, Yale nods at the driver of the second.

She should have been looking at its back door. A young man in a hat
with a tricolor cockade is opening that door and climbing into the back
seat, stealing the cab from her. "*Arrêtez-vous*, you crumb!" she shouts, but
the young man has slammed the door in her face. He leans forward to
speak to the driver, and the two cabs leave the curb nearly simultaneously.

Brennan laughs as if this is all a complicated prank she's arranged.
"Really, darling," she says. It's as if she assumes they are done now;
they will go back to the Y, have a bite, go to the dance, visit a club later,
have some cocktails, meet some men, ditch them, stumble home. "It's

just as well. This is all so unbecoming. Boys are supposed to jump through hoops for you, not vice versa."

For several additional seconds, Yale remains in the street, stunned as a cow hit over the head with a hammer. She watches the two cabs turn off the rue de Compiègne. She feels heartsick, as if it were Dub in the second of those taxis, as if Dub were being carried away from her forever. She glares at Brennan, who is still laughing, and then she glares at the uniformed fellow at the curb, a whistle in his one gloved hand, a crumpled pink franc note in the other, a bribe from the man in the cockaded cap. "That was my taxi," she says to him. He looks at her blandly, and she realizes she is speaking English. She's too angry to repeat herself in French. She wants to shove him. She wants to shove Brennan. Instead, she turns and runs back to the quai.

The Berlin train is gone, and the platform is empty except for the porter who is arranging suitcases, building a pyramid of luggage on his wooden cart, placing the little traveling case at the top.

Yale waits for Brennan to catch up. "Distract him," she says. "Get his attention."

"Will you stop?" Brennan says. "I am not going to distract the goddamn porter." She is going to leave, really she is, but then she thinks about Billy Wilcox. Or not really Billy, but his wife. Brennan is remembering the day Mabel came home. TB, Billy had told everyone in Palmyra, but he'd told Brennan the truth, that the Irish Curse had somehow fallen upon a wealthy woman without a drop of Irish in her. A Dutchwoman, a respectable clubwoman, a drunk.

Now Mabel was home again, and the dalliance between Brennan and Billy was, necessarily, over. But late that night, still in the habit of him, Brennan walked to his house. She had never gone there before, not with him and not on her own. They had rendezvoused in his car, parking by the water, visiting quiet lovers' lanes. Now, standing in the shadow of an old oak, she looked at the familiar Bearcat parked by the garage, the burgundy waxed and gleaming in the dark. She wished she could go to it, pet it as if it were a horse or a sweet loyal dog. Then she put her arm around the tree trunk and looked up at the only lit window high on the third floor.

Inside, she imagined, Billy and Mabel would be changing into their respective nightshirts. She knew what Mabel looked like, having seen her many times at the pharmacy. She was not fat, but she was well-fed, with a bust like a bureau drawer left wide open, a very proper woman who favored matronly purples and large feathered hats. Brennan had noticed all this, and she hadn't even cared about Mabel then. She didn't know that one day she was going to do something cruel to Mabel and that, after she did, she was going to justify her cruelty by deciding Mabel wasn't good enough, wasn't beautiful enough, wasn't smart and vivacious enough for Billy.

Although had she really been all that cruel to Mabel? In some ways, hadn't she been good to her? That same night, holding on to that oak tree, Brennan thought about what she would like to say to Mabel: These so-called friends of yours, these society dames coming by with their casseroles and soup, inquiring about your poor ravaged lungs—they aren't true friends. *I'm* your true friend. I kept your husband occupied and amused in your absence. I let him spend night after night telling me how much he hated you until that hatred was spent. At the same time, I made so few demands on him and his heart that the moment you deigned to come home—well, see for yourself how easy it was for him to return to you.

It had begun to snow. A girl from Palmyra, she wasn't fazed by snow, and she remained where she was, letting the flakes land on her head. She imagined they would sit on her hair, pristine, a white mantilla like the one she wore for her first communion. Of course that's not what snowflakes do, and she knew it. The snow melted and dripped down her forehead, making her feel all the more pitiful. Feeling pitiful, though, had been all right with her. To feel good was to be over him, never to have loved him, and if she hadn't, how could she justify the rest of it, a reputation shredded like an embarrassing love letter, a father's angry silence?

Another girl might not have stood for it, she wanted to tell Mabel. Another girl might not have let herself be gotten rid of so easily. Another girl might have whispered some things to those society dames. But not me, Mabel, and isn't that true friendship? I'm probably the best friend you'll ever have.

These memories sway her, she doesn't know why. Maybe she wants to demonstrate her loyalty, to prove she will not desert others as she's been deserted. Or maybe she is just being pragmatic. Maybe she only wants to hurry Yale along, get Yale to the part where she feels the same as Brennan—taken advantage of, left standing outside, nothing to hold on to but the bark of a goddamn tree. The sooner Yale gets her man, the sooner he'll disappoint her and the sooner Yale can get over him. Then it will be just the two of them again, twins on the town.

Deciding to stay and help Yale is the hard part. Seducing the porter, that's nothing. A tap on the shoulder of his brushed blue uniform. The arching of one pale brow.

"*Bon soir, monsieur. Le train pour Amiens, vient-il bientôt?*"

"*Ah, non, mademoiselle.*" The porter thrusts out his lower lip to convey the degree to which having to report this bad news to such an attractive young woman pains him. "*Il est parti il y a trente minutes.*"

As the two of them speak about train schedules, as Brennan pouts and fusses and the porter comforts her and offers alternative routes, Yale tiptoes behind him, reaches up, and plucks the little Vuitton from the top of the suitcase pyramid. Without looking back, she skitters along the quai, clatters across an iron bridge, crosses to the boulevard de la Chappelle, and continues along to the nearest metro station. It occurs to her that the streets are perfectly dark and she is perfectly unescorted. Never, Alban Bliss cried during one of his alarming sermons, does an Amen Girl walk the streets of Paris alone. Yale smiles and hurries onward.

CHAPTER FIVE

An Excellent Haut-Brion

THE HÔTEL CRILLON reminds one of a battleship these days, what with all those sailors milling about in the lobby. And there's an odor to it, or haven't you noticed?"

Trevor Hamilton is smiling as if he's just politely inquired about his dining companions' health. This, Colonel Stephen Lindsey reflects, is what happens when a person has too much wine with dinner. Even a professional diplomat begins telling the truth.

Lindsey and Hamilton—they're compatriots, these two. Liaisons to the small countries, an older American and a young Brit, they find themselves at the same parties, the same dinners, on the same trips through Bulgaria, Poland, Hungary. "Well, no, Trev," Lindsey says now, "I can't say I've detected any odor at the Crillon. Perhaps as an American I'm inured to our smell."

Hamilton laughs. "Gad, did I really say that?" He shakes his head. "I apologize. I've seemed to have forgotten the first lesson Lord Balfour ever taught me: *Un bon diplomat n'ouvre la bouche que pour boire.*" He fills his glass to the brim, raises it. "I believe what I intended to say is that I'm terribly pleased you agreed to dine at the British residence this evening."

"Where there are fewer men of rank," Lindsey says, touching his glass to Hamilton's.

General laughter, crisis averted, diplomacy in action. Dub Hagopian, the third party at the swank table, adds his glass to the other two. He is not one of them, but he's been their equal this evening, at least when it came to killing two bottles of wine. He too is feeling the effects, and he worries that he might also blurt out an unfortunate truth. He takes another bite of his steak to confirm his first impression. Only you Brits, is what he hopes he will not say out loud. You've come to Paris and what have you done? You've brought your own chefs.

The beef is inedible. Burnt, possibly boiled, nearly impervious to the knife in his hand. But the wine—the French wine is a different story. The wine is excellent, even Dub can tell. He knows he should stop drinking. But when will he have a chance like this again?

Also, it has been a very taxing day.

"Château Haut-Brion, ought-six," Hamilton says, although neither American has thought to ask.

"Very fine," Lindsey says. "But you know, my dear Hamilton, aromas or not, the Crillon's victuals are far superior to the Majestic's. You can't really mean we'll never have the pleasure of seeing you there again."

Hamilton reaches for a hard roll, genuinely hard, inside and out. "Actually, I've been frequenting the Griffon of late," he says. "Lunched there with Sir Wiseman just the other day. Who mentioned, by the way, how keen you Yanks are on a Greek zone at Smyrna."

Dub admires the way the diplomat, intoxicated though he may be, has moved the conversation from small talk to business. He turns to watch Lindsey, to learn from him. The colonel is nodding affably. "Yes, the Greeks at Smyrna, you Brits at Constantinople. And we'd be willing to have the smaller powers monitor the Straits."

Back to Hamilton, who has already finished his beef and is sucking on the sprig of parsley that decorated it. "Actually, we'd prefer you Yanks at the Straits." He smiles at Dub. "Have you noticed the cedar notes, Lieutenant? And the fragrance? Here, pick up your goblet. Sniff it."

Dub does what he's told. He's on edge, his leg jiggling under the table. He is aware of his lesser station, the likelihood of overstepping his bounds. He doesn't know either of these men very well. He met them a few weeks earlier, at a luncheon where, for the first time, he was translating for Lindsey. The conversation bogged down when it got around to the latest conflict between Armenia and the Azeris. Dub, seated between these two and across from Avetis Aharonian, hadn't eaten a thing. He'd been far too consumed with translating Aharonian's demand that the Brits replace their Governor Thompson with someone more sympathetic to Armenia. He'd found himself perspiring from the effort of softening Aharonian's angry rhetoric.

"We owe this boy a decent meal," Hamilton declared when it was over, nothing accomplished, nothing resolved, Aharonian glaring at Dub and then stalking out of the room by himself. And while Dub knew Hamilton's invitation was only a gesture, something you said, hoping to be turned down, he had accepted anyway, and Hamilton had not seemed put out. "Splendid," Hamilton said. "We'll do it at the Majestic, right after the first plenary session. I'll tell you what everyone wore."

Now the steaks have been removed and limp salads placed before them, and they indeed speak of clothes. Already the story about Clemenceau's casual attire is making the rounds. "And then," Hamilton says, "Lloyd George tips his hat and says to Clemenceau, 'I feel quite the fool; I was told we had to wear top hats,' and the Tiger tips his wreck of a derby and says, '*Oui, moi aussi.*'"

General laughter once more. Dub keeps intending to turn the conversation to Armenia, but so far all he's done is laugh and tremble and pretend to eat. He looks at his watch. He lets Hamilton refill his glass. And finally, pushing the drenched greens away, he gives diplomacy a try.

"You know, Mr. Hamilton," he says, "while we're on the topic of Constantinople, I wonder what your thoughts are on the Armenian situation."

"Were we on the topic of Constantinople?" Lindsey says. "I thought we were on the topic of Clemenceau's hat."

"Trev," Hamilton says, and for a moment Dub thinks the man is speaking another language. His brain tries to identify the language, to translate. "My name," Hamilton says. "Call me Trev." He dabs at his mouth with a napkin. He is the only one at the table who has cleaned every plate thus far presented. "Well," he says, "as to Armenia, I should imagine we'd like to see your people as Mandatory there."

Dub shakes his head. "My people? You want the Armenians as Mandatory of Armenia?"

"The Americans," Hamilton says. "Those would be your people, would they not?"

Dub feels himself color, says nothing.

"Right. Well, that's what we'd like. An American Mandatory over Armenia."

Colonel Lindsey spears a lettuce leaf, looks at the brown edges, puts his fork down. "We all want that, Trev," he says. "You want it, I want it, President Wilson wants it. Even Hagopian wants it, don't you, Lieutenant? But it's got a Chinaman's chance of getting through Congress."

"Other than the Mandatory," Dub says, "what are your thoughts regarding the conference? For example, will you reconsider seating Aharonian's delegation?"

Hamilton sighs. "Forgive me," he says. "I don't mean to sound exasperated. It's only that we hear daily from Mr. Aharonian, and now—just before I came to dinner as a matter of fact—I was told that our friend Nubar Pasha has written to the London *Times*. It's awkward, his going over our heads as it were to the public, when we've made our position quite clear."

Dub knows the letter Hamilton refers to. He and Boghos Nubar argued over the closure several nights ago, Dub advocating *Most sin-*

cerely and Nubar insisting upon *Believe me, sirs, yours very truthfully,* which made Dub cringe. "It is for my signature, not yours, is it not?" Nubar asked, and so he'd won.

"Well, you have to understand what Nubar is thinking," Dub says. "He turns to the people of England because they have been so supportive of the Armenian cause."

"Lieutenant," Colonel Lindsey says, with frosty amusement, "have you been promoted to a position of authority within my department of which I'm unaware?"

Dub blushes again, but Hamilton waves his hand. "No, it's perfectly all right, Stephen. I'm interested in what the lieutenant has to say." A platter of cheese has been placed before them. "But you might consider speaking to some of your own people about this, Hagopian. I've yet to hear Colonel House weigh in on Armenia."

"You're not likely to either." Lindsey has piled his plate with cheese, a food no chef can ruin. "Not that the colonel's confided in me, but my sense is he feels we have no place interfering with British plans in this matter."

Hamilton frowns. He's a dully handsome man, his features plain but even. His confusion becomes him, makes him appear smarter than he is. "What British plans are those, Stephen?" he asks. "I know of no British plans for the Republic."

Lindsey smiles. How readily Hamilton has walked into his trap. "Oh, but there *are* plans. In 1916, your prime minister made a pledge at the Guild Hall. Don't you recall what he said? I'll wager Hagopian does."

Dub feels called to the front of the class. He recites softly: "'Britain is resolved to liberate the Armenians from the Turkish yoke and to restore to them the freedom of which they have been so long deprived.'" He shrugs. "Something like that," he says.

"Something like that word for word," Lindsey says. "You Brits took on Armenia at least a year before we even entered the war. Why should we assume the burden now?" He is smiling again. "*Après vous, messieurs les Anglais.*"

"Touché," Hamilton says. "And yet surely you agree the situation is much changed since then. France and Italy have taken an interest in

Cilicia, while Nubar still clings to the fantasy it ought to be Armenia's. An Armenian state extending from the Black Sea to the Mediterranean. What can he be thinking?"

"That such a state is precisely what the French promised?" Dub says.

"The French," Hamilton echoes, and sees no need to say more. "But look, here's a thought, Lieutenant. If Colonel House is apathetic, why not turn to His Lordship for help?"

"I've spoken to Lord Bryce," Dub says.

The truth is they have had only one conversation, but it lasted long enough to count as several. The old man was passing through Translation, and, spying Dub's nameplate, he parked himself at Dub's desk and delivered a lecture on the history of the Armenian people. Did Dub know about the days when the Mongols ruled ancient Hayastan? Would Dub care to hear the lord's opinion on the question that has for so long divided historians, namely, was Armenia a tributary to Parthia or merely a client state?

"He's your best bet if you Yanks refuse to get involved," Hamilton says. "And don't misunderstand me. We're all sympathetic to the Armenian position. Not the Armenian land grab or their hopes for annexing Karabagh; that sort of imperialistic greed is a hallmark of dark days past, and someone should tell that to Aharonian. But, in general, we do mind awfully what happened to those poor people. During my own days in Turkey I saw things even more bloodcurdling than are reported in His Lordship's atrocity stories. And I say this without closing my eyes to the crimes the Armenians have committed by way of retaliation." He pauses, looks Dub in the eyes. "Indeed, I approve of such crimes."

Dub cocks his head to one side. It seems to him that Hamilton has just suggested that Armenians seek a route toward justice that does not include a stop at the peace table.

"It's astounding," Lindsey says, "when you consider the number of times Europe has broken its promises to the poor bastards, and yet they keep coming back, seeking more promises."

"Exactly," Hamilton says. "The Treaty of San Stefano. The Congress of Berlin. Disraeli's protests to Stambol. You'd think they'd grow weary."

"You'd think they'd stop playing the eastern game of martyrdom and vengeance," Lindsey says. He considers a nearly animated white pudding that has been placed before each of them, but finally sits back, pretending to be a man who has been sated, rather than bested, by his dinner. "You know," he says, relinquishing his utensils, "I witnessed something very interesting at the hôtel Royale the other day. I was there with some of the leaders of our budding democracies—Venizelos, Dmowski, several others—and the conversation turned to the pestiferous insurance agent who's been trying to knock Károlyi onto his rear end. I speak of Béla Kun, of course."

"The former Mr. Cohen," Hamilton says, white pudding in his mustache. "An oily little Jew in a moth-eaten fur coat."

"And so there we all were, discussing the Hungarian situation, when two soldiers from Chicago entered the tradesmen's lobby directly behind us. Now when I say from Chicago, I mean Chicago by way of some Polish shtetl. These gentlemen were conducting business at such a deafening volume we could no longer hear ourselves think. At which point Dmowski nudged me and said, 'You see those two? They're Béla Kun's brethren. If you ask them, they'll say they're businessmen, but they're actually smugglers. They've cornered the market in sugar.'"

"One never knows how to react to that strain," Hamilton says. "One part admiration to two parts indignation, I suppose."

"That's my point. They're impossible to stomach, but at the same time you have to admit they turn every adverse situation to their advantage. They don't take up arms. They use their heads." Lindsey taps his own. "The European ghetto becomes inhospitable? Move to Chicago. Cossacks rape your daughter and abscond with your fortune? Mourn for seven days, then get back to work and make another fortune. The Hebrew has been persecuted and his property expropriated since the beginning of time, and yet over and over he's risen above adversity, not by taking up arms but through his cunning. Why can't the Armenians do the same? Do they prefer martyrdom?"

"Well, the Armenians are Christians," Hamilton says. He grins. "No surprise that they prefer crucifixion to circumcision." He lifts a silver pot that has been placed on the table, pours a stream of gray liquid into a cup, offers the cup to Dub. "Coffee, Lieutenant?" he says.

CHAPTER SIX

His *You're Welcome*

CRUCIFIXION *as opposed to circumcision.* The two diplomats are still laughing at that one. All right, Dub thinks, and he smiles so they won't think he's a sorehead, a man who can't take a little good-natured ribbing. He refuses the coffee, downs the last of his wine, and counts the lessons he's learned at the table. From Lindsey, the lesson of passing the buck. From Hamilton—from Trev—the lesson that the British are going to do nothing. In other words, he's learned nothing he didn't already know.

Dub feels dizzy and defeated. Like his Armenian brethren repeatedly seeking European promises, he is someone who needs to have the same lesson repeated over and over before it will sink through his skull. Apparently he learned nothing from his time in St. Petersburg, the European betrayal he witnessed then. I'm such a fool, he thinks. He counts all the mistakes he has made just this one day alone. That wretched *poulet*. Going to the Quai d'Orsay. Attending this dinner. Opening his mouth. If, as Trev says, *un bon diplomat n'ouvre la bouche que pour boire,* what would he say about a bad diplomat? *Un amateur n'ouvre jamais la bouche,* for God's sake.

His biggest mistake, of course, and the one he's tried not to think about all evening, was trusting little Miss Yes. Damn her hide, he thinks, as he looks at his watch. She is an hour overdue.

He stands, and the floor seems to stand with him. "Oh, don't run off, Hagopian," Hamilton says, the voice coming at him distant and tinny. "It's nothing personal. One does the best one can. And Lord Calthorpe's written to the Grand Vizier complaining about the triumvirs lamming it in Germany, so perhaps there will be some arrests. That would cheer you, I presume. Besides, we've a splendid Château d'Yquem coming."

Out on the street, Dub leans against the Majestic's onyx walls and pats his coat pockets, feeling for his cigarette case. Damn, he thinks. He must have left it on the dining-room table. Another mistake, it upsets him as much as the others. He feels tears of frustration and shuts his eyes until he's certain they'll be dry when he opens them again.

He is drunk enough now to review not only the mistakes of this day but the mistakes of his entire life. He's engaged to a woman he doesn't love. He's best friends with a man he doesn't like. And what of the fact that he is carrying a 1908 Luger beneath his tunic so he might, if so directed, shoot a man he doesn't know? If he should ever get the order and the courage to actually kill that man, will the assassination turn out to be the worst mistake of his life? Or will it be something glorious, a deed that changes him, completes him, actually saves him?

How will he ever be sure? He supposes, with something like that, you just do it and see what happens next. You hope for the best. You trust Aram and you think of the atrocities. And if the slaughter isn't enough, if it sometimes feels distant, somehow not really directed at you, then you remind yourself that such an act will comfort Ramela. As for whether it's morally right, you don't even think about that. You can never figure that one out, you can never know.

Here's all a mere mortal knows for sure: he'll never be able to kill the tyrant if he doesn't know where the tyrant lives.

He opens his eyes. Where the hell is she? Has she forgotten she was supposed to meet him? It doesn't seem possible. More likely, she's gotten tied up with some YMCA emergency. A soul to save, a sandwich to slice. Even more likely, she failed to get the Turk's address and is too embarrassed to come tell him. Just that, nothing more.

Just that.

Unless she's at a police station, turning him in, spilling the beans.

Again he wants to cry for his past failures, his poor decisions. He wants to cry for his future too—first murder, then marriage—and for his more immediate future, which will entail driving to Aram's château and confessing the missed train. It was Raffi who found Kerim Bey buying tickets at that Berlin train station, Raffi who called Aram with the news. And now it's Dub who has lost him in Paris by sending a girl he barely knows—an *odar* no less—to do his work.

Although he'll leave that last bit out. No need to share every single piece of the story. I'm a U.S. soldier, he'll say, and I was given an order. It was your idea, Aram, that I enlist in the American army.

At least Raffi is still in Berlin. This is the only comforting thought Dub can muster. Let Aram gaze at Dub with grave disappointment, let Aram drum Dub out of the movement. At least Raffi won't be in the room, an observer both angry and happy.

So that's what he'll do: blame it all on Ned Harden. He feels slightly better, having fashioned an excuse. Still, there's no need to go to Aram's this very instant. He can delay an hour, even two. He thinks of the Deauville. A real drink. Perhaps a real woman. He begins walking, keeping one hand against the semiprecious wall of the hotel. He turns the corner, where he is met and nearly knocked over by a sheet of wind. This should invigorate him, but all it does is sting his eyes and revive his tears. He stops, leans against this side of the hotel, again with his eyes shut. He recalls something one French official said to another as everyone descended the stairs after the afternoon's plenary session. *"Mon cher, savez-vous ce qui va résulter de cette conference?"* the man had said. *"Une farce."*

He thrusts his fists into the pockets of his trousers. He means only to warm his fingers while waiting for the damned tears to retreat, but he feels a crushed pack of Fatimas. "Thank God for small favors," he mutters by rote.

His *you're welcome* is the snap of a lighter, the smell of fuel. His *you're welcome* is a naked woman carved in brass, a blue flame shooting from the top of her head.

CHAPTER SEVEN

Grips

HE DOESN'T RECOGNIZE the girl holding the lighter, but he's not interested in her anyway. He's interested only in the girl at her side. "Jesus," he says. "Where have you been?"

"Don't swear at me," Yale says. "We've been circling this stupid hotel for at least an hour."

"We?"

"*Oui*, we." Or perhaps the girl holding the lighter has said, "We, *oui*." In any case, it's some rudimentary French pun, and it's awful, and it seems a fair trade-off. This is what life is: the responsibility for avenging the slaughter of hundreds of thousands on the one hand; a pretty girl making silly puns on the other.

"My twin sister," Yale says. "Brennan White, meet Lieutenant Dub Hagopian. I'm afraid I have to tell you, Lieutenant, my sister is not very happy with you. The train was abysmally late, and now she's hungry and cold, and those horrible Tommies at the hotel door treated us like we were Typhoid Mary times two."

He is dizzy and overwhelmed and incredibly relieved. If he were a different sort of drunk, he'd be dancing Yale around in a circle, lifting her off the ground, swinging her in the air. "Sorry about that," he says. "The British are terrified of women bringing in diseases."

"Charming," Brennan says. She blows on her fingertips. Her nose is red. "I need a drink," she says.

"God, yes," Dub says. "Let me buy you both a drink." If they mention the tears, he'll blame the wind. "But first things first, hey?" He's got Yale by the elbow, urges her a few steps away, lowers his voice. "Did you get what I needed?"

Yale holds up a small traveling case. She shakes it, and the tag attached to the handle rattles. It takes him aback. It makes him ecstatic. It puts him to shame.

"Go on," he says. "You didn't actually steal his suitcase?"

She looks at the bag as if to confirm to herself that she actually did. "It seemed easiest," she says. "Rather than following him by cab. Of which there were none, by the way."

"Couldn't you have just jotted it down? The address?"

"Now there's an extraordinary thought," the twin sister says. But Yale is looking at him dolefully, an expression of hurt that makes him feel ungracious.

"Oh, don't mind me," he says. He wants to hug her. He wants to weep in her arms. He pats her shoulder. "You got the address. That's all that's important. It's wonderful, in fact. In fact, thank you. Really. Thank you."

His hand on her shoulder lies still. He waits.

"Might I have it?" he says.

She looks at the suitcase again, this time as if trying to assess its druthers—which of us do you prefer, him or me? But the truth is she's already thought this one out. Give him the suitcase and what additional need does he have of her? "Oh, that's all right," she says. "It's light as a feather. And I've never held something so fine. It's Vuitton, you know. So I'll just carry it a little bit longer. Now, where shall we go for those drinks? Do you know a typical café, Lieutenant?"

"Or brasserie," Brennan says. "I'm starving."

Now his shy grin, his head to one side. Yale is so glad to see the familiar gestures. She feels her head tilt too. She is so damned fond of this man. If she were alone with him, she might blurt out her feelings. I've missed you so much, she might say.

"How would you ladies like to dine at Maxim's?" Dub asks.

She doesn't confess her feelings, not then, but she does gasp with more enthusiasm than even Maxim's deserves. Oh, she and her sister would love to visit that famous establishment, she cries, and she steps hard on the word *love* as if it were the brake in a runaway car, the one and only thing that can save your life. And she loops her arm through his, grips him tightly as they walk along. The little suitcase too. She won't let go of either.

CHAPTER EIGHT

Senlis

MAXIM'S IS DARK, the door locked, and the handle removed—the French way of saying WE'RE CLOSED.

Yale turns to Dub, helpless, bewildered, batting her lashes. "But how can this be? It's well before curfew."

"Sometimes they run out of food."

"But I'm starving," Brennan says.

It comes out a wail, and Brennan is annoyed with herself for that wail, just as she's annoyed with Yale for those batting eyelashes. Her own trick, batting and simpering, and she sees what it looks like, hears what it sounds like, and, so help her God, she will never do it again.

"Lieutenant," says Yale, who has taken no such vow, "what should we do now?"

Dub says he has an idea.

He would not have had the idea had he been sober. But drunk, it seems like a grand idea, the best of ideas. He takes them first to the Crillon (sniffing the air in the lobby when he arrives, detecting no odor, repugnant or otherwise, deciding that Hamilton is batty, *khent*, barmy). Then, both hands resting on the blotter so he won't topple over, he confers with a young soldier behind a desk. After that, he leads the girls outside again, to an old green ambulance, a Fiat with slat wood sides. There are two torn brown leather seats bolted in the front. In the bed, covered with a flat roof, there is a long, thin wooden bench and nothing else—plenty of room for supplies and stretchers. The truck has no windshield and only one door, on the driver's side. To climb in, Yale and Brennan have to step up on the running board and slither past the spare tire mounted exactly where the passenger door should have been. Yale takes the front seat, the little suitcase held tight between her feet to keep it from sliding around with every bump and rut in the road. Brennan is on the bench, leaning forward, holding on to Yale's shoulders—the only way to keep herself from sliding around the truck.

As Dub leaves the rue Royale and drives through Paris, Yale leans back, allows Brennan to use her as ballast. She is using her own hands as a windshield. Every now and then, though the wind is cold and whipping, she peeks between her red fingers, and sometimes she sees nothing but darkness, but other times she can make out the dim outlines of bare trees or lampposts or the blue glow of a *refuge* sign still illuminated, still pointing to a shelter. Then Paris is behind them; on either side of them now are parks and estates and farms. If there is also destruction, houses blown to pieces, parcels of land stripped and shredded, most of the damage is obscured by the night.

"I know a great place," Dub shouts as he drives, first on one side of the road, then on the other. "Great food," he says, "and it's never closed."

BLACK'S GUIDE calls the walled city of Senlis one of the most picturesque places within easy reach of Paris. At the Château Royal, visitors can imagine attending the coronation of Hugues Capet in 987, witnessing the advent of the Capetian dynasty. Inside the city's twelfth-century cathedral, Notre Dame de Senlis, those same visitors can view the designs and innovations that later inspired the builders of Arles and Chartres. In early summer, they can meander along cobblestoned lanes where antique roses climb the walls of medieval cottages.

So many centuries gone by and not a thing changed. Oh, it's true that during the war the Germans occupied the city, shelled the cathedral, and burned hundreds of homes, that they also executed the mayor, M. Odent. But by 1919 the only Germans in Senlis are prisoners of war who spend their days cleaning up the mess they made, and the city is nearly back to its quaint old self. Very soon, if the city can hang on to the prisoners just a little while longer, the only ruins remaining will be the same ruins that were there not only before the war but before the death of Christ: the Gallic ramparts along the river Nonette and the old Roman amphitheater. "Small," Black's says of the latter, "but not uninteresting."

Aram and Seta Kazarian live on an estate several miles outside the heart of the city. To reach the Kazarian estate, you drive north until you come to a pair of large iron gates so intricately patterned they seem tatted by nuns rather than forged by blacksmiths. At these gates, you turn right and proceed up a driveway lined with sycamores and lindens until you reach a verdigris fountain that holds the remains of several rusty-leafed hollyhocks which, in summer, tangle up the fountain's base and fill its bowl. Should you continue straight at the fountain, you will soon come to a low stone wall surrounding a pond thick with lily pads and populated by turtles and ducks and a pair of swans, and then, if you continue around and beyond that pond, you will reach a thick and impassable copse where the men of Erinyes nail fezzes to tree trunks and take target practice. If you could then transform yourself into, say, a sparrow or a wood mouse, you could continue through the copse directly into the neighboring city of Chantilly. But if, at the fountain, you don't continue straight, if you bear left instead, then, several yards later, you will come to the Kazarians' half-timbered château, three stories tall, two hundred years old.

Only a half hour ago, Raffi Soghokian directed a taxi to make that left turn. If Dub knew that Raffi was in Aram's study right now, he would turn around and go right back to Paris. Instead, he drives the green Fiat onward, gulping the cold and sobering air while trying not to doze off or land in a ditch or otherwise kill himself and these girls.

If Raffi knew Dub was on his way to Senlis, he'd only be happy. He's dying to have it out with his old friend. That's why he's in Aram's study, pacing and fuming. That's why, when he picks up the framed photograph from Aram's desk—Raffi and Dub back in Providence— he shakes his head. "When I got off that train, Aslan," he says, speaking Armenian, "I could not believe what I was seeing. Or rather, I could not believe who I was *not* seeing."

Aram is reclining on a leather sofa. He has an afghan tight around his lower legs, and his disheveled mane stands up in the back like whipped egg white. He wears a crimson robe over his pajamas; on his feet, both of which stick out from the afghan, are dark blue embroidered carpet slippers. Until Raffi showed up, Aram was sound asleep on that couch.

He didn't realize he'd fallen asleep until Kevork knocked and then opened the door. Aram sat up, alarmed and confused. Raffi was standing directly behind the old servant. "I'm sorry, Aslan," Kevork said, "but you know this one. No peace if you deny him."

A burning pain in the small of Aram's back, a pain that seems always with him these days, kept him from rising. On bad days the pain twisted his backbone as if the human spine were a wet rag that could be wrung dry. On worse days, the pain continued up through his jaw and teeth and cheekbones and temples, as if the whole of him was that rag. Today was only a bad day, and he was able to keep his face placid as he motioned Raffi into the room.

Raffi charged in, knelt down, kissed the bearded cheek. "Asleep at nine, *Medz-hayrig?*" he said. "After all you've been through, you aren't going to start getting old now, are you?"

Aram smiled but turned his head away. He hoped his breath didn't reek from sleep. He hated this new habit of his, drifting off on the couch. He tried to remember exactly when he'd dozed off. He'd been reading a letter from the Berlin operatives, a plea for patience, restraint. "Let us see what the peace conferees do for us," the head of Erinyes-Berlin had written. "Let us remain coiled snakes, but, until we have our answer from the Allies, let us not yet strike." Pacific words that once would have made him rise up with frustration and fury had lulled him to sleep.

Aram despises being so fragile, a condition he doesn't blame on his age—he is in his late seventies now—but on Raffi Soghokian. Wherever he goes, Raffi brings worry and tension, and those, Aram thinks, are the things that make men frail.

"Sit down, dear boy," Aram says. "Don't pace. You make my neck hurt."

Raffi is too agitated to sit. "Aslan," he says, continuing back and forth, "promise me you will never again trust him with an important task. His head is with us, but his heart—or maybe it's the opposite. His heart is with us, but his head is in the clouds. I'm not saying this critically. I love him too. Would I let my sister marry him if I didn't? But it's a fact, Aslan. It's who he is. It's time to set him free. For his own good as well as ours."

Aram runs his hands over his beard. He wishes Raffi wasn't seeing him this way, so unkempt. He wonders if the leather buttons decorating the tufted sofa have left round impressions on his skin. He was having a terrible dream about St. Petersburg, about Kostya Kobakov, when Raffi came in. At least Raffi ended that dream for him. At least Raffi did that.

"All right," Aram says. He is speaking to his body, trying to rally his muscles and bones. He groans as he gets to his feet. Unable to straighten completely, shuffling the few steps to his desk, where along with stacks of papers and maps he keeps a crystal decanter, he says, "For this conversation, we need some Armagnac."

"Haven't you anything Armenian?" Raffi says.

Aram's hand shakes from the weight of leaded crystal. "You are not permitted to drink Armenian brandy when you're in France," he says. "Armenian brandy is to French brandy as the sound of the Armenian language is to the sound of French. We don't excel at every last thing, you know. Here, have a glass of perspective. You've never tried this before. Château Labaude. *À votre santé.*"

"*Genadzut,*" Raffi says.

Aram can't help laughing. "So stubborn. So stubborn."

Raffi smiles. His gold tooth glitters. He drinks, says, "It's good. Not as good as ours, but good."

"Stubborn and ignorant."

"Dedicated and loyal. Which is more than can be said for my dearest friend in the world."

Aram has been standing too long. He returns to the couch, covers his lap with the afghan, and holds his snifter up to the lamp. The glass is from a set of twelve, a recent gift from Poincaré. A consolation prize, Aram knows. The card may as well have read, *We are sorry, old friend, but no matter how many letters Nubar writes, no matter how many fits Aharonian throws, Armenia will never have a seat at the table.* Aram received a similarly lovely gift, a sterling tea service, after the St. Petersburg fiasco, the rejection of Djemal Pasha's astonishing offer.

Again, Kostya Kobakov's young, eager face flashes in Aram's mind. He should have melted that teapot, sold the silver, donated the proceeds to the cause, or even sent them anonymously to Kostya's widow and three boys, just as he should have smashed the crystal glassware, every bit of it, when it arrived. But he's kept it all. He likes sterling, loves crystal. Beautiful stemware is a reason to keep going, keep hoping. This is a world where some men rape and maim and kill, but this is also a world where other men know how to take God-given sand and fire, apply their own mortal breath, and create exquisite goblets.

Raffi interrupts Aram's thoughts, which is what Aram expects from Raffi. "Please try to concentrate, *Medz-hayrig*," he says. "I want to hear your view about this latest transgression. I want to know what you are going to do about him."

"It's probably my fault," Aram says. "Did I tell him the north or east station? They've been using both for the trains from Berlin. I may have gotten confused."

"Don't fall on your sword for him," Raffi says. "You never make mistakes."

"I never make mistakes? I'm the fellow who thought you two would work well together."

"How were you to know he would be so irresponsible? It infuriates me to think what would have happened if I'd failed to change my plans at the last minute. If I had not been on the Orient Express myself, we would be right back where we started. All our hard work to find Kerim Bey, *pffft*, up in smoke. We need to do something about him."

"Not yet," Aram says wearily. "For now, we'll just keep an eye on him. The leaders in Berlin wish to wait until all diplomatic avenues are exhausted. There is the new Republic to think of. At any rate, that's their refrain. So we will wait. We will play the role of politicians and diplomats just a little bit longer. I don't like it myself, but that's what we'll do."

Raffi finishes his drink, pours another. "Aslan," he says, "you know I wasn't referring to Kerim Bey. I meant Dub. We need to do something about Dub."

Aram frowns. He *didn't* know that's what Raffi meant. "Oh," he says. "Oh. Dub, we'll draw and quarter. Dub, we'll tar and feather. Quick, go ask Kevork if we've an old guillotine in the attic."

The pain in his back has sharpened. He wishes Raffi were, if not gone, then at least in another room. He wants to let his knees buckle; he wants to drop to the floor, squat there, forehead touching the floor-boards.

He has to wait for the pain to diminish before he can speak. "Raffi," he says then, "my dear son. Let me teach you how one leads men. First, one puts aside one's emotions. One looks at each situation calmly and rationally. You say that Dub wasn't at the station today? Yes, that might have resulted in a problem for us. But the fact is, *you* were at the station. So no problem arose." The pain is nearly gone now. "And you ask what would have happened had you failed to change your plans. But change them you did. The fact is, dear Raffi, everything has turned out fine. Thanks to you, we know where Kerim Bey is staying. The mission has been successful, and you have once again covered yourself in glory. When you return to Berlin, you will receive praise and a promotion and even better assignments. So why be distressed? Why not be eager to get on to the next problem? Sit down. Stop pacing. Tell me about the Berlin operation."

Raffi sits at the desk, his snifter balanced on the edge of one knee. The brandy sloshes from side to side as he speaks. "I can't bear to talk of Berlin," he says. "People dropping dead in the streets. They have nothing to eat. They fight over moldy bread. The blockade is very effective and very cruel." He stops. "But that's not what you're asking me. All right, Berlin. Well, we know where Nazim and Shakir are living. We have people watching them all the time, but as you say, the leadership wants us to do only that: just look at them and do nothing. So we spend our lives outside their windows or skulking in the corners of their filthy coffeehouses, where we get to watch them play backgammon with exiled Syrians and Algerians all day long."

"And the triumvir?"

"That's another story. After all this time we still don't have the first clue where they are. It's damned annoying because we're nearly certain the British know exactly—Talaat at the very least—but won't admit it."

"I did ask Poincaré to speak to Balfour," Aram says. "He says Balfour swears the Brits know less than we do."

"Balfour's lying. Did you read Bryce's last statement? 'Talaat ought to be hanged if only he can be caught.' Bryce probably believes it too. He's sincere, I think. He saw everything, after all. But the rest of them, they're frauds. They could have him in an instant if they cared to. We have no allies in this business. The atrocities served their purpose. Propaganda. Moral outrage. And now the war is over and the outrage is gone. I don't believe they truly want the criminals found or tried or hanged. I believe in the end we will have to do everything ourselves."

"If so, then we will."

"But not until Berlin says we can? No, it's a mistake. We ought at least to establish a deadline. A day by which, if justice has not been meted out by Europe, then we act. Or perhaps we should kill one of them, just to show what will happen if the world dares ignore us this time. Show them a little blood, this time not in our faraway mountains but in their own cities, their streets."

Raffi stands again. He's been sitting long enough. He's been talking for as long as he can tolerate talking. Dub is the man of languages. Raffi just wants to move around, find a target, pull a trigger the way he used to in the Caucasus.

He misses pulling triggers. Maybe later, he thinks, he'll go out to the copse, pin a fez to a tree, shoot it to ribbons.

CHAPTER NINE

Peacock Eggs

THE QUESTION IS THIS: Should they or should they not open the traveling case?

As they near Senlis, Yale, Brennan, and, to a lesser extent, Dub debate the question, screaming to be heard over the wind. It isn't much of a debate; they all quickly come around to the affirmative. Of course they will open the traveling case. It belongs to a rich woman; it might contain exotic perfumes or cosmetics or table linens, or, better yet, expensive jewelry that, Yale says, can be pawned and the proceeds donated to the fight for justice (which is how Yale has begun characterizing whatever it is these Erinyes people are up to, and Dub, so far, has neither corrected her nor agreed with her nor said much at all).

Brennan declares herself against selling jewels. "If there are valuables in there, they should go to you, darling," she yells. She speaks only to Yale, treating Dub as if he were a hired driver. "He only wanted the address," she shouts. "Anything else rightfully belongs to the person who took all the risks."

Shaking with cold, her head turtled down inside her coat, Brennan wonders if there might not be a muff of red fox inside the small case. If there is, that will be hers. She took a risk too, flirting with a potato-faced porter, aiding and abetting a cause she cares nothing about.

Though he says little about it, Dub also wants the case opened. He believes it may contain ill-gotten goods. Like Yale, he pictures jewels but stolen jewels, a suitcase full of wedding rings, brooches torn from garments, earrings pulled from lobes. Or what if there is something even more valuable inside; what if there is information? A list with the whereabouts of Kerim Bey's fellow lamsters. A postcard addressed to Talaat Pasha's German hideout. A diary in Kerim's own hand in which all his crimes are recounted and dated, a document stinking with hubris and guilt, providing irrefutable grounds for arrest. Mustafa Kemal's new government would have no choice but to conduct the trials it has promised. Executions would follow, carried out not by guys like Raffi or Dub but by an executioner: that is, a professional with a rope and gallows and a sealed court order.

"Of course we'll open it," Yale yells back, "but let's wait till we get where we're going. Let's see what Monsieur Kazarian says about it."

Monsieur Kazarian. Dub has filled them in on that much. Where they are going, who they will meet. Yale has never heard of Aram Kazarian, and while Dub is not surprised by this omission in her otherwise extensive knowledge of all things *Hai,* he is a touch disappointed, the way a scholar might be disappointed by an impressive autodidact who's somehow missed out on, say, Homer.

Yale's mention of Monsieur Kazarian, meanwhile, makes Brennan think about the true purpose of their trip. "What do Armenians eat?" she asks Yale.

Dub swerves around a deep hole in the road. "We gnaw on bark," he shouts.

"They eat rice," says Yale.

"I hate rice," Brennan says.

"You do not hate rice. Who hates rice? It's like hating water. And they eat lamb. Lots of lamb."

"As if anyone can get lamb these days."

"The rich can get whatever they want," Dub calls back at her, and this offends Brennan in a way that his previous, snider comment failed to. She throws herself back into her seat, covers her red nose with her red hands.

"Swell," she grumbles. "Dinner with rich revolutionaries."

Still, she gasps when she sees those iron gates. Even in the dark they are towering and complicated and beautiful. And she finds herself awed by the bare and sculptural sycamore branches canopying the driveway. And when they turn left at the verdigris fountain and a white peacock darts across the gravel and is, for a moment, illuminated by the Fiat's headlamps, she feels a jolt of emotion that shakes her to the core.

"Oh, did you see that?" she cries out softly, and then, minutes later, when she sees the château, she cries out again. "Jesus, Mary, and Joseph," she says, an oath from her mother's side of the family that has apparently stayed with her all these years and slipped out only now.

But, as it turns out, Aram Kazarian does not wish to open the traveling case. This is not simply because Dub has, in an uncharacteristic turn of events, brought unannounced guests with him. It's also because the address on the tag attached to its handle is not the address Raffi has reported to him.

"Where did you get that?" Aram whispers, while the girls shed their coats, hats, scarves.

"The wife had it when she got off the train," Dub says. "I waited until the porter's back was turned and then grabbed it and ran."

Aram's voice becomes a bit more urgent. "Raffi says he followed Kerim Bey to the hôtel le Marais. He says the family took up residence there."

Raffi nods, grins, glitters. "It's true, *tratsi*." He points to the tag. "Bernard Klein, it says. You've stolen some poor tourist's overnight bag."

When he first spotted Raffi in Aram's foyer, Dub wanted to climb back into the Fiat and drive away into the night, into the sea, somewhere, anywhere else. He'd taken Raffi's hand instead, given him half an embrace. "All I know, Aram," he says now, "is that Kerim's wife had this in her possession." He glances at Yale as he uses his fingers to comb the gray forelock out of his eyes.

"We'll discuss it when the three of us are alone," Aram says. He too glances at the American girls, these uninvited, unidentical twins. They harp at each other, the taller twin haranguing the shorter, complaining in English about her proximity to frostbite and malnutrition, perhaps even death. Aram herds the lot of them into the kitchen.

His wife is upstairs writing letters to her daughters. The bonne is in Paris with a klatch of other housemaids. The old servant Kevork has retired for the evening. But Aram is not incompetent in a kitchen, and late at night he sometimes feels better than he does in the mornings. Something about darkness rejuvenates him, and he feels hospitable as he pours a Bordeaux for all but Raffi, who has decided to continue imbibing the frightfully expensive Armagnac.

At the cast-iron stove, Aram prepares omelets, and the girls marvel as if the eggs he's cracking against the rim of a blue porcelain bowl were made by Fabergé. They haven't seen fresh eggs since the States, the smaller, darker twin tells him. The taller twin asks if these happen to be peacock eggs.

"Peacock eggs!" Raffi echoes with chilling disdain.

Aram arranges an omelet on each plate and adds a stuffed grape leaf and a chunk of the bread the bonne baked that morning. He puts out a plate of green olives. He apologizes for the absence of butter.

"I thought you said we could get anything here," the taller twin says. She is attractive in a contemporary way, Aram thinks, but she is also a crotchet. She is rebuking Dub, but it's Aram who places his hand on her shoulder.

"I am well off, my dear," he says, "but I'm not a magician. I can't produce butter when there is none in the country, just as I can't persuade my peacocks to lay eggs."

Brennan colors, but the disfigured hand on her shoulder is comforting and forgiving, and she is glad to be someplace warm. She and the others, all except Aram, start to eat. Aram remains by the stove, his lower back pressed against, soothed by, the heat. From this vantage point he watches Raffi, whose mouth is full and whose eyes are on Dub. He has asked Raffi and Dub not to speak of the suitcase in the presence of these girls, but he sees the expression on Raffi's face.

"So," Raffi says in his stilted English, "as I am understanding it, you are telling me you are at the train station this evening. And yet I am there too and am not seeing you anywhere. And believe me, *tratsi*, I am looking for you intensively. So tell me, please, precisely where on the platform you are positioned today."

"I was there," Dub mumbles. "Let's discuss it later."

"Yes, but where? Just tell me upon what number track you are standing."

Dub says nothing more, and Raffi smiles as if he now has his answer.

A gold tooth, Yale notices. She has never known anyone who has a gold tooth.

Egg in his mustache. That's what Brennan's looking at. It hurts her, this terrible waste of fresh egg.

Raffi is unaware that they're studying him, that Aram is studying him too. His eyes are only on Dub. "Confess," he says. "You are not there. From where you are acquiring this suitcase, who knows? But it is not from the train station this evening."

That's when Yale realizes who Raffi is. Fools rush in, she is thinking. But she can't help herself. "Dub was too there," she says, placing her fork on her plate, dabbing her lips with her napkin. "You might not have seen him, but he saw you. We all saw you." She doesn't like Raffi. He's not nice to Dub. His eyes are mean and angry, and there's that low-class gold tooth. And maybe she just wants to show off a little, get credit where credit's due. Maybe she wants Aram's attention.

She is successful with that last goal, at least. "Pardon me?" Aram says. "Is that right? You young ladies met the train also?"

Dub is holding his fork in midair. A piece of omelet dangles from a tine. Yale feels her neck heat up. "Well, yes," she says. "I'm sorry, how could you have known; it all came about so quickly. But, yes, we were assisting the lieutenant."

"Ah," Aram says. "How kind of you."

"I didn't have time to check with you, Aram," Dub says. "I had to—" He stops. He puts his fork down. He was going to explain that he had to attend the Peace Conference, but how can he say that when he's just claimed to have been at the station at the same time?

Yale wishes Dub would not try to handle this. He sounds so uncertain. His voice is straining; soon it will be squeaking. She might fall out of love with him if he squeaks. Worst of all, he is distracting her while she is trying to think of what to say next.

As is this Raffi. "This is one absurdity followed by another," he says. "I am telling you, Aram, Dub is not at the station, just as I am telling you that Kerim Bey is not going to the address on that suitcase, which I am also telling you belongs to some tourist who is right now having the heebie-jeebie fits in the *bagage grand vitesse*. I am swearing to you, never once am I allowing Kerim Bey out from under my vision. Kerim is getting into a taxi; I am getting into a taxi. Kerim is disembarking at the hôtel le Marais; I am disembarking at the hôtel le Marais. I am watching him register. I am watching him taking the room key and now, together with that wife and child, he is going up the staircase, and I am right behind him where he cannot see me but where I am seeing him the whole time."

Yale is willing to compromise. "Maybe they're staying at the hotel for only one night."

"Why would he not go directly to the address on the suitcase if that is really his home?"

"How should I know?" Yale says. "Maybe the apartment at the rue des Belles Feuilles is being painted. Maybe he doesn't like paint fumes."

"The apartment at the rue des what?"

Belles Feuilles. It's the address from the traveling case. Bell Fooey, Yale pronounces it.

"For this egregious mispronunciation alone someone should be shooting you," Raffi says. He is smiling his nasty smile at her, his twisted gold smile.

"Hey," Dub says, and Raffi aims the glare of his smile at Dub.

"I apologize," Raffi says. "I am not possessing your fine American manners. I am a peasant from the Dersim sanjak. But I am possessing a modicum or two of common sense. Why is Kerim Bey arriving in Paris today if his home is not to be inhabitable until tomorrow?"

"Maybe his lease in Berlin ran out," Yale says.

Brennan has finished her Bordeaux and most of her omelet. Her head hurts less than it did before. Her fingers have thawed to room temperature. "Maybe they were starving," she says. "There's no food in Berlin, people say. Maybe his wife said, 'Listen, Buster, we are going someplace where they have some food for this child right this minute and that's that.'"

"Dub," Aram says, "are you sure the suitcase belongs to the wife?"

"He's absotively sure," Yale says. "Positulely. We all saw the wife with it. Didn't we, Brennan? And they were the only people aboard the entire train with this kind of luggage."

"It's Vuitton," Dub says.

Raffi rocks back in his chair. It's a very old chair, the seat made of frayed caning, the legs spindly. He balances on one of those spindly legs.

"The question," Yale says, "is not if we're sure the suitcase belongs to the wife. The question is why doesn't Mr. Soghokian know it belongs to her? If he was there, if he saw them? How could he not know?"

Dub can't stop himself; he covers Yale's hand with his, tries to convey warmth, pleasure, pride. At the same time Raffi opens and closes his mouth. He wasn't looking at luggage, he finally says. Why would he be? He was too busy looking at Kerim Bey. He was looking at nothing but Kerim Bey.

"And you wonder why you didn't see Dub," Yale says.

She is beginning to relax. The sequence of events as they must have occurred has come to her now. As Raffi sputters and protests, she arranges, then holds those events in her head. She is like a child with a bouquet of balloons. Fail to hold on tight and the balloons will sail away; they will be lost forever. She tightens her grip, concentrating, letting nothing distract her. As soon as Raffi has finished his attempt to acquit himself, she begins.

"You see, monsieur," she says to Aram, "what happened was that the lieutenant knew Kerim Bey would never suspect my sister or myself, whereas he might suspect a man of the lieutenant's facial characteristics. So the lieutenant asked us to accompany him to the station so he could accomplish his goals while remaining out of sight. To avoid raising Kerim Bey's suspicions, you see. That must be why Mr. Soghokian failed to see the lieutenant. Because the lieutenant concealed himself so effectively. Then, when Kerim Bey left the platform to catch a cab, the lieutenant sent my sister and myself to chase after him, while he stayed behind with the luggage. Isn't that true, Brennan? Didn't we follow Kerim Bey to the taxi stand?"

Done with her omelet, Brennan is considering her grape leaf. She believes it is more than mere garnish. Still, if the little green roll is edible, how does one eat it? One's fingers? A fork? The wrapping seems merely decorative, dark and fibrous and unappetizing, but oily, bloody juices are seeping from that casing. An Armenian hot dog, she thinks, and then she thinks, What the hell. She thinks, Who are these people, and what does their opinion of me matter? She puts down her fork and picks up the small cylinder with her fingers. "Yes," she says. "Yale and I chased the evil Turk to the taxis." Then she tears at the little green roll with her teeth and gets to the ground meat inside.

Lamb.

"Yes. And so then," Yale says, "when Brennan and I got there, they—Kerim Bey and his family—they were situating themselves in the cab, and Brennan and I, we were all set to leap into the next one when Mr. Soghokian here bounded up and stole it from us. We didn't make a fuss over it, of course; we knew he was one of us because Lieutenant Hagopian had pointed him out on the platform."

Raffi, the last of them still to be holding a fork, throws his down.

Yale is as gratified by Raffi's rage as she is with the story pouring from her mouth. She is a golden nymph in a Versailles fountain; the purest of waters is streaming from her lips. She is the miller's good daughter in the fairy tale; she spews gemstones whenever she talks.

From Raffi's lips come angry snakes, crawling insects. "Aram, I am assuring you I am not doing such a thing. I am not seeing these two anywhere. And if I am, how am I to know they are one of us? And if I am stealing their taxi—but no, this is absurd. I am supposed to be chivalrous at that moment in time?"

"Well, of course no one wanted you to give up the taxi," Yale says. "Someone had to chase after Kerim Bey, after all, and what did we care who it was? But just admit you did steal it." The memory still irritates her. "You gave the man at the curb a franc, and then you jumped into our cab. Just admit it because it proves we were there. Or how else would we know all the details? Admit it, because it proves my version of things."

"It does sound like you, Raffi," Aram says. "Not that you did anything wrong."

"That's exactly what we thought too," Yale says. "We said to each other, Brennan and I, 'Oh, let Mr. Soghokian run around after Kerim Bey like a lunatic. We'll go back and help the lieutenant.' Of course, as it turns out, the lieutenant was right behind us by then. He'd snatched up the traveling case completely undetected and come racing down to the cab stand. He was so lickety-split about it, we could have easily held the second cab for him and still have kept up with Kerim Bey. So Mr. Soghokian wasn't really needed at all." She smiles at Aram. "But it all worked out in the end," she says.

"Maybe I am not noticing these two," Raffi says, "but I am absotively certain I would be noticing him if he is there."

"And yet," Dub says, "I was and you didn't." Beneath the table he presses Yale's foot, once, with his boot. Otherwise, he is still. Yale, by contrast, is out of breath as though she's reenacted the chase through the Gare du Nord right there in the kitchen. And Dub's foot upon her foot—she feels a thrumming inside and thinks of comic strips where hearts on springs burst through the chests of their lovestruck owners.

"Besides," she says, "look at the name on the tag. Bernard Klein. The same initials as Kerim Bey."

"She thinks Bey is his name," Raffi says.

"His given name is Kerim Borak," she says primly. She knows she sounds like the kind of schoolgirl who habitually reads ahead in the text. She *is* that kind of schoolgirl when it comes to Armenia. Ask me a date, she thinks. Go ahead, ask me.

It's a different question that Raffi asks. "How is an American *odar* knowing so much pertaining to the most obscure of the Ottoman refugees?"

She's never heard the word *odar* before, but she takes its meaning and knows she's been right all along to despise him. And she's not alarmed. She has long ago figured out the answer to this inevitable question, has only been waiting for the chance to provide it. "The gentleman the lieutenant met up with in the St. Louis Public Library?" she says. "Well, that gentleman"—and though she knows she is taking a chance, she believes it's only a small chance because she remembers everything Dub said in St. Louis, and one thing he said was that no one in Erinyes knew the old man with the guns—"he's my grandfather." She indicates Brennan. "*Our* grandfather. Maternal side."

Our grandfather. Brennan's eyebrow does not fly up. She doesn't even shake her head. She is so completely used to Yale by now. What she isn't used to is this messy delicacy, this stuffed bit of flora. She has already devoured hers, leaf and all. Now she takes Yale's right off Yale's plate. "If you're not going to eat this," she says.

Our grandfather. Dub immediately recognizes the expression on Yale's face. He's seen that expression earlier this very day. *The former French ambassador Harry White? Oh, yes, he's my father. He's my uncle. He's my cousin's third cousin.*

Aram notes it too—*our grandfather.* Part Armenian, part American, and he likes the girl's spirit. A pure Armenian girl (his daughters, his wife, Ramela) he'd protect, he would baby or relegate to the kitchen or keep busy with the children. But an Armenian girl with so much American in her—there are possibilities here.

The other one too, the crotchety sister, she also has gumption and drive. And a huge appetite, which Aram sees as related to the first two qualities. "Lieutenant," she is saying, her chin shining with grease, "are you going to eat your green thingamabob?"

Dub will slap Brennan's hand if he has to. He will stab it clean through with his fork. He takes his dolma in his fingers and devours it in two bites. Then he starts in on his eggs. He is suddenly ravenous, and, even cold and rubbery, Aram's eggs are far superior to the best British steak.

CHAPTER TEN

Parlor Games

WHAT ELSE would one do in a parlor, Brennan thinks, but play a parlor game?

That's where they are now, the Kazarians' front parlor. At some point while they were eating eggs and plants, the mistress of the house came downstairs in a long silk dressing gown and chided her husband for entertaining guests in the kitchen. She ordered them all to abandon their empty plates and repair to the more suitable front room. Brennan demurred. She and Yale should be getting back to Paris, she said, and she looked at Yale and saw that Yale could have throttled her for it, but in the end it didn't matter because Madame Kazarian said no. Madame Kazarian said, "My heavens, driving that machine on these ghastly roads in the darkness? I should lie awake all night fearing for your very lives. Do you not know there are buried mines and booby traps everywhere? No, no, for my sake, you must spend the night here, where we have many bedrooms and many empty beds. I will give you each a lovely nightgown. We have plenty of those also. Now, come have tea in the drawing room and tell me all about yourselves."

The parlor is done up lavishly in pale green velvet, the chairs all from different periods but all the same in their delicacy and great age. All quite uncomfortable too, with flat beaten cushions and wobbly legs. One feels very uncertain in Madame Kazarian's armchairs.

Far less uncertain in her hospitality. She offers tea but winds up pouring cognac. She asks questions about the twins' family. "My father makes airplane parts," Yale says. "My mother died ages ago," says Brennan. "Their grandfather is Armenian," Aram adds.

"And how did you girls meet our Dub?" Madame Kazarian inquires. She wishes to treat these girls as she hopes others treat her own girls. She has four daughters, all married, all scattered hither and yon.

"Yes," Raffi says, "tell us. We are nothing besides our ears."

"Raffi," Madame Kazarian says. "*Amot kezi.*" She smiles at the girls as if they are shy and need to be coaxed.

All heads turn to Yale. "We met at the Quai d'Orsay this afternoon," she says. "Our grandfather gave us a letter of introduction."

"And how are you knowing he will be at the Quai d'Orsay today?" Raffi says.

"Oh, we didn't. We'd gone there for fun. But our grandfather had described the lieutenant, and the minute my sister saw him she pointed him out. Didn't you, Brennan? Pointed him out even though you'd never seen him before?"

"It's true; I did."

"She just knew it was him."

"She knew it was *he*," says Raffi.

"Raffi," Madame Kazarian says, and Monsieur Kazarian says, "Of course. Because of the hair."

"And then I read the letter," Dub says, "from their grandfather, and I figured I could use their help, and I explained what we were up to, and the rest you know."

"You explained what we were up to?" Raffi asks.

Dub swears to himself. He is no good at this.

"Well," Aram says. He is sitting on a particularly awkward-looking chair, a tall back, low seat, stubby little legs. "It seems to have worked out." The word *inscrutable* passes through Yale's mind. Aram is still smiling, and yet Yale has a vision of him kicking Dub in the seat of the pants the moment she and Brennan are out of sight. There is something about this Aram Kazarian with his blue eyes and clawlike hands. He looks as if he can read minds, hers especially. She feels he knows everything about her just as she knows everything about Dub. But he has said nothing, has done nothing to make her feel this way. Even now he is only saying, as sincerely as can be, "We are a pragmatic fellowship. If something works to our advantage, we conclude it was the right choice."

Raffi would kick Dub right now if he thought he could get away with it. "This is absurd," he says. "Aslan! They are handing Dub a letter so right away he is telling them all about Kerim Bey? Some people are requiring to be tortured before they are divulging such secrets, but no, not him. With him all it is taking is a letter. *Khent es?* Anyone could have produced such a letter. Where is this letter? I would like to read such a persuasive document."

"Raffi," says Madame Kazarian.

"It's back in our hotel room," Yale says. "I'll be happy to show it to you, Mr. Soghokian. I only hope the maid hasn't thrown it away."

Brennan smiles. She is, she has to admit, having a good time. She is mildly drunk and there is a plate of chocolates from which to nibble between sips of cognac, and they are playing this parlor game and her side is winning.

She is nearly disappointed when the game is interrupted by a cry, sharp and birdlike, from the second floor.

"Oh dear," Madame Kazarian says to the ceiling, and the room grows immediately still. Then it comes again, now a sirenlike wail, now an unhappy hound dog.

"It's one of the new babies," Madame Kazarian says. She sighs as she stands. "Such nightmares that little thing has. *Le pauvre enfant.* Excuse me, please."

"Oh!" Brennan cries. She surprises herself by leaping to her feet. She is embarrassed as well, but it's too late to sit down, to pretend it never happened. "Oh," she says, apologetically this time. "It's just that I didn't realize. We've been talking so loudly. I'd have spoken much softer. But, oh—" They are all looking at her; she is looking only at Seta. "Oh," she says, "you have babies here?"

"I HAD FOUR little girls of my own," Seta says in the hushed tones of a woman who knows the consequences of waking a sleeping child. "This room belonged to the two eldest."

The three of them, Seta and Brennan and Yale, stand in the dark, moonbeams lighting their profiles, Yale admiring Seta. Aram's wife is in her late sixties and elegant, a small slim woman with large mannish features, nothing pretty about her, and she could soften those features, could do something with her coarse black hair other than pull it off her face and coil it several times around her head, but she doesn't. And yet she is very beautiful. It's her posture, her poise, her serenity. It is the fine cut of the silk gown she wears. Another improbable couple, Yale thinks, the deformed and disheveled Aram in his robe and pajamas, the petite and elegant Seta in silk.

Seta in silk, standing before a crib. In it, facedown, lies an infant in swaddling. The child has stopped shrieking. Now she only fusses. Seta pats the child's blanketed rear end, which is thrust into the air. "They grow up, they're gone," Seta says, speaking of her daughters. She does not sound sad about this. She is just telling these girls how life goes. Her hand slows as she speaks, and, nearly asleep now, the baby whimpers one last time. "This one we haven't bothered naming," Seta says. "A couple named Serabian is coming for her in a few days. I need to warn them. What a glutton for attention this little thing is. I could stand here the whole night patting her bottom, and she would be cross if I stopped at sunrise."

"I could do it, madame," Brennan says. She tries to duplicate Seta's tone, tries to keep her voice swathed in batting.

"Please," Seta says, and steps aside. "So," she says, "as I was saying, my own girls left, and then a few years passed and the house was so empty. But then came the boys, German soldiers. They billeted here. Not our choice, of course. Still, it was nice having children to take care of again." She raises her mannish squared chin. "Oh, I know," she says. "Aram is always telling me: say that around the wrong people, and next thing you know they'll have shaved your head for you. Well, no one would dare tell me what to say in this town. Or dare touch me. Not in Senlis. My family has lived here for generations. My father's rug business, you know. And, please, I didn't invite the Germans here, did I? And certainly I didn't try to stop them from leaving when it was time for them to run home like poor, defeated mice. And of course I was glad they were going home, because it meant the war had ended the way we wanted the war to end. But the truth is they were just lonely farmboys who missed their mothers and wanted nothing more than a good meal and some kindness. It wounded them to see the way they were portrayed in the posters. They were only children, and I would think of their mothers, and here am I, a mother myself. How could I not be motherly with them? I worry about some of them to this day."

She looks at Brennan, who is making small circles on the baby's back. "You could stop now. I think she is asleep."

"It's all right," Brennan says.

"There are others," Seta says. "Come, I'll show you. The older ones are even more cunning. They have more personality when they are four or five. Even when they sleep, you can tell."

They tiptoe from room to room. Cribs and trundle beds, dark-haired children, their lips wet and slightly parted, their breath heavy and audible, sighing, snuffling in sleep.

"After the Germans left," Seta says, "the house again was so empty. Aram is gone so often for his work. I became involved then with the rescue operations. All these little ones were either wrested from their mothers by the Turks or found in the desert during the death marches or else they were born into slavery. The little one in Araxie and Suzanne's room, we believe, is the child of a Kurd and an Armenian slave. We found no traces of the mother, but the baby was in a pile of straw in a bitterly cold barn covered with lice and mouse droppings."

"She won't remember," Brennan says. "She's too young to carry those memories."

"I should think you're right."

"Do you keep any of them?" Brennan says.

"Oh, my dear. We are too old to raise a new family. No, we find them homes. We place them in good Armenian homes."

They sleep among the orphans that night, Brennan in the room with the curly-haired infant, Yale in a room with a pair of wheezing toddlers. The bars of the toddlers' cribs shadow the whitewashed walls. Terrified of having to cope with two keening babies, Yale is careful not to make a sound as she changes into a nightgown that once belonged to a Kazarian daughter, a nightgown more delicate than any dress Yale has ever owned.

Raffi and Dub sleep in the room they regularly share when they stay here, so regularly that Seta calls it "the boys' room," while Aram returns to his study to finish his day's work. Before he can pick up a pen, he's asleep on the tufted leather sofa. Lately, he prefers spending his nights here on the ground floor to sharing a bed with Seta. Alone he can groan, curse, plead with God for relief or release, and no one is alarmed. When the pain takes over he can bite the case on his pillow, tear at it with his teeth like a dog, and Seta never knows a thing about it.

Seta stays up longer than everyone else. She gathers brandy snifters and arranges them on a silver tray and carries the tray into the kitchen, where she leaves it for the bonne to find in the morning. She looks at the omelet pan on the stove and decides to leave that too. She looks at the detritus on the cutting block, the grease and eggshells, an uncorked bottle of red wine. She leaves it all. She pulls the chain and turns out the electric light. Now that it's dark inside, she can see that outside it's begun to snow.

She does not turn on any lamps as she heads to the staircase. She walks skillfully through the darkness. Kitchen, dining room, parlor. She knows where every piece of furniture is. She was born in this house, raised here, married in the garden by the pond. She gave birth four times in the bedroom she's now heading to. She can navigate the house blindfolded.

She stops at Aram's study, listens to his harsh grunts. She loves him but does not miss having him in her bed. No one can sleep with a man who produces such sounds. Forty years was sufficient.

Climbing the stairs, she begins pulling hairpins from her coiled braid, feeling sections tumble down, brush the nape of her neck. Some pins slip and fall to the runner on the stairs. She turns on no lights. The bonne will pick up the pins tomorrow.

She knows the upper floor as well as she knows the first. That's why she stops so abruptly when she reaches the topmost stair. Looking into the general darkness of the hallway, she sees the shadows of decorative chairs, of ornate gold frames, of small tables and Chinese vases. She knows all these shadows.

But she is also seeing a shadow she doesn't know. The new shadow moves, it breathes. Seta shrinks back, presses herself against the wall. She holds on to the banister so she won't inadvertently shift her weight. She doesn't want the stair to creak beneath her. She doesn't want to give her presence away, let the shadow become aware of her, standing so near.

She peers into the hallway again. It's Dub, she sees now. The shadow is Dub's and it is subsuming another shadow, and that shadow is the smaller Miss White. Dub has the girl flat against the wall. His hands are pressing down on her shoulders as if to prevent her from flying away or, more likely, climbing his torso. He is kissing her—and Seta can't help it, the florid adverb comes to her before she can stop it—passionately. Kissing her madly. "Oh, Yale," he says between kisses. "Oh, Dub," she says in return.

Oh, Yale! Oh, Dub! Seta covers her mouth with both hands. She is afraid she is going to laugh so loudly she'll wake the whole house. The thought is horrifying in a comical way—Raffi would come running, and then he'd begin shouting, and then there would be all those crying babies.

Her hands still pressed to her mouth, Seta turns and descends the stairs, keeping to the oriental runner so her footsteps are muffled.

In the kitchen she leans against the messy cutting block as she laughs. "Oh, Yale!" she whispers, her tone mad and impassioned. "Oh, Dub!" She laughs for quite a while and then, wiping her eyes, pours herself some brandy. Nothing else to do now, she fills the sink, washes the dirty dishes. She scrubs the cast-iron pan, she cleans and dries the snifters. She decants the red wine. She should have done all this before. She is turning into such a lazy old woman. Cleaning tonight is the right thing to do; she will give the bonne, who has not had an easy time of it during the war, the gift of a less harried morning.

She is the sort of woman who, now and again, reflects on her life. It has been blessed from her first day to this day, but that doesn't mean she takes her blessings for granted. She is neither blasé nor ungrateful, and she likes conducting a bit of an inventory every now and again so she can marvel at her own good fortune. Her daughters, although far away, are all married and well. Their husbands, all four of them, have come home from the front. As for her German boys, they were not kept as prisoners but, at her behest, were all sent home and are with their mamas again. And upstairs in her house, an assortment of babies sleeps under warm blankets. The very fact that they are alive and at last unmolested is truly a blessing. They bless her home by sleeping in it.

And tonight, in her upstairs hallway, children are once again kissing and thinking that nobody knows.

She is terribly happy. She is energized by her joy. She might not sleep at all this night. Perhaps she'll watch the sun rise. She hasn't done that in ages, stayed up until the sun has painted the bare limbs in the copse a buttery orange.

She fights off a yawn. Such a sad world, she thinks. So often such a cruel world. And yet tonight all is well. Hands plunged in warm soapy water, she smiles. She does love it so when her house is filled with young people.

Part Six

CHAPTER ONE

The Hôtel le Marais

JUST AS YALE and Dub failed to see Seta in the hall of the château, so the next morning they fail to see Amo Winston in the lobby of the hôtel le Marais. Yale might have guessed about Seta. In that crowded château, it was likely that someone would come upon her after she stepped out of her room and just happened to run into Dub, Dub so sweet in his pajamas and bare padding feet and a towel slung over one shoulder. But who would ever have expected Amo Winston to be in the lobby of the seedy hôtel le Marais?

Amo Winston, for her part, is quite aware of Yale. She was on her way to deposit her room key with the clerk before heading off to the rue d'Aguesseau (her shift is to begin half an hour hence), when she spotted Yale at the front desk. Jumping back into the stairwell in the nick of time, Miss Winston stumbled and dropped the key on her booted foot. The key, solid brass and nearly six inches long to prevent guests from accidentally taking it home, injured Miss Winston's big toe. Now Miss Winston is concealing herself in the stairwell as she silently asks God to minimize her pain, while at the same time she thanks God for allowing her to break the key's fall with her person. Had that key landed on the stone floor instead, it would have clanged like a dinner bell, alerting Yale White and the man at her side to Miss Winston's presence.

As it is, Yale is oblivious to Miss Winston. Her only concern is the hotel register. Running a finger along its last pages, slightly smudging the signatures of the most recent arrivals, she looks for the name Bernard Klein. Her eyes skim over the other guests' names, and this is why she doesn't giggle when she comes to the couple registered as Mr. and Mrs. Romeo Julian. The name means nothing to her, that's how fast she's reading. She sees it, rejects it—it is not Bernard Klein—and skims on.

Oblivious.

And even had her eyes lighted on the name long enough to get the joke, never would she have imagined that the Julians were actually

Alban Bliss and Amo Winston. Not in her wildest and most grotesque dreams would Yale have pictured the lumbering, bellowing Mr. Bliss devising this sly yet tender tribute to his affiliation with Miss Winston. Nor would Yale have stopped to reflect, as Amo Winston has many times reflected, that the *nom de lit* alludes not only to love but also to the sorrow that will accompany the couple's inevitable parting. (His wife. His calling. His community standing.)

Yale's mind is on nothing but her morning's assignment, and she has barely noticed the section of Paris where she's carrying it out. She is in the Marais district, the French Jewish quarter. There are six-pointed stars stenciled on the windows of the restaurants, the butcher shops, the bakeries. The men on the street are heavily bearded, many wearing long curled sidelocks. Yale hasn't seen any of it. She has a job to do. Aram Kazarian has entrusted her with this one small task, and she is determined to carry it out brilliantly. She has gleaned that this is how one succeeds in Erinyes, how one gains the respect of its members. To succeed in the Y one must be a true Trinitarian. In Erinyes you just have to do your job well.

And be Armenian, of course. So perhaps it's not that different after all. But it feels different to her. "Aram, she's an *odar*," Raffi protested, when Aram (breathless with pain, desperate to be alone, and equally desperate to conceal his desperation) sent them out that morning. "Her grandfather," Aram said, by way of terse explanation. He was unable to muster more than those two words. My grandfather, Yale thought, remembering the man in the library, the flat hat, the string tie.

While Amo Winston's nine toes throb in sympathy with the one she has crushed, her brain works feverishly. At first she assumed Yale was here to spy on her, but between biting her lower lip so hard she's drawn a small speck of blood and offering prayers of gratitude for pain self-inflicted, Miss Winston has found a moment to persuade herself that this couldn't possibly be true. She and Mr. Bliss have been too careful. This little hotel he found for them is in a part of the city no one from the YMCA ever would visit.

And yet here is Miss White.

Amo Winston stops praying and starts putting two and two together. She recalls the confrontation she had with the two Miss Whites aboard the *Espagne*. The Jew and the Jew-lover, and now here is the Jew-lover and she's with—who else, but her Jew lover! For it's obvious that the soldier by Yale's side is her paramour; as Yale bends over the register, the soldier snakes an arm around her waist. And it's equally obvious that the soldier is a Jew. Amo Winston is looking at his profile, and that profile affords a clear view of his most telling feature.

Amo Winston is appalled not only because Miss White is having a dalliance with this Jewish soldier (she too is having a dalliance, after all), but because Miss White and her lover are checking into the hotel at nine in the *matin* when respectable people think only of work. Mr. Bliss returned to the Y an hour ago. Miss Winston was in the process of leaving. But here are these two, an AEF Jew and his little Y-lover, ready to slink into bed. Nine in the *matin*.

Yale has called the desk clerk over. Amo Winston stands very still, trying to hear what's being said. She can't, though; she can only see the clerk shaking his head. Now Yale confers with the soldier. Now the soldier nods and reaches into his pocket. The soldier gives the desk clerk several wrinkled francs. Now everyone nods and the clerk, at the same time, writes something on a piece of paper and pushes the paper across the front desk. The number of their room, no doubt. The hotel is fully engaged, but the soldier has bribed the clerk into giving them—what? The maid's room? The broom closet? The room Amo Winston has only just vacated?

But, no. Amo Winston is wrong. Yale slips the scrap of paper into her coat pocket, and she and the soldier walk out the door.

The coast finally clear, Miss Winston steps into the lobby at last. She gives her key to the clerk and hobbles out to the street. The January air is biting, but it is also the second sunny day in a row, and despite her aching toe Miss Winston is in a fine mood. She looks up and down the rue and, coast clear again, limps a few yards to the corner. She looks right, then left, and continues on toward the metro. She is eager to get to work. First to the clinic to see about this toe and then to tell the other matrons. Although—a conundrum. How to spread the news without exposing herself?

Lost though she may be in her dilemma, she has enough presence of mind to hurl herself against a patisserie window when a flock of local Jews pass by in their dirty black frock coats, their dirty black hats, their dirty black hair and beards. The men take up the whole of the rue des

Rosiers. It's as if they think there is no one else in the world. So rude, she thinks. So self-absorbed, so clannish.

That last thought taps her on the shoulder. *So clannish*. She wants to smack her forehead with her fist. Of course! she thinks. What has been wrong with her all this time? The way Jews stick together. You saw them every day in this part of Paris, speaking their private guttural language, all spit and phlegm. And their constant shoulder-to-shoulder. Eyes only for each other.

Besides, who else could stand to sleep with one?

Who else would defend one?

Twins, she thinks. Sisters, she thinks. Those girls are such liars, she thinks.

More than ever she can't wait to reach the Y. Never mind the clinic, never mind sharing secrets with other women. When she reaches headquarters she will go directly to Alban's room. She finally has a valid reason to interrupt the time that the Reverend Mr. Bliss calls sacrosanct: the time he devotes to his letters home. This will violate his most sacred rule, of course, and he'll be vexed at the outset, but she will explain, and then he will understand and forgive her. He could not reasonably expect her to keep this news from him until their late-night rendezvous at the Marais. The scope of this lie! The audacity of those two girls! Alban will want to know immediately. He will know how to intervene, perhaps how to save them. Plus the fact that one of them was at the hotel. He'll want to know that as well.

She will go to his room. She will knock on his door.

CHAPTER TWO

Yah-el

WHEN HE'S SOBER, Dub Hagopian is a careful driver. He maintains a safe speed. He signals with his arm extended out into the cold. Yale wasn't expecting such care from him, but here it is. Relieved of any duty to help him by shouting out warnings, she is free to help him another way. She kneels in her seat and looks into the back of the Fiat.

Brennan and Raffi have been sitting there, on opposite ends of the long wooden bench, since the quartet left Senlis. They have not said a word to each other or to anyone else. Now Yale's face comes at them, talking away. "Well, you owe me a martini, Mr. Soghokian," she says. "For a meager bribe of three lousy francs, the clerk told all. Yes, the Turk is staying at the hotel just as you said, but for two additional nights only—as I predicted. Then he moves to an apartment in the Trocadero. And guess what the address is?"

"The rooey Bell Fooey," Dub calls over his shoulder.

"So, Mr. Soghokian, where shall we go for you to pay up?"

"The Deauville," Dub says. "We'll all go tonight."

"We could go after lunch," Yale says.

Dub shakes his head. "I have to show my face at Translation. They'll think I've gone joyriding if I don't show up at all. Don't you ladies have to show your faces at the Y?"

Yale slides back down in her seat, faces forward. Shops and cafés on her right. The Louvre on her left, the exhibition halls still closed, but a thrill just to see the imposing gray stones. "Oh, it's all chaos there," she says. "Too many cooks at the Y these days. The good thing is, no one really cares what we do anymore."

"Our shift begins at three," Brennan calls. She holds on to the bench seat, trying not to slide off or closer to Raffi. "We have to be there by three."

Yale is back up on her knees. "And if we're not, what will happen? Will they put us overboard in a little lifeboat and leave us to our own devices?"

"None of this is making sense," Raffi says. He sits at the far end of the bench, looking outside, speaking to lampposts, to chickens hanging in windows, to nurses with long capes and winged hats. "Why are they living in a hotel if already they are renting a flat?"

"I'm telling you," Yale says. "It's the paint fumes."

He looks at her now, contemptuously. "Then answer this, you who have all the answers. Why are they staying in the third arrondissement if then they are moving all the way to the sixteenth? Why are they not finding a hotel in the same district?"

Yale sighs. Does she have to do everything for this guy? "Maybe they're trying to throw us off their trail," she says. "Maybe they know the owner of that hotel, and he promised them a reasonable rate. Maybe they want to see the place des Vosges. Maybe they first fell in love in that very hotel and are taking a few days to relive their glorious youth."

"Maybe they like how anonymous and hidden it is," Dub says. "It's where people go for secret rendezvous and trysts." He feels eyes. "Some of the fellows at Translation mentioned it."

"Maybe it's the only hotel in Paris with a vacancy," Brennan says. "Now that the Peace Conference is under way, people say it's impossible to find a room."

"Or maybe," Yale says, "they're just dopes."

Raffi, she thinks, is also a dope. He can't think ahead, he isn't imaginative, he has no talent for what if's and maybe's. He can't dissemble, can't hide his anger beneath a smile. And these, Yale feels strongly, are things a person in his line of work ought to be able to do.

She is going to be better at spying than he is. She is going to be better than either of these two men, the one already her enemy, the other already her love, though the word *love* has not been spoken between them.

"Come up," Dub says, when he parks on the rue Royale. He helps Yale out of the truck, does not have to help Brennan, who has already helped herself. "I'll show you ladies American HQ."

"And what?" Raffi says. "Again I am to be waiting in the cold like a lump on a log?"

Dub is feeling enthusiastic, upbeat. He does not want to be shadowed by Raffi, the purveyor of black clouds. "We won't be long. I'm just going to pick up the work on my desk. In the meantime, decide if you want to go somewhere besides the Deauville."

"How am I to be deciding this?" Raffi calls. "I am not the expert of nightclubs. You are forgetting I am eating rancid bread in Berlin all this time while you are gallivanting among your myriad boîtes."

There is something about the way he spits the word *boîtes*—Yale has to laugh. The sun is gone, and snow is beginning to fall again, slick and slippery, fat oversized flakes; the weather is playful and puppyish. Yale feels licked on the nose. "Watch your step," Dub says. Yale takes his arm and takes Brennan's as well, the three of them connected and safe.

She wonders if she looks fetching, as Brennan does, or merely bedraggled with snow in her hair.

"Have you ever made a snowman?" she asks Dub, as they clatter upstairs. It has just occurred to her that she never has. If it keeps snowing, she says, they can make one in front of the house in Senlis. The orphans might like to help. Of course, if they turn right around and drive back to Senlis, it will mean deferring drinks at the Deauville. Would Dub and Brennan mind terribly? Of course, there are wonderful drinks at the Kazarians' too, all those faceted decanters set about here and there, filled with colorful liquids. It would be fun to go back to the château, wouldn't it? They could taste every color and then make a snowman. Is there a word for snowman in French? *Homme de neige?*

"*Un bonhomme de neige*," Ned Harden says. He is jubilant. The word for snowman—he knows that one. He is the only one in the office this morning, has been sitting at his desk, feet up, reading an American newspaper. He rises when he sees the women, gives Yale a hug. "It's you," he says. "Miss White. My best friend. My savior."

He keeps an arm around her. He asks Dub how the first session went. How odd, Yale thinks, that they never got around to talking about the conference last night. True, they couldn't speak of it once they got to the château. But even on the way up. The most momentous event in the world, and they spent their time talking about a small valise.

"Apple pie," Dub says. He is such a different man here. He is assured, at ease. "Here are my notes." He removes a rolled sheaf of papers from inside his jacket.

"Can't thank you enough," Ned Harden says.

Both men are feeling expansive and inordinately fond of each other this morning. Dub sits on the top of his desk, plants his boots on his chair. "Can you read my scribble? And listen, just write it up. As if you were there. Let's monkey-wrench with history."

"Well, if you really don't mind."

"No, no, it's definitely how we should handle it. And, listen, you'll never believe it. It turned out to be a good thing one of us was there after all. Mantoux actually botched Lloyd George's tribute to Clemenceau. Lloyd George stands up and calls Clemenceau the grand young man of

France, and Mantoux translates it as grand old man. All kinds of hell breaks loose."

"Mantoux. *Quel idiot.*"

"Yeah, and then Wilson gets up and chin-wags for—no kidding—forty-five blessed minutes. You can take the professor out of Princeton, but—you know how the song goes. Everyone in the place was yawning except for Clemenceau, and that's only because the grand young man had literally fallen asleep in his chair."

Ned drops his jaw for comic effect. "Jeez, Hagopian, I wish I could have been there."

"You were there. It was all you. I don't want the official report to so much as mention my name."

"Well, that's really mighty white of you, Hagopian."

"No, it's fine. And tell House or Lansing, will you, that at the end, when you were walking downstairs, you overheard Jules Cambon say the conference was going to be a farce."

"That's awfully cynical," Yale says. "Isn't it a bit too soon to dismiss all hope?"

Dub smiles at her. He thinks of his dinner with Hamilton and Lindsey. He thinks of Djemal Pasha's offer in St. Petersburg. Peace proffered on a silver platter. Peace crumpled up and thrown away by the Allies as if it were a soiled rag. Kostya Kobakov looking down at his feet while he presented the crumpled rag to Aram. "Monsieur Kazarian," Kostya said, "I'd almost have rather shot myself than come to you with such bad news."

"No," Dub says, and Yale hears the shift in his voice, looks at him carefully. She sees the difference in his posture. His head is down. Gray hair flops over his forehead. "No," he says, "it's not too soon. It's hardly too soon. It's far too late."

"Oh, for Pete's sake," Brennan says. "It's only the second day."

She has been standing in the threshold, too grumpy to come inside. Now Ned Harden looks over at her, and, when he does, he steps back, hoists himself up, and sits on top of his desk the way Dub does. There is a framed photograph there, a Red Cross nurse he's been known to cut up with from time to time. He reaches around and tips the photo over. He smiles at Brennan and tells her his name.

AT THE VERY SAME TIME, only a few streets away, the doughboy assigned to work the front desk at 12, rue d'Aguesseau decides to abandon his station to play a friendly game of gin rummy with the Reverend Mr. Bliss and two other lay preachers. The doughboy leaves a sign by the push bell that says RING FOR SERVICE. Then he goes into the back and proceeds to beat the pants off the men of the cloth.

The doughboy is having such a lucky round, he's figuring on ignoring the bell should anyone ring it. But nobody does, not even Raffi Soghokian, although the information Raffi is seeking is within the purview of that cardsharp from Kansas, now six bits to the good.

Raffi is looking around the place, getting his bearings. The lobby is crowded with Y-girls milling about, carrying trays of coffee and biscuits. Servicemen play checkers and dominoes, read newspapers, write letters. Raffi buys a chocolate bar from a bowlegged brunette—the trouble with ever-shorter skirts: nothing's a secret anymore, not even the things that should be. He unwraps the chocolate and takes a bite. Then, without looking to see if anyone's watching, he goes about his business. He steps behind the front desk. He finds the ledger listing the Y-girls in residence tucked beneath one of the leather ends of the blotter. Flipping to the last page, he locates the two names he wants, the single room number he needs. He turns to the warren of mail slots behind him, takes the appropriate key. Dropping his candy wrapper on the floor, he trots up the stairs.

The fifth floor is as empty as the lobby was jammed. The door to the White girls' room opens easily, as if the lock recognized the key before it was fully inserted. Yale's letters are in the first spot he searches, under the mattress of the bed nearer the door. It's a substantial packet of mail he withdraws, pale blue envelopes tied with a ribbon, each envelope stamped with a St. Louis postmark. Tugging at the knees of his Russian uniform trousers, Raffi sits on the bed and shuffles through the envelopes.

At first he doesn't notice, but then he is surprised—no, more than surprised; he is flabbergasted—to read the name written in the upper left-hand corner of each one of those envelopes. He goes through all the envelopes again. The name above the return address is always the same.

After he has had a few minutes to think about it, however, if he remains surprised, it's only at his own stupidity. He should have guessed, by virtue of her extraordinary pushiness, her great big mouth.

Now he begins removing letters from envelopes. Each letter is one page long, none longer, none shorter, and the stationery is always the same too, a proper ecru, though the ink is a tawdry violet. The signature doesn't vary either. *With affection, Your Mother.* As for the greeting, it's slightly off. He thinks he must be misreading it. He thinks maybe it's the room. Shaped like a trapezoid, it's making him slightly dizzy.

He looks at the greeting again. He is not misreading it. Every letter begins this way: *Dear Yael.*

"Yah-el," he says out loud.

CHAPTER THREE

An Ugly Look

AS FOR THE CONTENTS of the letters, they would be unbearably dull except for the fact they contradict every last thing the girl said the night before. The mother whom Brennan claimed died ages ago writes of the father Yale claimed makes airplane parts:

> *Your father's factory has begun producing the new-style corset. This model minimizes the bosoms rather than the waist. It's an ugly look if you ask me, although I know you don't ask me. And yet it is a look that seems to have captured the fancy of your generation, and, knowing your tastes for contemporary garments, no doubt you yourself will be embracing it soon enough if you have not already done so. Although perhaps the fashion is different in France. One can only hope the stylish French woman has a higher regard for her bosoms than our own American girls do.*

There is no mention of Brennan, no *Send my love to your sister* addendum or even a hint that the mother knows her two daughters are in France together. There is no mention either of an Armenian grandfather, nor are there any letters from him.

In a bureau drawer, beneath petticoats and knickers and God knows how many pairs of gloves, Raffi finds a framed photograph of two older people. He assumes the woman is the affectionate mother. The man, then, is Yale's father, Mr. Weiss, who is apparently too busy making the new-style corset to dash off the occasional note to his child. In the photograph, Mrs. Weiss sits in a plain chair and looks ahead warily, as if she fears the camera is a practical joker that will, should she let down her guard, squirt a stream of lemon juice into her eye. The little father stands behind her, his hand on her shoulder, wire glasses wedged on the end of his large nose. He has a look of anxiety about him. Raffi sees none of Yale in the man. He sees her perfectly in the mother's little eyes and pugnacious chin.

He puts the portrait back where he found it. Once more, he sits on the bed, this time to gather his thoughts. The lie about her race he can almost understand. He would rather go to his grave than lie about his own origins, but he knows it's typical of the American *Hria* to deny who he is. Although—to try to pass as Armenian? That's a new one. And what about the claim that the two women are sisters, twins no less? What is the purpose of those lies?

It's the lie about the mother that troubles him most. He knows he can never forgive such a lie, will never forget that these girls could commit such casual matricide even if only in conversation. It's not because he gives a damn about their fat Jew of a mother. It's because there are bones of Armenian mothers scattered across the Syrian desert. There are bodies of Armenian mothers half buried in the silt floor of the Euphrates. In the air above Adana, there will forever be ashes of Armenian mothers.

Let their mother die. It's his vicious prayer to his vicious God. Let these daughters understand what it really feels like. He is thinking about the massacres now, that cruel parade of mothers. He is thinking about his own loss too, his older sister, his real sister, not a false sister like Yah-el's Brennan but his own Maro, mother to two little ones and maternal, always, to him. Maro, who bathed and dressed him when he was a child, who taught him to tie his laces, who fed him in the mornings and told him stories at night and who insisted his father send him to Christian school so he could grow up to be something other than a sheepherder. In the evenings he would sit on her lap as she worked with him on his English letters. Tall man with a big head and a cane: *R*. Fat pussycat with a little tail: *a*. A pair of hunchbacks wearing bow ties: *f f*. A little boy with a bright idea: *i*.

Memories, his little sister Ramela once told him, are like swallowing razor blades.

And you don't remember half what I remember, he had replied.

He searches the rest of the misshappen room for signs of Brennan White's true identity, but there are no clues. Either she receives no letters or she is the more professional of the two and knows to discard incriminating evidence. Still, what a team. Mata and Hari. The question is, what do they want?

When he steps out of the room, the door across the hall opens slightly and an older woman peeks out. She looks, he thinks, like a giant laboratory rat, her face slathered with white vanishing cream, her eyes pink from weeping. She sniffles and glares at him before she looks up at the ceiling with disgusted exhaustion. "Lord have mercy," she says.

"Yes," Raffi replies. "Wouldn't that be a nice change?" He tips his cockaded cap, even though by now the woman has slammed her door, turned the lock, and is safe within her room, where she has resumed her sobbing. Raffi can hear her as he walks down the hall.

Outside, the snow has stopped falling; the sun shines weakly. He is glad there will be clear skies and clean roads as he drives back to Senlis. He puts the Fiat into gear and takes off.

THOSE TWO GIRLS, he thinks as he drives. Are they gold diggers who have mistaken Dub for a wealthy man? Agents of the U.S. government? Are they employed by the Turks? At the Gare du Nord when Dub's back was turned, did they run up to Kerim Bey and whisper in his ear, "Careful, Effendi, they're on to you"?

He has to admit that most likely they are not spies. Most likely they are two dipsy dames in search of adventure. (From St. Louis, he thinks. And Dub so late that day, way back when. And Dub refusing to say why.)

This Yah-el, then. Just an American Jew mad for Dub.

Yet even as he keeps his eyes on the facts, he is blindsided by feelings. He thinks of Ramela waiting back home in Providence, and he feels heartache on her behalf, and he does with that heartache what he always does with his heartache. He fantasizes guns, bullets, swords, knives, revenge.

He is almost at Aram's front door when the snow resumes, blowing at him, lighting on his cap, his nose, his mustache. He parks, and Aram comes outside in his crimson robe and blue slippers. Raffi sees the confusion in Aram's eyes when he realizes it's just the one boy—and the wrong boy—inside the green truck. And in the eerie blue light cast by the blanketed sun, for the first time for a long while, Raffi also sees Aram. "*Medz-hayrig?*" he says, and the greeting comes out a question, because Raffi, for the first time, is seeing the old man's pallor, the skin yellow and flaccid, the silver mane as thin as the knees of a pair of old trousers. Along with alarm, Raffi feels an avalanche of tenderness. *Avalanche.* It's the word he comes up with, because he feels entombed in his feelings, yet they are as soft and lovely as snow. Snow is everywhere now, swirling around them. "*Medz-hayrig,*" Raffi says again, "let's go inside."

"Where is Dub?" Aram says. He is casting about the inside of the truck as if Dub may be bound and gagged in the back, as if it has finally come to this between these two.

"Off with American women," Raffi says. He reaches toward Aram, tries to urge him into the house. Aram shrugs him away. "And how have you wound up with this vehicle? Have you joined the American army?"

"No one else was using it."

"Steal from the AEF, that I don't object to. But do not steal from your brother."

Always, thinks Raffi, this concern for Dub. Dub the prodigal. Dub the *deumreuck*, the fuck-up who is betraying Ramela with this *odar*, this Yale White, this Yah-el Weiss. Dub who has allowed Aram to grow old and sickly.

"I didn't steal anything from anyone, *Medz-hayrig*. He wasn't using it, and I needed it."

"He knows you've taken it? He gave you his permission?"

Raffi wants Aram to look at him, not the truck. He wants to be allowed to escort Aram inside. They will sit by the fire and drink French brandy. In whatever language Aram prefers, Raffi will remind him of the first time they met. Do you remember, he will say, how I said I wanted to be *madagh* and you said, Go get some sleep?

My turn to take care of you. This is what Raffi wishes to say. But when they finally enter the house, stomping their feet, shaking off snow, Aram is also shaking his head and muttering, and Raffi is keeping his mouth shut. He asks no questions about Aram's health. He says nothing about the passing of power, the mantle of leadership. He doesn't mention lies or Jews or corsets. The things he planned to tell Aram he cannot bring himself to say. Nor will he tell Dub. Which means there is no one to tell. He will have to take care of everything on his own. He will have to keep his own eye on the Misses Mata and Hari. And when the time is right, when Kerim Bey is in his new home, believing himself safe, as willing to forget his crimes as the world seems to be—the grotesque march through the desert he helped organize and orchestrate—then Raffi alone will do what has to be done.

CHAPTER FOUR

To Whom It May Concern

A SECOND AEF vehicle arrives in Senlis an hour later. Aram looks out the window and sees it, a motorcycle slipping in the snow, driven not by Dub, who sits behind the driver, holding on tight, nor by either of the American girls, who are both in a sidecar, their hair dripping wet, their chins tucked against their chests, but by an equally drenched army captain, a huge albino with an overseas cap set forward on his head and a lead foot inside his boot, and no talent whatsoever for navigating snow-slicked driveways.

So, Aram thinks, Dub has brought an officer to arrest Raffi for stealing the Fiat. The pain in his back burns the length of his spine, and he clenches every part of his body he is capable of clenching—fists, toes, teeth, eyes, the humiliating parts too, the nether parts that are starting to join in, produce pain, leave blood—until the agony diminishes and, for a moment, he feels nothing but drained.

He does not rush outside as he did when Raffi arrived, when he still had some energy. He just observes the saturated foursome head for his door. He sees their humiliation. He knows what will happen next. Dub will come rushing into the foyer, dripping on the little oriental rug and shouting for Raffi, and then a fight will ensue. Aram can choreograph the fight. There will be no fists: they are grown men now, his two little boys. Instead they will throw words, each calling the other a Turk, each inviting the other to kiss this or that part of his body, the same nether parts causing Aram such distress.

The pain has returned but has moved into his stomach. What's wrong? Aram asks that organ. You were feeling left out? He limps to the foot of the stairs. He shouts up to Raffi. Raffi doesn't call back, but a baby starts to cry and Aram hears his wife groan.

SPRAWLED ON A BED he considers his own, Raffi is composing a letter to the YMCA. He is writing it in English, printing in capital letters for the sake of clarity and anonymity.

> TO WHOM IT MAY CONCERN: THIS MESSAGE IS TO BEHOOVE UPON YOU THE NECESSITY OF INITIATING FORTHWITH AN INVESTIGATION INTO THE BACKGROUND OF ONE PRESENT CANTEEN WORKER, NAMELY, MISS YALE WHITE, NÉE YAEL WEISS, OF ST. LOUIS, MISSOURI, TOGETHER WITH HER COHORT AND ALLEGED (BUT FALSELY SO) SISTER, MISS BRENNAN WHITE, ADDRESS UNKNOWN.

Then he takes a book by a French scholar and cracks its spine so it lies flat while he transcribes a passage, fiddling some with the language to make his own point. The book, which according to its jacket is recommended by both the *New York Times* and H. L. Mencken, is an attempt to warn Americans of the numerous pitfalls arising from the recent influx of Latin and Slavic immigrants to their shores. Raffi agrees with the author's theories up to a point, that point being the passage late in the text wherein the author describes the Armenian character as cringing. But it's a paragraph from an earlier chapter Raffi's copying now.

IS THERE ANY HOPE OF PRESERVING THE CHRISTIAN TRADITIONS FROM WHICH THE MORAL AND POLITICAL CHARACTER OF AMERICA EVOLVED WHILE THERE ARE ORIENTAL JEWS LIVING SECRETLY AMONG US? CAN THE CHRISTIAN RACE MAINTAIN ITS INTEGRITY WHEN JEWS CONCEAL THEMSELVES IN ITS MIDST AND WITH SEXUAL INTERCOURSE MORE COMMON THAN PEOPLE CARE TO ADMIT?

He is underlining that last part when he hears Aram's strained voice. He blows the ink dry, folds the letter in two, and tucks it in his pocket. Later he will decide how to sign it. Very truly yours, A concerned American. Sincerely yours, A loyal Y-woman. Believe me, sirs, yours very truthfully, Henry Louis Mencken.

Now he trots down the stairs and, as he does, he can hear the pounding on the door. He can see the motorcycle through the foyer window. He was thinking in English while writing his letter, and now he is swearing in English. "Shit," he says. He looks around and makes sure there is no little orphan within earshot. "Shit, shit, shit," he says.

At the bottom of the stairs, Aram, bent and grimacing, waits for him. "This is your doing," Aram says, pointing at the door. "I am too tired for this. You resolve it. Go ahead. What do you want to do? Shall we pretend no one is home?"

What Raffi wants to do is open the door fast, catch Dub unaware, charge at him, and knock him to the ground. Who are these girls? he wants to shout while Dub grovels in the snow. You *esh,* you shit, how could you have told them everything? And maybe he would do the same with this Yael—push her, knock her on her rear end. A man like Kerim Bey, a man she seems to regard as a buffoon, a harmless joke, would tear her clothes off, rape her, cut off her hair—her head—with his curved sword. Raffi wants to put his foot on her throat. Who are you? he wants to ask. What do you want from us?

He forces himself to remain calm. He remains calm for Aram. He glances at the door, ignores momentarily the pounding. "Well, we're in France, are we not?" he says. "I suppose what we should do is invite them in and offer them food and wine."

"You're growing up," Aram says. Raffi nods. He *is* growing up. Yesterday he arrived in Senlis to complain to Aram. Today he understands there is no need to burden Aram with every last thing. Tomorrow, before he catches the train back to Berlin, he will mail the letter to the Y. This is what the new mature Raffi Soghokian has learned: there are various ways to step on throats.

CHAPTER FIVE

A Girl's Adventures

SOMETIMES YALE THINKS she would like to be a girl reporter, someone like Clara Savage recording her impressions of Paris, writing newsy and humorous letters home for the popular magazines. But unlike Miss Savage, Yale would write about more than just Paris. She would also write about herself, about love and a young girl's dreams. The humor would arise from the flagrant stupidity of those dreams. The humor would arise from watching the young girl's dreams get dashed one by one.

What had she expected? She came to France in search of romance— the perfect setting, it would seem—but she made a critical mistake. She chose Dub Hagopian to be her swain. And Dub Hagopian, that sad sack of an Armenian, is anything but romantic. He never gets around to taking her to Maxim's. He immediately forgets he promised her cocktails at the Deauville. Certainly he never escorts her to any typical Parisian sights. For Yale, there are no trips to see the Jaconda ("the lady with the strange expression which every critic admires but none can analyse," says *Black's*). There are no ascents to the top of the Eiffel Tower ("safe, but not for those with weak nerves") or descents into the sewers ("interesting if not altogether pleasant"). There aren't even any moonlit drives, evening strolls, frivolous gifts. On St. Valentine's she is presented with no flowers, no candy, not even one of the chocolate bars she herself is selling that day in the canteen. Nor is she ever serenaded in the lobby of Y headquarters as so many other Red Triangle girls are.

No, with Dub Hagopian, a girl does only one of two things. She either sits in a an old green ambulance parked near the apartment of Kerim Bey and family on the rooey Bell Fooey, scribbling notes as if she were somebody's secretary (*Feb 22. Wife/son leave 11:00, return 13:00 w/1 bag groceries, 2 baguettes*). Or she spends time in the medieval city of Senlis getting to know an older couple who reside there, learning to make stuffed grape leaves (shiny side of leaf down, stem at bottom, dollop of rice and lamb in center, then roll, quickly, from stem to stern, jam into pan, and drown with bubbling broth) or spooning mashed peas into the mouths of dark and whimpering babies.

Occasionally there are moments of hope for the hopelessly romantic to cling to, moments of sweet pathetic hope. One morning Yale wakes in the room shaped like a trapezoid and discovers a poem slipped beneath her door (*White* rhyming with *she's all right; Yale* rhyming with *ain't she swell*), and she is touched and excited, if a little embarrassed, and she hides the ode under her lumpy mattress, preserves it among her letters from home, and is especially affectionate to Dub that evening when he takes her to the only restaurant he ever takes her, the dining room at the Crillon, with its mediocre food and unsettling aroma. But soon she discovers that the verse is the handiwork of an adenoidal marine she danced with after a recent sporting event, and she tears it to little pieces, not out of loyalty to Dub but because she's so angry at him for failing to be the poem's author.

Of course, hours later, without ever having told him she was cross, she decides to forgive him. Every day they're together, she decides sooner or later to forgive him. She has to admit she would rather spend time with her dreary lieutenant than all the poetry-writing marines in the world. Because with Dub there may be no romance, but there's something else.

With Dub there's adventure. The trouble is, she can't write articles about her adventures with Dub because these adventures are, first, top secret and, second, extraordinarily dull.

Feb 26. Wife/son leave 11:00. Wife/son return 13:00. 1 bag groceries, 2 baguettes.

"This isn't courtship," Brennan says. "This is political servitude."
Still, Yale has to admit that even if it is servitude, she doesn't mind it.
She likes being part of Erinyes. She loathes the never-seen Kerim Bey,
the way the murderer lives, the fact that the murderer lives. Besides, she
and Dub get a lot of talking done in the Fiat. They discuss their work,
the way colleagues will. They marvel at the spunk of Kerim's little boy,
who is always running or hopping or skipping or pogo-ing down the
street: that is, repeatedly jumping straight up in the air over and over
for no discernible reason. Sometimes the child sneaks up behind an
adult Parisian and imitates the unsuspecting stooge's gait: a three-year-
old loping along, hands thrust deep in the pockets of his little coat, head
down, muttering. The child's mother laughs and applauds. Yale and
Dub can't help but laugh too. They have to summon the image of
orphans the same age as that boy to revitalize their hatred for him, this
child of evil. If he gets in the way of a bullet meant for his father, they
tell each other—well, life is sad, life is suffering.

They marvel too at Kerim Bey, at the man's fortitude or fear or whatever it is that prevents him from ever leaving the flat. To go so long
without fresh air or sunlight . . . "Maybe he dropped dead in there when
we weren't looking," Yale suggests, and Dub says, "Wouldn't *that* be
convenient for all concerned." She has to lecture him then, tell him that
no, it would *not* be convenient, it would not be a good thing, that rather
it would mean Kerim Bey had forever escaped justice. Then they talk
about that—what is justice and should man mete it out as the modern
Armenian priests advocate or just leave it to God as the traditional
Armenian priests advocate—and while they're on the subject they ask
each other if there is a God, and they tell each other that of course there
isn't, and then they agree that this makes what they are doing even more
important because if there's no afterlife, no aftercourt, if there's just this
world needing to be set straight, then good moral people have no choice
but to take arms, take arms, again take arms, even though taking arms is
a painful thing for good moral people to do. And then they see the wife
and little boy again, at which point they shut up, slink down, Yale concealing her face behind the Fiat's big spare tire, as she writes on her pad.

Feb 27. Wife/son 15:00 from fishmongers.

Here's another thing she likes about ambulance-sitting: when they
aren't talking or arguing or jotting down the most trivial information

about Kerim Bey's loved ones and groceries, they are kissing. If it is a dark day, the streets empty, they also pet. Yale has stopped wearing stockings. It's the new style, going barelegged despite the raw weather, the only way to avoid limbs sheathed in snags and tears and runs. But she is older now than she was in St. Louis; she has motives beyond a devotion to fashion. Omitting stockings helps Dub get at her. In the Fiat, staring straight ahead, a comically blasé look on his face, a blanket over their laps, he can reach under her skirt and drive her mad.

She has no word for the part of her to which his hand travels with such alacrity and talent. He has several words for it, most of them French. She doesn't care what he calls it or her, is only pleased he is interested in both. It's a relief to find out he enjoys this sort of thing. A man so unromantic—one should make no assumptions.

He has reassured her, however. He is relentless in his pursuit of the part of her she won't call by any name. On their way to and from the rooey Bell Fooey, he drives the small roads to Senlis one-handed. He laughs, delighted, at her weakness for this play. She cannot begin to tell him how much she loves this touching. Literally cannot, because she is both too ashamed of herself and, in a way, too proud to talk about it. She will not even talk about it with Brennan. She can only suspect she is not like most girls. She is depraved, she is greedy, she is all those nasty names he has for that part of her.

So this is another impediment to her series of articles. How does one write about such depravity? She has never read anything, either humorous or serious, in which the heroine was so compulsively base, so exuberantly carnal. She has not expected to like this so much, to surrender so easily. Although surrender, she knows, is not the right verb. She is, after all, still a virgin. And furthermore, just as she is aware that some of her clothing purchases do not involve parting with cash (the mushroom-shaped *directoire* hat she wears daily now in lieu of her cap, the patent-leather belt for the new houndstooth fingertip coat she tosses over her uniform) and therefore cannot really be called purchases, she is also aware that her surrendering does not involve any initial resistance on her part. There was no initial warfare, not a single attempt at self-defense. How, then, can there be a white flag?

In fact, all she wants is for him to take more territory, if you will. Has there ever been such a phenomenon? A vanquished country begging its conqueror, Please, have a little more. Please, help yourself. Please, for the love of God, use the other weapons in your arsenal.

They sit in the truck, Dub smiling smugly and affectionately at her, Yale limp and damp. He puts an arm around her chummily. He looks at his watch, glances down the street. "Time to go," he says. The next team has arrived, other waiters and watchers, usually two middle-aged men named Sahagian and Gregorian to whom Yale will never be introduced but who, nonetheless, she feels she knows well. They look so familiar with their jet hair and big mustaches.

"You are going to get in trouble," Brennan says.

It takes Yale a minute to understand what kind of trouble Brennan is alluding to. "Oh, Bren," she says. "We're just sitting there."

"You could get arrested for just sitting there," Brennan says. Yale rolls her eyes, asks what on earth for. Brennan admits she doesn't know what for. Loitering, she suggests. Peeping Tommery. Anyway, she says, even if it's not illegal, whatever the hell Yale and Dub are up to in that truck, you wouldn't catch Brennan doing it. "And I," Brennan says, dancing from one end of the trapezoid to the other, "am the kind of girl you could once catch doing just about anything."

CHAPTER SIX

While the Getting Is Good

IT'S NO SURPRISE that they eventually leave the Y and move to Senlis. By the time this happens, they've already been given keys to the château and have slept over so often they have a room of their own. In the kitchen, they help themselves to food and drink. Yale sits with Aram for hours, listening to tales of his *fedayee* days. Brennan dabs dry both the mouths and the bottoms of dozens of orphans. "Who'd of thunk you'd like children this much?" Yale says, watching Brennan slop rear ends while cooing monosyllables in a falsetto, and Brennan looks at Yale with an expression that Yale admires but cannot analyze.

So not a surprise they wind up there. The only surprise is the precise series of events that leads to their move, events that begin on the first day of March, when Yale, slipping into the trapezoid shortly before dawn, also slips on an envelope.

She was at a dance—Dub working late on a project with Avetis Aharonian, another futile attempt to persuade the West to come rescue Armenia—and after the dance she went to the Follies with a group of girls and some doughboys, so she's tipsy when she enters her room, doesn't notice the envelope under her door. She is only focused on being quiet so she doesn't wake Brennan, who has been out, Yale knows, with Ned Harden and is now breathing noisily through her open mouth as she does when she falls asleep drunk.

Yale tiptoes into the room, steps square on the envelope, slides several feet, her arms flailing, until she grabs hold of a bedpost, which she uses to keep herself from crashing to the floor. Brennan mumbles, rolls over, and Yale, after catching her breath, bends to pick up the letter. This had better be good, she thinks, although, as she takes it to the window, she is already assuming it's another mash poem from the infatuated marine.

In the shallow haze of near morning, she can see that the envelope is addressed to both Brennan and herself. Curious now, she jags her finger beneath the seal, removes the letter, and skims its contents. Then she reads it again, start to finish, forcing herself to read slowly this time.

She leaves the light of the window, sits on her unyielding mattress. There, in the even dimmer light, her eyes strained and stinging, she reads the letter again, her disbelief and shame mounting. She is feeling a helpless fury, feeling near tears. "Dear Misses White," someone has typed with a fading ribbon that must have been inserted cockeyed because the top of every word is tinged with red. "There are times when we at the YMCA must recognize that among the several thousand workers we have sent to France, there are necessarily some who are entirely unsuited to this service."

Missed shifts at the canteen, inappropriate behavior on the dance floor, excessive drinking, disregard for curfew, a discrepancy between the number of cigarettes reported sold on their shifts and the amount of proceeds turned in. Their crimes, as set forth in the letter, are many, and the last of their crimes, named in a paragraph all its own, is deliberate misstatements on both their original applications.

The Y doesn't care what a person's religious affiliation might be, says the letter. It is deception, not creed, the Y cares about. All creeds are tolerated. Deception is not.

"After all," the letter explains, "we *are* a Christian institution."

She wakes Brennan then.

"But what did we do?" Brennan says, although Yale has now twice read her the list of the things they're accused of doing. "Yes, I know, but what did we do that half the other girls here don't do every day?" Brennan sits up in bed, flicks on the lamp. She wants to appeal the decision, she says. She wants to exercise their right to address the committee, explain their side of things. She reaches for her brass lighter, flicks the head of the brass woman, lights one of the cigarettes they've stolen from the canteen. What right? Yale wonders. What committee? "I don't know," Brennan says. She goes to the bureau, unscrews the lid to her flask.

"Let's just leave," Yale says. "Let's just go before sun-up."

"But, darling," Brennan says. "I'm so sick of being hustled out of town for doing the same things everybody else in the world is doing." The whiskey, though warm, is like a dive into the ocean on the coldest day of the year. Now she is alive, alert, braced. "And, really, I don't even understand what they're talking about here. What kind of misstatements did we make on our original applications? If there had been a box to check off—a have-you-ever-had-a-fling-with-a-married-man box—and I failed to check it, then all right, fine. But I didn't make any misstatements. I didn't. Did you?"

Brennan is on the move. She paces, she gestures, she tromps from one bizarrely angled end of the room to the other. She eyes their door each time she passes it, says she wants to go out, wake up anyone who might know something about this letter. The harridan across the hall, for instance. She wants to pound on Amo Winston's door; she wants to hurl invectives and ashtrays; she is *that* angry, she says. But Yale says she hasn't the heart for any of it.

While Brennan paces, Yale crawls into her own bed. There she sits beneath the blankets, fully dressed—jacket, long skirt, boots. She lowers her head. She fears she may cry. "You've known all along about my misstatements," she mumbles.

Brennan stops pacing, rushes to her side. It touches Yale, makes the urge to cry that much stronger. "Oh, darling," Brennan says, "do you mean your age? Oh, darling, really. What does it matter now? Anyone can come over these days; there are no more restrictions. Gangs of high school children are coming over with their teachers. Families on vacation are touring the battlefields. And anyway, Yale: my God, a woman lying about her age? I mean, honestly—stop the presses. I mean, really—if they tossed out every woman who lied about her age, the Y would be staffed only by nellies and Alban Bliss."

"Yes, but most women lie in the other direction," Yale says. "Younger, not older. And I suppose they do feel they have to bend over backward to keep the organization pure, given the political climate and the scandals."

She feels awful about the whole thing. Although, she reminds herself, it's hardly her fault that the Y's reputation has gotten so muddied up, all the news stories about what really went on during the war, misappropriated funds and the black-marketing of cigarettes by enterprising YMCA officials, all those true Trinitarians. Still, she can see why the Red Triangle feels the need to clean house, to sweep up.

Brennan can't see it at all. "That's exactly right," she says. "Important people are black-marketing cigarettes on a huge scale, and all we're doing is filching a few packs a day for our own personal use, which, given the ludicrous pay, is perfectly justified. So why are we the ones getting the boot?"

"Let's just go," Yale says. She has found a frayed corner of the blanket and is playing with the soft threads, running them against the palm of her hand. "Let's be gone before first shift."

Brennan sits on the edge of Yale's bed the way a mother might if her child claimed a fever on the day of an exam. "Darling," she says, and Yale recognizes a trace of the cooing, cajoling tone Brennan uses with the babies at Senlis, "it's not that I want to disassociate myself from you in any way, because I absolutely don't. But I didn't lie about my age on my application. I didn't lie about anything. And I suppose I'm simply wondering why they're accusing us both."

"There's the bit about drinking," Yale says timidly. "That might be you. Or maybe they just mean the twin business."

"I don't think so," Brennan says. "Look at how specifically they say misstatements on the original applications, plural. Look how they give that charge a whole separate paragraph. And before that, how they go on and on about our religious affiliation. That they don't care what it is, only they expect us to be forthright, et cetera, et cetera. Yale, I want you to know something. When I filled out my application, I put down the Catholic part. I swear I did."

Yale is twisting one of the frayed threads around her thumb. "I know," she says, "but you know what might have happened? There was that ridiculous time Amo accused you of being . . ." And she finds she cannot say the word that describes this part of her any more than she can say that other word, the one that describes that other part of her. But they are both in her head now, swimming around, pounding at her—what she is, what she is: Jewish cunt.

Brennan hoots like a disgusted owl. "Oh, come now. Amo didn't mean it, not literally. She was only trying to paint me as a bad Christian."

"But maybe she really does think it. And if she thinks it of you, then of course she thinks it of me. Twins, after all."

"She doesn't believe we're twins. She's never bought that. So she wouldn't think it of you."

"I think perhaps she does," Yale says, and she makes herself say it. "I think she thinks we're both a little bit Jewish."

"Why do you think that?"

Yale considers something like this: *Because, you silly girl, I am a little bit Jewish, that's why. Actually more than a little bit, and if you don't like it you'll have to get over it; you're officially stuck with me.*

"Because she said it, didn't she," she says. "Oh, it's so absurd, I can't stand it. Please let's just get out of here before we have to face everyone."

"Tell me the truth first," Brennan says. She inches closer to Yale. "Darling," she says. She places a hand on Yale's blanketed knee. "Darling, did you go and tell someone you're Jewish?"

She might have asked a different question. Darling, Brennan might have said, are you a Jew? But she has only asked if Yale might have claimed to be Jewish, and while it's a crazy question—who would make such a claim?—it's also a nudge in an entirely different direction.

"I suppose I may have," Yale says. "I suppose I may have been angry and wanting to shock some of the girls. You know how some of them behave as if people the least little bit different from them are just the absolute dregs? And I suppose feeling so close to Dub now—"

"He's hardly a Jew."

"No, but he's different. He's not Protestant. He's not even Catholic in the normal way. And what with me feeling so close to him—"

"And to me. Famine Irish."

"Yes, of course. And to you. So maybe one day at canteen I overheard some of them saying something nasty about—"

"Me?"

"Well, and maybe I wanted to make them think twice before spouting off anymore, before saying such lousy things and making assumptions about people who were different, and so maybe I piped up to shock them and shut them up and try to embarrass them. Maybe I piped up and said that I happened to be . . ."

Again, she can't say it, not even for the sake of her tale.

"Oh, Yale," Brennan says. She laughs, short and staccato. "I can just see it too. It's so you. Well, at least you didn't tell anyone we were colored." Her eyebrow shoots up. "You didn't, did you?"

"God, no," Yale says. She looks down. The loose strings at the edge of the blanket are wound so tight around her thumb she has cut off her circulation. The thumb is turning purple. She unravels the threads, sets her thumb free, watches the unnatural shade subside. "Bren," she says. "I'm leaving. It's not only them kicking me out. It's me wanting to go. I don't like it here. That lobby full of pamphlets and proselytizers and cocoa. I'm not like that. I don't believe in any of it."

"You don't believe in cocoa?"

She anticipates and talks past the joke, can't bear to go through the exercise, the laughing, the diffusion of what she's feeling. "Cocoa, no, I actually don't. And you don't either. We believe in gin and cigarettes, don't we? You especially. Don't let's look at it as being rode out of town. Let's look at it as turning our backs on them. That's so us, don't you think? Really, darling, I can't believe you're not jumping for joy. I can't believe you don't see this as a grand opportunity. It's the shove we've needed all along."

She has never seen Brennan so cautious, so ashen. "A grand opportunity to do what? To go home in disgrace? I can just see explaining to everyone that I was dismissed from the YMCA for lying about my Hebrew heritage."

"Who says we have to go home? The point is they don't want us. They had to come up with a reason to ditch us, and they didn't care how preposterous that reason was. Don't you see? They really don't want women like us. They wouldn't want women like your mother. They wouldn't want Seta or any of the orphans. They only take Catholics and Jews and whoever else because the government requires it. We can't stay on if that's the case. It's a matter of pride." She looks at Brennan. "In memory of your mother," she says, "we have to go somewhere else."

On the window ledge a pigeon struts about, its ruff silver and lilac. It looks into the room and trills like a mourning dove. Otherwise, there is no movement or sound, nothing at all to distract them. And then the bird flies off, and now there is only the kind of silence that makes you suddenly aware of hot water traveling through pipes.

And then, just as suddenly, Brennan is on the move once again, Brennan is up on her bare feet, opening closets, opening drawers, pulling out socks, underwear, throwing them onto the bed that still contains Yale. "If we're going," she says, turning again, swooping at the bureau, gathering up strings of beads, ticket stubs, gloves, laddered silk hose, all of this first in her arms, all of it then heaped upon Yale, "then let's go. Let's do it before sunrise. Let's do it before breakfast. Let's not have a whole scene downstairs about it, right? Let's get the hell out while the getting is good."

It takes no time at all. Brennan dresses while Yale dumps their belongings into valises.

"Don't forget all your black-market cigarettes," Brennan says.

"Don't forget your flask and obscene lighter," Yale replies.

They tiptoe downstairs, not wanting to wake Amo Winston. "Praise the Lord and pass by Amo Winston," sings Brennan, when they have successfully reached the staircase.

As it turns out they could have sung the parody full blast. Miss Winston is not in her room. She is awake and already down in the lobby, sitting on a sofa, tapping her foot, and looking unusually unhealthy and unhappy and having forgotten to take out one of her hair wrappers. She leaps up when she sees the two of them. She runs to them, forcing each girl to endure her embrace. She gives them each a container of cold cream to take on their travels.

She makes no secret of knowing all about their dismissal. "I've been up all night fretting over it," she says. "I tell you, it just isn't right." Brennan has to pat the poor woman's shoulder, assure her they're fine. "No," Amo Winston says fiercely. "You're not fine, and what is happening here isn't fine either." She follows them outside, limping as she has been for several weeks now. She waits with them, scouring the empty street for a cab. She leans heavily on a stick.

"Whatever happened to your foot anyway?" Brennan says.

"It's nothing," Miss Winston replies. "A broken toe. The great Alban Bliss himself told me it was of no importance and not to carry on so." She changes the subject from herself back to them, their plight. "You don't just throw people out on the street," she says. "You talk to people first. You give them a chance to explain. And what about a chance to atone? What about forgiveness? Sometimes, you know, a person may violate a sacrosanct rule for a very good reason. What about giving the person the benefit of the doubt? What about hearing them out? And what about, perhaps, considering that the rule itself is a bad rule? And even if it isn't—well, what about love and compassion? Aren't those the most cherished of all Christian values? I'm telling you this just as I told everyone else last night. This is so wrong. And where—and I said this too, I want you to know—I said, Where do you expect these girls to go? Two young girls in a city like this, and no rooms to let anywhere?"

A taxi has pulled to the curb. Amo Winston wants to send it away. No, she wants to get into it with the two girls. She wants to tell them everything. She wants to tell them all about the investigation, nearly six weeks long, and her role in it, their accuser, and then one day, their stalwart defender. She even wants to bring up the hôtel le Marais. She wants to let the pair know that the hotel may have a room available and that this room would be in a part of the city where the White girls would feel at home. (The Weiss girls, she reminds herself, recalling the anonymous letter that arrived in January, every word in bold uppercase so that reading it felt like being slapped in the face over and over.) But she can't think how to bring up the name of the hotel without explaining how she knows of it and how she knows that the younger Miss White knows of it too. She only hopes the younger Miss White will remember the place on her own. She hopes the sisters—no, not sisters, although they *do* apparently have the same name, both of them Weisses, and it's all so confusing—are headed there now. She hopes Yale's lover awaits her and will comfort and soothe her, which is more than can be said for certain other lovers she could mention. Maybe for these girls it *will* be fine. She hopes so, she does. She doesn't pray so, not knowing how to approach God on behalf of Jews, and not feeling overly fond of God these days in any event, but she stands on the curb with her right foot, her good foot, bearing most of her weight (which is diminishing daily should anyone care to know), and in the end all she does is wave good-bye as the twins' taxi heads to the Crillon.

SETA KISSES THEM in the French manner when they arrive at the château in the Fiat, accompanied by Dub and Ned Harden. They blurt out the terrible story to Seta. Thrown out, they say, due to vicious rumors, unfair accusations. They will stay with her in Senlis, Seta declares, as they have been hoping, perhaps even presuming, she will. She will brook no refusal, she says, and they offer none. They stow their bags in the room they already consider their own. They splash water on their faces, and Brennan peeks in on all the current babies. When they come downstairs again, Seta offers them breakfast: sweet rolls and hot chocolate. "Yale doesn't believe in cocoa," Brennan says. Yale says "Shut up" to Brennan and "Thank you" to Seta. Thank you, but no. "What can I get you to cheer you up?" Seta asks, and they shrug, they pout, they say "Oh, nothing, really," and "No, honestly, we're fine," and they sigh.

"Would you like an American breakfast perhaps?" Seta says.

The thought never occurred to them, but now that she's said it, they realize that's exactly what they want. They are dying for an American breakfast, they will give anything for an American breakfast, they have possibly, on some deep subconscious level, arranged this entire chain of events, beginning back in 1918 when each applied to the Y, just to get an American breakfast today.

But, "Oh, no," they say, and "You're really too kind, but we couldn't ask that of you," and "We would never put you to so much trouble."

"I would," says Ned Harden.

So Seta Kazarian sends the bonne upstairs to contend with the orphans, and she sets to cooking. She fries eggs. She throws thick slices of ham into a cast-iron pan. She pours black coffee.

It is all so much better after that.

Part Seven

CHAPTER ONE

Modern Art

DESPITE HARD TIMES and rationing, the new spring ensembles have begun to arrive in the shops. All of France heaves a sigh; no one could have endured a uniform for another minute. The new look is shapeless and short, and the colors are bright, even for men, who strut around now in red pleated trousers. Checks and plaids too.

Yale occasionally acquires new things as well. One day (with Brennan planning to attend a performance of *La Reine Joyeuse* with Ned and Dub planning to work late at Translation), Yale, who has no plans at all, reaches into a bin at a small shop and carries away the latest must-have accessory, a man's umbrella with a horn knob handle. If she feels guilty about it afterward, it's only because a more considerate girl would have stolen two, one for herself and one for Brennan.

Brennan is in need of an umbrella. Spring fashions may have arrived but not so spring weather, and Brennan is spending far too much time in the cold drizzle. Unlike Yale, Brennan rarely goes into Paris. She visits the city only when Ned shows up with theater tickets or restaurant reservations. Otherwise she no longer bothers.

Certainly she has no interest in fashion. Why wear the latest when your shirtwaist is always stained with baby food and spit-up? Why wear skirts of any length when you spend all your time outside in the rain, kneeling in the mud?

The reason she's kneeling in mud is that Brennan has devised a little project for herself and the orphans of Senlis, and this project involves digging in the herb garden directly behind the château. Given the unseasonable weather, the herb garden is bereft of any herbs save a few exhausted tufts of old chives. For the most part, the herb garden is just a patch of dirt in the shape of a huge fleur-de-lis.

"One of the German boys put it to bed for me last October," Seta says, while Brennan, in a pair of Aram's old trousers, digs in the garden with a trowel. Seta's head is cast downward and her shoulders are

hunched up. It has rained so frequently that whenever Seta steps outside she automatically adopts the posture of the recently drenched.

Despite the weather, so depressing, so enervating, Seta smiles when
she mentions this particular German boy. He was her favorite, the
youngest boy billeted in the château. The son of a Bavarian pig farmer,
he followed Seta around the house like an imprinted duckling as he
talked of how he missed putting his hands in the soil. She finally came
up with the idea of having him tend her gardens.

"One of the last things he did for me was plant grape hyacinths by
the stone wall near the pond," Seta says. "I don't know where he found
the bulbs. The garden shed, he said. I told him I had no recollection of
storing bulbs of any sort there, which meant that they must have been
very old bulbs indeed. I told him they'd never come up, certainly not if
he planted them in November. Much too late in the year. But he was
determined to do something for me before he and his friends had to go.
He stayed awake one entire night to plant them. It will be lovely, I suppose, should even a few come up." She looks to the sky. "Maybe this
weather will help those little flowers," she says. "Maybe the rain will be
like a gentle slap in their sleepy faces, waking them up."

She truly does hope the grape hyacinths bloom. She knows many of
her neighbors would have dug those bulbs up and thrown them away as
soon as the Germans were chased out of town. They would never have
accepted this gift from a German. "I don't feel that way myself," Seta
says. "I might even permit a repentant Turk to make amends by planting flowers." She laughs ruefully. "If only there were such a creature as
a repentant Turk."

Brennan smiles too, although she is only half listening. She is less
interested in flowers than Seta is. She was once charmed by flowers—
the bouquet of violets she caught on the *Espagne,* the roses that Billy
Wilcox occasionally gave her—but now she thinks flowers are empty
gestures, essentially useless. And she has no interest at all in Turks.
They lost the war, didn't they? They can do no more harm. Her passion
is for the here-and-now, and, more recently, for babies, for orphans.
And even more recently, for digging up little white stones.

When she told the family her idea—that's the term they all use now,
the family—everyone had scoffed, even Yale. Or, rather, especially
Yale. "Where did this crazy notion come from?" Yale asked, and Bren-

nan had to admit she didn't know. The modern art shows she's heard about, she supposes. The ones in Paris. Or maybe the idea came from boredom, from hanging around the house too long. She thought the idea might also have had something to do with the new batch of orphans who arrived only days after the White twins moved in. This batch consisted of a half dozen little girls who had been rescued from a Kurd's barn, mostly seven- and eight-year-olds who could remember nothing about life before or during the deportations, plus one sullen girl of fifteen who could remember it all, every last detail, but would talk about none of it. "Oh, dear Lord," Yale had said, after she met the batch and got her first good look at the fifteen-year-old, the glowering Shushan Khaladjian, with her long legs and wide hips and womanly chest, only her face that of a child, pale and round as pudding but terribly angry, the eyebrows bushy and knit together into one perpetual scowl and a sprinkling of acne over those eyebrows. "These girls aren't babies. These are actual people. They'll have wants and needs and opinions."

Seta said, "They will be much harder to place, especially the big one."

"We'll have to engage with them all the time," Yale said. "They'll join us for dinner. This is going to much more difficult and time-consuming than babies."

"I'll do it," Brennan had said then. "I'll eat with them. I'll engage with them."

But after only one day cooped up in the house with them, Brennan thought she would go mad, and that's when she came up with her project. She glanced out a window and saw that the rain had let up. "We're going to play in the garden," she said.

She herded them into the kitchen. Herded was the right word; the girls didn't understand the sounds coming out of Brennan's mouth, but, like sheep minding a barking collie, they figured out what she wanted. In the kitchen, Brennan helped them into warm coats, held mittens open so they could thrust their hands inside. She wrapped wool scarves around their heads, covering their hair and ears and the lower halves of their faces. The outerwear had once belonged to Seta's daughters, four overfed girls who'd grown up during the Belle Epoch. The sleeves of the coats hung to the orphans' knees. When the children trundled along after Brennan, they tripped over the hems. When they tried to breathe, they got wool in their mouths. But they had been trained all their lives to be docile and obedient and dependent, so out into the cold they waddled.

Brennan had them crouch by the herb garden. She distributed trowels, spades, broken teacups. "We are going to dig for little white stones," Brennan said. Then she said it in French because a foreign language seemed to be called for.

The girls looked at her blankly. She had to demonstrate what she wanted. They did their best to mimic her actions. They did all right. She had to teach them to reject the darker stones and the ones that were too big. She wanted the stones to be as uniformly small and as uniformly white as possible. Not stones, really. Pebbles. She didn't know how to say *pebbles* in French; the little girls didn't know French at all. Still, they caught on.

That evening, she had Dub translate for her. He and Ned came by most evenings now. They were part of the family too, and they came for dinner, stayed for brandy, and sometimes Ned played the piano. That evening, Brennan asked Dub to tell the little girls in Armenian what they'd been doing all day. The girls' Armenian wasn't all that proficient either. They'd been infants when the Kurd first acquired them. But Dub did his best, and he got the general idea across.

The general idea was this. Brennan and the girls would collect five hundred thousand small white stones, one stone for every person lost during the deportations. And they would wash the stones clean, and they would keep the stones in jars or in boxes, and eventually, when they had all five hundred thousand, they would place them into some sort of vast and transparent container. Brennan was imagining a huge fish tank, a glass aquarium.

"Explain that it's art," Brennan said. And when she saw the look on Dub's face, she said, "Then just tell them that we're going to make the world understand what five hundred thousand of something actually is."

"You ought to wait a little," Shushan said then. She'd been sitting in a corner. Nobody had guessed she was paying attention to the conversation. Nobody knew she could speak French, but there she was, speaking it. "They say that when Mr. Toynbee finishes his calculations, the final tally is going to be far greater than five hundred thousand."

Shushan hadn't gone outside with the others that day. What fool went out in the rain for no good purpose? But she had watched the activities from the kitchen window. She'd seen what they were doing out there, the little girls kneeling by the empty garden. At first she thought the girls were being put to work, were being made to dig for some sort of root vegetable. Then she saw they were amassing not vegetables but piles of small stones. She didn't think much about it. She assumed the stones were needed for some sort of domestic function. What did she know of the ways of the West? Nor had she thought to ask Brennan what she was up to. She could have asked. Since being rescued by people who spoke French, her own French was coming back to her. She had once been the spoiled child of wealthy parents. This was before the deportations began. She'd had a maid, her own personal maid. Not a housekeeper like Seta's bonne, but the kind of maid who dresses you and runs your baths for you and pares your toenails and speaks to you only in French.

"Some say the final tally will be over one million," Shushan said.

"What if we start with five hundred thousand," Brennan said. "We can always add later. It's good to have a goal."

"That's a whole lot of stones." Ned Harden rolled his eyes comically. He didn't like the grim tone of the conversation, wanted to cheer folks up.

"It's a lot of dead people," said Yale.

"What do you know about it?" Shushan said. Freed from the barn, her childhood haughtiness was coming back along with her French. "I am the only one here who has stepped over every last corpse. Sometimes I had to step right on top of them, like stepping-stones, so as not to burn my feet on the sand."

"There you are," Brennan said, as if her case had been made for her. "Stepping *stones*."

"It's horrible what happened," Ned said quickly, agreeably, though all the French was hurting his head, "but I don't understand the point of this project."

"The point of the project for *her*"—Shushan pointed rudely, intentionally rudely, at Brennan—"is to get those little brats"—she pointed equally rudely to the seven- and eight-year-olds who were sitting in a horseshoe on the floor, big-eyed and dumb—"out of the house for a few hours."

"To the contrary," Brennan said. "The point is to show the world what five hundred thousand of something looks like. If people don't grasp the magnitude, how can they care?"

"Yes, but how is that art?" Ned said.

Brennan didn't answer him. She didn't know where her idea had come from, but she knew it was important and no one would ever convince her otherwise. Someday, the huge aquarium filled with stones would tour the world. It would be displayed in museums. It would be placed in the center of a vast marble room that had been emptied for this special exhibit. People would wait in line to get in. They would be respectful and solemn, as if they were approaching a casket—which, in fact, is what they would be doing. And then they would look at the hundreds of thousands of pebbles inside the aquarium and they would see not only rocks but their own reflections. Then a guard would step up (or maybe it would be Brennan herself, Brennan the artist following her own creation from city to city) and encourage the people to dip their hands into the casket. Handle the stones, Brennan would urge them. Sift the stones through your fingers. Feel what five hundred thousand feels like. Feel five hundred thousand one by one.

As the other adults debated the merits of the contemporary art scene, Ned rehashing the old complaints about the Armory show ("If that's what Duchamp thinks a nude descending a staircase looks like," he said, mouthing the word *nude* so as not to offend, "it doesn't say much for his wife, does it?"), one of the orphans, feeling sleepy and bold and perhaps also having a sudden memory of events from a long-ago life, crawled into Brennan's lap. Brennan kissed the child's hair. Then she tipped the child backward and nuzzled her face against the girl's alarmingly flat belly and made vibrating airplane sounds. The orphan giggled, the other orphans clamored for a turn. Brennan embraced the orphans one by one. This was also what five hundred thousand feels like, she thought.

But, of course, an orphan—that was hardly art. You couldn't put an orphan on display in a fish tank. You could only give her a bath and put her to bed, which is what she did, ending the evening, at least her part in it, early.

IT'S AS IF Brennan has been given a job with a deadline. Each morning she gets up by 6 a.m. and makes American breakfasts for the skin-and-bone orphans. While they gorge, she lays out their coats, mittens, scarves, trowels, spades, and teacups. Then she heads out to dig with her own band of imprinted ducklings, along with one recalcitrant, ungainly goose—yes, Shushan has joined them now. They kneel in the gray mist and gather the most common of pebbles. They do this for hours, the operation accompanied by the murmur of their counting. One, two, three. *Un, deux, trois. Meg, yergu, yerek.* Each girl makes a pile of ten stones, then again and again, ten pebbles, ten pebbles, until each girl has one hundred, until each girl has two hundred.

It is boring and idiotic, the ducklings whisper to one another in a language Brennan will never understand, albeit a language she's happy to hear because at last they are speaking. It's boring, the ducklings are saying, but then one of them remarks that it's no more boring than tending the Kurd's goats, and they all agree. They prefer collecting stones to feeding his goats, mending his socks, fetching his water and wine. They prefer digging in the cold to sleeping in the cold. Besides, they've never been beaten bloody for spilling a jarful of pebbles.

Yale sometimes steps out the back door and watches the operation, which is the word Dub uses when he refers to the digging. If it's drizzling she stands under the eaves. She will not expose her new umbrella to the rain. It's too elegant, not really meant for that sort of thing. She presses her spine to the timbered walls of the château and shouts with her hands cupped round her mouth. "What about grains of rice instead? Five hundred thousand grains of rice? Wouldn't that be easier to get ahold of and more pleasant to run one's hands through?"

"You clearly know nothing about art," Brennan yells back.

"I know enough to come in out of the rain. What about white buttons? Wouldn't that at least be dryer?"

This is when Brennan teaches the girls another game. Now when Yale comes out, they all scream "Critic!" in unison and at the top of their lungs.

CHAPTER TWO

Springtime in Paris

ON APRIL FOOL'S DAY, the rain finally lets up, but—Ha! April fool!—only because there's a snowstorm instead. When Yale wakes up and looks outside her window, she thinks she may weep or perhaps tear her hair out, rend her garments, go mad.

By evening, however, the snow has melted, and the next morning she can smell spring. And in less than a week, spring has become more than merely a promising scent. In Paris, magnolia trees blossom, all the museums reopen, and children return to the streets with their hoops and balls and roller skates.

Also, Kerim Bey leaves his house.

And the next day. And again the next.

Every day now, for an hour or so in the late afternoon, Kerim Bey limps to a small park off the rooey Bell Fooey. His pace is slow, and he is never without his cane. Nor is he ever without his family. The wife and small son always follow him, modifying their pace so they remain a proscribed distance behind.

When Yale and Dub are on duty, they tag along too. Playing the part of neighborhood lovers, they stroll along holding hands, sometimes stopping to kiss, not necessarily because they are overwhelmed with desire but because, if they don't stop every now and then, they will overtake their quarry. That's how slowly the Turk and his small entourage proceed.

Once inside the park, Kerim Bey sits on a bench, always the same bench. Dub and Yale have their own bench too, close enough so they can watch Kerim Bey, sufficiently far away and screened by an unruly forsythia to prevent him from seeing them. The wife and son go off among the chestnut trees, the little boy chasing a ball or hanging from a branch or throwing a rock at a dog. The wife either watches the child or reads a thin paperback. Whichever she does, there's a wan smile on her face and a blank look in her eyes. She seems both contented and dazed.

"Look at that face," Dub says. "She's either an opium addict or just enormously stupid. We're harassing a woman who has no capacity to understand her husband's crimes."

"We aren't harassing her," Yale says. "We're keeping an eye on her. And I'll bet she understands his crimes perfectly."

Kerim Bey, meanwhile, sleeps in the sun. His head falls back, his mouth falls open. Sometimes his hat falls off his head.

"Look at him," Dub says. "He's a fat cripple. Let's say we do get to bring him to trial. The crossing to Turkey will kill him before he ever sees a courtroom."

"He managed to survive the crossing out of Turkey," Yale says.

This is part of her job: to help Dub buck up, stand pat, sit firm. The blaze in Adana, she reminds him. Who hired the thugs who started it? Who helped them bar the doors? So many children inside. And then, five years later, the murderous trek, the forced desert crossing. Who chased the people from their homes in his district? Who ransacked the empty houses? Who organized the firing squads? Who counted down, shouted *Ready, aim, fire*?

"Who told you about Kerim's crimes in the first place?" Dub says. "Do you think I've forgotten them?" The problem is that lately an annoying thought has begun to buzz him. The tragedies in the *yergir*. How, exactly, were they Dub's tragedies? How were they Yale's? Why are they seeking revenge?

"They would have been your tragedies if you'd been there," she says. A governess with a baby buggy strolls by. "You know they meant you. And I don't take kindly to that: someone wanting to hurt you. So of course I'm involved too."

"That's purely theoretical. Not to mention theatrical. The fact is, I wasn't there."

"Then look at it this way. The people whose tragedies weren't purely theoretical are no longer here to do anything about it. Shouldn't somebody do something on their behalf?"

The ever-helpful White twins, he thinks. Brennan planning to help the world comprehend the atrocities via half a million pebbles; Yale with her reasonable view of revenge. He should just leave it all to them. He could go off, sit in the sun, catch up on the news, fret about things that really mattered. An alarmed Ned Harden grabbed his sleeve just the other day. "Godfrey, Hagopian, I just got wind of the most disturbing news item. Did you know Harry Frazee's considering trading the Babe to the Yankees?"

Dub blames himself for Yale's infatuation with the cause. From the moment they met, he's been telling her too many stories. Of course she's all riled up. The atrocities in the East. His lethargic months in the Caucasus. Even the frustrating dinner with Hamilton and Lindsey. In some ways that story upset her more than the others. She has different standards for the West, she expects more of Europe than of Asia. She said, "But how can they refuse to give you your land when everyone knows they promised?" and she suddenly struck him as inordinately young, if adorably passionate, and his response was kissing, touching.

Aram has also told her too many stories. She tells Dub she can picture Aram as a young *fedayee* now, Aram straight as a tree, Aram in his tarboosh and sash and tinsel. She doesn't add that she can also picture him on the day he was captured by the band of Turks who held his palms flat against a stump and chopped off four of his fingers with their swords. Dub knows she does picture it, though. Sometimes when she's tending to Aram, he sees her cradling the fingers of her one hand with the fingers of the other, and then he knows she is picturing the day it happened, a sixteen-year-old boy, his blood and cries amid the Turks' laughter. The breaking of, the sawing through, four slender bones. He knows she's imagining all this because he imagines the same thing whenever Aram's hand clasps his, whenever Aram's palm rests on his hair. That's when it comes to him, as vividly as if he'd been there too: the surgery in the forest.

"My God, why?" she asked, after Aram first told her about it.

Aram had shrugged, "With the Turks it's not why but why not." He put his arm around her, held her because she was shaking with anger. "My father hadn't paid my army levy," he said. "There was a levy Armenians had to pay to avoid army service, and my father hadn't paid it. They came and they told him that if he wanted his son to be exempt from the military without paying the levy, then, fine, they would help make him exempt for good. There were four of them and they each took their finger of choice."

Gar oo chagar. Once there was and was not.

Neither Aram nor he should have told her such stories, and recently Dub has tried to back off. Now, when they are in the park, Kerim Bey snoozing, he tells her about himself. He tells her how he got his name. He tells her about the medals he won in high school. "The big French scholar," he says, laughing, and she smiles and nestles against him. She pulls away only when another governess with another baby buggy blocks their view of Kerim. She tilts her head so she can keep her eyes on the tyrant until the governess is gone. Then she relaxes into Dub again.

"Tell me more," she says.

"More about what? My illustrious high school career?"

"Maybe today about somebody else."

"Who?"

"I don't know. How about me? Tell me about me."

"Who am I to tell you about you?"

"Tell me what you think of me."

He smiles, messes her messy hair. Her self-absorption is one of the things he finds delightful about her. It's not necessarily conceit. It's more a hunger she has to figure out who she is. He thinks she would incorporate anything he told her into her image of herself. He could say, Well, let's see, I think you adore children, and the next thing you know she'd be pitching in with the orphans in Senlis, something that presently seems not to interest her in the least. She can even do this for herself. The way she told everyone she was Armenian on her maternal grandfather's side—she seems to have come to believe it as much as Aram and Seta do.

All this he likes about her. Watching her play the game of self-discovery. Watching her cheat as she plays it.

But today, as Kerim Bey brushes a fly off his nose as he dozes and dreams, Dub suddenly finds himself unwilling to assist her in the game. He feels put off by her question. *What do you think of me?*

At first he only teases her. "Do you think that's an appropriate subject for two soldiers on a mission? Do you think when Sahagian and Gregorian come here, this is the sort of thing they discuss? So, Sahagian, tell me"—he flutters his eyelashes, sends his voice sky high, a grating soprano —"do you think I'm beautiful?"

"I didn't ask if you thought I was beautiful."

"Why, yes, Gregorian, I find you excruciatingly beautiful. And now, Gregorian, darling, I've a question for you. Gregorian, do you love me?"

"I didn't ask that either."

"What did you ask? I've forgotten."

"You know what I asked."

"What do I think of you? I think you're very distracting. I find you a tremendous distraction."

"Why? Because I talk too much?"

"Yes," he says.

"No," she says. "Be serious."

"Why would you think I'm not being serious? You talk incessantly."

"No," she says. "Really. You do have feelings for me, don't you?"

"Is annoyance a feeling?"

"Dub," she says.

"All right," he says. "I think of nothing else but you. All day. All night."

She presses an accusing finger against his chest. "You're pretending you're joking, but you're telling the truth. I can tell everything about you, and I can tell when you're telling the truth. You *do* think about me all the time, don't you? Why is that, do you think?"

"I haven't the energy not to," he says.

He *is* joking, but then the melancholy returns to him all at once like a deluge, and he is soaked with his sadness. She doesn't see it, doesn't know everything about him after all. She laughs and kisses him, and he lets her; they kiss for a while, Dub with one eye opened and glued to the Turk. What does it mean, what does it say about him, he all the while wonders, that he can sit so close to that evil while kissing this girl? What does it mean that he feels more lust than unbridled fury? When he looks at the Turk these days he is not filled with hatred. The man is so used up, so obviously finished. Must Erinyes really punish him? The wife, such a stupid bovine. Must Erinyes really widow her? Today their brat chases a red ball. Does the brat have to be orphaned? And if he is orphaned, won't he grow up to seek vengeance himself? How will trials or hangings help? What will street murder change? Can't Dub just walk away? Can't he just take his girl to a ball game some afternoon instead?

He knows what he thinks of Yale. He knows what he feels for her.

He's told her the truth. She thinks he's joking, but he isn't. She distracts him. Even while she supports the cause, she makes him question the cause.

What does he feel for the Turk? If not hatred, then what? Pity, that's what. The same thing he feels for Ramela, his betrothed. The very same thing.

He is achy from sitting. What a relief it is to see Sahagian and Gregorian enter the park, these two men who look almost exactly alike with their belted trench coats, their mustaches, their scowls, and their galoshes, but each pretending he doesn't know, doesn't see the other.

CHAPTER THREE

The Rest of Their Lives Will Be Like This

SOMETIMES, on their drives back to Senlis, instead of steering the wheel with one hand, Dub pulls the Fiat to the side of the road so they can pet without running into a tree. Sometimes Yale imagines the rest of their lives will be like this, the two of them so mad for each other they will never quite get where they're going.

But this day he drives nearly straight through. He pulls over once, but it's only because she begs him to. "Crocuses!" she shouts, exaggerating her excitement, hoping to generate some excitement in him. He has been, this ride home, like a tire with a slow leak. The air seeps from him. "Look, Dub," she yells over the motor, "the first crocuses of spring." And she makes him stop, but he waits in the old ambulance while she gets out and pretends to be entranced by the heads of the flowers poking through rotted leaves.

"I thought you wanted to pick them," he says, when she gets back in.

"That's not what I wanted." She takes his hand and tries to coax it at least to her knee.

He won't do it. "I want to get into Senlis before the stalls shut," he says. "I want to buy some vegetables for dinner." It's ludicrous. When has he ever bought vegetables, when has he ever thought about helping with dinner? But he makes a sound like a chuckle, says, "All those open mouths," meaning the orphans, and puts the car in gear. He apparently hasn't noticed that her mouth is open too; that she's so stunned he's removed his hand, has actually yanked it out of her own, that her jaw has dropped. He studies his mirrors once, then twice, as if the road is congested with dozens of other wayward vehicles when the truth is there isn't even a horse cart to be seen, and they drive into the city proper, and finally, desperately, she takes his right hand from the wheel and places it on her skirted thigh. He lets it rest there, but she knows he's only feeling the material.

She never knew this was possible. She was taught it never could happen: that a girl might offer herself and a man might say no.

He parks near the grounds of the Château Royal. As they get out he reminds her that Hugues Capet was crowned there. "Just think," he says.

She *is* thinking, but not about Hugues Capet. She's worried she's done something wrong. She wants to tell him she was only joking, before, in the park. She wants to tell him that everything was fine the way it was. They don't have to talk about what he thinks of her ever again.

She doesn't say anything, though, not one word. He says he wants to take a walk in the waning sunlight, and she finds this encouraging. But beneath the old Roman wall at the edge of the city, she has a moment of alarm. They are standing there, hidden away, cooled by the wall's shadows, and when he turns to her, he seems ready to speak, and she knows he is about to say something important, and though she fears what it might be, she tries to encourage him with her eyes and the angle of her chin. Tell me, she thinks. Let's get it over with. But he only exhales loudly and dramatically and then takes her arm and leads her back into sunshine.

They descend the rue de Montagne. She tells him her shoes pinch. He says nothing. He points out the private gardens. "Yes," she says. "Faded gardens after a bitter winter. How lovely."

"Even faded, I find them beautiful," he says. "I gather you don't." It's as if he wants to imply that they are perfectly unsuited for each other. He sees beauty everywhere; she is dull and shallow. She suspects he is making a case against her. The lawyer in him is hard at work. Soon he will have a list. How could he have ever considered her?

At the bottom of the hill, by the bastions overlooking the river Nonette, he stops to look at the silver lichen in the ancient walls' interstices, to wonder aloud if she finds them as touching as he does—so soft, so gray—and instead of replying she throws her arms around him. He puts his arms around her too, but she is holding on harder, her legs begin to shake from the strain of reaching up, and she holds him fast and tries to think how to ask him what's wrong in a way that will make him forget that anything is, but before she can do it, he breaks from her. "Let's head back," he says. "It will be getting dark in a while." He says this as if darkness will interfere with what she wants from him.

She feels as blurry and burning as the edges of the sinking sun. She doesn't say a word, though. They walk along the medieval road until they are back in the city. They walk a bit more, and she can see the green motor truck waiting for them. They will drive to the château now. She wonders if he will even stay for supper.

"Do you want to go into the church for a minute?" he says. "Do you want to go in and have a small conversation?"

SHE HAS BEEN inside the old cathedral several times before, just to admire the architecture. She's never been in it when it's empty as it is now. The sexton is home eating his early supper, Dub tells her. The priests are off praying, and then they'll be eating as well. He has come here before at this hour, he says. Notre Dame de Senlis, all to himself. She tells him she never knew he did that. He doesn't respond.

The time of day the priests have their supper. This seems to constitute the whole of their small conversation.

Discouraged, defeated, she stops at a bank of white votives. She runs a finger, fast, through one of the flames. She has always found it remarkable, the way you can put your finger into fire, and if you are quick enough you won't feel a thing.

"For God's sake, don't do that," he says. "It's so disrespectful. Just because *you* don't believe. Really, what's wrong with you?"

She is chastened and frightened. Meekly, she follows him as he walks down the wide center aisle flanked by pews. She thinks of other churches she's been in. The Methodist churches in St. Louis where— years ago, it feels like—she attended funerals. The tourist attractions in Paris. Saint-Denis and the remains of shelled Saint-Gervais. Notre Dame de Paris, of course, another shrine to the Virgin Mother, although unlike this church, one that's never deserted. In fact, when she first got to Paris, you had to line up to get in. Once she and Brennan waited over an hour so they could attend a Te Deum of thankfulness for the end of the war. It was a cold day, people buying hot chestnuts from maimed soldiers just to warm their hands, but everyone excited and talkative. It was as if they were queuing up at the doors of a theater. And it *was* like a theater inside. Yale had expected God and saints and souls and candles, and she got some of that, the candles mostly. But what she really got that day was spectacle. First came the choirboys carrying the flags of every Allied nation. Then came the priests, at least a dozen of them. Finally, the star of the show entered, not God, but the cardinal in his crimson robe. The *oohs* and *aahs* made her think of parades, and parades made her think of Will Rogers, lasso tricks, fireworks. Words in the sky.

Notre Dame de Senlis is more modest than the famous Gothics. It is darker and cooler too, yet just as beautiful—even more beautiful if you value simplicity. And being in the cathedral all alone is a gift. This is what being in a museum after hours would feel like. Even though no one would be there to disturb you, you would still speak in a whisper. You would still be awed by everything you saw. But you would be able to cross the velvet ropes and stand as close as you could to every paint- ing, and you would examine every brushstroke, standing so close you could detect the false starts, the paintings beneath the paintings. And you would touch everything.

Here it's the confessionals she wishes to examine. She approaches the nearest and peers through the latticed wood screen. She can see the small bench where the priest must sit and listen. She thinks of wish- ing wells. She thinks she ought to squeeze a sou through the lattice- work and confide the wish she wants granted. *Let me have him. Make him love me.*

Add the word *God,* she thinks, and she'd be praying.

CHAPTER FOUR

Saints and Virgins

HE ISN'T WITH HER. While she paused at the confessional, he continued walking to the altar rail. He stands there now as if waiting to take communion.

She goes to his side, looks up. "It's awfully tall," she says.

"It just seems tall because the chancel is relatively narrow."

"It's very pretty."

They are so close to the pulpit. She wonders if he would laugh if she ducked under the rail and walked right up to it, stood behind it. She could flail her arms, ape Alban Bliss. Her voice would boom; she would shatter stained glass.

But he looks so serious. So unhappy. He hasn't brought her here to mock priests; she knows that. Although he hasn't brought her here to worship either. He doesn't believe, she knows that too. A sudden thought, another wish, comes to her. Could it be that he's brought her here because he knows she's uneasy in churches? Sometimes actually frightened by them? A girl might not receive roses or chocolate from Dub, but then, when she least expects it, she might receive a gift of this magnitude. A twelfth-century cathedral, all her own. *You see? There's nothing to be afraid of. No harm will befall you here.*

Would that explain his reluctance to touch her, to spoon on the drive home? The thought of the gift he was planning to give her—this church?

She tries to take it all in, to appreciate it. The clerestories on the ceiling. The books on the altar table, bound in old leather. She can see the subtle fissures in the stone floor. She is close enough to make out the embroidered hem of the altar cloth, white on white.

As she looks around, he takes one step back, then another to the side. He is standing directly behind her now. He wraps her in his arms. He pulls her back toward him. She takes a baby step backward so her spine rests against his chest. He leans over her, curls down and around her, rests his chin on her shoulder. Though she is not facing him, though they both still face the altar, she cannot be closer to him.

He whispers into her ear. He is going to tell her. *All for you,* he is going to say. *All for us.* This will be their small conversation: for you, for us, and at last the word *love.* She stands still. She holds her breath.

"I'm going to stay in Paris through the end of the conference," he says.

She doesn't move. She is still looking up. Her eyes are on one of the many images of the Virgin above the altar. The long doleful face. The sad flat eyes.

"It could be another year," he says. "It could be only a month. But whenever the Peace Conference ends, that's when they'll most likely be sending me home."

At last she understands. He is in despair, knowing he may soon have to leave France. He doesn't want them to be separated. He is about to ask the question a man asks a woman to prevent their parting.

He is holding her now, not only with both his arms but with one of his ankles wrapped around her right ankle. He's shackling her to him as if he's afraid she will run away. He is squeezing her against him. His chin is sharp on her shoulder. His mustache tickles her ear. She would like to shift, would like to break away, or at least to turn around within his arms. She would like to see his face when he asks her.

"Then," he says, and he is still so close, and he is still whispering, and the whispering reminds her of St. Louis, the library, the moment she first fell in love with him, "then, when I get home, the first thing I'm going to do is marry my fiancée."

She supposes he is waiting for her to squirm out of his arms, but she doesn't. She doesn't speak, still doesn't move. How is it, she thinks, that a tiny invisible virus, something like the Spanish flu bug, can kill a person like *that,* but one is expected to survive this sort of thing, so much worse, so much larger? And not only survive but survive gracefully, a good sport? It's staggering, really. Such a blow, yet still she's standing there. Although she does moan and the moan surprises and humiliates her, and she would clap a hand over her mouth except that he has her arms pinned to her sides.

"It's not that I want to," he says, "or even that I love her. You know how I feel. I love being with you, and I love working with you, but I've made a promise to somebody else, and I've got to keep it, and I'm going to keep it, so . . ."

She waits for him to finish, but he doesn't say anything more. She finds she can turn inside his arms now and face him. When she does, he kisses her mouth as if she has offered it to him. She pulls her head away, but only so she can tilt it back, present her throat. He kisses that too. Her eyes are open; she sees saints and virgins. "Don't stop," she says, and at once he stops.

"No," she says. "Really. It's all right."

"What is?" he says. "That there's someone else? How can it be all right?"

"I don't care about her," she says.

He says, "I care about her," and he lets go. He walks up the aisle of the church, out the door.

CHAPTER FIVE

Precious Cargo

H E WALKS AWAY. She has just absolved him of everything, and his response is to leave, and she understands why. It's because he's so good. He can't bear to hurt her, he can't bear to hurt this other girl. A man this good, how can she let him go?

Outside the cathedral, she catches up to him and snatches at his elbow. He pulls away, gets into the truck, and leans forward, his forehead on the steering wheel. He cradles his head in his arms.

She climbs in the passenger's side and sits down beside him. She rubs his back, small circles. "Hey, soldier," she says. "Do you realize you just left me standing at the altar?"

He raises his head. She smiles at him. He doesn't smile back. Such raw, red eyes. "I can't do this," he says.

His face, the eyes. "All right," she says. "All right. Then we won't."

"Thank you," he says, and drives them home.

On the way he explains the concept of *khosgob*. If you make a promise, you don't go back on it. Where he comes from, people take the idea of the word-tie very seriously.

"You come from Rhode Island," she says. She has been noble and self-sacrificing for at least ten minutes; it has made her irritable. "Just so you know."

"I know where I'm from," he says.

They don't say anything more, not even when he turns into the long driveway and both of them realize they forgot to buy vegetables. The climate seems different now that they are on the grounds of the château. Perhaps it's just dusk having fallen, but the sky is icy white. Only hours before they saw crocuses. Now it's ready to snow again.

At the verdigris fountain she reaches for the wheel. She is being playful but in an angry way, and he elbows her off. "Stop it," he says.

"No, let me steer to the house," she says. Again she grabs at the wheel, and again he pushes her. "You're not very much fun today," she says, being cute, being bratty, and he thinks, She is so angry with me; and then he thinks, Who needs this? and imagines getting out, letting her drive wherever she likes while he walks away. He will hitchhike back to Paris. He will claim French hooligans stole the old ambulance. He will desert the army, get on a boat, sail away, someplace exotic: Indo-China, Tahiti.

But no. If he were to go someplace else, if he were to run away, then it would all be so easy. He could just take her with him. And maybe that's what he should do. Why isn't that a viable solution? To turn the truck around, drive back to Paris. In his room at the Crillon, they could lie together on a featherbed. The next morning he could pack and then drive them to Spain. What if they did? The two of them gone. People wondering forever. *The damnedest thing. One day they just up and disappeared into thin air. Nobody's seen them since. Stole a motor truck too.*

Raffi would tell Ramela he was dead. Someone else would deal with Kerim Bey.

He knows one thing for certain. Yale is living inside him now. She has set up lodging inside his head in a way Ramela never has and never will, and she won't be going away anytime soon. He supposes this means he is crazy about her. Being crazy is having something inside your head that ought not be there, isn't it? He wonders when he first let her in. He thinks it was probably when she stood on her toes at the Quai d'Orsay and insisted he allow her to help him.

"All right, fine," he says. "Go ahead. Steer to the house."

"No," she says. She crosses her arms across her chest.

He says, "Oh, for God's sake. Come on. Go ahead."

"I don't want to anymore," she says. "You've taken the fun out of it."

"Fine," he says, and he releases the wheel, jogs the gear shift to neutral, takes his foot off the accelerator. The truck drifts off to a side of its choosing before it sputters and dies. They are on wet matted leaves now, a thin coat of plant debris over mud. Soon they will sink into the mire.

She doesn't budge. He is the one who relents.

"Hokees," he says, "please. Steer the goddamn truck."

She wants to know what *hokees* means first.

"My soul," he says. "My own beloved soul."

She makes a face as if such sentimentality repels her, but she also takes the wheel. He works everything else, the gears, the pedals, touching the gas as she turns out of the muck. How slowly they drive, and, as if they've discussed it, not to the château but to the pond, to the stone wall by the copse, the two of them exercising as much care and caution as they possibly can, as if they have been charged with transporting precious cargo and neither quite trusts the other to do the job right.

By the wall they park, get out, enter the woods. They use their coats as blankets. Yale lifts her head. She watches Dub's hands and his face. He undresses her only to the extent necessary. An unbuttoning here, an unhooking there, a general rearranging, a pushing, a pulling, a folding over, and through it all she helps only in the most cursory ways, by raising her hips or, when a sleeve needs removing, offering her arm. Mostly she just watches. She loves the way he is gritting his teeth. She loves how his nostrils flare—a nice touch of the dramatic. His skin turns red, that's how hard he's working, yet his eyelids flutter as if he is peacefully sleeping, having sweet dreams. Then he pushes harder, and she cries out, and he covers her mouth with his hand. For a moment he lifts himself off her, his head rising, his spine curved, his body a question mark. "It's all right," she says through his fingers, and he removes his hand, and she apologizes, even though she is the one who's been hurt, even though tears are dripping sideways down her cheeks, into her ears.

By the time they've finished, he is the one with tears in his eyes. It makes her laugh. "Oh, Dub," she says. They sit up, adjust their clothes. He puts his arm around her.

"I guess we'd better start packing for hell," he says.

"Always consigning us to hell," she says. "Another man might have mentioned love at this point."

CHAPTER SIX

Springtime in Berlin

A COUNTERTERRORIST MOVEMENT is comprised of three arms. The intelligence arm keeps track of the persons the movement has marked for murder. The technical arm gathers and develops the weaponry needed to carry out the murders. The political arm endeavors to persuade the world that the murders are just.

Since October 1918, the month when the primary architects of the Armenian massacres fled to Europe aboard a German warship, Raffi Soghokian has lived in Berlin, where at separate times he has participated in all three arms of the counterterrorist movement known as Operation Erinyes.

It was Raffi's choice, the Berlin assignment. He could have opted for France, spent more time with Aram. But Berlin was where the escaped murderers were hiding; it was therefore the only place where Raffi believed he could fulfill his life's dream, his calling—to be a full-time professional vengeance seeker.

And yet how quickly he grew unhappy in Berlin. It was not only the city's desperation. It wasn't only that he missed Aram. Nor was it that the big prizes—Talaat, Enver, Djemal—remained exasperatingly elusive.

The reason for Raffi's unhappiness in Berlin was the same reason so many are unhappy wherever they reside—he hated his job. And his reasons for hating it were no different from anyone else's. He resented competing with other eager young men for the best assignments. He disliked spending so much time with co-workers not of his choosing, not to his taste. Plus, the hours were long, the pay inadequate, and the tasks he performed boring and repetitive.

Above all, he loathed his boss.

He might as well have stayed in Rhode Island, he thought, might as well have continued working for Acme Plating.

The leader of the Berlin branch of Erinyes was a small Russian-Armenian, sleek and dark as a seal and not much older than Raffi, who went by a nickname that was difficult to translate into English but came close to meaning the Spreader of Horror. "Don't mistake me for Aram Kazarian," the Spreader of Horror told Raffi when they first shook hands, "with his bags of money and his soft heart for bourgeois Americans." The Spreader of Horror smiled. It was a narrow smile, a mean smile, a sneer's first cousin. "How old is the lion anyway?" he asked. "It's hard to believe he's not dead yet." He laughed at this joke. "I don't know how it works in gay Paree, Comrade Soghokian, but here's the way we work in Berlin. I give the orders. You follow the orders. Can you do that, Comrade Soghokian?"

He had been assigned, as he had requested, to the intelligence arm of Erinyes, and he had followed the Spreader of Horror's orders until the January day he realized the man buying tickets for the Orient Express to Paris was Kerim Bey. Then something took hold of him, and he went to the station the next day, got on the train too. "You will receive praise and a promotion and better assignments," Aram had said to Raffi, and Raffi had thought how ironic it would be if the monster responsible for the church-burning in Adana should also be responsible for the greatest advance in Raffi's career. But when Raffi returned to Berlin only several days later, he was greeted with no praise, only fury. "Who told you to leave the country?" the Spreader of Horror demanded. "Once Kerim fled our jurisdiction, it was Kazarian's job to keep up with him. We had other things planned for you to do here. Your absence inconvenienced us."

"Aram is short-handed," Raffi said, a mistake because the Spreader of Horror began laughing, joking: short-handed, so true, three fingers short of a right hand, one finger short of a left. Raffi felt the Mauser in the waist of his trousers. He bit his lip with his gold tooth. He thought, Yes, Aram is short-handed. And suffering and dying and relying far too much on Doubleday Hagopian. And yet, Aram in France still accomplished what you in Berlin couldn't. It's Aram's men who have cornered Kerim. He waited for the laughter to end. He said, "I didn't want to risk our losing Kerim completely. A decision had to be made on the spur of the moment. I had to act."

The Spreader of Horror was unmoved. "It was France's problem, not yours. If the old man botched the job, people on my level would have dealt with it. We might have temporarily lost Kerim, but we'd have been able to shore up the movement. New leadership. A more effective chain of command. For which you have no respect."

On the train back to Berlin he had fantasized being asked to help find Talaat. Instead he was assigned to a lesser Turk, an exile named Halim. It irked him. Not that he would have minded shooting Halim. The guy had deported thousands, they had it in writing—the orders, the secret memoranda. The guy was a bastard, they were all of them bastards. It was just that Erinyes already knew where Halim Bey lived.

Where was the intrigue, the need to use one's intellect and cunning? Raffi sat by the window of a coffee shop all day long and watched the criminal's house. The man never ventured outside. They already knew that. So why watch the residence? Did the Spreader of Horror fear the mortar and bricks would tiptoe away if no one kept an eye on them? At least Dub Hagopian got to leave the rue des Belles Feuilles after a few hours went by. Raffi had to spend an entire day, eight hours, in a coffeehouse run by a Zionist who, though sympathetic to the Armenian cause, still expected Raffi to part with at least a few coins when he occupied a table in his establishment. The result was that Raffi spent all day drinking coffee. At mealtimes, he ordered a slice of cake. By day's end he was tapping his foot, jogging his leg so rapidly and compulsively that coffee spilled from cups on adjacent tables.

Across the street, serene and still, Halim's house remained affixed to its foundation. The only movement Raffi ever saw there came at dusk: a maid turning on a lamp in the dining room, Halim's wife gliding into the parlor. She was Anatolian but wore western dress and twisted her hair into a chignon. She was as serene as the house. He often saw her arranging fresh flowers in a vase.

She never lowered a shade or drew a curtain. It was as if she knew Raffi was out there with orders to watch but do nothing more, and she had decided to taunt him, to put on a show. Any Berliner walking by could have seen her performance too: spring flowers being fussed over, while the rest of the city starved. It was as if these people weren't happy unless they were tormenting someone. Raffi began longing to shoot the wife as well.

On the final day that Raffi worked for the intelligence arm of Operation Erinyes, he had finished his last cup of cold coffee and pushed aside a dry torte at the same time Halim and his wife began gnawing on what looked to be lamb chops. Another Erinyes man had entered the café and taken a seat. As if a six o'clock whistle had blown, Raffi threw down his money and left the shop. But instead of returning to the cold-water flat he rented from one of the wealthier members of the Berlin branch, he did something he had only previously imagined doing. He crossed the street and then, partially shielded from view by an evergreen, he stood to the side of Halim's brightly lit dining-room window, removed his pistol from the band of his trousers, and aimed directly at Halim's face.

That's all he did. He didn't shoot, he just stood there. A tableau: *Revolutionary with Gun*. He stood there until he heard the sleigh bells on the door to the coffeehouse jingle.

The other Erinyes man had bolted out of the shop, waving his arms and hissing like an angry cat. Raffi saluted the man and returned the pistol to his waistband.

He went home then. No one else had seen his pantomime. Halim, the wife, their maid—none of them suspected a thing.

So where was the harm in what he'd done? He had no intention of firing, he told the Spreader of Horror. He only wanted to show the other Erinyes man how easy it would be. Sure, maybe it had been his way of asking a comrade what the hell they were waiting for. But he hadn't done a thing, not a damned thing.

They demoted him anyway. He didn't go quietly. "Do we have to wait until he gets away?" he said. "Is that what you want? For them all to give us the slip the way Kerim Bey nearly did?"

The Spreader of Horror, seated behind his large desk, looked up. He sneered. Then he looked down again. He returned to his paperwork. He was writing a memorandum to the Allied Powers at the Peace Conference. He had come to believe that the right prose would persuade Wilson to appoint him a delegate, even though both Aharonian and Nubar had been repeatedly rebuffed when they asked for the same thing. But the Spreader of Horror was a man with big dreams. The Spreader of Horror planned someday to be president of the new Republic of Armenia. And as long as he and the Allied leaders all happened to be in western Europe at the same time, he didn't see why they shouldn't begin forging a relationship. He wished to show them how reasonable, how western, he could be.

"Kerim Bey did not give us the slip," the Spreader of Horror demurred, struggling to keep his mind on his memorandum.

"Yes, thanks to me he didn't," Raffi said.

"Thanks to a number of persons, as I hear it." The Spreader of Horror put his pen down. He looked up once again. "Listen to me, Soghokian," he said. "We can shoot Kerim Bey tomorrow if I decide that's what we should do. We can shoot him and Halim Bey and Dr. Shakir and Dr. Nazim in the next five minutes, should I order it. It's not what I want. It's not in our best interests at this point in history. The new regime in Turkey has at last acquiesced to the British demand that there be tribunals. We have an obligation to wait and see what the Turkish courts do concerning the Berlin fugitives. We have to allow the Allies to exercise every option to secure a legal solution before we take other action."

"I can tell you right now what the Turkish courts will decide," Raffi said.

"You are having trouble understanding me, Soghokian. Let me speak slowly. I give the orders. You follow the orders. I make the decisions. You do what you're told."

Raffi was not in the mood. "You're clinging to a political solution when you don't understand the first thing about politicians," he said.

The Spreader of Horror nodded. He removed his glasses and cleaned each lens slowly, carefully, with a cloth. He had seen powerful men do such things—smile when they were angry, nod when they meant no, slowly slowly clean their glasses and say things like "I give the orders; you follow the orders"—in plays back in Russia. "Perhaps you are right, Soghokian," the Spreader of Horror said. "Perhaps your strength lies in the political realm."

That was it for Raffi in intelligence. He was reassigned the next day to the political arm, where he lasted most of one meeting. "Let me play devil's advocate," an old professor had begun, and Raffi had covered his ears with his hands. "Why do we need someone to advocate on behalf of the devil?" he shouted. "The devil is the enemy. Why are we sitting here trying to see his side of things instead of going out and killing him?" The old professor and his cronies laughed nervously. Before anyone shot anyone, they explained, it was necessary to come up with a set of guidelines to govern such shootings, to make sure they were morally just. They read to him what they'd come up with to date:

1. Reprisal is legitimate when all available means of nonviolence have failed.
2. Reprisal is legitimate when the suffering inflicted *upon* the injured party does not exceed the suffering inflicted *by* the injured party.
3. Reprisal is legitimate when it is preceded by formal notice of the planned action.

"I like the last one," Raffi said. "Yes, let's send little notes to all the Turks in Berlin. *My Dear Effendi: Tomorrow at one we plan to blow your worthless brains onto the sidewalk. If you could please meet us on your front steps at the aforesaid hour it would be most appreciated.*"

The professors were nonplussed. We need standards, they said. We are Christians, they explained. This was Raffi's big chance. He told them the story of the paper ladle. *Beloved Armenians, hear my words and understand my meaning.* They'd all heard it a thousand times, they said, but he shouted them down. He gestured where Aram would have gestured. He bellowed where Aram would have bellowed. "Where guns and swords make noise," Raffi screamed as others had screamed before him, "of what significance are appeals and petitions?"

"Please don't yell," the professors said.

In a slightly softer voice, Raffi moved that the political arm vote itself out of existence.

The next day he was with the technicians. They met in a dank basement where it was necessary to wear several sweaters to keep from shivering all day, but it wasn't that bad because, given the absence of windows and daylight, the technicians were also spared the sight of the frustrating world spinning around them. Also, there was a sense of accomplishment down in the basement that Raffi had never before experienced in Berlin. It was exhilarating when, as a result of fiddling with some pins or a spring, a gun that had been misfiring suddenly made a large hole in an empty tin can. Or when you mixed this and that and came up with a tiny bomb. Raffi was fascinated by how small bombs could be. Cottonwood, that was the essential ingredient, but in lieu of cottonwood, any sort of tinder drenched in any sort of fuel did the trick. A cigarette lighter plus threads from your trousers or lint from your belly button. It was astonishing, all the inanimate, innocent things you could teach to blow someone to pieces.

Raffi was grateful to the technicians for the practical skills they taught him. He admired their enthusiasm for clever killing, their conviction and passion that was so much like his own. Still, he was very much aware that their passion was confined to a basement. They never went out; they never blew anything up besides all those hapless tin cans. After he left the third arm of Erinyes, this time of his own volition, he asked the Spreader of Horror (whose office he'd barged into without an appointment) what good it was having the most up-to-date bombs, all the 1908 Lugers and Mausers in the world, if you never used them?

The Spreader of Horror ordered him to stay put, to remain in Berlin. "Don't shame yourself by running like a child to Aram Kazarian," the Spreader of Horror warned Raffi.

Raffi asked the wealthy fellow whose miserable flat he was renting to deliver a letter for him. On the front of the envelope he printed the Spreader of Horror's given name. Inside, on formal stationery borrowed from the wealthy fellow, he wrote:

I have learned that reprisal is legitimate when preceded by formal notice of the action planned. Accordingly, please note the following: I am off to Paris. I plan to take action.

CHAPTER SEVEN

The Gare de l'Est

RAFFI RETURNS to Paris on a train that deposits him at the Gare de l'Est. Coincidentally, the British diplomat Trevor Hamilton is at that station on the very same night, awaiting the arrival of the very same train.

The British diplomat is there to meet an old school chum he's not seen for at least a decade. Despite the intervening years, Hamilton spots his old friend right away. The man hasn't changed since their school days; he is as handsome and fair as Hamilton remembers. The two men shake hands warmly, repair to the station's café, and sit at a small round table.

The old chum is a German emissary who has come to France illegally and must return to Berlin as soon as he can. The next train to Germany leaves in fifteen minutes. He checks his watch often.

"The treaty is impossible," he says, after the briefest exchange of greetings. He speaks flawless English. His faint accent makes him sound regal.

"I know," Hamilton says. "It's the bloody French."

"But you can't just throw up your hands and say it's the bloody French," says the German. How calm and professional he sounds, a learned man imparting wisdom to an inferior. "You must change their minds. The reparations they want are prohibitive. Their demands for the Saar are extraordinary."

Hamilton warms his hands on his coffee cup. He looks at his fingernails. They appear waxy blue in the night. "The war has done something to the weather," he says. "All the mustard gas, one supposes. Spring's come so late this year. And then there's the coal shortage." He takes a sip of coffee, tastes water. "Several of us motored to the Front last week," he says. "All those fields, the lush farmland—all gone now. Simply gone. One lad picked up a box of fuses. Said he was going to use them as chess pieces. Turned out they contained fulminate of mercury.

There were some larger ones he let be. Wouldn't fit well in the hand, he said. Later we were told those contained TNT. Children all around us, mind you, playing trench war. Anyone could pick the bloody things up."

"Perhaps the reasons for anger are also the reasons to put anger aside and make a just peace," says the German.

"Tell me how to make a just peace under the present circumstances." Hamilton has meant to lower his voice, but instead it has risen. "Everything's all bollixed up at the conference. Clemenceau's not been himself since the assassination attempt. Wilson's not been himself since finding out Colonel House gave away his precious League of Nations. He's acquired this godawful tic. It drives one mad just to pass him in the hall. Lloyd George, meanwhile, is busy wining and dining his charming secretary, and Orlando is obsessed with annexing Fiume."

"The Council of Four. Upon whom we rely."

"What's more, they meet only in secret now. All one can do these days is sit in the Ministry and eat macaroons."

The German looks at his watch. "Then at least tell me this. When will the blockade be lifted? No macaroons in Germany. No food, milk, or medicine. German children are literally dying in the streets."

"There are no plans to lift it, I'm afraid."

"And how much will reparations amount to in the end?"

"The Americans say twenty-five billion. We say one hundred. The French say two hundred."

The German checks his watch once more. He rises and puts his fedora on his head, covering his flaxen, pomaded hair. He smiles slightly. "Very well," he says. "I shall report that the British are four times as mad as the Americans, but only half as mad as the French."

Hamilton stands too. He recalls the two of them as boys, kisses under sycamores, blankets on cold, empty beaches. Now he doesn't so much as pat the man on the back.

"Trev—" the German says.

Hamilton has begun to weep. "No, it's true," he says. "There will be no peace." He looks up, wishing the German would reach out, dry his tears. The German only looks at him coolly. "And I suppose I shall never see you again," Hamilton says.

Raffi is sitting at a table nearby, waiting for the train to Senlis. He can't hear the two men, but he watches them. It's easy to spy on them;

they have eyes only for each other. A tête-à-tête, their heads close, their voices low and anguished. A lovers' quarrel, Raffi thinks, when the prettier one runs off.

Now the darker one is giving Raffi a sidelong glance. Raffi hurriedly finishes his coffee and returns to the concrete quai. He seems to be the only person on the platform who is waiting for a train. All the others are the usual allotment of beggars and prostitutes. Gay Paree, as the Spreader of Horror called it. Raffi peers down the track. He wishes for the impossible: a train to arrive early.

Paris in this frigid, corrupt spring. And yet the city is so much better off than Berlin. The day before, when he was preparing to leave that tormented city, there were riots and executions in the gutters, child rebels and factory workers ripped apart by soldiers who had never relinquished their machine guns. All this in bright daylight. And at night came the baiting and beating of Jews. A soldier, drunk on the afternoon's victory over the Bolsheviks, had offered him a Jewish girl. He'd had one arm around her waist, which she was trying to pry off. She wore a long wool skirt and a white blouse with a ruffle at the neck. She had no coat. It was clear she'd been pulled minutes ago from a nearby house. Raffi imagined her washing dinner dishes or practicing at a piano when the doors to her apartment were kicked suddenly open. She was bleeding from the mouth and carrying on, not whimpering prettily or asking for mercy but shrieking like a banshee and trying to bite the arm of the hooligan who was holding her and bouncing her breasts for Raffi's amusement. The hooligan was laughing. They were always laughing, these thugs. They were the happiest men in Europe.

Raffi had kept walking. Only when he'd gone several blocks, finally stopping before a dance hall, did it occur to him that he should have accepted the girl and taken her someplace safe.

He went inside the hall. It was painfully loud in there, but he wanted a drink. He had one, then a second. He felt around inside his pocket, located his train ticket. Tomorrow, he'd be out of this place. Still, he ordered a third shot of whiskey.

CHAPTER EIGHT

Tea

THE DAY RAFFI SOGHOKIAN heads to France is an equally exhausting day for Yale White. Early in the morning, Seta bundles up all the little ducklings and embarks on a journey to Le Havre, where she will put them aboard a boat to America. Once across the Atlantic, the little girls will be distributed among rich Armenian-Americans who are willing to take them in and raise them. The ducklings leave behind approximately three thousand small white pebbles, all washed and stowed in hat boxes. They take with them the ability to giggle, cuddle, and explain the merits of avant-garde art.

Seta has gone through this particular pain before, letting go of children who were never hers to begin with. She has learned she needs an immediate distraction, and what she plans to do, after calling adieu to the ducks, is spend a few nights in Le Havre with a daughter who lives in that city. She will dote on her grandchildren. A perfect cure.

"Try to enjoy the quiet," she says to Brennan and Yale. She kisses each of them. "Another batch will arrive soon. The silence will not last."

In the meantime, it will just be the twins and poor Shushan, for whom no family has been found. The thick brows. The acne. The perpetual glower. She is a girl who does not take a pretty picture.

To protect Shushan from having to watch the ducklings leave for a happier life, Brennan has taken her outside to dig. To prevent Brennan from thinking too much about the ducklings, Shushan has suggested they find a new spot to dig in, a spot with no memories attached. And so they are digging today near the stone wall by the pond.

Sometimes Yale has joined in the activity just to be sociable, but she never lasts long. Really, it's the most tedious occupation. Sitting in a truck for hours while staring at a door that rarely opens is far more stimulating. Waiting tables at the Y was more scintillating. "I suppose I'm just not the creative type," she hears herself saying, after several minutes of digging, piling, counting to ten.

On the day the ducks leave, she doesn't bother to go outside at all. Dub has told her he's needed at Translation, so there's no spying on Kerim that day. This leaves Yale unemployed, and having nothing to do makes her feel low, especially with the weather so gloomy again, the house so still. In the early afternoon, there is a visitor who turns out to be a doctor summoned by Aram, scheduled for a time he knew Seta would be away. After the doctor leaves, Yale steps into the study with Aram's afternoon tea and finds him weeping against the back of his hand.

He composes himself upon seeing her. "I'm not bawling for myself," he tells her. He has grown a full beard since she first met him; it's as if his head is swathed in fine silver. "I'm ready myself. But poor Seta. She so adamantly pretends all is well. I can't imagine how she will face up to things when the time comes."

"And Dub," Yale says. "Dub doesn't want to face it either." She realizes too late that it's a clumsy thing to have said. She's implied that all the rest of them know he is dying, have known for a while, and have come to accept it, and although it's the truth she shouldn't have said so. Aram's eyes fill again. She curses herself. This is what comes of telling the truth.

But then Aram takes a breath and smiles at her, and they have a little discussion about what the doctor has told him. They talk about the likely escalation of pain and the application of morphine. She smoothes his afghan while he speaks. She clears off the low table he has pulled alongside the leather couch. She knows he appreciates the elegant lines of the tea service—a gift from Poincaré, he has told her, trying to conceal his pride in having such a famous acquaintance—and she wants the service to look its best, no clutter around it. He helps her tidy up by issuing instructions. Put the map over there on the desk, if you please. Kindly tear up those papers and toss them away. Pour a little of that brandy into the tea, if you will. No, my dear girl, a touch more than that. You can be a bit generous with a dying old man.

He is so slight now that there is plenty of room for her to join him on the couch. She sits by his calves and looks straight ahead, out the window. She can see Brennan and Shushan in the distance, the two of them kneeling by the muddy border against the stone wall. "I don't know about my sister's project," Yale says. "I think she's scared all your herbs away. Only the chives have come back so far. And now she's after the garden by the pond."

"No, it's all for the good," Aram says. "They work the soil at the same time. A little bit of art, a little bit of weeding."

"Is it better than what Dub and I are doing?" she asks. "Let's say they manage to dig up all those stones and put them in a glass tank and send them around the world. Let's say people actually go and see what five hundred thousand looks like. Will that accomplish more than we will?"

He tries to sit up. "Weak as a kitten," he says. "Can you believe I once leaped off horses and knocked men to the ground?"

She says she can, and he smiles. This is her talent with Aram. She makes him smile. Her humor, her intelligence, her charm—he says it's her Armenian side coming out. He attributes everything he likes about her to her Armenian grandfather. Sometimes she feels defensive, says, "My paternal grandparents were important too."

"Well," he says, responding now to her question. "I would like to hear your opinion. You tell me which is the more valuable, your sister's project or your own. But first, what is it you think you are doing?"

She is surprised and pleased that he refers to spying on Kerim Bey as her own project. "I don't know," she says. "We're watching. We're watching and waiting."

"Exactly right. But watching and waiting for what?"

"I don't know. I used to think we were waiting for Kerim Bey to be indicted in Turkey, and then we would say, *Yoo-hoo, over here, come and get him.* But now I don't know."

"No," Aram says. "You are exactly right again. We are waiting for indictments. We are waiting for Turkey to hold trials."

"Forgive me," she says. "But do we honestly think that Mustafa Kemal will do that?"

"No," Aram says. "Honestly, we do not."

"So we're waiting for them to do what we don't believe they'll do?"

"Exactly. And as soon as they don't do it, we'll stop waiting."

She smiles. "And then what?"

"No, no. You tell me."

Speaking slowly. Wanting to get it right. Wanting to help. "Perhaps we ought to appeal to the British. If the Turks refuse to indict the criminals, the British should set up the international tribunal they're always talking about. I think the Brits are our best hope."

"Once again you are correct," Aram says. "Yes, we will turn to Britain. Of course, Britain won't lift a finger. Oh, she'll say a great deal, and Lloyd George will repeatedly use the word *deplorable*. Do you know what it means when a man says that something is deplorable? It means that this thing is so ghastly, the speaker must take a moment to bitterly denounce it before going on with his life. No, I assure you, in the end Britain won't hold any trials. And so she will be no different from the Turks she deplores."

He has more to say, she can tell, but he's stopped by a racking, choking cough. He reaches for his handkerchief and spits a thick black substance into it. She averts her head. The coughing, the spitting continue. She wants very much to leave; she thinks she should. Instead, she puts her hand on Aram's foot. She sits there looking away from him, looking out the window, all the while holding on to the great man's toes.

Even when the coughing fit ends, she can't look at him. She doesn't want to see his face scarlet from effort. She doesn't want to glimpse the soiled handkerchief. She doesn't think he wants her seeing those things either. "I should go," she says. "You should rest."

"First won't you pour me another cup of tea?" he asks.

"The tea is ice cold," she tells him.

"Omit the tea, then. And consider a cup for yourself. If you wanted to stay just a bit longer, I could tell you a story about England."

He wants her to stay. She doesn't know whether to feel flattered or trapped. She prepares their refreshments. She sits at his calves. He reaches for her hand, pats it. She loves him, she does, but still—the missing digits—she recoils and pulls away.

CHAPTER NINE

St. Petersburg

THE FOLLWING IS A TRUE STORY. It happened in St. Petersburg, in the frigid month of December, in the heartbreaking year of 1915. Check your history books if you don't believe it.

Your history books will also remind you that at this time the Ottoman Empire, led by Talaat, Enver, and Djemal Pasha, was winning the war in the Middle East. Talaat Pasha had secured a route through the Balkans. Enver Pasha, having decimated the British in Gallipoli, was readying to march on Iraq. Djemal Pasha was occupying Syria, where he was very content.

Djemal, in fact, was more than content in Syria. He was besotted with the place. He wanted to stay there forever, put his feet up, relax. In short, Djemal wished to retire.

And so Djemal Pasha came up with a plan. He sent a note to his enemies, the Russians. He offered them the deal of a lifetime. If the Russians would agree not to interfere with his peaceful life in the desert, he would defeat Turkey for them.

Here's how he would do it, he said. Rousing himself one last time, he would rally his armies and, without any help from the West, without bringing harm to the head of a single Allied soldier, he would attack and destroy Talaat and Enver, his brother triumvirs. Then he'd surrender.

As simple as that. And there was more. As an additional gesture of goodwill, he would give the West the great city of Constantinople. And, all right, he would throw in the Straits of the Dardanelles too. Those prizes, the cause of so much strife, so much death—he would just hand them over. Turkey and all the trimmings presented to the Allies on a silver platter.

And one more thing. He would also immediately end the Armenian deportations.

All he wanted in return was to be sultan of Syria. Nothing else.

Naturally, the Russians didn't believe a word of it. What commander who is winning a war offers to defeat himself? It's as absurd as if the stronger of two boxers suddenly turned his fists on his own nose and knocked himself out while his opponent stood in the ring scratching his head and wondering what to do next.

Clearly the offer was a ruse. Or perhaps Djemal was insane. In either case, the Russians turned him down. Thank you, but no, thanks. Really, we couldn't. Back to your corners, and, when the bell rings, come out fighting.

But the offer continued to nag at them. What if Djemal had actually meant what he said? Stranger things have happened, though no one could think of any. But, still, what if this offer was genuine? It couldn't be genuine. But what if it was?

And so a meeting was arranged, the Russians enlisting the help of a certain Armenian freedom fighter, an old *aslan* who happened to be in the Caucasus at the time. The old *aslan* had been trying to persuade another reluctant general into battle. Now he was dispatched to Syria, where he could not only talk to this new reluctant general but also look him in the eye.

In the end, the *fedayee* came to believe the pasha. He left Syria for St. Petersburg, where he would tell the czar of the pasha's sincerity. On the way there, he stopped briefly in Bitlis, where he rescued his American son from the dreary life of a soldier serving with an army at rest.

Oh, St. Petersburg, that magnificent city that no longer exists! Women swept through the streets in gowns of fur. Chaliapin sang at the opera house. No matter that three feet of snow lay on the ground. The sledge ponies wore wreaths of fresh flowers.

And yet, there were small signs of what was to come. One day, a shooting in the street, blood on the snow. The next, a wild-haired fellow preaching revolution on the same corner. And the next day, while the mass at St. Isaac's concluded with a prayer for the Imperial Family, a prayer so heartfelt that tears slipped down the worshippers' faces, rumor had it that the czarina and her children had fled the Winter Palace and were sharing a small house outside the city with a man called Rasputin.

But the *fedayee* and his American son, having no reason to fear anything, not with the startling offer of peace they were bringing, headed directly and eagerly to that grand Winter Palace. They sat in the office of the foreign minister. They were surrounded by great Russian leaders. They repeated Djemal's offer: Russia's enemy overthrown, peace restored on her southern border, the gifts of Constantinople and the Dardanelles, the end of the Armenian deportations.

"Will you agree to Djemal's offer?" the *fedayee* asked the Russians.

"What's not to agree to?" the Russians replied.

Waiting now to hear from the other Allies, the *fedayee* and the American soldier remained in the city for several more weeks. They were entertained during those weeks by a third secretary to the foreign minister, a young man named Konstantin Kobakov. They had meals with Konstantin Kobakov's family beneath a portrait of the czar. Kostya. They went to church with him. They skated with his children.

It was Kostya who summoned them to the palace in early January, Kostya whom they found sitting behind the foreign minister's grand alabaster desk like a little boy playing at being a grown-up. The foreign minister could not be there to meet them, Kostya said. None of the other ministers could be there either. He had therefore been asked to convey the news. They laughed at his formality. Kostya opened his hands wide. He began to speak. Nothing came out. He began to sob. It was not quite the foolish spectacle it sounds. He was Russian. One got used to their tears.

France, it turned out, wanted Syria for herself. England, despite losing all her battles in the Middle East, still hoped to acquire that part of the world. As for the deportations—well, Djemal and his emissaries had made a miscalculation there. They thought that when the Allies said that saving Armenians was one of their critical objectives, that the Allies had actually meant it.

"You," Kostya said to the American boy. "Look at you. Such a young man. Why are you even here? God has given you half a coat of armor. He is telling you to do what you need to do to secure justice for your people. He is saying if you do part of it, he will be at your side. He will help with the rest."

Take arms. Take arms. And again, take arms.

Then Kostya Kobakov turned to the old *fedayee* and said, "I'm sorry,

Monsieur Kazarian. I'd rather have shot myself than told you their news. It's simply deplorable."

That is essentially the end of the story. The American sailed home to Rhode Island. The old *fedayee* stayed on several more days, loose ends to tie up. Then he went back to France, where he now made his home.

CHAPTER TEN

Loose Ends

ARAM'S STORY ENDED unhappily for most of its characters. The war with the Ottomans lasted another three years. The deportations, the slaughter, the torture in the desert continued. Poor Djemal never became sultan of Syria.

Still, one man's unhappy ending is another's happily-ever-after. Talaat and Enver never learned what Djemal had tried to do to them. That was good news for Talaat and Enver, and even better news for Djemal. And look what was happening now. France was getting Syria after all. England was taking the rest of the Middle East. Just as they wanted.

As for the moral of the story?

"If you want something done right, do it yourself," Yale says.

"Yes," Aram says. "Once again you are correct."

"No politics. No politicians. Just put on your half coat of armor and sally forth."

"Well put," Aram says.

"That's fair," Yale says. "Nobody can say it isn't."

"How many times can we negotiate with such faithless men?" Aram says.

"I know," Yale says.

"Again and again and again," he says. "And always the same results."

"Exactly," she says. "Again and again and again. And yet here you are. Negotiating once more."

"And this time the brutality is so heinous, civilized men can barely bring themselves to describe it."

"And yet, because you are civilized men, you wait for the world to mete out justice."

"If my voice was still respected, we would not be waiting."

Aram's head falls back against his pillow. His eyes close. Telling the story has depleted all his strength. Yale takes the teacup from him. She smooths the afghan. How quickly he's fallen asleep.

Several minutes go by before he says, his eyes still closed, still apparently asleep, "Shoot the messenger." Talking in his sleep; he does this sometimes. "Shoot the messenger," he repeats. She smiles. *Don't* shoot the messenger is what he means. "Nazarbekian was right," he says. He lies so still, he's like a corpse with a few last things to get off its chest. "In his tent he told me, 'Stop killing boys. Start killing the politicians.'"

So lucid. Perhaps he's awake, just resting his eyes. "Like Princip with the Archduke," she says. "Although look where that got him."

Now Aram opens his eyes. They are so blue. Every day they startle her anew. "Shoot the messenger," he says again.

He looks at her expectantly. It seems he is giving her an order. She surveys the room, tries to see if there's something he wants.

"Can you imagine how angry I was?" he says. "And he was the one they sent to me. Not the czar. Not Lord Balfour. Not the foreign minister's first or second secretary. And I was a soldier. Had they forgotten? I did what I had to do. What my general told me to do."

"Aram," she says. She pats the back of his hand lightly. "*Medz-hayrig*, are you awake?"

"Nazarbekian. My general. He was the one. Shoot the messenger, he said."

"I don't understand," she says. "You were the messenger, yes? You were bringing a message from Djemal Pasha. What happened? Did somebody try to shoot you?"

He is suddenly as frustrated as a child whose baby talk can't be deciphered by the new nursemaid. He is furious, on the brink of a tantrum. The extent of his rage is nearly funny. "No," he says, seething. "*He* was the messenger: Konstantin Kobakov."

"Someone shot Konstantin Kobakov?" she says. "The politician?"

He simmers down then. "Someone," he murmurs. He closes his eyes.

These waking nightmares. She supposes they will happen more and more frequently. One of the things she's learned from Aram is that dying can be a very slow process. She hadn't known, but now she sees. Aram's body is a house of cards. Each day when she comes into the study, another card has fallen. But just one card. Each day the structure is weaker. Each day she tells herself the kindest thing she could do would be to knock down the whole flimsy structure, one fell swoop, over and done with. Instead, she brings tea and watches as he comes apart slowly, so slowly.

"All right," she says. She is crooning the same way Brennan croons to her charges. "It's going to be all right," she says, but he's already sleeping. She neatens his afghan once again. She tends to the fire. She arranges the cups on the tray.

The brandy hasn't agreed with her. She needs to put something nourishing into her stomach. Or perhaps all she needs is fresh air. She makes herself head to the door. As she carries the silver tray, the sterling teapot, past the window, she looks out at Brennan and Shushan. They are far away, small, but still at it.

For a moment her thoughts wander to this Russian, this Kostya who dared tell Aram the killings in the desert would continue. Apparently shot dead for telling him that. She looks back at Aram asleep. Well, nothing to do about it now. So sorry. How deplorable.

She tries to think what to do with the rest of her day. She considers changing into trousers, joining Brennan and Shushan. She considers letting today be a day she sides with artists. Instead she puts the tray down on the low table, sits by Aram's feet, and stares out the window, waiting for the inevitable drizzle.

Part Eight

CHAPTER ONE

Lullabies

H AVING TO SAY good-bye to the little girls. Confirmation that Aram is dying. The fate of this person, this stranger, this Kostya. Discovering that all of civilized Europe, even England, is base and self-serving.

And that's only the first half of her day.

Dub arrives in the evening, Ned Harden in tow. With Seta away, the bonne has taken some time off, and Brennan and Yale are doing the cooking. Yale heats up broth for Aram's dinner, stays by his side as he eats. She wipes dry his beard. He is restless, cranky, doesn't feel like talking. How grateful she is.

As for feeding the others, it's like playing house. Two sisters, their beaus, and one little niece gathered around the dinner table. The sisters make sausages and white potatoes and dolmas, an entire meal of boiled food. And yet it's all delicious and lovely, with Shushan lighting the candelabra and Ned Harden offering a good-natured Protestant grace. For dessert there is cake the bonne baked the day before, and after that there is a pitcher of martinis. They know brandy would be more proper at the end of a meal, but martinis are what they want. Shushan is allowed to sip from Brennan's glass, and there is much laughter at the appalled faces she makes.

Then come several games of hearts and, later still, Brennan clumsy at the piano but managing to beat out the popular songs of the day, the number-one song especially, and all of them sing it over and over until even Shushan knows the words and sings along in her heavily accented English, "How you vill keep them down on farm after they see Paree?"

Ned is the first to call it a night. He sleeps in Raffi's vacant bed. Dub and Yale go upstairs next, each with a gin-filled brandy snifter. They can still hear Shushan, her dark husky voice doing her best with the tune. She is soloing now, as Brennan pounds the keys. "Never vill they vant to rake and plow. And who in deuce can parley-vous big cow?"

A nice night, then. A nice night to make up for a disturbing day. And now Yale is in her room, in the narrow bed that once belonged to a Kazarian daughter, and Dub is in another narrow bed, his pushed beside hers, and his arms are around her, and her own arms are looped around his neck.

They have been together every night since their tourist stroll through the medieval streets of Senlis, since their visit to the cathedral, their tryst in the copse. They have never spoken of his fiancée since then. Neither thinks there's any need to. Each thinks the other understands the situation perfectly.

On this night, although it is late April, it is very cold again, and they are slow to undress. Dub is only holding Yale, stroking her hair and telling her about his day at Translation. She seems interested, insists she wants to hear it all, so he tells her. "Did Ned really say that?" she says, and "Oh, Dub, that's awful," and "My God, that Major Kendricks is such a prick, isn't he?"

She will do anything to prolong the conversation, to prevent herself from blurting the question knocking about in her head: Darling, do you happen to know the fate of a man named Kobakov? Or is Aram just hallucinating again?

She doesn't really have to do much to keep Dub talking. He's going on and on about the situation in Karabagh now, Armenia's skirmishes with the Azeris, the refusal of the new English governor, Shuttlesworth, to listen to reason. He has barely stopped to take a breath when the door to the bedroom swings open and Brennan and Shushan come rushing in, shrieking and laughing. Brennan, at least, should know better, and Yale is about to deliver a prim lecture on the niceties of knocking, but she doesn't bother because the invaders are too drunk to listen to lectures. The invaders are whooping like loons and dancing like lunatics, and both are wearing a similar costume: tremendously oversized men's silk pajamas.

Yale has never seen this expression on Shushan's face before. She is giddy, silly, happy. "Look vot ve find," she cries, leaping about the room, a frantic marionette swathed in orange, a dancing persimmon. Her pajama sleeves flap like bright wings. She has cuffed her trouser legs at least a dozen times so they will clear her bare feet, but as she twirls the delicate silk unfolds by itself, and she trips and stumbles and laughs. Brennan wears a nearly identical get-up: bright red, Mandarin neckline, frog closures.

"Fools," Yale says, disengaging from Dub. Brennan and Shushan are up on the beds with them now, standing and holding hands, dancing, bouncing. Buffoons who have to grab at their waists to keep their pants up; clowns who keep stumbling over Yale's legs, Dub's big feet. Gin drunks who occasionally, perhaps purposely, fall onto their rear ends and bounce back to their feet.

"You're going to break the beds," Dub says.

"How you vill keep them down on farm," Shushan sings.

"The springs will break," Dub says. "The slats will splinter."

"Yes," Brennan agrees, still bouncing, "and everyone will blame you and Yale."

"Where did you get those pajamas?" Yale says. She wants a pair too. She wants to jump on the beds with Brennan and Shushan. "Are they Aram's?"

"Are you kidding?" Brennan gathers the excess material at her waist in one hand, illustrating that these are the pajamas of a hugely fat man. "We opened the little Vuitton," she crows. "Shushan and me. We couldn't stand it a second longer." She sees Dub's face. "Opening it," she says, clipped and professional, though she is still hotfooting it about in her bright red pajamas, "was imperative for the safety of the household."

"Oh, really?"

Down on her knees, back up on her feet. "What if there had been a ticking bomb in there?"

"Ticking for three months now?"

"Oh, Dub, what's the diff?" Gasping for air now, thoroughly winded. "I was careful not to scratch the lock. I used one of Yale's hairpins. If you don't blab, no one will ever know. And this is all that was in there. Believe me I looked, I felt the fabric. I investigated thoroughly. This was our lousy haul. A half dozen pairs of big fat pajamas."

Dub is beginning to feel uneasy, a prickling along his neck, a squall of worry coming his way. "Aram wanted the suitcase left alone," he says. "Come on. Go take those off now. We've seen the performance. Put them away."

"Aram's been so tired lately," Brennan says. "You know he's completely forgotten the suitcase ever existed." She drops to her knees at the foot of one bed. "What do you think, darling?" she asks Yale. She gestures to herself. "Don't they give me an air?"

Only Shushan is still jumping. So much energy in her leaping, Dub thinks. Like Nijinsky when he went mad onstage. And the way her eyes shine, the way she bares her teeth. Such a ferocious girl. And so brave. Far less squeamish than he is. Wearing that fiend's silk pajamas would sear Dub's flesh. He can barely imagine what they would do to a girl like Ramela. But here is Shushan, the one who actually lived the catastrophe, and she is frolicking in them, gaily, childishly, her womanly breasts bouncing.

And singing. Out of breath, out of tune, one word per leap. "Who–in–deuce–can–parley–vous–big–cow?"

"You both have to try on a pair too," Brennan says. "So should Ned. Do you think he's asleep yet? Let's wake him up. We'll take a photograph of all of us and send it to the rooey Bell Fooey. Kerim will open the envelope, and there will be all these Armenians and Americans wearing his pajamas. Wouldn't that be a scream?"

It seems to Dub it would not be. "Put them away," he says.

"But, Dub, they were just sitting there serving no purpose," Brennan says. "If we took a photograph and sent it to him, it would be art. It would be a provocative assault by means of art."

"Brennan," Dub says, "you are so full of shit. Go be full of shit for your own cause. Leave mine the hell alone."

Shushan's jumping has slowed, but she is still laughing. Yale knows that her laughter isn't a reaction to the conversation. She can't understand what Dub has just said to Brennan. Too much English and it's being spoken too rapidly. No, Shushan is laughing, Yale thinks, because she's a girl of fifteen and she's woozy from jumping and having no bedtime and being fed too many sips of gin.

"Or," Brennan says, as if Dub hasn't spoken, "we could dress animals in them. That would even be better. Pigs and geese all wearing his silk pajamas. It will humiliate him. You two don't get it. Humiliation is much better than whatever you have planned. It lasts longer than anything else there is."

It's the look on Brennan's face that sobers Shushan up. She looks at Brennan and sees what Dub can't see, the anger and grief behind the smile. Shushan not only sees Brennan's anger, she is certain Brennan's anger is caused by Brennan's deep love for Shushan. Shushan is sure that Brennan knows what she endured in that barn.

But she won't think about the barn. Instead, she thinks back to the day before yesterday, the last time she and the ducklings and Brennan all dug in the herb garden together. They'd been out several hours, and then it started to pour as it so often did. The ducklings shrieked and laughed, and Brennan opened her coat wide, turned herself into an umbrella, and the ducklings huddled against the lining of her coat, and they all ran like mad for the house. Only Shushan didn't move. It was like being in one of those bad dreams where your legs stop working. She remained on her knees. The rain was coming down harder, falling from a cloud directly over Shushan's head. Rivulets of mud soaked her trousers. She curled her body over her small pile of stones. The wind grew stronger, colder. Shushan's teeth chattered. Even the stones seemed to shiver. She reminded herself that she didn't care about stones. It was just something to do, a way to fill time, get in on the small talk and gossip. She knew no one would ever care about these stones, this silly enterprise. But she also couldn't bear the thought of leaving the pebbles unguarded, susceptible. What if the storm washed them away? She had worked so hard to gather them, these stupid, insensible stones. She had gathered more than fifty that morning. She tried to push the stones into a single pile. She tried to pick up the entire pile with her wet hands. Rain dripped off her nose. A bolt of lightning cracked against the pond. She was afraid of lightning, and she looked up, and when she did, the stones fell from her cupped palms, were absorbed by the herb garden. Back where they came from, lost to her, and she began to cry. Quickly, she wiped away the tears. She could tell the tears from the raindrops. She got to her feet. She tried to run. It was difficult, the mud so slick, the boots she was wearing too big for her. It was difficult to take even one step. She was afraid of falling.

She might have stood there forever if Brennan, in her guise as human umbrella, hadn't come back for her, hadn't wrapped her up and taken her inside.

As if she had not stopped crying that rainy, muddy day, Shushan starts crying now.

Yale has watched it happen, has seen how seamlessly Shushan's uncontrolled laughter has turned into sobs. And when Shushan throws herself at Brennan, Yale is watching this too, and she sees how seamless this part is as well. One second Shushan is at this end of a bed; the next, as if in defiance of the laws of gravity, she's in Brennan's arms. And then she pulls away and flings herself at Dub.

Dub has no idea how he's wound up holding the girl. He has never seen anyone so convulsed. His collar is saturated with her tears. The tears are like a waterfall, a torrent, and of a quality he's never known tears could be. They are thick and glossy like glycerin lozenges. If he touches one of those tears, it might adhere to his fingers, coat his skin forever.

He risks it. He touches her wet cheeks. *"Eench eh?"* he says. She wants to hear Armenian, he is sure of it. That's the only reason she'd leave Brennan for him.

"Pan mah cheh," she says. *"Chem kider eench eh."*

"All right," he says, "if you don't know, you don't know." Through the fine silk of the pajamas, he feels her breasts pressed against his chest, the thatchy mound pressed against his thigh. Still, she feels like a child to him. "You know, don't you," he says, "that I spent a lot of time in the East. I saw the villages and the people chased from their homes, and I know what happened to the ones who didn't get out. I've heard all the stories. There's nothing you could tell me that would make me think ill of you. You can tell me what's wrong, and I will never think it's your fault."

She raises her head. He has accomplished what he hoped to accomplish, the cessation of her tears. She wipes one cheek completely dry with the sleeve of Kerim Bey's pajamas.

"Did you ever kill anyone?" she says. She doesn't wait for an answer, doesn't need to. He's embarrassed. She's sized him up, he thinks, she knows what he's made of, knows what he's lacking. "I have," she says. She wipes her nose. She sits back in bed. She has wriggled herself into the most comfortable spot on the mattresses, the very center, between Dub and Yale.

"What is she saying?" Brennan asks. "Shushan, speak French. *Que dites-tu?*"

"J'ai dit que j'ai tué quelqu'un," Shushan says. She is boasting, arrogant, angry. *"J'ai tué mon bébé."*

They are quiet until Brennan says, "Yes, of course. Of course there would have been babies."

"That was the whole point in taking girls," Dub says, very contained, very calm, a historian imparting an interesting if little known fact. "The whole point was to produce babies."

"I took it one night and left it on the mountain," Shushan says. She is in control now. She is prideful. The things she saw. The things she survived. She is back to herself, back to Shushan. And she wants to be the focal point of her own horrid story. She wants all eyes on her. "Nobody cared," she says flatly. "It cried all the time. It was a girl, and he had too many of those already. He wanted a male, so even he didn't care."

They are all exhausted by then, some from jumping, some from anger, some from telling their secrets. Shushan is still leaning against Dub. He strokes her arm. Even Ramela has never made him feel so protective and, at the same time, so angry that he knows he could tear a man apart. But then, what is surprising about that? What has Ramela ever lived through, what pain has she ever experienced firsthand that was not self-inflicted? Meanwhile, Shushan is thinking about the rest of her secret, the part she didn't tell—that the reason she left the baby was not only because it cried but also because she despaired of their rescue and wished to spare the child this life. And then rescue had come, *it had come,* and only a mere week later.

It's a wearying thought. She yawns and lies down. She rolls over as if she is in this bed all alone. She commandeers a pillow, wraps herself in the blankets. She takes Dub's littlest finger in her fist and closes her eyes. She falls asleep though the electric lights blaze.

CHAPTER TWO

Exclusively Our Red

To avoid stepping on buried land mines, it is wise to keep to the center of the road and walk only in the ruts left by cars and carts. Raffi likes having a legitimate reason to strut down the middle of roads. He feels like a drum major leading a parade. He basks in the admiration of the stars and the moon.

He is on his way to the Kazarians' château. Nearly midnight of this day, which began with his escape from the Spreader of Horror, and he's ecstatic to be done with Berlin. He's equally happy to be out of Paris. In Senlis the brisk night air is so clean. It's the absence of smoke, the absence of people, the absence of ideas and theories and strategies. The road belongs to toads and crickets and, of course, to Raffi himself.

As much as he's enjoying the night, he's looking forward to the warmth of the château. He imagines what life will be like once he starts living full-time with Aram, once he relieves Aram of all the draining obligations of running the French division of Erinyes. Life will not be all glamour and heroism, he knows. He will put himself in charge of Aram's menu. He will make sure that Aram is fed, warm, and never alone. He will personally stoke Aram's fire.

Aram, he will explain to anyone who comes to the house with pressing business, must be allowed to rest. How else will he ever get well? And then he will say, You can, however, speak with me.

He knows how he'll establish his authority. Using Aram's name, he will call the French operatives together. He will tell them of the new role he is taking on. But before that, so they will not deem this an untenable coup, he will do something grand to gain their respect, to let them know they are being led, once more, by a man of action, by Aram Kazarian's true heir.

When Raffi reaches the château, tired but content, the house is thoroughly dark. Being the only person on the grounds who is awake doesn't make him uneasy, though. Rather, it makes him feel paternal both toward the old couple he assumes are upstairs sleeping and toward the old timbers themselves. Soundlessly, he lets himself in. He removes his shoes. At the door to Aram's study he hears the old lion's troubled breathing. So, Aram is not in bed with Seta after all. Raffi opens the study door just enough to discern Aram on the sofa, under an afghan. Just a sliver of Aram, just a small curled version of this once great man. Raffi would step inside and poke at the fire, but the room is warm, tidy as well, and Raffi decides that for now he will let Aram be.

On the second floor, he throws open the door to his room and stops in his tracks as soon as he sees the white-blond American captain in his bed. He retreats a few steps, closes the door again, stands in the hallway. Then he presses his ear to the other doors until he hears the sound of male sleep. Slowly he opens the door to that room. In a slash of moonlight he can make out two narrow beds pushed together. He waits for his eyes to adjust to the darkness, and at last he sees that asleep in those two narrow beds is—everyone.

Yale and Brennan and Dub and another girl too, younger than the others. They are—he is relieved to see this much—fully clothed. The young girl and Brennan wear pajama tops so bright they nearly glow in the dark. And those pajama tops are buttoned up to their chins. At least there is that.

Still, he can't imagine what he's stumbled upon.

He breathes himself into the room. Deftly, he taps Dub on the shoulder. Even when they are out in the hall, Dub sleepy and sheepish, Raffi manages to restrain himself. He does not raise his voice, does not raise his fist.

"What in God's name is this?" he says, a heroic attempt at a whisper. "What are you these days, a sultan with a harem?"

"Not now," Dub says. "It's been a long night. You have no idea. What the hell are you doing here?"

"All you need to know is that I *am* here, and I am staying here, and I am going to prevent whatever it is that is going on in there. And why are those American girls here?"

To find out the American girls are living here now, that Seta invited them, gives Raffi a pain deep in his stomach. He will attend to this intrusion, this exploitation of Seta's generous nature tomorrow. "And the other one?"

"An orphan."

He is horrified. He is furious.

"You don't understand," Dub says. "You're misinterpreting everything."

Yale steps into the hall then, her face creased from sleep, troubled from bad but easily analyzed dreams. Dead babies drowning in swirling waters, hundreds of them, and she with only one pair of arms. "Dub," she says, pouting and bleary. She sees Raffi then. He is turning to Dub. "I will be downstairs," he says. "I'll wait for you. I want to talk to you about someone you seem to have forgotten." He descends the staircase, is swallowed up, disappears.

"Oh, hell," Dub says.

"Why is he here?" Yale asks. Dub doesn't respond. "Come here," she says. She takes his hand, leads him into the bedroom that Brennan and Shushan usually share. On one of the beds is the little Vuitton. Two other pairs of Kerim's pajamas—royal blue, royal purple—are strewn about. She stuffs them into the suitcase, latches the clasp, puts the suitcase out into the hall. She closes the door on it and on everyone else. "Lie down with me," she says.

He sits on the edge of the mattress instead.

"What is it?" she asks. *"Eench eh?"*

"I don't know. Raffi. He wants to talk to me. Now."

"So what? Who cares?" She waits. "Talk about what?"

"Who knows? My many failures and transgressions."

"I love your many transgressions," she says.

"He wants to talk about his sister."

"Oh," she says. His poor dead sister. The church fire. Kerim barring the doors.

He hunches over, curling his spine until he can rest his chin on his knees. She puts her fingers in his hair at the nape of his neck.

"Have you noticed your black is beginning to gray?" she asks. "It's so tragic. Soon you're going to look like a grumpy old man from either profile, not only the left."

"Tragic?" he says. "It's hardly tragic. God, I can't wait." He straightens up, suddenly enflamed. "I'm so sick of this aberration."

"Your friend Kostya liked it," she says. "You told me so in St. Louis."

He is startled by that. "How do you know about Kostya? How do you know his name?"

"Aram told me."

"He was killed in the revolution."

She feels her heart turn over like an engine.

"He was a good man," Dub says. "When the whole world turned its back on us, he at least cried. Now I have to go downstairs and listen to that one cry about nothing."

"Not nothing. His poor sister."

"No," Dub says. "He has another sister. He wants to talk about his other sister."

"Oh," she says. "How come?"

He covers his face with his hands. Too dramatic, she thinks. Too feminine. "I should have told you long before," he says.

They have not talked about his fiancée since the time in church, but now she realizes she has never, not for a moment, stopped thinking about that girl. How else to explain her immediate comprehension of such a cryptic confession? And on this night when she is so tired of confession.

"Say something," he says from behind his hands.

She says, "It's been a lousy day."

"I know," he says. "I'm sorry."

She says, "What's the worst thing that's ever befallen you?"

He has to look at her to understand she is not alluding to Ramela. "In the Caucasus once—" he begins.

"No," she says. "Not things you saw or heard about. Not things that happened to Aram or your neighbors or even your parents. Not bullets that whizzed past your head but hit someone else. I want to know about the bullets that have actually hit you."

He doesn't answer.

"None," she says. "Though you keep trying to jump in front of them."

"We're all hit sooner or later," he says.

"So why can't you wait?"

"You're right, of course," he says. "It's something to think about, all right. But for now, why don't you go back to sleep? I'll get rid of Raffi and come back up."

"No," she says. "Either stay with me now or don't come back." She starts to cry a little. She presses her fingers to her eyelids. "Oh, damn," she says. "How infuriating. I don't think anyone who hasn't killed a baby gets to cry tonight, do you?"

"Hokees," Dub says. "You go to sleep. I'll go talk to him for a second, and then I'll be back. We'll figure life out in the morning."

"Don't mind me," she says. "It's only gin and lack of sleep. It isn't you. Look." She holds up her palms. "Not a bullet hole to be seen. I'm fine. I'm unscathed. You go ahead. It's a fair choice. He's been your dear friend your whole life. And now to find out he's nearly your brother-in-law."

That makes him angry. As if he's got a right to anger, she thinks. "Look," he says. "The situation—yes, I may have omitted some information, some of the particulars, but the situation remains the same. I told you about my obligations. Nothing's changed. It's just that you know her name now."

"That's true," she says, though it isn't true. Everything has changed, and she *doesn't* know her name. "Still," she says, "it's how I feel."

"But why now? God, why add to everything now? Wasn't I engaged to her yesterday?"

"Because I know her name now, I guess." Though she doesn't.

IN THE DARK parlor, Dub sits on a bony chair and listens to Raffi. "We've had this discussion before," he says, as soon as Raffi takes a breath. "We've had it in Providence, we've had it in Russia. I've told you. When I'm a husband, I'll be a good husband."

It is nearly two in the morning. Even Raffi is worn out. He has said what he needs to, has delivered his speech on loyalty, fidelity, commitment. It has bored even him. Now Dub is talking, and Raffi knows he should be listening, but instead he gazes up at the dark ceiling beams speckled with traces of dusty white. Powder beetles, he is thinking, as Dub makes his counterarguments and excuses. This old house needs him so desperately.

Now he is looking down at the carpet. Threadbare in spots, a hank of fringe missing from one section when, years ago, a Kazarian daughter decided to give it a haircut. And there's an obscene cigarette lighter on it, fallen off a table, lying by his boot. He picks the lighter up, runs his finger over the body of the female figure hammered into it. While Dub talks, Raffi flicks the lighter to flame several times. He does this without even knowing he's doing it. He stops when he catches himself.

"Listen," he says, cutting Dub off. "Listen, this isn't the point. I know you will be a good husband someday. I know that if you marry my sister you will treat her with respect. And I understand needs and urges and all that. What I don't understand, and what I am asking as your friend, is how can you spend so much time with this girl?" He points to the rug. "Look at that red, would you, please? You know that red comes from Armenia exclusively, don't you? How can you be with someone who doesn't give a damn about the red in our rugs?"

"Because I don't give a damn about the red in our rugs," Dub says.

"What do you care about if not your own culture, which is slowly being wiped off the face of the earth?"

"I care about Babe Ruth staying with the Red Sox," Dub says.

"Fine," Raffi says. "You want to make jokes. But you know, if you were to tell Ramela about your devotion to this asinine baseball team, she would be devoted to them too. She would build them a shrine. She would go to church twice a day and pray for them if you asked her to."

"I know," Dub says.

"While this one, this *Hria* from St. Louis, no matter what you tell her about your love for these Red Sox, she is never going to love them just because you do. She is too American, too stubborn. She is too self-ish. She will remain in love with her own team, the—I forget who."

Dub has heard him. It's just that he thinks Raffi doesn't understand the word. He assumes Raffi thinks that in English the word *Hria* is some sort of generic insult, another word for *slut* or *homewrecker*. He almost corrects him. *You don't mean Jew,* he almost says. Instead, he continues to talk baseball. "The Cardinals," he says. "The St. Louis Cardinals."

"Cardinals? Really? So, you with these Red Sox and this girl with her red birds? In both cases red, but in both cases the wrong red." He leans forward, points down to the right red, says, "You understand what I am telling you? She will never love those Red Sox just because you love them. She will never be that kind of wife."

"I'm marrying Ramela," he says wearily.

Raffi raises his hand. "And if you were to have children with her, you will not only be getting an inferior wife. You will not only be kill-ing my sister. You will be completing the job Talaat began. You will be helping in the effort to erase your own people."

He's done now. He stands up. He has spent the day fleeing Ger-many, he has walked all the way from the train station. Now he walks to the staircase. "I'm going to bed," he says. "I'm going to find a room up there with nobody in it, and then I'm going to sleep."

He means to leave it at that. He's about to climb the stairs, could be out of the room in less than five seconds. But he doesn't leave the parlor. He has to say the rest of it first. He won't sleep at all if he keeps it inside. He'll pace all night, he'll seethe, he might burst in on them, strangle someone.

Dub can't see him. He can only hear the voice, their secret language coming at him in the dark. Increasingly loud despite the slumbering household. "All I ask is this. You keep writing to Ramela. You tell her nothing about the Jew from St. Louis. You keep your promises to her. That's all I ask. In the meantime, fine, amuse yourself with your *odar*. But know she's no good. Know that nothing she's told us is the truth. Her name? A fabrication. The other one? Not her sister. Her mother? Perfectly alive. The father? He makes underwear."

"All right," Dub says into the dark. "It's late. That's enough."

"Yes," Raffi says. "More than enough."

"That's been my plan all along," Dub says. He says it although Raffi, climbing the stairs now, is unable to hear him. He says it in Armenian, in a whisper. He says it to scare himself and persuade himself. He feels drained as he talks to himself. It's as if somebody else is talking. Voices in the dark. A language he no longer understands even as he speaks it. "To marry Ramela," he says. "I never said I'd do anything else."

CHAPTER THREE

Yale, He Says

WHEN HE GETS into bed, she rolls from him as if fitfully dreaming. "Yale," he says. Full voice. Not a whisper. He repeats her name, shakes her shoulder.

"Go away," she groans.

"What does your father do?"

She knows right then; she knows. She covers her head with the pillow. "What time is it?" she says.

"Late. Early. What does your father do?"

"All right." She sits up. She takes the pillow, holds it in front of her, a shield. "What do you want? Are you trying to calculate my dowry? Compare it to Raffi's sister's, make a decision that way?"

"Does he manufacture airplane parts?"

The answer to that question is, of course, yes. But she's too tired for yes. "My father?" she says. "My father is a textile manufacturer." She makes a sound, derisive, not quite laughter. "And what does your father do?"

"You told me he makes airplane parts."

"I know what I said."

"What about Brennan?" he says. "What does her father do?"

The same laugh. "I don't know. I hear he's a pharmacist."

"Then—well, do you have the same mother?"

"You think we're twins with different fathers?"

"You're not sisters at all?"

The sky is pink. She can see his face. "What?" she says. "Am I supposed to be ashamed of myself? Of course we're sisters. Of course we're twins. Just not the way most people are sisters or twins. Oh, don't look at me like that. You lied too."

"I never did. Not like that."

"Lies of omission."

"You go to a less horrible level of hell for lies of omission."

"Again, he's sending me off to hell."

"What do you care? I thought Jews don't believe in hell."

How is it she has no explanation at the ready? She takes a breath, holds it for as long as she can. The dearth of oxygen changes nothing. It doesn't sharpen her senses, nor does it take her out of the world, not even for a moment.

"Well," she says. "Are you asking me a question?"

"I suppose so. Yes."

"You have somehow been given the impression I'm a Jew, and you would like me to confirm or deny it."

"It's not that I'd care one way or the other."

Now, there's a lie of commission. "How nice. How very tolerant. But I'm not."

"Yale," he says.

"I'm not. My parents are. Their parents were. I'm not, though. I don't believe in any of it. It's always been something that's had nothing to do with me. Always."

"I just want to know the truth," he says.

"If you start to think of me as a Jew, you won't know the truth. You'll be thinking about someone who isn't me, because it's not who I am."

"But your parents are. Their parents were. You can say whatever you want, and the world will still say you're a Jew."

She shakes her head so vigorously she strikes him with her hair.

"But it's true. In 1915 there were all these Armenian-Americans returning to Turkey. They did it routinely, you know, to do business. Rug importers, going back to buy stock. And the Turks grabbed them and shot them too. Or clubbed them to death, or however they were killing Christians that week. These guys, they could shout they were Americans forever. They could wave their passports in every *mudir*'s face. It didn't matter. It didn't change anything. Their parents were Armenians. Their grandparents were Armenians. They were Armenians."

"So you're going to let the Turks settle this?" she says.

"I just want to be able to trust you," he says.

All right, she tells him. Here's the entire truth. She comes from Missouri. He comes from Rhode Island. Originally, they came from the apes.

"What's your name?" he says.

"All this time and you don't know my name?"

"Please don't."

"I'll tell you," she says, "because it's you." Even then, it takes a moment before she can say it. "Don't call me that, though. It isn't really my name. I won't come running."

"It's nice, though," he says.

She lies down again, the pillow on her face. She talks through the down and the linen. "Well," she says. "Now we know each other's deep, dark secrets. And mine affect you only to the extent you wish to let them, while yours affect me irrevocably."

He lies down next to her. He takes the pillow away. If she tries to throw him out, he will refuse to leave the bed. He will argue, and he will use his superior strength. But she doesn't do anything. Of course not, he thinks. She never starts fights unless she knows she can win.

CHAPTER FOUR

April 23, 1919: Nine a.m. at the Château

IT'S NINE O'CLOCK the next morning, and Brennan White's never been so hung over. At first she can't figure out who's sleeping next to her, breathing on her. The mess of dark hair. The mandarin collar the color of persimmons.

Then the night comes back to her: Shushan's confession. Brennan would like to cry then; crying, she feels, would be an appropriate, even pleasurable response to the revelations of the previous night, but she is too dehydrated from gin and vermouth, she couldn't produce tears if she tried. She decides to go downstairs instead. She will brew some coffee, or what passes for coffee in this sorrowful world. She sighs as she gets out of bed. She wishes a good cry were something you could buy in a store, have on hand for times when you need it. A good cry and good coffee. Both wrapped up, taken home, stored on a shelf for mornings like this one.

NINE O'CLOCK that same morning, and from his couch Aram Kazarian looks around his study. He doesn't know why he isn't in his own bed. He would like to go to his bed now, but he can't recall where his room is. Then he remembers—it's in the rear of the house (the crumbling walls, stained ceiling, the bed he shares with his younger brother, he of the horned toenails). Don't let the bedbugs bite, people say, but they do. Also, he needs the chamber pot, but he can't seem to find it. He must have looked for it during the night and failed to find it then too, because the trousers he's slept in are wet and cold, and he begins to cry, tears of rage and frustration and fear. He shouts for his mother, but she doesn't come, and now he is worried. There are such dangers at night. Men with curved swords coming in through the doors and windows. Piles of teeth and bones are buried in the herb garden.

The teeth belong to a *mudir* he waylaid in the mountains. The old Turk had begged for his life. All right, Aram said. He was sixteen, already known for his bravery and bloodlust. He knocked the Turk on his back. His compatriots held the Turk's limbs. Aram knelt on the Turk's chest, his full weight on those old ribs. He had a pair of horseshoe pliers. He was prepared. He began yanking teeth from the *mudir*'s mouth. As he did he shouted the names of men who had disappeared. They all knew the old *mudir* had been in on it. Aram squeezed the pliers, twisted, yanked. "An eye tooth in exchange for Tash der Manelian. A dog tooth for Lev Saroian." His voice echoed. "And this wisdom tooth for Manoog Kazarian." From the *mudir*'s mouth, such screams, so much blood. "Not a tooth for a tooth," Aram said, "but a tooth for an entire body. For a father. You see how merciful we Christians are?"

That was why they came after his fingers. Not anger over an unpaid army levy. To get their quid pro quo. But the trouble was, no one knew who'd gone first all those centuries ago, so no one knew which side got to go last. No one could ever figure out when the exchange was completed, when they could all call it quits.

Aram is cold and wet. He shouts for his mother, but she doesn't come. And the patterns on the rug have turned into long red water snakes and the snakes slither toward him. He is afraid of snakes, and he is afraid of teeth, and he is lost in the mountains, and his mother is gone.

NINE O'CLOCK in the morning, and Dub Hagopian and Yale White have just finished making love. They've been awake all night, arguing, talking, confessing, and Dub has told her all about Ramela, has betrayed Ramela in every way he possibly can. Yale is fascinated, wants to hear more, but Dub has no more to say. By telling Ramela's secrets, he has come to realize he knows nothing else about her. Yale knows her better than he does. "You see, the reason she does these things is she knows they keep you attached to her," Yale says. (Typical Jew, thinks Dub, overanalyzing, overintellectualizing everything.) "She carves a slogan into her arm with a sewing needle before she sees you the way other women spray perfume on their wrists. It's the way she gets ready for a date with you."

"But she knows I won't marry her so long as she's doing that," he argues.

"One might conclude, then," Yale says, "that marrying you is not what she truly wants."

"You don't know the first thing about Armenian women," he says. "Your type, I know, is more ambitious and dominant in the family. Our women want nothing more than, first, to get married and, second, to please their husbands. They come from a tradition of arranged marriages and living under the roofs of their mothers-in-law."

"Talk about going to hell."

"What do you think she wants if not to get married?"

"Perhaps just to know someone is out doing something for her."

It's true, of course. That has always been their bargain, his promise. His blood shed so she doesn't have to shed hers. When he thinks about it, he's never made any promise to her but that one.

And yet she sheds her blood all the time and he has shed none at all.

NINE O'CLOCK, and Raffi Soghokian sits on the floor of Aram and Seta's bedroom, the only room where he was able to find a vacant bed the night before. It felt like sacrilege when he climbed under those sheets, yet he can't remember ever sleeping so well. Now, on the floor, he's lost in concentration. He barely dares to inhale.

The calendar on the wall reminds him that today is the twenty-third of April, tomorrow the twenty-fourth, although, God knows, he doesn't need a reminder. He is keenly aware of the date, the anniversary of the day, four years earlier, when Kerim Bey gathered all the male Christians in his *vilayet* and had them shot one by one. The same thing was taking place at the same time in all the other cities and villages in Turkey. Governors, police chiefs, officials like Kerim issuing decrees.

Teachers, doctors, shopkeepers, poets, painters, bank tellers, storytellers, rounded up, lined up, shot. The end of all poetry on a single spring afternoon.

To Raffi's right is the obscene cigarette lighter he found in the parlor the night before. He slipped the lighter into his pocket while talking to Dub. He played around with it before going to sleep. It disgusted him, and he had no doubt about who had brought it here, yet there was something magnetic about the lurid contraption. A person couldn't resist working it, flicking it on and off.

He's taken the lighter apart. Here is its small fuse. Here is the cylinder for the fluid. He has already drained that cylinder.

To Raffi's left is his Mauser. Its chamber is open, and several bullets are lined up on the floor. Raffi takes one of the bullets and cuts the shell above its brass edge with a pocket knife, exposing the powder. "Careful," he hears one of the Berlin technicians tell him. "Jostle the cap and you blow yourself up."

His hands are steady as he pours the powder into the lighter's empty cylinder. Next he adds the tinder. He gathered it earlier, going outside in his bare feet. Plenty of dry grass to be harvested.

Someday, when it's a less critical matter, he plans to try all this again with his belly-button lint. He just wants to see if that really works.

But for now, he is done. He leaves the bedroom. He is heading to Aram's study downstairs. He plans to slip in without waking Aram and borrow the little Vuitton suitcase that Aram has kept there these past months. Raffi has figured out how to put that suitcase to use. But oddly, he sees the suitcase sitting in the hall. He tries the clasps, and they spring open. He looks inside and sees a pile of pajamas.

Back in Aram's room now, he examines the top, bottom, and sides of the suitcase, slitting them with his knife, checking for papers, contraband. Finding nothing, he folds the pajamas and replaces them in the suitcase, neatly, prettily. He wonders if he's ever felt anything so soft as this blue, this purple silk. He drops the lighter in the suitcase, closes it firmly. Then he slips into an old robe of Aram's and heads downstairs, suitcase in hand.

As he does, he passes the room where Shushan sleeps. Nine o'clock in the morning, and she dreams of people she has not allowed herself to think about for years: mother, father, grandparents, siblings, cousins, aunts, uncles, schoolteachers, store clerks, neighbors, a priest, a congregation, a baby. A pleasant dream, and Raffi's eyes on her don't disturb her. She won't give up this dream so easily.

When he walks into the kitchen, Brennan laughs. Robe, bare feet, traveling case. Raffi looks like an absentminded tourist.

CHAPTER FIVE

Nine a.m. Elsewhere

IN LE HAVRE, Seta Kazarian sips chocolate with her daughter while grandchildren in various stages of dress vie for her attention.

In Chantilly, the bonne wakes up disheveled and hopeful in the bed of her deceased husband's brother.

Having slept well in the charming Senlis château, Ned Harden drives the green Fiat back to Paris.

On the rue des Belles Feuilles, Kerim Bey exercises his bad leg. Sitting on the rug in his bedroom, he stretches the leg out in front of him and slings a towel around the arch of his foot like a stirrup. He pulls the ends of the towel and feels the pain shoot up his calves. A German doctor told him this was just the thing to revive atrophied muscles. The doctor was affiliated with a spa in the north country, a salty mineral bath, and when Micheline demanded they leave Berlin, Kerim Bey suggested they move to the spa town. He pictured himself in the steam baths, wrapped in long white sheets. He pictured the German doctor catering to his every need. But Micheline announced they were moving to Paris. She wanted to live in her homeland. She wanted to be near her elderly parents. She wanted to raise Hassan in France, not in Germany. Kerim could come or not, it was up to him. She didn't care.

Kerim cared. After so many years of living apart, after so many years of war and horror and failure, he wanted a simple life; he wanted to be with his wife and with this late-in-life child, his heir, their miracle, his redemption. He gave in immediately. His fault for falling in love with and then marrying a European. Everyone had warned him against it. A dreadful career decision, one that had required him to be more brutal than he was by nature just to prove himself to everyone else. But there's nothing he can do about any of it now. Nothing, he thinks, and he pulls harder on the towel, lifts his heel an inch off the floor, and mutters in pain.

NINE O'CLOCK in the morning in western Europe is four o'clock in the morning in Providence, Rhode Island, where Ramela Soghokian sits by an open window and contemplates the silver streetcar tracks embedded in Smith Hill. Nine o'clock in the morning in western Europe is three o'clock in the morning in St. Louis, Missouri, where Esther Weiss stands on her front porch, watching over her sleeping neighborhood, her sleeping garden, and wonders what is happening in western Europe that day.

She has only to look in the paper. In England, former soldiers who can't find work sit in the roads and stop automobiles. In the Autonomous Republic of Nagarno-Karabagh, a member of the British mission meets with the Azeris and urges an invasion of Armenia. In Germany, people scrounge for food. If you still don't believe that the war didn't end five months ago, ask the captains of all those Allied ships blockading the North Sea. Ask any German mother.

Or ask this fellow here, this towheaded son of a Bavarian pig farmer living several miles south of Munich, who, at nine o'clock on this morning, is yawning and stretching, and then, remembering where he lives, rolling over again, returning to sleep. What else is there for him to do with his days but sleep them away? No work, no food, all the pigs long ago sold or stolen or slaughtered. Why get up when there is nothing to do until five that evening?

Because while the rest of the world may be on the go by nine in the morning, five in the evening is when the day begins in Bavaria. At five in the evening, Bavarians get ready to go to their meetings. Attending meetings is the new Bavarian pastime. Everyone belongs to one political organization or another.

Most of the people the boy knows are Bolsheviks, which is lucky for them as the Bolsheviks are now in power in Bavaria. Last week it seems they were all in prison, but now they've taken over the Assembly and seceded from Germany. Bavaria is officially the Bavarian Soviet Socialist Republic.

This boy is not a Bolshevik, though.

Nor is he a Socialist wringing his hands while calling for reform of a more moderate nature, nor an Imperialist weeping at the mention of the Kaiser's name, nor a Democrat committed to preserving for the prosperous what little prosperity remains, nor a Sparticist reciting angry verse, nor a Unionist willing to die for the people, nor a member of the Peasants' League.

So many things one can be in Bavaria these days, so many parties to choose from, and this boy has made his own choice, and if that choice doesn't seem wise today, it will seem wise soon enough. Although, give this boy some credit—his choice isn't calculated. He isn't trying to side with the eventual winner, isn't looking for power or position. His choice comes from the heart because this boy is an idealist, and so he has joined the idealistic Thule Society.

Where else would a true patriot throw in his lot? This boy is a romantic, a dreamer, and what he dreams about as he goes back to sleep is a Utopia where the citizenry looks exactly like him, blond and blue-eyed and pure and Nordic, if perhaps a little less scarred from adolescent acne.

So at nine in the morning the boy sleeps, but come five in the evening he will rise and put on the Thule insignia, an ornate hooked cross, the same ancient and eastern swastika that decorates the borders of the slithering rug from which Aram Kazarian is, right this moment, recoiling. Strangely enough, the boy is actually familiar with that very rug, given that he was once billeted in Aram's château. But the boy never thinks back to those days. He doesn't think about the château or its carpets, certainly not of the mistress of that house, an aristocratic woman with whom he may have fallen a little in love. She did not love him in return, however, so why should he think of her? He did everything for her, protected her from the filthy plots of the others, tended her gardens devotedly. But she did not realize he was protecting her, never even knew she was in danger, and she never loved him, and he knew this because she did not say a thing when he told her he was leaving. "Don't go," he wanted her to cry. "I won't let you, I'll hide you, you must stay here with me." But she didn't say any of it, and the night before he left, he stayed awake imagining her waving good-bye and then, the moment he was out of sight, disinfecting the sheets of the bed in which he had slept. He had to get up then, had to leave that bed. He went out into the night and visited the garden one last time. He told her he had been planting grape hyacinths, tiny bulbs.

But, as we've said, he doesn't think of those days any longer. These days he looks only to the future. Tonight, he will walk to his meeting, where he and his friends will plan that future, and on the way there he will run into others and they will sing songs of revolution. There is one song everyone in the Thule Society especially loves these days, though the lyrics are improbable and apolitical and the Reds sing it too. Still, it's a good song, and it's the most popular song in Bavaria on April 23, 1919, and he will sing it with his friends as he walks to his meeting.

Come with me, my little countess.
Why worry what tomorrow will bring?

CHAPTER SIX

A Flashback: The First Day of the War (or, The Hungry Assassin)

LET'S RUN THROUGH it quickly, hundreds of years of history in five sentences:

1. Up until 1858, the Ottomans ruled Bosnia-Herzegovina.
2. Thereafter, pursuant to the Treaty of Berlin (of paper-ladle fame), Bosnia was governed by Austria-Hungary.

3. Then, in 1908, the Austrians actually annexed Bosnia.
4. This annexation infuriated the nation of Serbia (because Bosnia had a large Serb population). And so:
5. Six years later, when Austria's heir to the throne, the Archduke Franz Ferdinand, announced that he and his wife, Sophie, would visit Sarajevo, Serb insurgents decided to send several adolescent boys there to kill him.

On the day of Franz Ferdinand's visit, the young assassins took up their stations throughout the city. One assassin hurled a bomb at the archduke as his car went by, but that attempt failed, resulting only in the assassin's suicide by cyanide pill and a change in the motorcade's route.

Upon hearing of the failed attempt, another of the would-be assassins, a sixteen-year-old named Gavrilo Princip, deciding the jig must surely be up, abandoned his position on the Appel Quay and walked down a side street to buy something to eat.

Imagine his surprise when, upon leaving Schiller's Delicatessen with a sandwich, he saw the archduke's touring car directly in front of him. The driver, it turned out, had made a wrong turn and was now stopped by the curb in front of Schiller's, getting ready to back up.

Princip looked at the car, removed the gun from his pocket, and fired. The bullet killed Franz Ferdinand and then (and this part was a shame) continued on through Sophie, killing her too.

Thirty days later, the Great War began.

What became of Gavrilo's sandwich? Sitting on the rue des Belles Feuilles in a black transport truck he's stolen from behind the Crillon and a bit hungry himself, Dub wonders about that. He knows the assassination of Franz Ferdinand was noble and necessary—a people's rights being trampled, the world as usual not giving a damn—but he can't help envisioning the actual killing as a vaudeville scene. A bumbling boy in a baggy checked suit and enormous bow tie is about to take a bite of a sandwich the size of his head when suddenly he is face-to-face with the guy he's supposed to be shooting. The hungry assassin looks at his gun in the one hand, his sandwich in the other. His head swivels back and forth. The gun or the sandwich? The sandwich or the gun? To bite or to shoot, that is the question.

On the vaudeville stage, the boy would give a Jewish type of shrug and opt for the sandwich. Or maybe he'd get mixed up, bite down on the gun barrel and try to fire the rye bread.

In real life, Dub imagines the assassin must have dropped the sandwich in the gutter and probably didn't think of it again until late that night, when he found himself in a jail cell, alone and starving. At the time of the shooting, there would have been no chance to think or plan ahead or anticipate how hungry he'd soon be.

Still, Dub thinks, there might have been enough time for a feeling. Dub wonders what that feeling might have been. Probably surprise. Possibly righteous anger. Maybe even spine-chilling terror. But, on the other hand, Princip might have felt ecstasy. God had, after all, delivered the sedan right to him. God could not have given him a clearer sign, a heartier endorsement.

April twenty-third is a balmy spring day, and the rooey Bell Fooey smells of magnolia blossoms. The scent makes Dub think about the unfurnished cell where Gavrilo died last year. The boy had been in solitary confinement from trial to conviction to death. He had been intentionally deprived of things to see, smell, hear. Nor was there anything for him to touch but concrete.

Four years of hard. Four years of cold. A senseless existence. But also four years of knowing that he had done right. Although certainly it must have crossed his mind once or twice that he hadn't helped Bosnia or Serbia one whit. Nothing had changed for his people. And it also must have occurred to him that he had personally caused the grisliest and most pointless war the world has ever known.

Also that he'd killed the duchess and orphaned her children.

Still, he must have reminded himself every day that he'd done right. If he ever began to doubt this, he could have remembered the way the car had stopped right in front of him. So shoot already, God said to Gavrilo. What are you waiting for, an engraved invitation?

CHAPTER SEVEN

A French Sailor Suit

DUB DOESN'T KNOW what he's feeling, but he knows what he's not feeling. He's not feeling happy. This used to be fun when Yale was with him. The way Yale would take notes: they were like kids playing spy. They were like scientists out in the field, gathering data, strictly observing.

Now, having decided to do this, he's nervous. There, that's a feeling. Apprehensive and antsy and determined as well. Is determined a feeling? He is going to keep one—if only one—promise to Ramela before writing her the unpleasant letter he's been composing in his mind. He's going to make her world just a little bit safer. Maybe his own blood won't be spilled, maybe it will be. But blood will be spilled today, of that he's certain.

He takes a deep breath, hoping the fragrance of magnolias will calm him, but along with that scent has come the smell of gasoline. There's also the harsh city jangle: speeding taxis, clumsy autobuses, awkward people chasing them. Dub taps his fingers on the steering wheel. He runs his hand down his shirtfront. He feels uncomfortable out of uniform. He misses the weight of his U.S. collar disk. He has never realized before how often he played with the doughnut-shaped buttons on his AEF tunic. But no need to risk implicating the army in this. He is dressed like a clerk now, an invisible assistant to a man of no importance.

He checks his watch. He runs through a list. He calculates how old Shushan must have been when the Kurd impregnated her (the babe a few months old plus nine months in the belly subtracted from fifteen, and Shushan could have been as young as thirteen). He reminds himself of the number of days a baby can live without food or water (seven days without food, three without water, statistics he remembers from some grim but abstract conversation a long time ago). He thinks of Shushan spread and helpless beneath the Kurd. He gives the Kurd Kerim Bey's face.

When the Turk's western wife and child emerge from the apartment and step into sunlight, Dub slides down in his seat until they pass by. They are headed toward the corner. They stop only once, when the child insists on picking up a petal that has fallen from one of the magnolias. It's a large white satin petal tinged with scarlet and shaped like a canoe. The petal in his free hand, the child nods like a potentate, and he and his mother walk on, turning left onto Victor Hugo.

Dub sits up again. Both the wife and the child were dressed up. The wife wore a cigarette coat and, though it is a beautiful day, the sky blue and faultless, she carried a knob-handled umbrella, the same type Dub has seen Yale carry at times. This, Dub thinks, is a good sign. Not as good as the archduke's car stopping right in front of you, but still a good sign. For the wife to be so gussied up means she must be going someplace special, must be visiting someone important, and so most likely won't be home anytime soon. And she'd done up the child too. He was wearing a little boy's version of a French sailor suit, short horizon blue pants and a flat-topped cap with long ribbons streaming down the back. A cunning get-up, a kid dressed to be fussed over, admired, and pinched. Grandparents, Dub guesses.

He tries to think of Kerim Bey with hatred again. But now he finds himself thinking how the sight of his child in that costume must have hurt him. Maybe looking at his child in that outfit hurt more than anything Dub plans to do to him. Dub imagines the Turk kissing his son good-bye, smiling but thinking, So, it has come to this: my child parading about like a fop French marine.

It's not the first time Dub has suspected that killing the deposed tyrant, the fat old cripple, will be almost a redundancy, the same as stabbing a corpse. Such an act might live in the memories of witnesses, and surely it will forever haunt its perpetrator. But what impact will it have on the corpse itself?

Dub's nerves feel on fire. He feels exactly the way he used to feel when forced to recite in school. A bad case of stage fright, that's what he's got. *You're on,* and he reaches for the small Vuitton traveling case he found on a chair outside the kitchen before he left the château this morning. He didn't wonder how the traveling case made its way down the stairs and onto that chair. Shushan. Brennan. Perhaps even Raffi, who was at that moment in the kitchen eating eggs. He didn't say a word to Raffi, had no wish to talk to him. He looked only at the case, understood how it could help in his plans, and took it as he stealthily set out on his travels—a walk to the train station, the metro to the Crillon, a quick stop for this truck, and now here, at the Turk's.

CHAPTER EIGHT

The Assassination of Kerim Bey

H ERE'S THE FIRST thing he didn't plan for: on the front steps of Kerim's building, the concierge puts up a fight. She herself will bring the suitcase to Monsieur Klein, she says. She will not permit a stranger to disturb her tenant. Her tenant wishes no visitors at all. No, not even those returning lost property. Her tenant has been quite definite in this desire. He has made himself very clear.

Very clear, she repeats. Very clear, she says again. She might have gone on and on—very clear, very clear, very clear—but Dub finally figures out what she means and offers her enough francs to make his own wishes even clearer. Now they are friends. Dub is her countryman, after all. The tenant is a foreigner. "Where are you from?" she asks Dub. "Let me guess. Is that a southern accent you've got there? Are you from Marseilles?"

"Yes," he says, and she looks him up and down, smiles girlishly. So now he knows that he has spent too much time with her and she will be able to identify him if he is apprehended after he does what he is going to do. This skinny hag in her housecoat, her unfettered breasts, a long black hair growing from a mole under her lower lip—she will be the eyewitness if he is arrested, his executioner if he is convicted. Good, he thinks. That face of hers, it makes a man more determined to pull things off flawlessly. When he gets upstairs he will not hesitate, he will not reconsider. When he finishes what he's here to accomplish, he will not waste a moment feeling regret. He will run down the stairs, dash around the corner, go immediately AWOL in this stolen truck. He and Yale will disappear. Spain, he thinks. Anywhere, so long as he never sees this hag's face again.

He smiles at her. He enters the building. He jogs up the stairs to Kerim's apartment.

Standing to the side of the door, he pauses to catch his breath. He puts his free hand in his pocket, holds on to the Luger. For a moment he has a vision of Aram's hand, the two fingers, and this fuels his anger. The poor schoolboy, he thinks. The boy had done nothing; it was his father who had failed to pay the military tax. The animals held Aram down for the fun of it, left him with a hand that looked like a gun itself. He imagines Kerim Bey as one of those heartless surgeons. He takes his hand from the Luger and knocks on the door, twice and loudly.

At first he thinks Kerim Bey is not home, although that's impossible. He has been watching the front door since the last shift retired. And yet there is no response. Dub pounds, becoming bolder the longer there is no answer. Then, at last, he hears footsteps, an uncertain shuffling punctuated by the thump of a rubber-tipped cane, and he stops knocking at once, returns his hand to the Luger in his pocket. He wants to run, has to fight to remain on the doorstep. He hears the voice now, suddenly close, thick from sleep or medication. Or drink, Dub thinks hopefully. He likes to think of Kerim as weak and a hypocrite, a traitor not only to his electorate but also to the laws of his God.

"Who is there?" Kerim calls in heavily accented French. "Madame Patenaude?"

He should have shot right through the door. So easy, so efficient, over and done with, no pleading eyes ever looking into your own. But he never pictured doing it like that, a cowardly attack through a closed door. He has a script to follow, and he is too scared to deviate from it, so he shouts his first line. "I am from the Railroad Authority, monsieur. I've a small bag that you seem to have left at the Gare du Nord."

"What is it? My bag? Describe it, if you please."

The door was supposed to open now. Dub takes a breath. He feels his hand, sweaty on the grip of the Luger. He describes the suitcase.

"Oh, yes, yes!" the Turk says. There is a lilt to his voice. Such excitement over silk pajamas. Although they are, of course, fabulous silk pajamas, obviously custom-made, and no doubt they remind the fat cripple of happier days. "Yes, that's it. My little traveling case."

"Exactly," Dub calls back. If they keep shouting like this, other tenants will soon be sticking their heads out, an entire building of witnesses, of executioners.

"Leave it on the mat," the Turk calls. "I will retrieve it later."

Dub presses himself flat against the wall. He wishes he were not so alone. He longs for Yale, someone to share his feelings, this combination of fear and exasperation. "I can't, monsieur," he shouts. "I am ordered by my superiors at the Railroad Authority to return with a signed receipt."

"Pass the receipt under the door," the Turk yells. "I will sign it and pass it back to you."

He has not anticipated this. Now he's ad-libbing. "I can't do that, monsieur."

"Do not worry. I will pass to you also a gratuity."

Dub looks around as if he might find a prompter. "No, monsieur. I am afraid I cannot do it like that."

"But why not?"

He cannot for the life of him come up with a good reason why not. Again, he wishes for Yale. If she were here she would be shouting a string of compelling reasons why not, each one more plausible than the last.

The thought of her inspires him. To be inspired—it means to take in air, to take in life. This is why they have to be together, why he has to choose her. "Because I am required to witness the signature," he calls. "All these rules, this bureaucracy. You know how it is, monsieur. Government men. They should all be shot."

He imagines Yale laughing at this. He smiles at the thought of her laughter. Crazy, to be trying to amuse her when she isn't even with him. Crazy for him to be smiling right now. Smiling while his legs shake. Smiling while his heart pounds and he is consumed with the stinging need to piss. The smile fades as he thinks these thoughts. Now he thinks about nothing except how badly he wants this to be finished. He wants to knock down the door and charge into the apartment. But, just as badly, he wants to run down the stairs and out the front door, like a child pulling a prank on a neighbor, a child ringing a doorbell and then running as if for his life.

The silence continues. Then the thick voice at last. "Very well. One moment, if you please."

Dub lets out the breath he didn't know he was holding. He hears the dance of tumblers. He takes the gun from his pocket, though he knows it's too soon.

The door opens slowly and Dub has to wait another beat before he throws himself forward, forcefully, furiously, and he hurls the suitcase as he does, hurls it as if he were pitching a baseball, throws the suitcase so hard it flies into the apartment and smashes into Kerim Bey, hits him right in his face. An unintended target but a stroke of good luck, a sign from God, perhaps, as Kerim Bey cries in pain, loses his balance, falls backward, winds up on his knees.

Gun already drawn, Dub kicks the suitcase out of his way, then turns and closes the door behind him. Then he bulls his way fully into the apartment, the room shabbily furnished, the sofa and chairs draped with colorful shawls and scarves, prettied up with little throw pillows, all these dizzying and conflicting patterns in womanly shades: pinks, lilacs, pastels.

Dub pushes the kneeling old man with his free hand. The Turk's body is large and bulky but there is no strength to it. As Dub has suspected, the Turk is a corpse. Dub pushes him again, and Kerim falls against a Victorian settee covered with fringed paisley, and then the old Turk sinks to the floor, where he lies on his back on an Armenian rug and cowers.

The rug. Dub barely glances at it and yet he knows it, can describe it in detail, even the parts hidden by armchairs and the settee, even the part concealed by the fat Turk himself. Dub knows the rug the way he knows his mother's face, the back of his hand, his own name. He knows how it has been made, that the yellow comes from Armenia's pear trees, the browns from the husks of Armenia's walnuts, the red—the *vortun karmir* Raffi spoke of last night—from the shells of the female cochineal beetle, a creature found nowhere outside the *yergir*. He knows the rug's story by glimpsing the border design, a row of *S*'s. The *S*'s represent fish spines and water snakes; the rug therefore celebrates water, and water is life. Dub doesn't have to think about any of this. He knows what he is standing on the same way he knows how to separate oxygen from carbon monoxide.

And splayed on that rug, splayed on that red, is his enemy, this fugitive, this killer, this Turk whose own spine is bent like an *S*, this helpless, revolting spectacle, and now is the time to kick him, beat him, use the handle of the gun before using the trigger. Now is the time to shout slogans: *Vive les Arméniens, vive, vive, vive!* Now is the time for gloating and extracted confession and torture.

The Turk is entwining his fingers, lifting his braided hands. Dub thinks about slicing the fingers off and taking them home to Aram. Or, better yet, sending them to Ramela along with his cowardly letter of apology. Or perhaps he should send them to her before he sends the letter. Doing that would be like giving a woman an exquisite diamond ring, knowing that after you jilted her, after she recovered from her shame and heartache, she could hock the damned thing and live off it the rest of her life.

But he can't do any of it. He can't beat or kick or pistol-whip the man. And slicing off a man's fingers, tearing off parts of a living creature's body—he can't begin to imagine how one actually commits such offenses.

The problem is the man on the floor isn't Kerim Bey. He's not even a man. He is a sad creature, not really human. He is a turtle on its back, a june bug flailing in a puddle. Dub can't stand it another second. "For God's sake, get up," he says.

The Turk grunts as he grasps the leg of a table and uses it as a crutch to hoist himself back to his knees.

"Don't kneel in front of me, for Christ's sake," Dub says. "Stand the fuck up."

"I am unable to stand on my own, sir." The voice is as muscleless as the body. "I have phlebitis and also in this leg atrophied muscles." Tentatively, he holds out a hand. "If I had some assistance, sir, I could comply—"

Dub takes an automatic step away from the trembling hand. He aims his gun at the mewling head. "Then stay on your knees," he says.

In later years, on the rare occasion that he allows himself to remember this shameful day, Dub never has to think, *Oh, if only I'd thought to say this,* or *Damn, if I'd only thought to say that.* Everything he could possibly say rushes through his head right then and there, each vicious phrase presenting itself like a candidate in some sort of inhuman pageant.

Where is your curved sword? he wants to ask the kneeling Turk. After I kill you, I'm going to use it to sever your head and leave it on the doormat for your wife to find when she comes home.

Where is your wife? he wants to ask. Do you want to hear what we have in store for her after you're dead?

Where is your child? No, don't fear, don't worry. We're merely going to raise him a Christian, the one true faith, the only true faith. We're going to teach him to love Jesus and hate you.

Unlike the Turks, Dub knows he can't do any of these things. He can't even say any of these things. He can't kick the man or spit on his head. He can't even manage to say, You're a man with a child; how could you have treated other men's children so cruelly? And that's something he genuinely wants to know. How could you have done all those things when I can't even do this one thing?

Where is your God? he wants to say. Off on holiday with our God, he thinks.

But he says nothing. It's the Turk who is talking, and he's rational, even persuasive. "You don't understand, sir. We were at war, sir, don't you see? We had no soldiers to protect the desert caravans. We hadn't the means to keep marauders away. All we wished to do was move a population that was providing sympathy and arms to our enemy, transport them to a place where they could do us no harm. You can't fault us for that. It was imperative to move rebels away from the Russian border. Even today, your own Boghos Nubar is asserting that Armenians fought on the side of the Russians, that the Armenian populace in Turkey functioned as a de facto belligerent on the side of the Allied forces. Am I not right? Does he not assert this?"

It is true, Nubar does, indeed, assert that very thing. Dub has edited the letters to Poincaré, the London *Times,* in which Nubar has said it.

Dub could argue with Kerim Bey. He could cite written evidence too. The letters, the documents in Talaat's hand. The reports of eyewitnesses, of Morganthau, of statesmen, even Germans. But Dub isn't here to refute Kerim's speech, that carefully rehearsed litany of pathetic excuses and shadings of truth and outright lies. And even if he accepted Kerim's arguments pertaining to 1915, what about 1909? And what about 1896?

And what about and what about and what about? But he hasn't come here to play lawyer. At last, he has no desire for arguments, courtrooms, trials. He has come here to do this, to take action. Not for Raffi, not for Aram, not for the men of Erinyes. Not for honor and not for the new Republic of Armenia. But for Shushan and her unwanted girl baby. For Ramela and her scarred flesh and her dead sister. For Yale, even for Yale, a girl who cradles her fingers when she looks at Aram. For Seta, for Aram's daughters, for any daughter Dub may have someday. For these women, Dub sights along his arm. He checks the angle of his wrist. He locks his elbow.

He says, "Do Mohammedans confess? Do you unburden yourselves before death?"

As Kerim Bey prays, tears slip down his cheeks, tears upon tears, but the tears don't move Dub. Like the Turk's explanations for massacre, for slaughter, the tears strike Dub as too automatic, another manipulation. They are as unappealing as a long trail of ants.

Then the Turk looks up. "Forgive me," he says. "I am so sorry. Forgive me."

Dub narrows his eyes.

"Terrible wrongs," the Turk says. "What does it matter, the why of it? I am so ashamed. I am so sorry."

Dub falters, then he catches himself. Another breath, and he has to start all over again. He sights along his arm. He readjusts his angle. The Turk is beginning to cry again. Before he can, Dub shoots.

Part Nine

CHAPTER ONE

Another Last Day of the War

Raffi cannot find the traveling case. He has looked everywhere.

He left it right here on this chair. He is sure of it. He brought it downstairs, meaning to hide it in the wine cellar until it was time to use it tomorrow, the twenty-fourth, the day on which he would kill Kerim Bey in the most clever manner, thereby impressing all the members of Erinyes–Paris. But before he could take the suitcase down to the cellar, the smell of ham got to him and he put the suitcase on this chair and detoured into the kitchen. Who could blame him for that moment of irresponsibility? For months he had been slowly starving to death in Berlin.

Resting a suitcase on a chair. Who could have imagined the consequences? The house was dead quiet at nine in the morning, no one up but Brennan, who was cooking. She told him the giant albino American was already long gone. He asked about Dub and Yale. Dub had left too, Brennan said. Raffi went to the window. Sure enough, the Fiat was no longer there. Dub and the albino must have piled in hours before. That meant the only other people in the house were Aram and the orphan girl and Yale, all still in bed. So where was the harm in putting the case on the chair and going into the kitchen and eating the meal that Brennan had just prepared? Who is that for? he asked, and she said, Oh, what the hell, take it, and he did.

She didn't mind, really. If she fed him, she could get rid of him all the sooner. He ate standing up, and she watched him chew, hoping to make him uncomfortable, to deprive him of some of the pleasure of fried eggs, salty meat. She was, to say the least, not pleased he was back. She supposed he had the right to be here too, but he felt like an intruder. She called the château home now. She raised her children here. He was not a member of her family.

Still, she tried to talk to him; she tried to be polite. She told him about the orphans who'd been placed, the ones he ought to have remembered. She told him about her art project. He made an allusion to the number of Jews in the fine arts. She thought, It must be something I'm doing. Maybe people think I'm cheap, somehow.

"Say 'Thank you, Brennan,'" she said, when he finished the meal, but of course he ignored her. He left the room. Then he came right back. "Hey," he said. "Are you maybe taking something of mine from the chair outside?"

She told him no. She said, "I've been standing right in front of you the whole time, for Pete's sake." She thought, This is going to be crummy, him always around, accusing us and calling us names.

She made porridge for Aram. She ladled it into a bowl and set up a tray for him, which she carried to the study. She sat by Aram's side. He didn't eat much. He was not really awake. She tried to help him, to feed him as if he were a baby, another one of her ducklings. He opened his mouth several times, let her dab at his chin with a napkin, but then he lost interest. He spoke to her as if she were his mother. *Mayrig,* he called her (she knew that word), but the rest was Armenian and she couldn't help him. Gradually she understood he wanted to show her a picture or maybe a map. Not that he had a picture or a map, but he held his hands as if he were holding a sheet of paper, and he pointed out things, though she didn't know what. *Trés bien,* she said several times. Eventually he rolled the paper up, his fingers working in the air. No actor, no mime could have been more convincing. She believed there was a map just as sincerely as Aram did. She believed that map was as real as she was, as real as the walls, the porridge, the gods and goddesses. Some things one could *see* were real; some things one simply *knew* were real.

Still, she could not get out of the study quickly enough.

She went upstairs and stuck her head into the room where she'd slept the night before. "Get up, darling," she said to Shushan. Shushan groaned. Her first hangover, thought Brennan. Her first crying jag too. "Come on," she said. "There are people to see and pebbles to dig." She stepped into the room and closed the door. Standing before a mirror, she wet her fingers with her own saliva, and made spit curls. A Jew! she thought as she looked at her fair, freckled skin. The world was mad. *J'ai dit que j'ai tué quelqu'un.* Had the child really said that last night? Best never to mention it again. Into the trash bin with Billy Wilcox and her

Red Triangle insignia. The past was nothing. The present was every-thing. And the future. All hopes for the future. "We need to keep an eye on Aram today," Brennan told Shushan. "He's not feeling himself."

When Raffi burst in, Brennan screamed. Not out of modesty, hardly that, just the surprise of the door flung open. "Jesus," she said, her hand at her heart. Shushan stared blandly at him. He frowned at her. She was still wearing the Turk's orange pajamas. He thought she looked like an American jockey.

The suitcase, he said. What had she done with the suitcase? "Oh, for the love of Mike," Brennan said. "I don't have it. We left it in the other bedroom last night."

"It was not in the other bedroom this morning. It was in the hallway."

"Then Yale must have put it in the hallway. Why all the com-motion? There's nothing in it but pajamas. Believe me, I looked very thoroughly."

"Last night, you looked. Maybe there is something more in it this morning."

"Not unless you put something more in it. I haven't seen it at all."

"You haven't taken anything from it? You aren't concealing the suitcase from me and maybe removing something from it? Maybe something you think is belonging to you or that Yah-el?"

She threw her arms up in the air. "The only thing I took were paja-mas." She indicated Shushan. "Aren't they gay, though? Later, we're all going to put on a pair and take a photo and send it to the Turk Dub is tailing. Our little foray into artistic vengeance. Letting him know he's nothing but a mockery."

Rocks and pajamas, her answer to wholesale slaughter. A series of jokes, her response to the deaths of people who still came to him, one by one, in dreams. He couldn't stand her. What did she dream of? Dresses and hats and colloquia on modern art, she the chief panelist. Making a name for herself on the bones of his people. For a moment he hoped she *had* found her lighter. He would hand her a cigarette himself, run out of the room, plug his ears with his fingers.

"Now go find something to do with yourself," Brennan said. "In this room, ladies are dressing." He stalked off, and she called after him. She said, "And don't you dare wake up Yale."

HE WENT downstairs again, searched Aram's study quietly, desperately, while Aram moaned in his sleep, but he left empty-handed, near tears. He found the bonne, who was just arriving, hours late—the household was going to hell—and quizzed her. He summoned old Kevork from the fruit orchard and grilled him.

He went back upstairs. Brennan and Shushan were leaving their room now, each dressed in her work gear. "Come dig with us," Shushan said.

"Can't you see I am looking for something important?" he said.

"We are too," Brennan said. "Anyway, he needs to stay here with Aram. Yale will take over when she wakes up." She turned to him as she had before. "And don't wake her. We all had a miserable night."

As soon as they were gone, he went into the room where Yale lollygagged in bed. She looked up at him, sleepy. She was tangled in sheets, one breast exposed, and the length of one leg. She saw him then and, as Brennan had, she screamed. She pulled the sheet to her clavicle.

"Where is the little suitcase?" he said. She was relieved this was all he wanted of her. She didn't trust him, she didn't like him, she didn't put anything past him. And she was annoyed too, to be woken for such a trivial matter after she'd gotten not one minute's rest the night before. Also, his sister was on her mind. Still, she answered him, starting to go through the events of the previous night, to recount the suitcase's various adventures. He cut her off. "I am aware of all this," he said. "What business are you having to be taking it from Aram's study in the first place?"

"I didn't take it," she said. "Shushan took it."

"If this is true, then you are instigating this behavior in her. You and your alleged sister."

She saw how he was looking at her. She knew then that he was the one who'd exposed her to Dub. She drew the sheet from her clavicle to her chin. "The last place I saw it was out in the hall," she said. "Now, can you please let me be?"

BY NOW HE has looked under every bed. He has looked in the kitchen, checked the bathtub. He has been to the wine cellar twice. But the suitcase is nowhere, and over and over he returns to the chair. He puts his hand on the cushion as if the suitcase might still be there but in an altered state, turned invisible. He does this again. Touching the cushion. He swears in every language he knows. Then he sits in the chair and starts to sob.

He's done with that, thank God, by the time Yale comes downstairs, dressed in her nightgown, an open robe thrown over it. She sees only that he's unhappy. "Oh, Raffi," she says. "Are you still on the suitcase? Honest to God. It's nothing but pajamas."

"No," he says. "It is not nothing but that."

She sees now he's been crying. She is dumbfounded. "Brennan looked inside it thoroughly, Raffi. She said there was nothing else."

"That was yesterday. Yesterday there was nothing else. Today there was maybe something else."

She considers this. "What else?"

He smiles ruefully, the gold tooth flashing. A desperate man, he thinks of himself. For the first time in his life, he understands the American expression about strange bedfellows. "There is maybe a little bomb in it now," he says.

She feels her heart revving. "Why," she says, "would anyone have put a little bomb in it?"

"Maybe as part of a plan."

"A plan."

"Maybe a plan that is involving your cigarette lighter," he says. Then—what the hell—he tells her the rest. How he planned to take the suitcase to Paris the next day, the anniversary of the slaughter, and leave it in the Turk's hall. That's how simple his plan was. No knock on the door, no calling hello. Eventually the Turk will open his door and find it. After that he will bring it into his home and open it. He will empty the contents, not only his ridiculous nightclothes but also the obscene western contrivance. There is something about that contrivance that's impossible to resist, Raffi says. He was sure the Turk would pick it up. He was equally sure the Turk would feel compelled to flick the wheel. Raffi acts out a thumb running along the flint. "He would make a flame," Raffi says. "And then—"

"*Boom-boom,*" Yale says.

"And I would be miles away."

"It's an all-right plan," she says. "Unless it blew the wife up. Or the boy."

"Any of them would suit my purposes. What do I care?"

"Then it's a very good plan."

"Was," he says.

Unwanted thoughts are coming to her. "Maybe Dub took it," she says. "Before he went to Paris."

"No. The truck is leaving before I am downstairs. The suitcase is still here then."

"I thought he was going to take the train today," she says.

"No," Raffi says. "Brennan says she is seeing him going by the truck."

She feels relief and then the heat of her own angry tears. She blinks until they're gone, and all that's left is the heat. "That lighter belonged to Brennan," she says. "What right did you have to take it?"

"What right did you have to the suitcase? And in any event, such a disgusting object should not be in this house. Just as you should not be in this house."

"I was invited," she says. "Seta invited me. I'm more help to her than you. I take care of the orphans. I take care of Aram. We've done more for the victims of the massacres than you ever have. We've done more for Aram in just the past few weeks—"

"You are not even knowing Aram Kazarian," Raffi says.

"You're the one who doesn't know him," she says. "He's told me secrets he's never told you."

She is prepared to go on, to hint at what these secrets might be, but before she can, he has left his chair and has hit her. He has slapped her so hard that she has staggered back and fallen against the corner of a buffet, its sharp edge jagging into her hip, and this hurts more than the blow. It also knocks her off balance, and she slumps down to the floor. Once there, she stays there, huddled in a corner between the buffet and the wall, her hand to her cheek.

"You hate that they love me," she says. "You hate that *he* loves me."

"He is fucking you," Raffi says. "This is not the same as loving in my culture. He is fucking you, but he is marrying my sister."

"He is never marrying your sister," she says.

He stands over her. The edge of the buffet, the volume of his voice, the obscenities he's using: it all hurts much more than the slap. But she can't move her hand, can't take it from her cheek. "You can scream until you wake the dead," she says, "and your sister will still be crazy. She'll never live up to her end of their contract. And as long as she doesn't, he won't marry her. I know him. He's given himself an escape hatch. He won't throw his life away."

Raffi crouches over her, his arm rising without his permission, the fist longing to come down, and it is only at the last instant he makes himself stop. "What is this contract?" he says.

She has raised her other hand to protect herself. She is squinting at him from between her fingers. He lowers his arm. She lowers hers. She explains his sister to him.

His fist forms again, and she recoils. Then, like ice into water, he loses all shape. His legs don't support him, and he has to sit down. He sits next to her, the two of them squeezed between the buffet and the wall, barely enough room for one. They can't even rear back sufficiently to look at each other.

"She rips up her arm?" he says.

"You know. The awful thing she does with sewing needles."

"Sewing needles?" he says.

She will never be able to say how it happens, her head against his chest, his chin on her head. All she can say is that they sit like this for a long time.

"Will you really kill him tomorrow?" she says.

He says that he will.

"Even if you don't find the suitcase?"

"I will use a gun. I was being too clever. It was stupid."

"I didn't really believe we were going to kill him. I thought we would just bring him to justice." The phrase sounds ridiculous. Cops-and-robbers. A dime novel.

"You won't kill him," he says. "*We* will. I will. Justice. Tomorrow."

"I could go with you," she says. She is thinking of Shushan. She is thinking, she admits, of his sister. Not the one who died. The other sister. The care she requires from others. The one thing that might make her feel safe, go away. "I know all about him. I hate him too."

"No," he says.

"Because I'm an *odar*?"

"Yes. He belongs to us. It's our battle."

"No," she says. "It's what they did to women. Shushan and your sister." The one who died, she means. "And your sister's daughter." The white communion dresses. "The outrages. All against women."

"Armenian women."

"Then we should go together." She points to him. "Armenian." Points at herself. "Woman." She says, "God said he would deliver Sisera into the hands of a woman."

"Who is this Sisera all of a sudden?"

"From the Bible. A tyrant. Killed by a woman." She gestures wanly toward her temple. "With a tent peg."

"Fairy tales," he says. "You want to pretend you're a woman in a fairy tale. You should go back to America."

"I live here," she says.

"In Berlin, they are starting in on the Jews." He thrusts his head back and it hits the wall. She winces for him. He winces too. "I made a terrible error in Berlin last night," he says. "There was this Jewish girl. Like you. She is haunting me now, along with everyone else. If I don't find that suitcase, who will be haunting me next? I can do nothing right, it seems." He sighs, tries to do one thing right. "You should leave Europe," he says.

She looks up at him then. He twists until he can see her face. "Oh, no," he says. "You can see where I am hitting you."

"It hurts too."

"You must understand why he is having to marry her," he says. "More than ever now. If we are punishing the past for what it did to Maro, we must at the same time provide a future for Ramela."

"What about me?" she says.

"I thought you wanted to be *madagh*," he says.

"I do," she says, although it's a word she's never heard. She closes her eyes and hears him whispering something, she doesn't know what. Yah-el, he is saying, Yah-el, but so softly she isn't able to tell. She thinks he's praying for his sisters or for the return of the suitcase, the bomb he's put in it. She thinks, What are we all doing, what are we doing? until his voice and her thoughts are drowned out by the sound of an explosion in the hyacinth garden.

CHAPTER TWO

Going West

THE BULLET Dub fired at the Turk struck its intended target. Kerim Bey's words ceased, and he screamed. He looked at Dub, and Dub saw those eyes, drowning, red-veined. Then those eyes looked heavenward. Then they looked downward. Then the Turk held out his palms, and his eyes went to those palms. He saw they were not bloodied. Slowly he pressed the clean palms to his chest. He looked at them again. He showed the palms to Dub.

They were still clean. His eyes asked a question, pleaded for an explanation.

Dub looked to the settee. The Turk looked too. Only then did he see where the bullet had gone. It had torn through a velvet throw pillow. Little white featheres were snowing onto the settee's cushions.

NOW, AS RAFFI and Yale sit side by side in Senlis, Dub continues his rampage. He pivots and fires into the Turk's bedroom, killing four satin pillows arranged on the Turk's marital bed. Another pivot and one step forward so he can see into the second bedroom, see between the slats of the crib, and Dub aims at and murders a tiny blue pillow of eyelet lace.

The Turk gasps. The place where his son lays his head every night. "What do you want from me?" the Turk asks.

"Get out of here," Dub says. "Take your wife and your brat, and get out of France. I am so damned sick of thinking about you."

Six pillows gunned down, and not a single neighbor appearing to have noticed. At least no one has left his apartment to come by and investigate. This is good news for Dub, although he isn't cheered by it. If he were not such a coward, he would turn the gun on himself. That's how disgusted he is, how full of self-loathing.

He leaves the apartment, crosses the street, heads toward the black truck at a brisk pace. He doesn't know much, but he knows this for sure: the only thing more ignoble than assassinating throw pillows would be getting arrested for assassinating throw pillows, becoming famous for it.

Kerim Bey, meanwhile, is sitting on the carpet in the front room of his apartment. His legs are still shaking; there is no point in his trying to stand or even crawl to the settee. He has the small case in his lap, though. He is nearly embracing it.

"Oh, I know," his wife said, on their first night in France, when he could not find his blue silk pajamas. "The big case was so full I moved your night things into the small case, and now it seems the baggage office has misplaced it." She could not understand his despair; she herself was relieved that nothing more important was missing. And he could not explain. It had made their nights in the hôtel le Marais, an old rendezvous spot of theirs before they wed, fraught with tension and recrimination. "Oh, why must you always fuss over such petty matters?' she said, before turning over to go to sleep. "Either the case will turn up or we'll buy you new pajamas. After what we've been through, one would think you might have some perspective on what is important in this world."

Now Kerim Bey opens the clasps, lifts the top. The red and orange pairs are missing, he sees right away, but not, thank heavens, the purple and blue. He reaches in and removes the royal blue bottoms. With his fingers, he rips out the stitching in the thick hem of the right leg, thus freeing the diamonds and rubies he sewed in there before leaving Constantinople. He watches as they tumble into the suitcase, into the folds of silk. He wants to scoop them out, but his hands are shaking as badly as his legs, and he is afraid he will drop them. If they fall into the nap of this rug, they might be lost forever, that's how small some of them are. A cigarette, he decides. Due to the phlebitis, he rarely smokes anymore. But here on the table by the settee are his wife's cigarettes. He will have just one. It will calm him. Then he will proceed to the second royal blue leg and set free the gold, all the hoops and rings.

He looks for his wife's matchbook. He doesn't see it. This is when a small naked woman catches his eye.

DUB IS SITTING in the truck, trying to catch his breath. He is also trying to comprehend the enormity of what he's just done—or rather what he's just failed to do. Now Kerim Bey will understand that he's being watched and he will flee (Dub did, after all, command him to flee), and all of Erinyes' hard work—trailing him, watching him, making sure he was where they could find him—will have been for naught. Dub feels sick. He doesn't understand himself.

He is turning the key in the ignition when something else he doesn't understand happens: an explosion from the building he has just left. This time all the neighbors do come running. They've been affected this time, the blast so loud it's shaken family portraits off walls, filled kitchens with smoke, knocked a teacup from the hands of an elderly widow who now cannot stop crying.

Behind the wheel, Dub sees the concierge standing on the sidewalk as her tenants pour from the building. He puts the truck in gear, slams his foot on the accelerator, and gets the hell out of there.

BUT THIS EXPLOSION, the one that blows Kerim Bey's head off, is not the same explosion that has stilled Raffi's prayers in Senlis. The explosion in Senlis, the one that causes Yale to disentangle herself from Raffi, to run into the yard in her nightgown, has occurred down by the hyacinth garden near the pond, and only Shushan Khaladjian has witnessed it.

Trouble is, Shushan won't say what happened. The reason is—although this is part of what she won't say—she doesn't know which language to use for the telling. At first, there's no one to tell but Raffi, and Raffi wants her to say it in Armenian. But Brennan didn't speak Armenian, Shushan reasons, and so it would be disrespectful to Brennan to tell the story in a language Brennan wouldn't have understood. Besides, Raffi didn't like Brennan. Why should Shushan have to endure his false sympathy?

Later, people from the city come to the house, and they want her to tell the story in French, and she would, Shushan would, except that the more they scream at her (they are frustrated and frantic and they think that if they bellow in her face she will suddenly start answering their questions), the fewer French words she remembers. So she doesn't talk to them either.

She would tell it in English, but her English is poor. Besides, Yale is

the only one left in the house who would want to hear it in English and
Yale is in bed, her eyes closed, her mouth lolling open, because the doctor has given her something powerful to make her shut up, because it
was very clear she was never going to stop screaming if left to her own
devices.

So what's the point of Shushan's making the effort to talk about it?
And what is there for her to say? It's a story like any other story, like
every story she knows. Brennan's life is like any other life. Shushan's
mother, her father, her siblings, her grandparents, her cousins, her aunts,
her uncles, her maid, her priest, her schoolteachers, her baby. *Gar oo chagar,* she used to whisper to that baby. Once there was and there wasn't.

CHAPTER THREE

Magic

THE STORY SHUSHAN refuses to tell would, if she told it, go something like this: Brennan was at the far end of the flower bed, kneeling by
the stone wall near the pond. There were no flowers in the flower bed,
and Brennan seemed surprised by this. She expected there to be tiny
green fingers of grape hyacinth leaves poking through the soil. But
there was nothing except the soil itself, dark and rich, with the tines
from last fall's final hoeing still visible, like comb tracks through bril-
liantined hair.

Shushan, at the other end of the wall, was bored with digging. She
was bored with all things Armenian, now that she thought about it. The
night before she had cried hard over all things Armenian, but today, she
decided, it was time to look to the future. She would no longer waste
her time with stones. What did she care if the world never figured out
what five hundred thousand of something looked like? The five hundred thousand were gone. Why didn't Brennan just send the museums
a big box full of nothing?

Today would be her last day of digging, she decided right then. Tomorrow, she would go to Paris instead. She would ask Brennan to take her, and if Brennan said no, if Brennan insisted on being more Armenian than Shushan was, then, fine, Shushan would go to Paris with Yale. And in Paris she would buy a short skirt and bob her hair. She wanted to be like Brennan. She didn't want Brennan to be like her.

As she daydreamed about Paris, a pair of swans that had been sleeking along the pond now lumbered ashore. Shushan had never seen swans out of water, and she was amused by the sight of them, how ridiculous they looked, padding about on their huge orange feet, not having the first notion of what to do with their necks. Then the male swan began chasing the female, and the two of them looked even more ludicrous, running and flapping and squawking. The female's beak was wide open and her skinny black tongue was sticking all the way out and vibrating with fear. She ran toward the flower bed. The male was right behind her.

Shushan picked up some of her pebbles and began pelting the male, who wasn't the least perturbed by the onslaught. Although pebbles were bouncing off his wings and hitting the back of his head, he kept chasing the female until he finally caught her. He mounted her from behind, and she screamed and kept running, this time with the male on her back. Shushan threw some of the larger pebbles, but the male wouldn't break from the female. They ran in crazed circles, all the while the male inside the female. Shushan thought then of something the Kurd once told her when he was inside her like that. He told her that the male cat's penis had thorns all along it. When the male cat withdrew from the female, he tore her apart. "That's why they howl all night," the Kurd said, laughing as he huffed in her ear. The female swan screeched again. Shushan wondered if fowl were thorned like felines. She lifted a big rock that she'd dug out of the bed, and she threw it as hard as she could at the swans, now a single whimpering creature. The rock missed completely, didn't even come close to hitting the male. It landed near Brennan, who was dipping her trowel in the earth, oblivious to all the drama, and it fell to the grass with a dull thud. Shushan saw the rock fall, and she saw Brennan look up, perplexed. Then, before Shushan could call out to Brennan, explain where the rock had come from, a geyser of dirt was coming at Shushan, and within the spew were hundreds of little white pebbles arcing toward her like shrapnel.

Then the sky turned white as milk and the air turned gray with dust, and Shushan flung herself to the ground and buried her head in her arms. Only then did she hear the sound of the explosion. She knew the sound must have come before the shrapnel, but it seemed to her that it had come after, such a powerful sound, so forceful a thundering that it killed both swans. The sound killed the swans, and it lifted Shushan off the ground and, just as she had thrown the big rock, so it threw her to the lip of the pond. She landed with the same dull thud as the rock had, and when she opened her eyes, she was swaddled in mud, and she knew the mud had saved her, the soft mud into which she had apparently wriggled deep, like a worm.

Brennan was not so lucky. It was as if she'd been erased by the thunder. Shushan opened her eyes, and as the dust dissipated and the sky returned to blue, she saw that, other than the addition of two mangled swans and the absence of Brennan, everything was as it had been. It was like a magic act. A shimmer of cymbals, a gasp from the crowd, and—*poof!*—the magician's lovely assistant is gone.

B Y E A R L Y E V E N I N G the château and its grounds are crawling with men: doctors and politicians and Armenian freedom fighters and German prisoners of war with shovels. Also small Indo-Chinese dressed in black, who, like elegant hound dogs, try to sniff out more buried danger. If Shushan were to tell the Indo-Chinese the story she has so far refused to tell anyone, they would explain that what happened today was no disappearing act. One only needed to know where to look. In the branches of a chestnut tree. Beneath the umbrella of a toadstool. Under a leaf. On the roof of a shed. Everywhere, there's plenty to find, and it will be found by these men, who, like the German boys working nearby, know the war isn't over. They know it because, if it were over, they would not still be disarming the French countryside, harvesting little white fingertips and khaki brown sleeves. And this knee. And this toe. And this fragment of scalp, the hair black on one side, ginger-beer yellow on the other.

CHAPTER FOUR

Dinner That Night

WAS SHE SMOKING a cigarette?" Raffi asks. Shushan has relented at last; she will answer select questions in Armenian, preferably questions that allow a monosyllabic, monotonal response. Meanwhile, she is ignoring the leftovers Dub has heated up, served to Aram, offered to them. No one at the table—Raffi, Dub, Shushan—is hungry. The three of them are supping on their old fallback, gin. Shushan puts her finger into Dub's glass, sucks it dry. She wonders how gin would taste heated up. The only thing more comforting than gin right now would be soup.

"Shushan," Raffi says. "I asked you something. Was she smoking?"

A stupid question. She was always smoking.

"And how did she light the cigarette?"

A stupid question. He knew about her cigarette lighter.

Dub has never seen Raffi so undone. His eyes are swollen from crying, the eyelashes are slick from his tears. My God, Dub thinks. Was he in love with Brennan?

"Are you positive, Shushan? Think hard. Did you see the lighter in her hand?"

"I don't know," Shushan says. She licks her thumb. "She always used it."

"But did you see it today? Did you actually see it today?"

"Leave me alone," Shushan says.

Raffi looks at Dub, who, Raffi thinks, does not look anything like Dub anymore. Earlier, while Yale slept her drugged sleep—she sleeps it still—and men ran about the grounds, digging and grimacing and yelling for silence, Dub had gone to the bathroom, emerged shaved and shorn. Cut this short, his hair no longer looks dramatically two-toned. It's simply black tipped with gray. Raffi tries to ignore this new clean-cut look, which he finds disconcerting. He tries to remember it's only Dub he's addressing. "She had that piece of obscenity with her," he tells Dub. "That lighter. I'm certain of it. I'd taken it last night, and I put it somewhere, and then this morning, first I had it and then, suddenly, I couldn't find it again. She must have found it when my back was turned. She must have taken it. I asked her about it. I asked if she had it. She denied that she took it. I would have stopped her if she'd told me she had it. I would have explained. But you know her. The two of them. Compulsive liars, and so, of course, she lied to me and then she used it out by the pond to light her cigarette."

"That's not true," Shushan says. "You didn't ask if she had her lighter. You asked if she had the little suitcase. You're the liar."

Raffi looks to the heavens. "The lighter was inside the suitcase."

"No," Dub says. He is tired and confused. Two explosions and no explanation for either. Yale sound asleep—no one to talk to. "There were only pajamas in the suitcase."

Raffi throws up his hands. It's a very Brennan-like gesture. "Are you listening to me at all?" he says. "I'm telling you I put the lighter inside that suitcase. With the pajamas."

Dub holds up one hand, a traffic cop, the guy in charge. But he's in charge of nothing, he's only puzzled. "You put the lighter in the suitcase?"

"Yes, yes, yes."

"But . . ." He can't think of what to say. "Such an odd place to hide it."

Raffi covers his eyes with his hand. "Are you hearing a word I'm saying? I rigged it first. I rigged it. A little gunpowder. A little tinder. A little flick of the wheel. You see? I rigged it, and then I put it in the suitcase, and it was meant for Kerim Bey, but she must have found it and taken it and used it—"

He understands at last, everything falling into place, and he should feel anger, fury, but he feels only tenderness. Dear boy, he wants to say. Oh, my dear boy. He puts his hand on Shushan's hand. He looks into Raffi's eyes. "I know what happened now, *tratsi*."

He planned to tell no one, certainly not Raffi, what transpired in Paris that morning. But now he tells them the story. He tells it his own way. It is not the Armenian way—*once there was and was not*—nor the American way—*once upon a time*—nor God's way—*in the beginning*. It is the opposite of God's way. How else would one mistheist tell another mistheist a story? He begins with the ending.

CHAPTER FIVE

How the Jews Got Their Names

ONE LAST STORY.

Several days after the explosions, while Raffi drives Aram to Le Havre, where Aram will spend his final weeks alongside his wife in the converted attic bedroom of the home of his daughter; and while Shushan interviews for the position of housemaid at the home of a prosperous importer of oriental rugs in Chantilly; and while Dub is in Aram's study, trying to decide which papers should be burned in the fireplace, what evidence must be destroyed so nobody ever puts two and two together and comes up with one missing black transport truck, Yale is drowsing in the same narrow bed she's been drowsing in since Brennan's death. She finds the bitter draft the doctor has prescribed quite effective, especially when she washes it down with the expensive Armagnac that Aram was unable to take to his new home. Yale cannot bear to waste that Armagnac, which is, in her by now fairly expert opinion, far superior to anything else she has ever drunk.

She is considering whether or not she can open her eyes, heavy and sticky from sleep, for even a few minutes, when there is a knock on her door, and Kevork, the old servant, peeks cautiously in. "Mademoiselle," he says, "there is a friend of yours wishing to see you."

She assumes it's Ned Harden, who comes nearly daily, but the next thing she knows Kevork has ushered in Amo Winston. It feels like a bad if somewhat absurd dream, Amo sitting on her mattress here in Senlis, Amo clutching her hand and weeping.

Even worse, Amo has brought a man with her. The man is short and chubby, hook-nosed and bearded. Except for his YMCA uniform, he's a Jew straight out of the pages of the Thule Society's least-restrained pamphlets. "This is Rabbi Blau," Amo Winston says. "I heard there were no Jewish churches in this town, and I thought you might need someone to talk to, so I invited the rabbi to see you."

"Senlis is actually a city, not a town," Yale says.

"It's a *beautiful* city," says Amo. "And I thought you might like to speak to a man of your faith."

Yale feels woozy and thick-tongued, but she is able to say this much: "The Y threw me out because of my faith."

"But that's not actually true," Amo says. "I understand why you'd think that, but it's not actually the case."

"They threw Brennan out because of my faith too," Yale says. She is not really being accusatory. She is only making drowsy, drugged conversation.

"I was actually quite involved with that very decision, Miss Weiss," says the rabbi. The name he has called her doesn't rile her. He speaks so slowly, a singsong cadence that could never make anyone angry, that only makes her long to roll over, close her eyes again. "It was not your Judaism that anyone objected to."

She manages this much emotion: "The bunk it wasn't."

"But it wasn't. It was certain inconsistencies, if you will, between your application and your actual circumstances."

"Bunk," she says, near dreaming again.

"But it's true," Amo says. "Oh, Yale, if you had only told the truth in the first place, none of this would have happened, and you'd still be living at the Y, and Brennan would still be alive."

If her head were clearer, this remark might have upset or angered her, but foggy, her thoughts ambling about, Yale sees Amo's point, and so she says nothing.

"You should be glad we discovered those confabulations, Miss Weiss," the rabbi says. "What if we hadn't and the telegram regarding Miss White had been directed to your family instead of hers, under the assumption that unmarried twin sisters shared the same address?"

She can see his point too. "That would have been something," she murmurs.

"I'm sure you never stopped to consider the power of lies," the rabbi says. Amo nods solemnly. My God, Yale thinks, she's in love with *him* now. And she thinks it will be times like this—*Guess what Amo Winston's up to these days, darling?*—when she will miss Brennan most dreadfully.

"There's a story I'd like to tell you, Yale," the rabbi says. Or perhaps he's called her Yael but has pronounced it so it rhymes with *jail*.

"It's the story of how the Jews got their names. I used to tell it to my own children when they were young."

The story is long and the manner in which it is told is patronizing and belittling, but its highlights, which years later Yael will tell her own children (*Once upon a time,* she'll begin), are these:

First, the Jews got their names directly from God. God named Abram Abraham and Sarai Sarah. Next, the Jews got their names from fighting with God. Jacob wrestled all night with the Lord, and the next day the Lord named him Israel.

After that, though, things changed. The names of the Jews were no longer gifts from God but insults from governments. Lords of a different type insisted the Jews take last names. How else to find them at tax time, how else to find them when it was necessary to conscript them into their armies?

Some Jews took the names of their tribes: Cohen, Levi. Wealthy Jews purchased beautiful names: Lillenfeld, field of lilies. Poor Jews accepted humiliating names: Gross, fat. Some Jews took the names of their towns, although if the Christians living there objected, then those Jews had to take the names of barren sites nearby: Berg, mountain; Wald, wood. And some Jews took the names of their professions, although if the Christians working in those professions objected, then those Jews had to take the names of their tools. Not tailor but scissors: Sher. Not carpenter but nail: Nagel.

"In one town," the rabbi says, "the mayor was an efficient man. He called all the Jews to the town square. He had the city officials divide the square into quadrants with big ropes. Then he assigned each quadrant a color. In whichever quadrant you stood, that was your name. Red, Blue, Black, White. Roth, Blau, Schwartz, Weiss."

"And they lived happily ever after," Yale murmurs.

The rabbi smiles. "I'll leave you two ladies to talk," he says. "May I first kiss your cheek?" Yale lifts her limp hand. The rabbi takes the hint, shakes it. "I'll wait for you outside, Miss Winston," he says. "And Miss Weiss, I want you to think about my story and your name and what it means."

It means I was in the northeast square of the quadrant, she thinks. But she nods. She is warm and logy and intoxicated.

"He's a very great man," Amo Winston says, after he's gone. She reaches into her large purse and pulls out a milky white glass with a candle in it. "I thought you might need this."

"Thank you," Yale says.

She reaches into her purse again. "And I thought you might be out of face cream."

"That's sweet."

"If you want—I've been talking to the rabbi about how these things work—I could drape a cloth over the mirror."

"All right," Yale says. Amo wishing to cover the mirror—Yale must look a fright.

Amo whisks the sheet off the second unused bed in the room, arranges it over the glass. "Shall I light the candle?"

"All right."

"Shall I say the prayer?"

She will have converted by summer, Yale thinks.

Amo prays in a language Yale doesn't know, and then, when she's done, begins to weep. "I am so sorry," she says. The tiny flame in the milk glass dances. "I am so sorry for your loss." Snuffling, she blows her nose with the handkerchief she keeps in her sleeve. "When you apply the face cream, you don't need to use the mirror. Just locate your cheekbones with your fingers and rub in a gentle circular motion."

"Okay," Yale says.

"And never pull at the skin near your eyes. That's how we wrinkle."

Yale promises she won't. And then she can't resist, she gives Amo a going-away present. "Although," she says, "I don't really have to worry about wrinkles yet. You were right about my age. I'm not even nineteen until August."

Amo smiles through her tears. "Yes, I know. I know everything. Still, we're never too young to start after wrinkles."

After Amo leaves, Yale gets out of bed. Her legs are weak, but she wobbles to the mirror. She pulls off the sheet and she looks at herself. Pale and in need of a good washing, but otherwise not so bad. She drops the sheet onto the floor.

The candle she leaves alone. Candlelight, she has no objection to. She runs her finger once through the flame. Then she goes back to bed and sleeps for another week.

CHAPTER SIX

Requiem

N OT LONG AGO the family was large and chaotic, a dozen members: Aram, Seta, Yale, Brennan, Dub, Ned, Shushan, five little ducklings. The day they go to Brennan's memorial services, they are only three. It's hard to take it in, so Yale doesn't.

Instead, she keeps busy. The house in Senlis has been evacuated while the Indo-Chinese and Germans search it for hidden explosives. Meanwhile, Ned has been sent back to the States and Raffi has also sailed to America, carrying a letter from Dub to Ramela. When the poor girl tries to read it, Yale imagines, her brother will be talking to her nonstop, explaining the many ways in which she will be much better off with a man other than the one she chose on her own. The more he thinks about it, Raffi told Dub before he sailed, the more he is certain he must have been insane to let Ramela pick her own husband. He blames it all on America, he said. He needs to stay there, keep his eye on it.

Now it is only Dub and Yale and Shushan. Dub and Yale have temporarily moved into an inn on the Senlis square. Each day they read the newspapers, French and American, the smallest print, the most obscure columns, but so far there has been nothing about a stolen army vehicle and its relationship to a monstrous crime, although there has been lots written about the crime itself. A wealthy foreign businessman, a M. Bernard Klein, has been blown up in his home amid a mysterious rainstorm of gems. The body was found headless but bejeweled, sparkling. The case has captured the public's fancy.

It has overwhelmed Dub. He doesn't want to go outside. He doesn't want to talk. He says he's fine but then he says little else. All day long he lies in the sagging bed at the inn and stares at the ceiling. Yale sits by his side and reads from guidebooks she's bought, one for Spain, one for Portugal. "Or we could just go home," she says. "Whatever you want." He says he doesn't want to go home. She says that's fine, she doesn't either. She tells him she thinks Portugal sounds romantic. They'll fit in there. They are both dark Mediterranean types. She thinks they can get away with it.

Shushan is living in an attic room in the house of her new employers in Chantilly. She seems sanguine about it. She is too drained to get angry these days. Housework is just what she needs, she says. It fills her days, exhausts her. She sleeps well at night.

On the morning of Brennan's mass, Shushan waits for Dub and Yale outside the inn. She is wearing a new ensemble, one of the new all-the-day-thru dresses in navy blue. Her hair has been cut to her chin. Her thick bangs hide her brows and her acne. Very fashionable—and still she looks dull and deadened.

"Is it the outfit washing her out?" Dub asks Yale. He is feeling fairly dull and deadened himself. When he finally fell asleep the night before, his nightmares featured severed heads and the sagging breasts of the concierge. Ramela made an appearance as well. He has dreams like this nearly every night. He wakes up not only in a fearful lather but thoroughly embarrassed. He can't believe how simplistic his nightmares are. It's as if his dream mind thinks his waking mind is an idiot that needs everything spelled out for it. "She looks awful," Dub says of Shushan. "Worse than when we first got her." But when he is close enough, he holds her at arm's length to admire her—he has seen people do this—and says, "Is that a new dress? Don't you look pretty."

"All right, then," Yale says brightly. Who else is left to be the mother? "Are we all set? Shall we go?"

"I don't want to go," Shushan says.

"Now, darling," Yale says. "None of us wants to go. But the city has organized this for Brennan and we have to be there. What would people think if we weren't? They'd think Brennan was friendless and unloved."

"Why do we care what they think?" Shushan says.

Her difficult adolescent daughter. But it's all right; they are already walking by then. The cathedral bells have begun to chime. Yale wonders where the piece of bell Brennan took from the Western Front is these days. She wonders if taking that bell had anything to do with Brennan's fate, if it angered some god of church bells. She tells herself to stop thinking this way. She tells herself to stop looking for explanations.

The threesome has fallen in step with the townspeople, everyone in somber colors, their voices hushed. Yale knows this mass is not really for Brennan. The city has used her death as an excuse to allow everyone to come together one more time. Since the end of the war, the citizenry has tried so hard to be plucky. They've pulled themselves together, returned to work, gone on with their lives. Now at this mass they will get to fall apart once again. They are looking forward to it. Lavish tears, mutual comfort. They will pretend it's about Brennan. Such a young girl, people who never knew her will say to other people who never knew her. Such a blameless life, and this is the thanks she gets. Well, at least it was fast. At least she didn't suffer. And then they will say, Not like my poor son. Not like my poor husband. And they will tell their stories one more time, and it will feel so good.

Inside the cathedral, the children's choir is singing a hymn that is solemn and moving. Yale looks around, sees that there have been no special seats reserved for the truncated family. Yale, one of the few in the cathedral not yet teary-eyed, is miffed to learn it. If she had known the town wasn't going to make the least little effort, she might indeed have stayed home. She already feels stiff and awkward, isn't sure how to answer the questions she fears will be put to her. *Now, do I understand correctly that the late Miss White was your sister?* How will she reply with Dub standing next to her, monitoring all she says? It's true she has promised him she will turn over a new leaf. It was the condition of his marriage proposal: I will marry you if—no more lies. She agreed at once. She tried to explain the rationale behind the earlier lies. At the same time, she neglected to confess her true age. Jewish, he seems ready to put up with. But eighteen? He's told her so many times that this was part of Ramela's problem. She was just so young, too young.

Yale plans to tell him how old she is soon, any day now. She plans to stop lying, she really does. She will turn that leaf over; she just doesn't know how to determine the precise moment to begin. Shushan, for instance, doesn't know about anything yet. Doesn't know Brennan was never her sister. Doesn't know she and Dub plan to marry. Yale can't just set the record straight when answering the questions of inquisitive strangers, not if there's an innocent family member standing at her side.

She wanders toward the bank of votives. A crush of people are lighting candles for loved ones. Everyone is patient and polite. There's only the slightest bit of jockeying each time a space opens up. Yale doesn't join the crush. Every evening, at the inn, she lights the milk glass candle Amo gave her. She murmurs Brennan's name under her breath. That's her prayer: *Mary Brennan White, amen.* Even that bit of ritual would make Brennan raise an eyebrow. Brennan would never have wanted this requiem mass. If the townspeople really want to honor Brennan, they should all go bowling.

Yale looks around for Dub. She wants to tell him her bowling joke. She can't find him, though. She pushes through the crowd. She sees him then. He's near the confessional, the same one she peeked into the last time they were here. She remembers the wish she made then. *Let me have him. Let him love me.* And she does have him. And he does love her.

But the fact that the wish has come true—this is no miracle, no blessing, no answered prayer. It's only that she articulated a goal and then went out and made it a reality. It has nothing to do with God or fairies or angels or fate. She knows this.

Dub, however, doesn't seem to know this. It makes her so sad. She has tried to assuage his guilt about Kerim Bey. You didn't mean to, she has said. It was an accident. It was Raffi who did it; can't you see that? Can't you see that by feeling so bad about it you're actually taking credit for something Raffi achieved? Or her second approach: he had it coming; he struck the first blow; it's not called murder when it's an act of war. Or her third approach: it's over and done with; you can't change it, so let's just go on. Whatever her approach, it doesn't matter; he won't listen. He won't let her absolve him. He cries out in his sleep. He holds her too tight. And now he is looking at the confessional.

If he goes in there, if he is that weak, if he prefers a priest's incantations to her own words of comfort, she will not marry him. She tells herself this even though she knows it's the biggest lie she's ever told. Of course she will marry him. She loves him, she will marry him, her acceptance of his proposal did not come with any ifs. But oh, how she hopes he will not go in there.

As she stands watching him, fretting over him, Shushan comes up to her. "Look at him," Shushan says. She says it in her weary monotone, in her everything-hurts-but-who-cares voice. She says it with a tinge of disgust. "Who is he?"

In the end Dub walks away. He won't risk it, confessing such a crime to a priest. Anyway, he knows there is no absolution for him, for anyone. Freedom fighter or murderer: some will call him one thing, some will call him the other. It's up to him to decide what he'll call himself, not a priest in a confessional. Priest is just a word too.

Still, he thinks, it's a heavy burden. Maybe he will visit a more remote church when they get to Spain, to Portugal; maybe there he will confess in a language the priests don't quite comprehend. Just to hear himself talk about it. Revolutionary or murderer. Just to hear which word comes out of his mouth.

He rejoins Yale and Shushan. "Where have you been?" Yale says. He says he was outside talking to the sexton. He says they ought to find seats now. Soon they won't be able to sit together. Yale takes his arm.

Because the pews are crowded, Shushan sits directly behind them. She doesn't mind. It gives her a chance to study Dub. The nape of his neck. The flesh that attaches his ears to his head. His hair is so very short. When she said, "Look at him," she meant it quite literally. Look at him. Do you even recognize him? Because Shushan doesn't. No mustache. Such short hair. And recently he has rubbed hair coloring into it. The hair is uniformly jet now.

The services have begun. The entire church goes down on its knees. Only Yale and Dub remain seated. "Armenians don't kneel," he whispers to her.

"Neither do Jews," she says.

Shushan is kneeling like everyone else. Kneeling, she is that much closer to Dub, and she is struck by the change a haircut can bring about. Dub looks so ordinary, so average. He could be a stranger. He could be a tourist. It fills Shushan with both regret and envy. He could be any American boy.

TIMETABLE

Kerim Bey is not a historical figure, although seven prominent Young Turks did indeed flee to Germany shortly before the end of World War One. Erinyes is also fictional. It was, however, inspired by an actual organization that called itself Operation Nemesis and claimed responsibility for the assassinations of six of these seven fugitives. Nemesis functioned very differently from my invented Erinyes, and most of its members were victims of the massacres. For readers who may be interested, the following timetable provides a summary of Nemesis' activities.

Oct. 1918　　Immediately before Turkey surrenders, Talaat Pasha, Enver Pasha, and Djemal Pasha (the ruling triumvir of Turkey), Dr. Shakir and Dr. Nazim (the men alleged to be the primary forces behind the massacres), Djemal Azmi, the governor of Trebizond, and Bedri Bey, the police chief of Constantinople, all flee to Germany.

Nov. 1918　　The war ends.

Jan. 1919　　As the Paris Peace Conference convenes, Britain's Admiral Calthorpe instructs Turkey to "have proper punishment inflicted on those responsible for treatment of prisoners of war and Armenian massacres."

Mar. 1919　　Turkey begins arresting those responsible for the massacres.

Apr. 1919　　Turkey hangs Kemal Bey, the lieutenant governor of the Yozgat Sanjak, for his role in "the murders, looting, and rapes" of "small children and defenseless Armenian women in the deportation convoys." The hanging foments unrest in Turkey, which, in turn, strengthens the Nationalist Party of Mustafa Kemal (Atatürk).

May 1919   Turkey sentences Djemal Azmi to death in absentia for having facilitated, among numerous other crimes, the "torturing and killing" of Armenian men and the rape of Armenian women, who were subsequently forced "to walk for months over a route such that the deportees were totally and absolutely exhausted." Djemal Azmi is not then, or ever, extradited to Turkey.

June 1919   The Treaty of Versailles is signed, formally ending the war with Germany.

July 1919   Turkey sentences Talaat Pasha, Enver Pasha, Djemal Pasha, and Dr. Nazim to death in absentia. None is then, or ever, extradited to Turkey.

Jan. 1920   Turkey sentences Dr. Shakir to death in absentia, calling him "the man who employed, planned, and led these pyres of human beings." He is not then, or ever, extradited to Turkey.

Aug. 1920   Turkey signs the Treaty of Sèvres, thereby agreeing to turn over to an international tribunal all those accused of planning and carrying out the massacres. Turkey never complies with this provision.

Jan. 1921   Turkey annuls the verdicts against all the Berlin fugitives.

Mar. 1921   In Berlin, Soghomon Tehlirian, a member of Operation Nemesis, assassinates Talaat Pasha with a 1915-issued German army pistol.

Nov. 1921   Britain releases all Turkish prisoners in her custody in exchange for half as many British prisoners held by Atatürk's Nationalist Party. Britain describes her actions as "deplorable but necessary."

Dec. 1921   In Rome, Arshavir Shiragian of Nemesis assassinates Said Halim, one of the more prominent prisoners released by Britain.

Apr. 1922   In Berlin, Shiragian and Aram Yerganian of Nemesis assassinate Dr. Shakir and Djemal Azmi.

July 1922   In Russia, Stepan Dzaghigian, Bedros der Boghossian, and Aruashes Kevorkian of Nemesis assassinate Djemal Pasha.

Aug. 1922   In Russia, Enver Pasha dies in battle. It is rumored he was killed by Armenian forces.

July 1923   The Treaty of Lausanne replaces the Treaty of Sèvres. Not a single one of its provisions pertains to war crimes against Armenians. Lloyd George calls this omission an "abject, cowardly, and infamous surrender" on the part of the Allies.

Aug. 1939   The night before the invasion of Poland, Adolf Hitler assures his generals that the world will not long object should they treat the Polish citizenry brutally. "After all," Hitler says, "who today speaks of the annihilation of the Armenians?"

1944   The United Nations coins and defines the word *genocide*.

A NOTE ON SOURCES

A novel is an act of the imagination, a story told strictly from the point of view of characters the author has made up. As such, it is not meant to provide an objective account of any historical event. Because my task here is that of the novelist and not the historian, I have made no effort to be unbiased or to present every side of every story. Furthermore, the gulf between the Turkish and the Armenian positions as to what actually happened in 1915 and why it happened, a gulf that has not diminished over time, is not something I am qualified to debate or to reconcile. However, the vast majority of historians and genocide scholars who *are* so qualified agree that a deliberrate extermination of more than one million Armenian Christians absolutely did occur in 1915 and 1916, and after reading much primary and secondary source material on both sides of this issue, I found no reason to doubt their conclusions.

With very few exceptions, the characters in this book are *not* based on any actual people. And while, in my effort to transport the reader to another time, I did try to respect historical and geographical facts to the extent that I could, I also deviated from them whenever I felt that doing so would serve my invented characters and their story. If my characters needed a cathedral to be deserted when, in reality, it might have been populated, I emptied the church. If my characters wished to play in a park, I placed a park on the street where they lived.

That said, I would like to acknowledge some of the sources I turned to when trying to give this imaginary world an air of authenticity. I would also like to point out those places where I intentionally changed or ignored the facts as I understood them.

In writing about St. Louis in the early 1900s, *A Tour of St. Louis* by Joseph A. Dacus and James W. Buel and *I Remember You, St. Louis* by Arthur Proetz were particularly helpful, as was Jean M. Gosebrink of the St. Louis Public Library, who provided me with photographs and drawings circa 1918 of the Central Branch Library. As for the claim that hot dogs, ice cream cones, and iced tea were invented for the 1904 World's Fair, this is embraced by many sources and rejected by many others.

Railfans, responding to questions I posted on the Internet, shared loads of information about train travel in 1918. I'm grateful to them all, especially Tim Zukas and Ori Siegel.

Given that I speak no Armenian, I relied on friends and books to help me put the right words in my Armenian characters' mouths. I owe a huge debt of gratitude to the Charkoudian family. Bethel Bilezikian Charkoudian provided me with phrases and suggested appropriate transliterations, although any mistakes or inconsistencies are certainly my own. Arax Charkoudian, via her niece Karoun Charkoudian, provided me with the phrase for arranged marriage (*word-tie*). I also borrowed Armenian phrases from Peter Balakian's moving memoir, *Black Dog of Fate*, and from two powerful novels, Carol Edgarian's *Rise the Euphrates* and Micheline Aharonian Marcom's *Three Apples Fell from Heaven*.

In writing about the postwar Armenian revenge movement, I learned a great deal from Jacques Derogy's *Resistance and Revenge: The Armenian Assassination of the Turkish Leaders Responsible for the 1915 Massacres and Deportations* and *Stay the Hand of Vengeance: The Politics of War Crimes Tribunals* by Gary Jonathan Bass. I also relied on Professor Bass' work in creating the timetable that precedes this section.

I found information and, I suspect, a great deal of lore about the *fedayee* in *Armenian Freedom Fighters* by the nineteenth-century *fedayee* Rouben Ter Minasian, whose story was translated and edited by James G. Mandalian. *Memoirs of a Lost World* by Lascelle Meserve de Basily and *Caucasian Battlefields* by W. E. D. Allen and Paul Muratoff both gave me a sense of life in prerevolutionary Russia. The Allen/Muratoff book also provided remarkably detailed accounts of the fighting in the Caucasus during World War One and also of General Nazarbekov's reluctance to engage in battle only days after his victories in Urmia and Baskale. I have, however, very much invented General Nazarbekov's history, personality, and motivations for the purposes of this book, rendering him an essentially fictional character.

Other helpful material concerning Armenian freedom fighters, Armenian immigrants in Rhode Island, and other aspects of Armenian culture during the early 1900s included "The Black Company," an article by Gregory Mason published in *The Outlook* of July 1916 (which also provided the details pertaining to the *Kursk*'s crossing to Russia); *The Armenians in Rhode Island* by Ara Arthur Gelenian; and *Torn Between Two Lands: Armenians in America, 1890 to World War I* by Robert Mirik. I also visited Heritage Park, a Web site celebrating the lives of survivors of the massacres who subsequently immigrated to Rhode Island, and I practically memorized *The Armenian Community in Providence* by S. Hagopian (originally published in the June, July, and August 1937 issues of *The Hairnek Monthly* and now available at a number of online sites).

The Der Hayr's sermon about the Christian sword is adapted from Khachator Abovian's *The Wounds of Armenia* (1841). The full passage, however, goes on to say this: "I agree, we must have all of these. But, I tell you, when you don't have a good sword they cut your throat, snatch your children, seize your belongings, and enslave you. This is how it goes. What can you do?"

Raffi's story about the tortured Vartapet is a compilation of various events alleged to have taken place in Turkey during the early 1900s. According to a number of sources, particularly the aforementioned Heritage Park, the fire in the Adana church was an actual event.

Alban Bliss' sermon in the *Espagne*'s chapel and his views on women's suffrage were adapted from "A Straight Talk to Women," an article by YMCA lay preacher Gipsy Smith, which appeared in an issue of *Good Housekeeping* shortly after the war. In all other respects, Alban Bliss is my own creation and isn't intended to reflect the views or, heaven knows, the conduct of Gipsy Smith.

William Klingaman's *1919: The Year Our World Began* contains fascinating information about that year, from weather conditions to the ins and outs of the treaty negotiations to life in postwar Bavaria. Two other books that were invaluable resources were *Peacemaking 1919* by Harold Nicolson and *Unfinished Business* by Stephen Bonsal. In fact, material in these two memoirs furnished a lot of the dialogue—including, alas, the anti-Semitism of some of their statements—in Hamilton and Lindsey's conversation with Dub at the Majestic Hotel.

The imperialistic dreams of the Allied Powers listed in the section called "Meanwhile, over in France" are as reported in *The Supplementary Volume to the Great War: History from the Armistice November 11, 1918, to the Ratification of the Peace Treaty* edited by Louis E. Orcutt and published in 1920, but are also augmented with data found in atlases and other primary sources from 1920. The list is not complete, but gives a fairly good idea of what the nations attending the peace conference wanted.

Nguyen the Patriot, whom Dub sees on the first day of the Paris Peace Conference, would later be known as Ho Chi Minh. During the conference, the young man resided in Paris and was given an audience with the Allies, where he futilely pleaded for self-determination for Vietnam.

Passages from letters attributed to the men from Erinyes pleading for a seat at the peace table are actually passages from letters written by the Armenian representative Boghos Nubar Pasho and sent to the French government in December 1918 and also printed in the London *Times* in January 1919.

I altered the lyrics of the song "That Little-Good-for-Nothing's Good for Something After All" just a bit. The actual line is "she's joined the Red Cross," and not, as I have Brennan and Yale sing, "she's joined the Y.M."

Raffi's letter to the YMCA contains several lines, slightly altered for context, from *America Comes of Age* by the French scholar Andre Siegfried, a book that wasn't actually published until 1927 but was, in fact, favorably blurbed by Mencken and the *New York Times*.

The quoted lines from the letter booting Yale and Brennan out of the YMCA come directly from a YMCA defense of its workers against broadbrush accusations of embezzlement and black marketeering. (In 1918 the Y's name was still spelled with a period after each letter, but for the modern reader's convenience, I've omitted that punctuation.)

Erinyes' rules of reprisal that annoy Raffi so are actually rules proposed in "Reprisal" by Frits Kalshoven, an article reprinted in *Crimes of War: What the Public Should Know*, edited by Roy Gutman and David Rieff.

The St. Petersburg events are based on an incident described in David Fromkin's *A Peace to End All Peace: The Fall of the Ottoman Empire and the Creation of the Modern Middle East*. According to Fromkin, Djemal Pasha secretly offered to overthrow his fellow triumvirs, surrender Turkey, hand over Constantinople and the Straits of the Dardanelles, and end the Armenian deportations, all in exchange for control of Syria, but France and Britain rejected this offer, preferring to preserve their hopes regarding the Middle East. Fromkin reports that an Armenian revolutionary named Dr. Zavriev carried the message from Djemal to the Russians; obviously, I inserted Aram and Dub in Dr. Zavriev's place and did a lot of fictionalizing, including throwing in the murder of poor Kostya. I do wish to note that although I tried to find a second source to confirm Fromkin's reporting, I was unable to do so.

Much of the information in the chapter "How the Jews Got Their Names" comes from "Our Heritage: Surnames" by Ruth Schultz, an article that appeared in the Fall 1990 issue of *Inside Magazine*. I've read elsewhere, however, that the story about the mayor, the rope, and the quadrants isn't really true.

Other helpful material included Andrei Bitov's *A Captive of the Caucasus: Journeys in Armenia and Georgia;* Paul Dickson's *War Slang: America's Fighting Words and Phrases from the Civil War to the Gulf War; Against Forgetting: Twentieth-Century Poetry of Witness,* edited by Carolyn Forché; Philip Gourevitch's *We Wish to Inform You That Tomorrow We Will Be Killed with Our Families: Stories from Rwanda;* Philip J. Haythornthwaite's *The World War One Source Book;* Edward Hopkins' *History of the Y.M.C.A. in North America;* Victor Klemperer's *I Will Bear Witness: A Diary of the Nazi Years, 1933–1941* (which helped me give voice to Yale's denial of her Jewish heritage toward the book's end); Hans Konig's wonderful novel *The Death of a Schoolboy;* Rubina Peroomian's *Literary Responses to Catastrophe: A Comparison of the Armenian and the Jewish Experience;* Nicole and Hugh Pope's *Turkey Unveiled: A History of Modern Turkey;* Frank Schoonmaker's 1928 guidebook, *Come with Me Through France;* the 1920 edition of *Black's Guide to Paris,* edited by Charles Mathon; Frederick James Smith's "The Celluloid Critic" column in the January 18, 1918, issue of *Motion Picture Classics;* and Simon Wiesenthal's *The Sunflower: On the Possibilities and Limits of Forgiveness.*

ACKNOWLEDGMENTS

While working on this book, I received generous financial support from the James Michener/Copernicus Society of America and from the Wisconsin Institute for Creative Writing's James C. McCreight Fiction Fellowship funded by the Ed and Lynn McCreight Family Trust. Ed and Lynn also befriended me, encouraged me, and, from time to time, bought me lunch. I am immensely grateful for all this help.

Bethel Bilezikian Charkoudian, along with her husband, Levon Charkoudian, and their daughter, Karoun Charkoudian, expended an extraordinary amount of time to help me, a complete stranger when this project began. Peter Balakian (whose *The Burning Tigris* provides a detailed history of the massacres), Thisbe Nissen, Ron Wallace, Mark Baechtel, Marilynne Robinson, Sara Becker, and Jesse Lee Kercheval were invaluable readers at various stages in the writing process. Mark Tavitian, Mickey and Jayne Rosenberg, and my colleagues in the Program for Creative Writing at the University of Wisconsin offered support at every stage, as did my family, especially my mother, Claire, my brothers, Gene, Gerry, and Matt, and the inspirational trio of Max Friedlich, Andrew Mitchell, and Madeleine Mitchell. I also wish to thank Eric Simonoff for giving the book its title, Jenny Minton for giving it a home, and Deborah Garrison, her assistant, Ilana Kurshan, and the other professionals at Pantheon for giving it their all.

As for my husband, Don Friedlich, who encouraged me to give up my day job—I could not be more grateful or blessed.

Finally, I would like to acknowledge the special contributions of two friends. Shortly after I began working on this book, Claire Sanford invited Don and me to vacation in her family's home in Hawaii. There, much to Don's chagrin, I found stacks of magazines from the mid-1800s through the present and spent many gorgeous afternoons inside, reading pristine issues of *Vogue*, *Good Housekeeping*, *Motion Picture Classics*, *Harper's*, *Current Opinion*, *Life: The Humor Magazine*, and *The Outlook* from the early

1900s. All these magazines helped give me a vivid sense of the times, and one happened to contain the recruitment announcement for YMCA workers that now (in edited form) appears in the novel. That serendipitous discovery helped give me faith in my project. I thank Claire for giving me access to this extraordinary collection.

Years before I ever thought about writing a novel, my friend Sheila Haggerty handed me a thick sheaf of letters written in 1919 by her great-aunt Wera ("Wee") Nathan when Wee was a YMCA canteen worker in France. Although Yale White's story is not Wee Nathan's, the spirited tone of Wee's correspondence, plus a brief reference in one letter to an encounter with an Armenian who'd lost his family in the deportations, captured my imagination. While I was writing *The Last Day of the War*, Wee Nathan died at the age of 106. I am told she was lucid and feisty until the end. Many thanks to Sheila for sharing Wee's letters with me; I would not have written this book without them.

ABOUT THE AUTHOR

Judith Claire Mitchell teaches creative writing at the University of Wisconsin. A graduate of the Iowa Writers' Workshop, she is a recipient of a James Michener/Copernicus Society of America Fellowship and was a James C. McCreight Fellow at the Wisconsin Institute for Creative Writing. She lives in Madison with her husband, Don Friedlich. This is her first novel.

A NOTE ON THE TYPE

Pierre Simon Fournier le jeune, who designed the type used in this book, was both an originator and a collector of types. His services to the art of printing were his design of letters, his creation of ornaments and initials, and his standardization of type sizes. His types are old style in character and sharply cut. In 1764 and 1766 he published his *Manuel typographique,* a treatise on the history of French types and printing, on typefounding in all its details, and on what many consider his most important contribution to typography—the measurement of type by the point system.

Composed by NK Graphics, Keene, New Hampshire
Printed and bound by Berryville Graphics, Berryville, Virginia